The Life We Remember

Between Worlds
Book I

ANNETTE OPPENLANDER

First published by Annette Oppenlander, 2024
Averesch 93, 48683 Ahaus
First Edition
Visit the author's website at www.annetteoppenlander.com
Text copyright: Annette Oppenlander 2024
ISBN: 978-3-948100-55-1 eBook
ISBN: 978-3-948100-56-8 Paperback
All rights reserved.

Except for brief quotations in critical articles or reviews, no part of the book may be reproduced in any manner without prior written permission from the publisher. The story, all names, characters, and incidents portrayed in this production are fictitious. No identification with actual persons (living or deceased), places, buildings, and products is intended or should be inferred. No part of this content was generated by or with the help of artificial intelligence (AI).

NO AI TRAINING: Without in any way limiting the author's [and publisher's] exclusive rights under copyright, any use of this publication to "train" generative artificial intelligence (AI) technologies to generate text is expressly prohibited. The author reserves all rights to license uses of this work for generative AI training and development of machine learning language models.

The rights of Annette Oppenlander as author have been asserted in accordance with the Copyright, Designs and Patents Act 1988.
Editing: Tanya Coats Konerman
Design: fiverr.com/akira007
© 2024 Annette Oppenlander

Also by Annette Oppenlander

A Different Truth *(historical mystery – boarding school Vietnam War Era)*
Escape from the Past I, II, III *(time-travel/gaming adventure trilogy)*
Surviving the Fatherland: A True Coming-of-age Love Story Set in WWII *(biographical – WWII and postwar)*
47 Days *(biographical novella – WWII)*
Everything We Lose: A Civil War Novel of Hope, Courage and Redemption
Where the Night Never Ends: A Prohibition Era Novel
When They Made Us Leave *(WWII young adult)*
Boys No More *(WWII – collection)*
A Lightness in My Soul *(biographical novella – WWII)*
The Scent of a Storm *(WWII and German Reunification)*
So Close to Heaven *(biographical – Napoleon Wars)*
When the Skies Rained Freedom *(Berlin Airlift)*
24 Hours: The Trade *(biographical novella – WWII)*

German

Vaterland, wo bist Du? Roman nach einer wahren Geschichte *(2. Weltkrieg/Nachkriegszeit – biografisch)*
Erzwungene Wege: Historischer Roman *(2. Weltkrieg – Kinderlandverschickung)*
47 Tage: Wie zwei Jungen Hitlers letztem Befehl trotzten *(2. Weltkrieg – biografische Novelle)*
Erfolgreich(e) historische Romane schreiben *(Sachbuch)*
Immer der Fremdling: Die Rache des Grafen *(Mittelalter – Gaming Zeitreise)*
Als Deutschlands Jungen ihre Jugend verloren *(2. Weltkrieg – Sammlung)*
Bis uns nichts mehr bleibt *(amerikanischer Bürgerkrieg – Abenteuerroman)*
Ewig währt der Sturm *(2. Weltkrieg – Flucht und Vertreibung)*
Leicht wie meine Seele *(2. Weltkrieg – biografische Novelle)*
Endlos ist die Nacht *(amerikanische Prohibition – Abenteuerroman)*
Das Kreuz des Himmels *(Napoleon Kriege – biografisch)*
Zwei Handvoll Freiheit *(Nachkriegszeit/Berliner Luftbrücke – historischer Liebesroman)*
24 Stunden: Tauschgeschäfte *(2. Weltkrieg – biografische Novelle)*
Das Gegenteil von Wahrheit *(Vietnamkrieg/Militärinternat – Abenteuerroman)*
Ein Schimmer am Horizont: Zwischen den Welten *(Auswandererroman)*

"We believe...that marriage should be an equal and permanent partnership, and so recognized by law; that until it is so recognized, married partners should provide against the radical injustice of present laws, by every means in their power..."

"If a woman earned a dollar by scrubbing, her husband had a right to take the dollar and go and get drunk with it and beat her afterwards. It was his dollar." –Lucy Stone, feminist (1818-1893)

CHAPTER ONE

Löwenstein, Württemberg, Germany, November 1848
Mina Peters bent low to wring out the bedsheet. She hated washing and this time of year—the first snow had come early—was particularly trying. Her hands had lost all feeling in the frigid water, the skin of her fingers chafed and painful. Drying would be the next challenge, but how could she not wash the filth, after her husband, Roland, had thrown up and soiled their marriage bed. It wasn't the first time and wouldn't be the last. A sigh escaped her. If her mother were alive, she'd never... Why had she ever agreed to marry him?

"Wilhelmina, where is my damn dinner, why don't you cook something for once in your life?" Roland stood, hands on hips, in the doorway to their modest home, a cabin with a thatched roof, just large enough to hold their bed, a cooking space and an eating nook.

"Coming," she hurried, though the sheet still needed another good squeeze before she'd drape it near the firepit. Back home they'd cooked on a cast-iron stove with two spaces for pots. Since marrying Roland, she'd had to learn to prepare meals over an open fire. In the beginning, she'd burned everything, and she still hesitated to leave the boiling pot unattended.

She squeezed past Roland into the gloomy space, trying not to breathe his stench, a mix of alcohol and body odor. He needed a bath, badly, but whenever she approached the subject, he waved her off or worse, started yelling at her. The nightly visits, he kept up despite his drunkenness, were unbearable.

"Why didn't you cook dinner, woman?"
It isn't dinnertime yet, she wanted to say. He was early again, which meant, he hadn't worked a full day and wouldn't get paid much. What

little coin was left, he mostly took to the pub. She scanned the meager stores of flour and potatoes, the shriveled onion sitting by the hearth, the small sack of oats. She'd need to search for wild plants again, a skill her mother had taught her, when she was a little girl. A half mile from the village, along the edges of the forest, grew patches of earth ivy and meadow daisies.

"I need to go to the market soon," she said, peeling the onion on a wooden board, she did all her kitchen work on. "We have hardly enough for tomorrow."

Roland sagged onto the only comfortable chair in the corner, eyeing her suspiciously. "What did you do with the money, I gave you Monday?"

Her hands hovered midair as she weighed her answer. "That was a week ago, Monday."

Roland coughed, cleared his nose with thumb and forefinger and wiped the mess on his pants. The way they looked, he'd been doing it for months. In her parents' home they'd used handkerchiefs. She needed to find another pair of pants—

"...dreaming," Roland said, pulling her back from her thoughts.

"What?"

In a swift movement, he appeared next to her. "Heavens, woman, you're good for nothing." His dirt stained and work-calloused hand landed on her forearm, made the knife, she'd held, drop onto the board with a clatter. "You're not fit for a wife," he hissed. "Make me something to eat. Now!"

He let go and returned to his corner while Mina picked up the knife with a shaky hand. This was only the second winter with this man, and the prospect of spending the rest of her life with him made her want to jump in the river. She forced herself to concentrate on fixing the soup, boiling oats and onion into a slimy stew.

Tomorrow, she'd visit the market to buy potatoes, pretty much the only thing, they could afford. At least Roland didn't know about the Taler, she'd hidden behind a loose stone by the fireplace. Otherwise, it'd already be wasted on the cheap, yet strong swill made from potatoes, the men drank at the Hirsch, the village pub.

"Was that so difficult?" Roland pushed away the clay bowl, wiping the back of his hand across his mouth. He rose and pulled on his jacket. "I'll see Tom for a bit. Don't wait up."

"Have you asked him about work this winter?" Mina knew it was a risky question with the potential of sending him into one of his fits. To her surprise, he remained calm.

"Not yet, but he's well connected. Surely, he'll know of someone." He gave her one of those rare smiles, she'd once relished during their courtship.

When Roland left, Mina heaved a sigh, scrubbed the bowls and pot with sand, and sunk onto the stool by the fire. Already, the room was cooling, but she was hesitant to waste more wood when all she'd do was go to bed.

As a day laborer, Roland had no formal skills. He was young, twenty-five, not much older than she, but already his body showed the signs of hard labor, the skin of his face ruddy from working outdoors and too much liquor. From spring to fall, he worked for a variety of farmers who themselves often leased the land they worked from the estate owners. But Roland hadn't even been able to secure a tenancy nor was he interested in learning a new skill.

She remembered her wash and rushed outside where it was growing dark fast. They'd have to sleep on the bare mattress tonight as they didn't own a second set of bedding, but it couldn't be helped. She draped the wet cloth across the chairs and table, changed into her night gown and crawled into bed.

She felt bone tired, yet sleep wouldn't come. At home, she'd have done needle work or sewing, or read one of her parents' precious books, sitting by the open hearth. Here, she didn't have money for decent candles or lamp oil, making it impossible to do anything useful. And the winter was just beginning. Besides, Roland called her needle work nonsense and a waste of time. To him, so she had found, a woman was meant to clean and cook and have babies.

Another sigh rose into the darkness. She had no intention of getting pregnant, not now. It was too hard, and she wasn't willing to bring a child into this world...into this life with Roland. She rose again, lit the tallow lamp and made her way to the opposite corner where dried bundles of chamomile, mint, sage, buckhorn, and yarrow hung hung from the ceiling. She opened a clay pot, filled with dried brown seeds, took a spoonful and ground them with a round stone. Then she placed the mixture in a cup of water and drank it down. Roland didn't know that wild carrot seeds prevented pregnancy, but she was thankful for Mother telling her.

It seemed like a lifetime ago when they'd gone on excursions, studied and collected plants. Mother had kneeled next to a patch of white frothy blooms that looked as delicate as the lace she'd once seen when a traveling peddler had stopped in Löwenstein. "You must be careful with this one, Mina," Mother had said. "The wild carrot has several lookalikes like the poisonous water hemlock, so study it with care." She'd proceeded to point out its unique features and, after looking around to make sure no one was near, had whispered to her of its special quality.

Mina set down the cup and closed the ceramic pot. She hadn't found quite as much as she'd liked and worried, she'd run out before the next bloom. No matter how much drink Roland had in him, it didn't seem to reduce his manly prowess. If he could just invest as much interest in finding and keeping work, she'd breathe easier. Her hand traveled to her belly which was flat and hard. Roland could never know about her little trick, as soon as their wedding night, he'd talked about raising boys who'd help him work the land. What land?

With a scoff she returned to bed, massaging her freezing toes under the cover until she fell asleep.

She awoke from pottery breaking and Roland's curses. A moment later, he sagged onto the mattress. A wall of alcohol fumes hit her nose as a rough hand grabbed her nightshirt.

"Where're you, woman," he slurred. He yanked harder, fingers twisted into the coarse linen of her gown. All she wanted was to scream, to tell him to leave her alone, but no sound escaped her. Instead, she pulled off her shirt, the cold air hitting her skin like an ice bath.

Roland grumbled something like, "Oh, what the..."

She felt him fumble with his pants, waited for the inevitable.

It didn't come. He took a deep breath and slumped down, his left shoulder painfully trapping her arm. The heavy breathing turned into snoring while Mina carefully pulled away. She redressed and laid in the dark, listening to the grinding gasps next to her. She had no idea what time it was, but sleep refused to come. When the neighbor's rooster crowed, she slipped out of bed, got dressed and went outside to fetch water. A layer of hoarfrost covered the ground, each step crunched. She needed the cold this morning: to chase away the fog in her head and clear her thoughts. The icy air pricked her skin and attacked her nose and ears. She pulled the scarf closer around her face and shoulders and headed to the well.

Down the narrow streets with identical modest homes, though few as rundown as hers, people stirred. Across the street, Harald Steiner was already cutting wood, stacking each log neatly under the overhang of his roof. He lifted a hand in greeting. Next door, Frieda Lutken who'd lost her husband to consumption last year, was leaving the house and only threw Mina a brief glance. Ever since her husband's death, she'd been silent, her face pale and ever more gaunt. Mina had stopped by a few times, but Frieda did not invite her in, nor did she accept any help. She just shook her head and smacked the door in Mina's face. By the way she dragged herself up the lane, she'd soon join her husband.

It's what she wants, Mina told herself. Still, she felt helpless...as helpless as she'd been, watching her own mother die.

"Morning Mina." The voice was chipper despite the freezing drizzle and for once, Mina smiled and turned on her heels to face her friend, Elise.

"You're off early," she said, waving her close. Elise, who wore a smart skirt of dark green linen and a heavy felted wool coat on top, waved her basket. Unlike Mina, she had married a farmer who was growing potatoes and rye. Even if they didn't own any land, they had plenty to eat.

"Going to the market, before it's all gone." Elise frowned, eyeing her closely. "You look terrible. It's Roland, isn't it?"

To her surprise, Mina felt her eyes sting with tears. She shook her head to push them away and produced a half smile. "If you wait a moment, I'll come with you."

Luckily, Roland was still asleep as she returned the empty water pale and grabbed her basket and the remaining coins, two Groschen and seven Pfennig.

The market assembled around the village well, surrounded by a few houses and city hall. A half dozen vendors were here this morning, not even half of what Mina was used to. Two dozen women and children sat and lounged on the ground, head and feet wrapped in rags. The children, some no older than one or two, stared at Mina and Elise with large eyes. These people were begging, the poor, some openly with hands outstretched, others just staring as if their hunger had laid a cloak of stupor over them.

Mina forced herself to turn away. She wanted to help, but then her fingers cramped around the little purse that was way too light to last through the week. To her dismay, her favorite potato farmer wasn't here, nor his neighbor who sold eggs and butter. Not that she could afford them.

She followed Elise to a different stand.

"You're lucky I've got these," the woman behind the cart was just saying. Her hands were as muddy as the heaps of potatoes, she was selling.

Elise shook her head. "Looks like we're rich. I better tell my husband."

"Three Groschen for five kilos?" Mina cried. "That's twice what is was last week.

The vendor took one of the spuds and eyed it closely. "Haven't you heard, they've been going bad overnight. In Heilbronn half the vendors are missing, many lost everything last summer. Right before the harvest, the plants wilted and then, the potatoes turned to mush." She threw the potato back on the pile. "Who knows what the new year will bring. We may be ruined, too."

Behind them, six or seven women had lined up, listening and whispering to each other. "We better stock up then," one of them said. She pulled out her coin purse and moved next to Mina. "You going to buy or just gawk?"

Mina swallowed. Chances were, the other women would buy out the only potato offerings. But she'd wanted to get a sack of flour with the money, carrots and onions, too, maybe a bread. She did a quick calculation in her head and moved her shoulder just enough to regain the front spot.

"Just give me enough for two Groschen."

Her bag was terribly light, when she returned home. Elise had hurried off to tell her husband about the exorbitant prices. They delivered larger quantities to the wealthier merchants and townspeople as far as Heilbronn, the big city twelve miles from here. Talk about failed harvests wasn't new. For the past two years, rumors had spread of people leaving their homesteads to look for new opportunities in the city.

Roland sat on the bed, holding his head with both hands. "Where've you been?," he grumbled. "There's no water."

Mina held up her basket, but Roland didn't seem interested. He attempted to get off the bed and sank back down. So much for going to work at a decent time. He'd be terribly late, even if he started now. "I'll fetch water and make you something to eat."

"I can't eat, don't you get that?" Roland straightened again, this time his legs held. "My head is about to come apart. Damn schnaps."

Mina turned her back to hide her disdain. Was she supposed to feel sorry for him, for going out and getting drunk over and over again? On the way to the well, her stomach growled, reminding her that she hadn't eaten.

Back in the cabin, Roland still sat bent over, cradling his head. She poured water into the pot and added oats for a plain gruel.

"Potato prices are going through the roof," she said to cut the silence. "There was only one vendor and she told us that the harvest has been lost even for many large farmers."

Behind her, Roland spit. "Damn potatoes. I've heard it, too. Soon, there won't be any work left, you'll see. Everyone lands in the poorhouse. People are leaving all over the place."

"Did you talk to Tom?"

"About what?"

"You said, he may know of work in the area this winter."

"Why don't you mind your own business?"

Mina suspected that he didn't remember any of their conversation from last night, the cheap and strong schnaps was burning a hole in his mind. She turned her attention to the sack of rye flour that looked gray and emitted a foul smell. Unable to afford bread, she'd picked up the rye after the vendor assured her that it was good enough to bake bread. After stoking the fire, she began mixing flour and water, added a few dried herbs, wild garlic, mint, lemon balm and nettles. The loaf remained gray and looked unappetizing, but Mina quartered it and laid each piece on the flat stone, she used for baking.

"I'll have bread soon, you can take it with you," she said, turning her attention back to Roland. "How about I'll make you some tea? It should help with your stomach," she hurried. Her husband had put on his shoes, but otherwise sat motionless as if he hadn't heard her. "I used the last coin today."

With a groan, Roland rose and at first, she worried he'd turn on her—it had happened a couple of times—so far the bruises on her chest, wrists, and neck had healed quick enough and nobody had noticed, not even Elise.

"I better go." Roland pulled on his coat and hat and opened the door without a second look.

"Good-bye," Mina mumbled to herself. She turned the loaves as the aroma of baking reached her nose. Again, her stomach grumbled. She'd have to control herself and only eat one and leave the remainder for this evening. Roland would be famished and it'd be dangerous.

Listen to yourself, the voice in her head commented. Whatever happened to that bright and funny girl you used to be. Mina looked around the room, really looked at it, the rough-hewn bedposts, the blackened firepit, the assembly of mismatched pots. She'd landed in a hovel, and now she was going to starve through the winter.

Her throat closed as if bony fingers were squeezing it. She gasped and pulled on her coat and hat, took one of the small breads, and rushed outside. She had to get away. Her legs, weak as they were, grew tired in minutes, yet, she forced herself to march on.

Only when she saw her childhood home did she stop. Shaded by an ancient oak, it stood a little uphill by itself, a lath and timber structure, old but strong. Three glass windows faced the fields and road, its roof made of silvery shale like the scales of a fish. As a child she'd played in the adjacent barn or the courtyard with its own well, had helped her mother in the vegetable garden, fed the chickens and played with the cat.

A rain shower brought her back. She shivered and wrapped her head with the shawl. As she looked up again, a rivulet of smoke rose from the chimney and called to her.

CHAPTER TWO

Skibbereen, County Cork, Ireland, November 1848
Davin Callaghan rubbed his hands on a piece of cloth and inspected the farthing-sized blisters at the bottom of his right fore- and middle finger. They'd filled with blood and would soon pop, but he still had a good three hours of work in front of him. He'd been sloppy, not taken care of his hands. Why had he agreed to help Mark with the roof in this weather? How could he not? Mark had been there for him last year...

Davin swallowed and grew aware that it had begun to snow again. With a rough movement, he pulled the hood of his coat over his head and grabbed the hammer once more. He'd split the timbers, cut out holes and now forced wooden peg into the openings. It was still his preferred way of binding two boards together.

By the time he finished, it was dark. Lantern in one hand, he climbed down. At least they'd be ready tomorrow for the rye thatch already waiting inside the walls. Davin called a greeting to the man, Mark had instructed to guard the house. People were so desperate these days, they stole whatever they could, either to use themselves or trade for sustenance.

It was becoming unbearable to just walk through town. Half the homes were empty, people having died or left when the hunger grew too great, the others still occupied, housed large families, gaunt from malnutrition. The potato harvest had been bad or utterly lost for the third year and money had run out. Here and there a soup kitchen sprouted, financed by the English or by wealthy Irish landowners, but it wasn't enough. He'd lost most of the carpentry work this year because there was no more need to build anything. Mark had been lucky to find a patron, willing to build in the dying village. Never mind, he was English.

Head low into the wind, Davin spit. After the day roofing, he was famished which only increased his anger. Everybody knew that the English were intentionally killing off Ireland. The potato famine was one thing, but instead of helping and keeping the other food in the country, nearly all grain and other food were exported to England. What was left, was sold at exorbitant prices, prices Irish peasants could not afford. Worse, out of desperation, they were eating their seed potatoes, set aside for the next year. And if they had no money to buy food, they surely didn't have money to pay a man to do carpentry. He had to look elsewhere.

He sighed with relief when his parents' house came into view. By now the snow had crawled down his neck and soaked his shoulders and back. After draping his drenched coat near the fire and taking off his boots, he joined his da' at the table.

"You're late," his mother said, patting him on the back. She silently set a bowl of stew and a mug of watered-down ale in front of him.

"Wanted to finish the framing," he said, digging in. He'd supported his parents all year because the small plot of potatoes had failed last year and by midsummer it was clear, there wouldn't be any harvest this year either. So, Davin had traveled all over to do woodwork and sent home, whatever he could.

Still, he noticed how the shine had gone from his father's eyes. He was a tall man, proud with a full head of coarse red hair, Davin had inherited. Now, Da mostly sat idle around the house and instead of working a man's job, he helped his wife with the washing.

Davin realized that his mother had lost weight, the top of her dress now as loose as the skin on her throat.

"I may have to go away for a while." Davin's words stood in the room like strangers not to be touched. "The English are building railroads. I could get better pay, send it home to you."

"The lease payment is due in January," his father said. "Word is, if we don't pay, the landlord will take over."

"I've heard they kick tenants out and destroy their houses." Mother's voice was low as she joined them at the table, a mug of sage tea in her hand.

Davin half turned to the firepit where the dinner pot sat—empty. He swallowed his question for a second helping and focused on his parents. "I hate'em like you do, you know that. But I've got to do something, find a paying job."

"You're a carpenter, we saw to it that you learned a skill." Mother's mouth worked, a sign, she was close to tears. Davin knew they had sacrificed for years to finance his education. Most sons just worked the fields alongside their fathers, but his Da had always said, that it wasn't a future, as if he'd foreseen what was happening.

Davin also knew that his mother had suffered multiple miscarriages and after he was born, had never gotten pregnant again. Even now, he felt her gaze on him like a warm glow. It was all he could do, not to jump up and embrace her, tell her, things would work out fine. He was determined to support his parents with every breath he took. It was the least he could do.

"Mam, you know there isn't any more work, nobody can pay me. They don't even have enough to buy food."

His mother lowered her head, but he knew without looking that she was crying.

"When will you go, *mac*?"

Hearing Da call him *son* in Irish made Davin's heart squeeze together painfully. They were trying to hang on to their identity, no matter that the English were ripping the heart out of Ireland.

"Soon, just finishing the house for Mark, getting my pay. I heard at the pub, there's an Irish gang near Liverpool. I'll send word, it'll be aways." Just getting to Dublin would take a couple of weeks, maybe longer if the weather got worse. He didn't want to worry his parents, so he rose and stretched his aching back. "I'm turning in."

While he peeled out of his work clothes and put on his nightshirt, he heard his parents whisper in the other room. His space was tucked behind the wall, no more than a compartment with his bed and a stool. He'd helped his father build the walls when he'd turned fifteen, one of his first projects, working with wood.

Even from here he sensed the sadness of his mother, how it made the air heavy and hard to breathe. He was bone tired, yet he wanted to run out and get drunk. That's what men did these days, drink *poitín*, homebrewed moonshine, made from whatever was available, and forget. If only for a few hours.

Who could blame them? But it wasn't for him, he had things to do, and he'd rather fall over dead than waste his life on liquor. Not after the sacrifices his parents had made.

Except he didn't see a future. The light in Ireland had turned off, it was black as coal, impossible for him to see where he should turn. The English railroad would pay the bills and then what? His parents owned nothing except for the few pieces of furniture, they had no future. Where did that leave him? He'd thought he'd be building a good life, not rich, no, that would be too much, but a solid existence, working with wood. He understood wood, how it bent and cut and fit together. It was a puzzle, he enjoyed. The smell of the sawdust, planning and splitting. He could draw a structure in his mind, see it grow into a building before his closed eyes.

Unlike his future.

CHAPTER THREE

Mina

"Papa, it's me," Mina cried when she entered the home.

Her father, a stained rag in his hand, entered the hallway. "I'm fixing breakfast." He shrugged, looking lost for a moment, the sparse hair on his head shaggy as if he'd just gotten up.

Mina took the rag and led him back into the main room where a fire roared and the smell of something burning rang alarm bells. Inside a pot, something cooked furiously, the bottom blackened. She moved the pot aside and turned to face her father who stood, arms hanging in the middle of mayhem. Table and counter were covered in dishes, dirty cutlery, and pans. Her mother's best tablecloth lay in a heap on one of the chairs. The air was thick with smoke and spoiling food.

"Oh, Papa, what happened?"

He shrugged. "I'm just not managing." He pulled a hand through his wispy hair and sank on a stool. "Since your mother...I miss her so." His eyes sparkled with tears as he hung his head.

Mina fought down her own sadness and went to work, secretly scolding herself for not stopping by more often. Life with Roland was such a drain on her energy, she hardly knew how to get through each day. If she were honest, she'd admit that she couldn't bear her father's questions about her life.

She threw away scraps, warmed water and scrubbed dishes and pots, wiped down table and oven and swept the floor, while cooking her father a hot breakfast with oats and some dried apple, she found in a forgotten tub—while her father watched her quietly sipping tea.

"How do you do it, Mina?" he said, when she served him the

steaming bowl. "I'm such a burden."

"Nonsense, I just have more practice." She turned to fetch more water, when a hand landed on hers.

"Sit with me, child."

She nodded and sank across from him, watching him eat. Since Mother's death two years ago, he'd aged ten. The skin under his eyes appeared puffy and gray, his clothes just hung on him. Whatever happened to the strong man, she'd grown up with?

When he laid down the spoon, their eyes met. "What's going on with Roland? I haven't seen him since your wedding. And *you*..." he hesitated and seemed to search for the right words, "look tired and sad."

Like you, Mina wanted to say. Instead, she forced a smile. "I'm fine, Papa. It's just hard right now, work is sparse, harvests have been bad." She sighed. "You know all that."

"I wish, Roland would try a little harder. By God, you deserve it."

She bit her lower lip. How could she tell her father about Roland's drinking, the abuse and rough language? She needed money, but she'd never ask her father for help. Not if she were on her deathbed.

"We'll manage." She rose and picked up his bowl and spoon. "But you've got to take better care of yourself. Promise me."

"I know, I—"

"Promise me!"

"I'll promise." A sigh escaped him. "She was all I had. Life without her is empty."

Mina returned to the table and patted her father's shoulder. "I miss her too."

His gaze fell on her right hand. "I know she'd be happy to see you wear her ring."

Mina gave the gold band on her ring finger a whirl. It was all she had left from Mama, a gift, her father had given her for the wedding. Her mother wouldn't have approved of Roland, she was sure of it. But after her death, they were all upset, her father in his own world and she...what had she done? Run off in her grief, married an idiot.

"I'll stop by more often," she said, thinking that the right thing to do would've been to invite her father to her home. But she was ashamed of the hovel she lived in, ashamed of Roland and what he'd reduced her to.

Her father smiled weakly. "Promise?"

She nodded and reluctantly straightened. All she wanted was to stay and take care of her father. "I better go, have to do some cleaning and cooking as well."

He accompanied her to the door. "Take care of yourself."

Her heart ached as she climbed down the steep path, the last look of her father that of an old, shriveled man who would soon lose the will to live—like her neighbor.

The road she lived on seemed considerably worse than even a year ago. Four houses stood empty, people having died or left to head north to take one of the ships to America. Supposedly, life was better there. Some families were receiving letters, telling of rich soil, freedom, opportunity, and plenty of food.

Other than in the past, these vacant houses remained empty. The little gardens grew wild, moss-covered shingles and entries, vermin moved in, then mold and decay. Nobody wanted to live here, not when the fields were dead and people starved.

She opened the creaky gate and immediately noticed that the front door stood ajar. Alarmed she rushed inside. "Roland?"

No answer. The house was empty, but something had definitely happened. They had had little, but now even that was broken. Her clay pots lay strewn on the floor, her carefully collected dried herbs, mixed with broken shards. Chairs and table were on their sides, the bed turned over, blankets and the freshly washed sheet on the ground.

She remembered the door, checked its lock. Nothing was broken. Had she forgotten to lock up and somebody had ransacked everything in search of valuables? The fire was out, allowing the cold to creep inside. She needed to get firewood, make it warm and then clean, sort out her herbs. Where would she get new pots, she couldn't afford any. Her thoughts spiraled and she felt dizzy.

She remembered her shopping from this morning, the potatoes and grain. It was still there in the wooden box as was the one gold ducat in its rocky hiding place. She sighed with relief and went to work.

Around five o'clock she made dinner, potato soup with bits of onion, a sampling of herbs. She contemplated baking another bread from the spoiled rye—the three small buns from this morning were missing—but decided against it. When the church tower rang six times, she ate her share and eventually fell asleep sitting in her chair.

She awoke from the door banging shut. Roland was back, looking even more disheveled than usual.

"What happened? Are you all right?" she asked through the fog of her sleepiness.

Her husband didn't answer, just sank heavily onto the stool by the fire to take off his shoes. "What do you mean?"

From those words she knew he'd been drinking again. "Did you see Tom?" When he didn't answer, she continued. "Somebody broke in today, the house was ransacked, most of my pottery is broken. She gazed at the sad remains of her collection.

"What do you mean?" Roland got up to investigate the soup pot and moved to the table. "Better get me some of that."

"Of course." Mina hurried to fill a bowl and set it in front of him. "I don't have bread. It was missing, too."

"Where were you earlier?"

"You came back?" Mina poured two cups of peppermint tea and sat down across from her husband. Instead of an answer, he noisily slurped down the soup, once in a while wiping a sleeve across his mouth. A terrible thought entered Mina's mind. He'd returned and not finding her, being angry about the world again, had exploded in a fit. It would make sense. The door lock was intact, nothing was taken except for the food she'd made. "Did *you* do this?"

"Do what?"

"Ravage our home."

The answer lay in his eyes as he finally met her gaze. "So what."

Mina abruptly rose and went to the fire pit. Like this morning, the walls were moving in on her, the air seemed to grow thin as if Roland's moods were snuffing out her will to live. She forced herself to take deep breaths while she added another log to the fire. "I can't believe you did that. Why?" She'd only mumbled the words, but Roland was upon her like a flash.

"What was that?"

For once she did not shy away, but stood with straight shoulders to face him. "Why did you tear apart our home? It's all we have. I worked all afternoon to sort it out."

Roland squinted with fury, but there was also an element of surprise. Maybe he wasn't used to her acting unafraid. "I was angry."

You're always angry, because you can't get your act together. "About?"

"Tom said, he can't help me this time. I've got no work lined up and—"

"Did he pay you for the last days?"

Roland shrugged. Before he said anything, she knew, he'd taken it to the pub. "I've been asking around all afternoon, nobody has anything."

Mina sank on the stool by the fire. "I'm out of money. I'd hoped you would bring home enough to shop for food again before the weekend." She scanned the meager content of the storage box. "This won't last."

He dug into his pocket and held out a hand with a single Groschen and four Pfennig. "It's all I've got left." Remorse swung in his voice and for a moment, Mina felt sorry for him. But that didn't last long, because she knew he'd brought this onto them by his own actions. And now Tom refused to help. He'd been Roland's friend for years, had stood by him despite the drinking. Something had happened, something Roland wasn't telling. Or Tom was simply tired of a friend who lost every work, he'd ever taken on.

She rose from her chair, feeling like her bones were filled with rocks. All she wanted was to lie down and sleep—forget.

CHAPTER FOUR

Davin

When Davin arrived at the construction site the next morning, the thatcher and his helper were already there, bundling the tough rye stalks. It was an art, he didn't understand and after a short greeting, he climbed on top to check his handywork, make sure that the support structure was sound, all pegs in place. He methodically moved from joint to joint until he was satisfied.

"Look, who's about." Mark's voice easily reached him, so he climbed down to embrace his longtime friend.

"I'm done. Just wanted to check it over in daylight."

"Good work, as usual." Mark, broad shouldered with a sandy mop of hair, smiled broadly, exposing a hole where his upper right front tooth used to be. He'd lost it in a fistfight, pulling apart a couple of men in the pub. He put a hand on Davin's shoulder and said, "Sorry, I don't have anything else. It's getting tougher by the day. Half the people are leaving, the other half die."

Davin nodded. One had to be blind and deaf not to notice. "I'm going to head to the railroad. Pay is better."

"They'll work you hard," Mark said thoughtfully. He pulled out a purse and counted twelve pounds. "That should do, I hope."

Davin stuffed the bills into his jacket pocket. He'd already calculated that the lease on his parents' place was eight pounds, which left them four to cover the time until he'd get paid by the railroad. "Thanks, man. You know you can count on me, when you line up another building project."

Mark's brows drew together. "I wish I'd feel optimistic. I always did. Until this summer when the potatoes went bad again. The country is falling apart and everyone with it." He gazed at the thatcher balancing on one of the roof beams. "I never thought I'd say this, but I may take one of those ships to America."

Davin knew that Mark wasn't married. It wasn't quite clear to him why, but he'd never been too interested in the lasses, insisted they'd take his strength and his money.

"I don't think I could," Davin said. "This is my home, besides, ma and da need my help."

Mark nodded, his expression now serious. "Of course, just promise me to move before it's too late."

Too late for what, Davin wanted to ask. But at that moment, the thatcher called to Mark, so they shook hands. "Take care of yourself and if you leave, drop me a note."

Near the market, a group of women and children in tattered clothes called to him. They had the gaunt faces of the starving, large eyes, cheek bones sharp and that look of despair about them. These days, half of Ireland seemed to be on the road, looking for food. Davin's hand wandered into his pocket, where the pound notes lay waiting. He couldn't afford to give any away. Besides, it was dangerous to show that he carried money. People were desperate and couldn't be trusted.

On a whim, Davin entered the Red Paddy, the local pub, which had been there for decades if not centuries, a darkish smoky place frequented by Skibbereen's villagers. Despite the morning hour, half a dozen men stood by the bar counter, nursing ale. He felt like drinking whiskey, but knew it was a bad idea. He didn't want to flash his pound bills, besides, it'd raise eyebrows. Hardly a soul could afford the "good stuff" right now.

So, he nodded to the locals, one of them his neighbor, Finn Boyle, a fifty something man and tenant farmer like his parents, and ordered beer and soda bread.

"A bit early, isn't it?" Finn said, moving a little closer. "Never see you here."

"I'm done with a job," Davin said, moving backwards a couple of feet. The man reeked like rotten garbage.

"What're you going to do then?"

"Work the railroad, I think." Davin took a sip from his beer. "Great Western Railway."

"You going to England?" Finn, who'd obviously already had too much, grinned. "I heard it's backbreaking work."

"I don't mind. I've got to help my parents keep the farm."

"You think those rotten potatoes ever grow again?"

A good question, one that millions of Irish asked themselves. "Maybe once we know what causes it."

"I heard the Americans brought the disease to Ireland, though I wouldn't put it past the English, just to finish us off." Finn took a hearty swig from his glass and smacked it back on the counter.

Davin didn't answer. The beer was making him hungry, so he devoured the bread. Already, he felt the alcohol swirl through his blood.

"You hear that, boys," Finn shouted. "Davin here is heading for England. Let's drink to that."

Everyone hollered and lifted their glass to toast. Davin took another sip.

"Better be careful, over there," one of them said. "My cousin writes, they're breaking rocks all day."

"How you getting up there?", a man with a bulbous red nose asked. Davin knew he was the town drunk, spending every dime he made in the pub.

"Walk, I suppose." Davin waved at the barkeep to order a stew. No point, going home on an empty stomach.

"Weather is awfully cold." Finn scratched his head. It was obvious he hadn't taken a bath in months. "It'll take two weeks, at least, just to Dublin."

"It'll get worse," the drunkard commented, downing his beer. "You could buy us a beer before you leave, as a good-bye."

Davin quickly calculated in his head. The pub was nearly empty and the six or seven ales wouldn't set him back much. "All right, then, let's have another."

Again, the pub erupted in enthusiastic shouts. "Good boy...best of luck...to the lad...," they cried.

He finished his drink and began eating the stew, mostly cabbage and potatoes, while a second glass appeared in front of him. It was true, he hadn't given much thought to his travels which would be hard at the best of times. The temperatures were dropping, and he'd need shelter every night or he'd freeze to death. But waiting until spring was no option. He loathed to sit idle and several months doing nothing while watching his parents being depressed and the poor fill the workhouses and die of hunger was not for him. He'd have to plan carefully, though. Take a blanket and ration his food.

By the time he finished his stew, his glass was empty, but already somebody else had ordered another round.

Finn was hanging on the counter now, having downed a couple of shots. "Just be careful, lad, promise me that," he said over and over.

Davin downed the third glass because all of a sudden, he wanted to get home. Outside, the snow was getting thicker, thick white flakes danced in the wind. Ma would have the fire going and he looked forward to a talk with his father. It'd cheer him up.

Davin called the barkeep as the pub erupted in cheers, somebody else ordered another round.

"You going already," Finn slurred.

"One more, come on, Lad, it's ugly outside." The fellow with the bulbous nose was carrying glasses to his fellow drinkers and placed one next to Davin.

"Wife is going to beat me anyway," another man cried, lifting his glass, causing a wave a raucous laughter.

"To the wives," several of them hollered.

Davin lifted his to play along. The room was slowly moving up and down, as if the stool were bucking him. He put a hand on the counter to steady himself. Damn liquor.

The barkeep appeared. "What can I do for you?"

"I want to pay." Davin realized that he was having trouble speaking clearly. The stew was sloshing in his middle, causing him to belch. He'd meant to pull out one of the bills, but the entire stash appeared and slipped from his hand. He quickly bent to pick them up, separated one and put it on the counter.

"Having a windfall, eh," Finn said, his gaze remaining on the pocket where Davin had stashed the bills.

Davin leaned closer, hoping the others wouldn't hear. "Got paid for a job. It's all for my parents' farm, the lease is due."

"Lucky bastard." Finn's eyes were red now and greedy. He watched as Davin slipped the change coins into the same pocket. "Should've learned me self some carp...carpentry."

Ignoring the man, Davin finished his beer and pulled on his hat. "Better go."

"Happy travels," Finn called after him.

The icy wind hit Davin like a wall. He wrapped his jacket tightly around him and head low, marched off. Except it wasn't very straight at all. Every step seemed to wobble, and his sight felt milky like walking through fog. The more he tried to focus, the more his vision quivered. Everything was white and fuzzy as if he were walking inside a cloud. He didn't realize he'd drunk that much.

A grinding noise turned into sharp pain, the ground rushed up to him and he knew nothing.

"Can you hear me?" The ruddy face of a stranger hung above Davin like a strangely lit lantern. He could see every wrinkle, even the little blue veins on the man's cheeks. Davin's skull felt like bursting as he tried to determine where he was. "Lad, better get up before you freeze to death." The man, wrapped in a checkered shawl, pulled him to his feet. "You're bleeding. What happened to you?"

Davin touched his head, realizing that his hat was missing. On the back, where the sharp pain was worst, something felt sticky and wet. When he looked at his fingers, they were red.

"I got hit over the head," he whispered. He cleared his throat and this time louder, "Did you see anything? Somebody running?"

The man shook his head. "Better get yourself inside somewhere. I'm staying at the inn, if you need to rest for a bit." He extended a hand. "Malcolm Murphy, glad to meet you, I'm on my way north to Dublin."

Davin took the man's hand. "I live nearby, not to worry."

"All right, lad, farewell then." The man turned and left Davin standing in the whirling snow. That's when it hit him. His hand slid into his right pocket where he'd stashed the pound notes. His pocket was empty. Like his left.

They'd robbed him, hit him over the head and left to freeze to death in the snow.

A terrible fury gripped him, one he'd never known. His gaze focused now, he also noticed how cold he was. He should return to the pub and ask around, but inside his head swung a hammer. The next moment, he bent low to puke out the stew.

The cold had penetrated his skin and was cutting into his bones. Soon, he'd be too frozen to move. Hugging himself, he stumbled forward...toward home. He'd have to tell his parents, have to tell them, they'd lose the farm.

Because he'd been stupid and reckless.

CHAPTER FIVE

Mina

Roland had gone out early to ask around again. He'd left her alone that night, maybe because he knew he'd taken this too far or maybe because for once, he'd been half-way sober.

Mina had not even gotten up to make breakfast, had lain facing the wall with open eyes while Roland rummaged around the kitchen in search of something to eat. She didn't care if he went hungry. Until this very moment, she'd done whatever he asked, had been a good wife.

After the door closed, she slowly rose, washed her face and hands and stoked the fire. There was still that spoiled rye flour, she'd make into another loaf. Maybe she'd eat it all herself. She smiled grimly while she sorted through her dried herbs, what was left of them.

Soon, the little house filled with the aroma of baking bread. Her stomach gave a painful rumble as she tried to distract herself. Even if she'd use that last ducat, if she were sensible and planned well, it'd push off the inevitable by a few weeks at most. And then what?

What would become of them? She'd passed by the overcrowded poorhouse, had seen the begging people at the market, more every time she went. Deep in thought, she pulled on her warmest shawl and basket in one hand, entered the street. A fine glittering of ice covered the ground and she slipped and nearly fell. She had to be crazy, but sitting in that cabin was not going to do anything, except drive her mad. She pressed her lips together and headed down the path, out of the village.

Along the forest which belonged to one of the aristocrats, ruling the land, she left the footpath. She'd passed by here a thousand times, picking flowers. Now she was looking for something else and there it was: the creeping Jenny, dark-leaved and low to the ground, was hardly noticeable this time of year. But Mina knew that it was a nutritious plant best harvested in the spring when it carried beautiful blue flowers, good for tea and treating ailments. But they could also eat it, even if it was bit sharp and bitter tasting. At least, it'd fill them...if she could find enough for a meal. One meal. She sunk to her knees and began picking the leaves. It was slow work and soon her legs shook with cold, and her feet grew numb. Still, she continued until the basket was half filled.

She'd dry some for tea and add the remainder as flavoring to a couple of soups. She looked into the overcast sky that had taken on the color of ash. *Thank you, Mama.* The air smelled of snow and the wind had picked up.

The cabin was empty and judging by the state of it, Roland hadn't been back. Just as well, that gave her time to fix a soup in peace. Her thoughts wandered to her father, who struggled to deal with his loneliness. She was married and felt just as isolated. Everybody was struggling so much, they had no time to visit or share their lives with others.

Outside, snow had begun to fall, covering the ugliness of her life in a white blanket. It was growing dark even earlier, the church bell had barely rung four times. Christmas was coming and it'd be a sad affair. She had nothing to give because both Roland and her father had no use for the little baskets she sometimes wove from willow and a variety of vines. She scoffed. At least, Roland couldn't break those.

Humming to herself, she sorted through her supplies and inspected the bundle of willow, sitting in the back corner. It'd need soaking which meant she'd have to go to the well through the snow—

The door swung open and banged against the opposite wall. Roland rushed inside, snow whirled, accompanied by a gust of icy air.

"Close the do—"

"Mina!"

Mina had never heard such urgency in her husband's voice. She rushed forward as Roland threw the door shut. He shook himself and removed the hat. A bloody gash cut across his cheek and his lower lip was swollen.

"What happened?" she cried.

"Listen," Roland took her hands in his, "listen to me. We've got to go. Now!"

"Go where, what did you do?" Mina's voice was shrill in her ears. That same expression of despair, he'd carried last night, showed in Roland's face now. She knew in that moment that he'd done something terrible, something that would send him away or to the gallows. Her heart raced as she fought to calm her breath. "Tell me what happened."

Roland ignored her and moved to the bed, rummaging underneath where they kept a couple of bags and an old suitcase. "Help me pack."

"Where are you going?"

He rushed back to her, squeezed her left wrist painfully. "*We* are going...*together*!"

A terrible anger took hold of Mina as she yanked her hand free and took a step back. "Unless you tell me what happened, I won't move a finger," she said, fighting to control her breath.

Roland groaned. "Woman, we don't have time for this."

Mina stood her ground, in fact, she moved next to the fire poker, in case he'd attempt to grab her again. Across the divide, they eyed each other.

Roland looked away. "There was a fight...in the pub. We were playing cards, I was winning."

Mina's thoughts raced. What was he wagering, if he didn't have any money? She forced herself to remain silent...to wait for the inevitable.

"One of the players, Harald, you know from across the street, accused me of cheating. It got loud and they tried searching me. I fought them off and Harald stumbled and fell...hit his head." Roland's voice had grown quiet, so quiet, Mina leaned forward. Still, she wasn't prepared for the last part. "I think he's dead."

"You pushed him?" Mina's voice was just as quiet now.

Roland shrugged. "I don't remember, everything went so fast. One minute, we were all sitting there having a good time. The next, Harald lay in his own blood."

"We need to tell the police." Mina knew it meant traveling to the big city, but surely, they'd be able to explain.

"No...I mean they're sending somebody to Heilbronn. That's why we have to leave now."

"I don't understand, you said, it was an accident, why—"

"I can't stay." Roland's voice shook. "They'll accuse me of murder, I'll go to prison or worse."

"You said it was an accident—"

"It was, but..." Roland finally looked up and met her gaze.

What Mina saw in his eyes made her shiver. A lie stood there as clearly as if it had been written across his forehead. "But what?"

"We should move someplace else. Work here is done anyway. We'll start over." He rummaged through his pocket and handed her a crumpled piece of paper.

Mina smoothed it out as she flew over the lines. Beneath the drawing of a sailboat, it read...

General Emigration Newspaper
For interested parties who intend to emigrate to the free American States

Mina's hand sank. "You want to leave Germany?"

Roland nodded enthusiastically. "I've been thinking about it for a while. Many families have left already and there's no good work here anymore. We're going to starve like those souls on the street." A bit of color had crept into his cheeks. "The other night, an agent for Hapag-Lloyd was in the pub. He said there're ships leaving from Bremerhaven all the time. We just need to get up there and..."

"What about my father?"

"He's old, I don't think he'd make it."

"Of course, he wouldn't want to go." New anger brewed inside Mina. "I can't leave him here alone, he has nobody."

Roland squinted and by the way his eyes flashed, Mina knew he was running out of patience. "We can't wait."

"But we can't afford the trip. Surely, it's expensive."

"They've got the redemptioner program. I'll just agree to work for an outfit for a few years and in exchange they pay for the voyage. They also said, we'd receive a piece of land afterwards."

"Just like that."

"Just like that." Roland took a step forward, but he was smiling. "Don't you see, Mina. It'd be real new beginning, we work hard, build a cabin, raise cattle and horses. You get chickens"

Mina had heard about resettling in the new world. Half a dozen families had left the village last summer, more this year, it seemed half of Württemberg was clearing out—King Wilhelm I. had not been able to stop the bad harvests and famine. There'd been letters read aloud about lush pastures and friendly Americans, how they helped each other settle and grow new neighborhoods, all German, all working together to build new communities. Little German towns in America. It sounded too good to be true.

"I need to wait for father..." She realized she would be willing to try something new, but not while Papa was still alive. It'd break his heart—

"We cannot wait!" Roland stood quite close now and Mina was stuck against the wall. "We're leaving tonight." The old threatening undertone was back in his voice, and she knew she'd have to tread carefully.

"The weather is terrible," she said quietly. "How will be get to Bremerhaven?"

"On foot, if we have to," Roland said. "But I heard there're ships traveling the Rhine."

"Those cost money, too."

Roland pulled a fistful of coins from his pocket. "Remember, I won tonight. This will get us to Bremerhaven."

"Don't we have to get permission from the authorities to leave?" Württemberg's King was afraid, too many people were leaving and required its citizens to apply for emigration which could take months.

"We'll send them a letter later. Now we need to pack."

Mina lowered her head. She felt beat, kind of empty. She wouldn't have time to say good-bye to her friend…and what about her father? A journey like this one took time to plan. Instead, they were running…like fugitives…like they were guilty.

CHAPTER SIX

Davin
Davin's fingers were so stiff, he hardly was able to open the door.
　His mother rushed up to him. "What happened to you? Your head." She gently made him sit, investigated the back of his skull.
　He began to cry, silent tears rolled down his cheeks, dripped from his chin. "I was robbed, Mam," he said after a while. Never in his twenty-four years had he felt so humiliated, so utterly frustrated...and disappointed with himself.
　As his father stoked the fire and helped him take off his shoes, Davin told them about stopping at the pub. "The money for the farm, it's all gone."
　His mother covered her eyes with both hands, his father sighed heavily. "We'll have to write to the landlord. Maybe he'll see reason, extend the deadline." His father was pretty strong for near sixty, his shoulders brought, and his arms muscular. Except in the last few months, a persistent cough had appeared, keeping him up at night. He never talked about it, but Davin swore that he was in pain.
　As he sat across them, he knew he had dealt them a terrible blow. Da abruptly rose and put on his outside clothes. "I'm going to the pub, ask around."
　"I'll come with you." Davin straightened though the movement sent darts of pain into the back of his head and the room grew foggy. With a groan he sank back down.
　"You're in no shape to go out," his mother said, throwing his father a warning glance.
　Davin knew that look, he himself had experienced off and on. Ma

hardly used words, she could do it all with her expressions. His father obviously knew it too, because he grumbled something unintelligible and headed into the storm.

Less than an hour later, he was back, covered in snow and shaking with cold. "Damn weather," he said quietly. Davin was lying in his bed, but with the open space, he heard every word. "I asked around, nobody has seen anything. Finn was pretty drunk, but he swore that nobody followed Davin after he left."

"What are we going to do?" His mother's voice was low, yet Davin heard the distress in it as clearly as if she'd sat next to him.

"I'm going to write to the landlord." Feet shuffled and Davin turned to his side, pressing a fist into his mouth to keep from crying out. Even if the landlord gave them a reprieve, which was unlikely these days, not after the second year of lost harvests, it'd only postpone the inevitable. How could they ever repay what they owed?

He wanted to jump up and head out immediately, get to England and start sending money home. It was the only option.

Davin's father had sent word to the gendarmerie, but nothing was being done. All of Ireland was in the grip of the famine and desperate people did desperate things. That also meant committing crimes and Davin knew he'd been foolish, had made it easy for the thief to take him down.

While the wound on his head healed, his heart continued to ache with regret. He wanted to return to that moment when he'd entered the pub, tell himself to keep walking home. But it was no good. It was done and he'd have to live with himself.

Within days, all three lined up for the soup kitchen. It was the first time and Davin felt ashamed. But shame had nothing to do with it. His belly ached from the constant gnawing and while he was better dressed than the fifty or sixty souls waiting in front of them, he was just as desperate. He took the hot cabbage soup with shaky hands and slurped it down like the others.

His father had pleaded with him to delay until his head was better, but the longer he waited, the weaker he'd get. A letter arrived from the landlord.

Ma watched it laying on the table in front of her, unable to lift her gaze and just as unable to read it. "Let's wait until your father get's home."

Da had gone out again to ask around for odd jobs. Davin knew it was useless, nobody was hiring, not even younger, stronger men.

Ireland was dying in front of his eyes.

But when his father returned, he looked almost hopeful. "They're hiring near Cork," he cried, joining them at the table, "building roads."

"That's at least three days walk," Davin said.

"Your shoulders are bad, it's breaking and hauling rocks all day." Ma looked dejected and scared at the same time.

Davin patted her hand. "Pay is bad, too. I heard you hardly get more than a few meals."

All three eyed the letter on the table until Davin's father finally opened the seal.

He squinted at the writing, neat even lines, undoubtedly written with an expensive ink pen. "He can't wait." The letter tumbled to the table where Davin picked it up.

Regrettably, the lease is due as scheduled. To cover rising costs, it has increased to nine pounds ten shillings. An agent will stop by in the first week of January to collect...

Davin's hand sank. No use to read the remaining lines, undoubtedly some empty wishes for their health. The English were cutthroats who'd dance on his parents' graves, on the graves of the entire country. The old fury was back, and he opened the button of his shirt collar.

His mother shook her head. "We're heading for the workhouse."

"I'm leaving tomorrow," Davin heard himself say. "My head is well enough." It was a lie, he still had terrible headaches and his vision blurred accompanied by waves of nausea, forcing him to halt what he was doing until it passed.

But he could not wait. It'd take long enough to reach Dublin, he'd likely have to work to afford the passage across to Liverpool. Not to mention the question of food and housing along the way.

Ma just looked at him, that caring, loving expression, he knew so well, now mixed with a worry frown.

His father leaned forward, his work hardened hands folded. "I could come with you."

"No," his mother said. "It is too hard. They need young men on the railroad."

"Ma is right," Davin addressed his father. "It's at least a two-week march to Dublin, the English won't hire you anyway."

Davin left at first light. He'd packed a few things, an extra sweater, a change of underwear, a towel. It was more than most owned these days and he felt thankful to have clothes at all. They'd hugged quickly, Davin forcing himself to remain calm, despite Ma's wet eyes and his father's heavy sighs.

"I'll write from Dublin," he said. "Don't give up, I'll send money before Christmas."

He abruptly turned, opened the door and stepped onto the icy road. Fifty yards away, he threw a glance back at the house where his parents still stood, watching him. They didn't wave, just stood there, Da with one arm wrapped around Ma, almost like ghosts ready to dissolve at any moment.

With a shutter, Davin lowered his head and trudged into the morning. Last night, he'd visited Mark one last time. Word had gotten around and Mark asked him to stay for tea. Davin had filled his stomach, hardly able to speak. Seeing Mark brought it all back, his recklessness, the moment when he realized he'd been robbed and the utter devastation he'd felt. Still felt. It was like a poisonous cloud choked him.

Mark poured another tea after Davin had declined the poitín. "The railroad, is it?"

"I would've gone anyway, but now I've got to hurry. My parents are losing the farm."

"I think the English love it, taking our farms, taking back the land."

"They must be some calloused bastards." Davin took a sip, his fingers soaking up the warmth of the mug. It was true, except for the landlord's agent, he'd never met an English man in his life.

Mark downed the poitín and poured another. "They are, lad. I've met my share of rich lords. Not the poor though, they're just as bad off as the people here."

"Makes you wonder, what goes on in their heads." He took a deep breath. "Say, I'm desperate—"

"Here." Mark placed a pound note in front of Davin. "I knew you'd stop by and I'm sorry for what happened. But that's the best I can do, my order books are empty. Not sure, what I'll do in the spring." He scoffed. "Might have to join you on the railroad."

"I thought you were heading to America."

Mark scratched his grizzled chin. "Maybe so, will decide in the spring."

They'd shaken hands good-bye, Mark giving him an encouraging pat on the back. "You'll succeed, lad, just be on your toes and never lose hope."

Now that he was trudging up the path, it was exactly how he felt:

losing hope. There was no way to earn enough money to pay the landlord in time. His parents would have to move to the workhouse and maybe, if he were able to send enough over time, they'd afford a small cottage. He'd do what was needed, if he'd break his back doing it.

By the noon hour he was famished. The unaccustomed walking through foot-high snow was wearing him out. The snow slowed his progress and the constant wind cut into the skin of his face. He couldn't feel his toes and his nose and eyes burned. He'd soon look like old Finn with blue veins and pocks all over his cheeks.

Twice he saw the still forms of women, one or two children by their sides, frozen in the snow, perished in the middle of nowhere, nobody grieving, nobody burying them, impossible because of the frozen ground. Like millions before them, they were poor and thus forgotten, snuffed out by history as if they'd never existed.

He kept his eyes straight, called a greeting when he passed someone, few even acknowledged him, likely too exhausted to muster the energy. They appeared to be in worse shape, eyes huge and glassy in their faces, often blue-tinged bare-skinned legs and questionable shoes. Soon, they'd lie down like the women and children, he'd passed earlier.

There was nothing romantic about traveling, maybe if it had been spring or summer, when the fields and trees were so green, it hurt the eyes. Maybe then would he have enjoyed it a bit. But in this weather, with the pressure of finding money, so his parents wouldn't starve to death, it was a grind that never seized.

By the evening, he stopped in a workhouse, hoping for a meal and a straw bed. Both were offered free of charge, and he stuffed two soda rolls into his pocket for later. He kept the pound note in a leather bag on his chest and except for his hat and coat, never took off any of his things. Even those and his bag, he carried with him inside the workhouse, afraid, somebody would steal them.

He could not afford to make additional mistakes. Not now!

CHAPTER SEVEN

Mina

Mina and Roland had made it to Heidelberg, a grueling four-day walk through the snow-covered landscape. At night, they crept into a barn and buried in the hay, several times coming upon other travelers, heading the other way. Roland never looked over his shoulder, but Mina sensed his nervousness. Anymore, she doubted his story, knew something worse had happened, something he'd be accused of, if they caught him.

She'd wanted to leave a note for her father, but Roland had torn it up and thrown it into the fire. "No notes, I don't want anybody to find out where we're going."

"But nobody knows anything. At least, let me see Papa to say good-bye." In the end, Roland had conceded to pass by his house. But she never went inside, not only because Roland didn't allow it. She realized she didn't have the strength to tell him that she'd be far away for a while. That's what she told herself. After a few months, when things had calmed down, they'd return and she'd take care of her father, she'd visit him daily and help him find hope again. Let Roland dream of a faraway country. Until now, he'd never finished anything he started.

Behind the glass, she'd watched her father sit at the table, studying a piece of paper. After a few minutes, he looked up and she saw the tears. He didn't seem to notice his wet face, just stared into the distance, mumbling something as if his wife were there in that shadowy corner of the room.

Roland had impatiently tugged at her sleeve and after one last look, she'd followed him into the night.

Now they were staying at some cheap inn at the outskirts of town, ten or twelve people squeezed together in a room with nothing but a bit of straw. The air was thick with the odor of unwashed skin, but nobody was desperate enough to open the window and cool down the room even further. They slept huddled together after eating a watery cabbage soup, at least it was cheap.

Her nose stuck against Roland's chest, she thought of her house and who would take it over while they were gone. Until now she'd despised living in the cabin, but now, from a distance, she knew it had been a place to call home. Likely, it'd sit empty until they returned. Behind her, a woman coughed, a deep roaring sound as if her chest were filled with wet cloth.

Why couldn't she fall asleep like the others? Roland just closed his eyes and fell immediately into deep slumber. No matter how tired she was, she lay there and fretted. They had hardly spoken during the march, not only because it was too cold, but she realized, they had nothing to say to each other. At least, he was leaving her alone right now, sharing the room with strangers and lying in a freezing barn.

"Wake up." Mina opened her eyes. Roland waved a baked roll in front of her face. "Eat that, so we can leave."

She peeled out of her blanket and regretted it immediately, the now empty room was nearly as cold as the outside. She got to her feet and picked the straw from her skirt. "I'm going to the outhouse and find some water."

"Hurry up." Roland looked as grumpy as she'd ever seen him. He had no opportunity to seek solace in drink. Even *he* knew they needed the few coins to travel. And he was obviously scared enough to want to put distance between them and home.

Mina swallowed a rebuke and climbed down the wooden staircase, no wider than a couple of feet. The host was wiping the counter with a rag, about as grimy as his own clothes. Mina asked for directions and after washing her hands and face, hurried back upstairs. She patted her chest, where, inside her undershirt, the gold coin lay wrapped in a piece of cloth.

They hadn't stepped outside yet, when the hunger pains returned. Sleep seemed to be the only time when she had any peace.

"Do you know what it costs...traveling on the Rhine?", she asked as they followed a wagon, piled high with traveling trunks. Alongside walked four adults of varying ages, all wrapped into shawls, wearing hats and sturdy boots. It was a good thing because this morning, the air itself felt frozen and with each breath, the little warmth, she was producing, evaporated.

Roland mumbled something, so Mina addressed the woman who was walking behind the wagon. She looked to be her own age, not much older than twenty, with deep blue eyes ringed by long lashes. But Mina was mostly drawn to the woman's expression, that little smirk in the corners of her mouth as if she were enjoying this adventure.

"Good morning, are you by any chance heading to Mannheim to take a boat?"

The woman smiled broader now and exposed even teeth. Despite the shawl covering her hair, she exuded beauty. "We are, my family and I are traveling to Bremerhaven and then across the Atlantic."

"May I ask what the ship's passage north costs?"

A tiny wrinkle appeared between the woman's brows. "Let me ask." She hurried forward, calling, "*Vater*, what is the price for a passage on the Rhine?"

The man said something, Mina didn't understand, before the woman returned. "He says around a Taler and twelve silver Groschen per person."

The man in front turned to face them and called, "I hope they haven't changed the price, in fact, it may be less because fewer people travel in this weather." He resumed his walk as Roland hurried to join his side.

Mina waved. "Thank you."

"You are going to America, too?" The beautiful woman eyed her curiously.

Mina shrugged. "I don't think we will. My husband wants to..."

"But you'd rather stay home."

Mina threw a glance at the woman. The smirk was back. "Yes, my old father is back there in the village."

"He surely understands if you're seeking a better life. Everybody is starving. *Vater* said it is the only way to secure a good future for the family." The path in front of Mina blurred and she lowered her head. A gloved hand appeared in her vision and patted her cheek. "What happened?"

The lump in Mina's throat grew. She wasn't used to a stranger's kindness and all of a sudden the pressure of the last days demanded release. Her eyes welled over. "My father...I didn't..." she stuttered.

"You didn't tell him?" Mina shook her head. "Dear God, you poor thing." The gloved hand moved around to her shoulder. "I'm so sorry. You must write to him, explain your reasoning."

Mina wiped her face which had grown even colder from being wet.

"Here." A white handkerchief with a pretty lace border appeared in her vision. It seemed far too nice to use for blowing a nose. "Go ahead, take it. I've got half a dozen. *Mutter* insisted. We've been planning this journey for two years."

Mina dabbed at her tears and stuffed the little cloth in her pocket. "Thank you." She felt almost disappointed when the arm disappeared from her shoulders.

"I'm Augusta."

"Mina." They looked at each other and Mina felt a little warmth return to her limbs. "If you planned for such a long time, why are you traveling in winter? I thought it was best to cross during the warm weather."

"*Vater* thinks it's getting crowded. People have to wait a long time and he figured it would go much quicker this time of year."

Ahead, Roland was talking to Augusta's father while the other women listened. Mina was glad to have time to herself, only occasionally she glanced at Augusta who seemed deep in thought.

"Do you have an admirer?" Mina asked after a while.

Augusta vehemently shook her head and cried, "no."

"So, you do have one."

Augusta laughed though it sounded close to tears. "I did." She nodded at her father. "It was not a good match, so *Vater* refused to allow us to marry." She pointed over her shoulder. "He's back home."

"I'm sorry."

"What about your husband? Is he a good man?"

Mina thought about their hasty departure, the drinking and his anger toward her. She lifted the small pack that was all that remained from her old life. "We left in a hurry. I'm not sure how we'll get north. Roland wasn't working much before we took off."

"Why didn't you wait?"

Mina shrugged. In her mind she saw Roland enter with that expression of panic on his face. "He got impatient."

Ahead, the men called out and pointed ahead. In the distance, a wide band of water was visible. "It's the Rhine," Roland cried.

"Not much farther," the two women upfront said. "This must be Mannheim."

Augusta gripped Mina's hand. "The first part of our journey."

They headed toward the port where boats and ships lined up along several quays. People of all ages, dressed in everything from fine garments to rags packed the streets and milled along the water's edge.

Beyond, the pewter-gray waves of the Rhine River awaited. Mina shuddered. Would she really be able to step foot on a ship? She couldn't swim, what if she fell—

"Isn't it glorious?" Augusta's eyes were wide with excitement. She clapped her hands as she looked toward the line of sailing ships. "I wonder which one we'll take."

Mina tried a smile, failed as Roland was rushing toward her. "I'm going to accompany Stefan to the port. You should go with the women to the inn." He pointed at a two-story building, sitting back from the street.

Without waiting for a reply, he hurried off after Augusta's father and was immediately lost in the crowd. Two dozen people crowded the entrance to the inn.

"Where're you going?" One of them, an older man in a fancy suit, a thick gold chain hanging from his pocket, said. "We're all waiting here." The women around him threw Mina and Augusta angry glances, muttering insults.

Augusta didn't seem phased. "I'm sorry, dear sir," she addressed the man, "I did not know." She pulled Mina with her to wait in back.

"I doubt we'll find beds here," Mina said. Secretly, she knew that they'd never be able to afford a room, not this close to the port.

"We can't leave though," Augusta answered. "*Vater* and your husband will not know where to find us. We might as well wait here."

An hour later they reached the reception desk. The fancy man and his group had disappeared down the hall.

"Your name?" The receptionist said. "You reserved how many nights?"

Augusta and Mina looked at each other. "We didn't reserve..." Mina said.

A look of disbelieve came over the man's face. "Dear ladies, you surely know that it is impossible to find rooms without a reservation." He pointedly looked over Mina's shoulder and nodded at a man behind her. "Next."

"Damn," Augusta said once they were back outside. "I'm afraid, this will be difficult. Hopefully *Vater* will get passage for us today."

Augusta's grandmother leaned against their cart, while her mother was helping her drink from a cup. "There is no room here," Mina said, asking herself why she hadn't thought of asking her father to come along. He was no older than Augusta's grandmother and likely in better shape. She swallowed the bitterness in her throat and looked toward the port. No matter that it was winter and freezing cold, thousands seemed to want to travel.

The sense of feeling lost rolled over her and in that moment, all she wanted to do, was to return home.

CHAPTER EIGHT

Davin

Every day, it seemed to Davin that he grew slower, his legs heavier and colder. The winter weather was not letting up and he worried about frostbite on his face and toes. The boots he wore were far from waterproof and had no chance to dry in the damp conditions of the places he slept. On the fifth night, he was not able to get into a workhouse and the soup kitchen, he'd passed two hours earlier was now out of reach. He rubbed his chest where the pound note rustled softly. He could buy a meal, sleep in a warm bed. But that meant, spending a portion of the money and once the bill was broken, the rest would follow quickly. No, he had to be strong.

On the outskirts of the village, he crept into a stall with a handful of sheep. He squeezed in-between them, glad for their warmth. To distract himself from the gnawing in his middle, he daydreamed of his parents moving into a nice home. One he'd pay for with the wages from the railroad.

In the morning, he washed his hands in the sheep trough and snuck outside, worried some poor farmer was going to hit him over the head. At a well in the center of the next village, he drank his fill, though the icy water chilled him to the core again and the ache in his belly made him lightheaded.

On a whim, he knocked on the door of a home, one of hundreds of gray stone buildings, a tiny garden and a handful of chickens behind a wire fence. A band of smoke rose from the chimney and was immediately torn away by the wind. This morning, it felt even colder than usual.

The door opened a crack and the face of an ancient woman, her head covered in a shawl, became visible. "Yes?" Despite her looks, her voice sounded like that of his mother.

"Excuse me, mam, I'm wondering if you could spare a bit of bread. I'm on the road to Dublin and I've got nothing to keep me going," Davin said with a shaky voice.

The woman eyed him from the shadows, neither spoke nor moved and he waited for her to slam the door shut in his face. What did it matter? He didn't even blame her. He had to look rough, likely stunk of manure. He hung his head and turned away with a "Sorry to disturb you."

"What is your name?" the woman asked his back.

He turned again. The door had opened a few more inches. "Davin Callaghan, mam, I'm from Skibbereen, County Cork."

"I know where that is. Come on in then and take off your boots."

Davin nodded and slipped through the door. He peeled out of his coat and his numb fingers fumbled with the laces. Now on socks, he hesitated. The woman had moved to the hearth, her back to him. "Sit, lad, sit."

He sank on the chair, thankful to sit at a real table. Immediately, he was transported back to his parents' home and the memory of their worried expressions.

"I'm grateful, mam."

The woman turned. In the shadowy house, she looked even older, her face crisscrossed by a field of wrinkles. Still, her eyes were wide awake and watched him curiously. "What's a lad like you doing on the road in this weather?"

"I'm a carpenter, but there's no work anymore, so I'm heading to Liverpool and from there to the railroad."

The woman added oats to the pot on the fire and stirred before she turned to him. "You want to work for the English, those murdering bastards?"

Davin shrugged. "I've got no choice. My parents will lose the farm, if I don't."

"You left your parents in Skibbereen?"

"Aye, mam." The old woman clucked her tongue before she poured milk into an earthen mug and set it in front of him. "Drink slowly." She cut a slice from a loaf of bread and handed it to him. Then she sat while a small groan escaped her. "Damn old bones, they're stiff as old wood. My knees don't bend in this weather." She took a sip from a mug and smacked her lips. "Damn English, the only reason, I'm still here is because *mo shíorghrá*, my dear husband, smart geezer he was, had paid off the land."

Davin chewed the rye bread and closed his eyes because the feeling of food sliding down his throat felt like heaven. The chair legs scraped on the stone tile made him look up. The old woman was slowly rising before giving the pot a whirl. She wobbled to the corner where a couple of wooden boxes sat, rummaged in one of them, and returned to the table with two apples. "Here, eat something fresh."

He chased the bread with the apple, chewing quickly. The skin was wrinkly, but the inside was still juicy and full of flavor. When had he last eaten an apple?

She sank back on her chair. "Gave up potatoes three years ago. Couldn't work the land any longer. It seems now it was a good decision." She shook her head and looked toward the tiny window. "Damn potatoes are killing the country."

"Do you have any children?" Incapable of slowing himself, Davin picked up the second apple.

The woman's gaze returned to him. "Had a little girl once, Myra was only four when she died. Got a fever and just burned up." A raspy sigh escaped her. "It never stops hurting. I had no more children after that—a blessing and a curse."

"I'm sorry, I'm the only one in my family. Ma never..."

"It's for the better. Look at what this famine is doing, entire families are dying of hunger, those who have any sense left, leave." She leaned forward, eyed him closely. "You should leave, lad, while you still can. Go far away. Ireland is dying."

"My parents need my help."

"You could help them more if you have a good life. I'm sure that's what they want for you. Those English," the old woman clucked again, "they don't deserve our help. All they do is make slaves of us."

Davin nodded. She was right, but what could he do? He needed to earn money...quickly. The landlord wouldn't wait.

The woman straightened again and ladled the steaming oatmeal into two bowls. She added a spoonful of something red to each and handed him his portion. "Blackberry preserves."

They ate in silence, once in a while Davin glanced at the old woman across from him. She seemed far away, likely in her thoughts with her lost child or dead husband. He scraped the bowl and finally leaned back. He was full to the brim, as full as he hadn't been in months.

"Thank you for sharing your table, for helping me," he said.

Already, he felt the urgency again to take off again and hurry north. Until his gaze fell on the beam above the entrance door. It looked rotten, the wood gray and soft. It'd be only a matter of time before the front of the house would cave in.

"I could fix that for you." He pointed at the wall. "If you have any other wood to replace the beam."

The woman waved dismissively. "Leave it, lad. I kind of look forward to this life to be over."

Davin rose. "I'll be eternally grateful for your help. Just think you'd been gone." He took the old woman's hands, small and wrinkled like her face, in his. "You're old, lonely...but today you were my sun."

The old woman's dark eyes shone and there was even a hint of a smile. "You're a good lad with a good heart. Look in the shed...behind the chickencoop."

It was early afternoon before he left, his pack filled with a loaf of bread, six apples, four boiled eggs, and a sliver of cheese. He'd lost time and yet, he felt good to have made a friend and maybe having brought a bit of joy to the old woman. They'd helped each other, brought a bit of warmth to this harsh world.

At dusk, he reached Mallow. The town's main street was deserted, the wind had built six-foot snow drifts in places. Davin searched for an open shop and found a mostly empty pub called The Olde Fiddle, which was as gloomy as it was outside.

"Would there be a soup kitchen in town?," he asked. "Or a barn to spend the night?"

The barkeep scratched his nose. "Not from around here, I take it."

"Skibbereen, heading to Dublin."

"You might try the city building though it's likely closed by now." He glanced at the wall clock. "Murphy may give you a place, if he likes your face."

"Where would I find this Murphy?"

"Old codger lives a half mile out of town. Watch for the stone walls on the right. Can't miss it."

Davin longingly watched the man pour ale for a patron. The pound note inside his chest rustled. It'd be so easy—

"Want to order something?" The barkeep looked at him expectantly.

"Sorry, no, I'm on my way."

The wind outside gripped him anew as he turned right, down Main Street. Most everything was closed, certainly the city building. He sniffed, but there was no sign of a soup kitchen or even people walking the road like him. Where was everyone? It was dark as he followed the road, and the quarter moon gave hardly enough light to keep him on the road. He should've stopped earlier, should've looked for a barn. Now it was too late. How in the world was he going to notice rock walls—half of Ireland's roads and pastures had them—when he could barely see his own feet? He stumbled forward, wishing himself back to the old woman's home.

He'd propped up the opening, removed the old wood and fashioned a new cross beam. He was proud, how well it'd fit into the space. She'd offered him to spend the night and start in the morning afresh, but he'd refused, nervous again about wasting too much time on the road instead of earning a living to save his parents. Now he was in a bad spot because of it. The temperatures had dropped well below freezing and unless he found shelter, he'd freeze to death.

You're a damn idiot, Davin. Can't you for once think ahead? He looked into the night sky where a cloud slid past the moon. In the deepening shadows he made out the path and hurried on. On his right was no rock wall, in fact, everything around him seemed like a black void, ready to swallow him. He'd wander off someplace and in the spring some farmer would find a frozen and emaciated body. He thought of the dead, he'd passed along the road, some of them still walking, but so weak, they might as well be corpses. If he wasn't careful, he'd become one of them.

Thicker clouds moved in front of the moon, and it grew pitch black again. He stopped in his tracks, unsure what to do. He could return to town, break his pound note and ask the barkeep for a spot in the storage room. He looked over his shoulder, shook his head. When he turned his gaze forward again, he noticed a tiny sparkle to his right. He blinked, thinking he was seeing things. But the twinkle was still there. He closed his eyes, opened them again.

There was something out there, some light source. He stumbled forward and smacked into rock, pain shot up his knee, but it didn't matter. This had to be the wall. He felt for the rough stone that ended at his hip, turned sideways and one hand touching the wall, staggered forward. Off and on, he blinked to make sure he still saw the light which didn't move and slowly grew larger.

When the light was directly to his right, the wall ended. He moved straight toward it, one arm out in case he'd walk into another obstacle. Something smelled of dung as his ears picked up the rustling of animals, maybe goats or sheep. But he didn't have the energy to creep into another barn. The light grew brighter, and he recognized the outline of a window...then a door. He'd reached somebody's home.

Without hesitation, he knocked. "Hello?"

After what seemed like an eternity, the door flew open and the barrel of shotgun pointed at him. "What do you want?"

"Sorry, sir, I'm...the barkeep..." Davin tried to remember the name of the pub, but his mind was empty.

"Did that son of a bitch send another clapperdudgeon." The man, dressed in ill-fitting pants, a badly mended jacket, with a gray grizzle on his chin, eyed him suspiciously.

"I don't need food, just a bit of straw somewhere. It's frightfully cold tonight." As if to emphasize his words, a gust of wind blew open the door until it smacked into the wall.

"Damn winter," the man said, still watching him. Was there a softening in his eyes? Davin couldn't tell.

"I'm heading to Dublin, looking for work as a carpenter to help save my parents' farm, name is Davin, sir."

"Davin, eh?" The gun barrel sank toward the ground. In a quick movement, much quicker than Davin had thought possible, the man waved him inside. "All right, then, come in before I lose all the heat in this place."

The room reminded Davin of the old woman's house, a single space with a stone hearth. He moved to the fire to warm his numb fingers.

A small smile crept onto his face—obviously, he'd passed inspection.

CHAPTER NINE

Mina

The hours passed in slow motion while Mina and Augusta's family were waiting for the return of the men. They watched hundreds of travelers enter the inn and return with disappointed expressions, while others moved in with a sense of superiority.

Mina wanted to smack them in their arrogant faces, but then who was she to question anybody's motives. Roland's and her travels were nothing but a headless escape.

By the time, Augusta's father and Roland returned, it was afternoon.

"I was able to get passage three days from now," Stefan said, looking dejected. "Until then every vessel is booked solid. They're even using small ships, but it isn't enough." He looked at his family and Mina. "What is going on, why are you out here?"

Augusta's mother clapped her hands. "Oh, you fool, we're waiting for you, of course. Do you think there are rooms available when all the ships are booked?"

Roland pulled Mina aside. "We've got to talk."

While Augusta's family discussed what to do next, Mina followed Roland to the road. "I wasn't able to book tickets," he said, not meeting her eyes. "It's more than three Taler." He shrugged, looking dejected. "I don't have it."

Didn't you know that before we left, Mina wanted to shout. Instead, she stared at the man she'd married, who'd turned out to be very different than she'd expected. "Why don't we go home then. It's only a few days—

Roland grabbed her by the upper arm and squeezed. "No!"

"You're hurting me," Mina cried.

He let go of her. "I can't return, don't you understand that?"

Mina massaged her arm. "What really happened that night?" Instead of answering, Roland watched Augusta's family who still huddled together. "I could ask Stefan for a loan, though I'm not sure he's got enough extra."

"I'd rather you wouldn't." It was out before Mina realized and immediately, Roland was upon her again.

He bent low and hissed into her ear. "I'm going to do what I want, woman. Stay out of it."

In that moment, Augusta and her family were walking their way.

"We'll head back a bit to find a place to stay for the next few days. Will you join us?", Augusta asked, her expression carrying that smirk again.

Roland put a little distance between him and Mina and loudly declared, "Of course, nothing we can do right now."

As soon as they walked off, Roland returned to Stefan's side while Augusta moved next to Mina. "I heard your husband didn't buy any tickets."

"He didn't have enough money." She thought of the gold coin resting on her chest, which would've easily bought the ticket. She smiled grimly, glad they were heading back the way they'd come.

If Augusta was surprised, she didn't let on. They chatted about cooking and the strains of traveling, the weather and the terrible harvests. It was as if Augusta were the sister, Mina had never had. She'd miss her when they went home.

They finally found a room at the Ox Inn, nearly two hours back. Every other place had been full with not even a space in an outbuilding.

While Augusta and her family moved into the inn, Roland and Mina rented shelter in the barn. It wasn't much, but it was a roof over their heads and Mina was exhausted from the long walks. Surely, Roland would see how crazy his plans were, if he couldn't afford to buy passage.

Augusta's father had invited them for dinner, so they met back inside the inn. "They've got potato soup and venison roast," Stefan announced. He ordered six portions, ale for Stefan and himself and apple cider for the women.

Mina hadn't eaten this well and fancy in years, not since going out with her parents for her sixteenth birthday. She was soon full, the unaccustomed meat and dumplings heavy in her middle.

To her dismay, Stefan ordered more rounds of beer and Roland soon had glassy eyes and was talking so fast, she wanted to sink beneath the table from embarrassment. She longed for bed, hoping to head home in the morning.

At some point, the waiter stopped to point out another visitor with a beard and curly gray hair. To Mina's surprise, Roland got up and unsteadily walked over to the other guest.

"What is he doing?" Mina asked Stefan across the table. She was stuck between Augusta and her mother on the bench.

"Apparently, that man is an agent for Hapag-Lloyd, you know, the shipping company."

Mina sat there as the food in her belly seemed to expand. The pressure was so great, she excused herself and scrambled to the outhouse, where she threw up her dinner. Her legs felt heavy as rocks, and she wanted nothing more than to lie down. But that was not an option. Not while Roland hurdled them into the next disaster.

She forced herself to return to the restaurant, afraid what she would find. Roland was still sitting across the agent, reading some kind of paper. He was nodding while the bearded man kept talking.

"Here she is," Roland shouted when he discovered Mina. "Join us, dear, let me introduce you to *Herrn* Singer. This is Mina, my wife." The man rose and tipped his hat, before he turned his attention back to Roland. Another half-empty beer stood in front of him.

"I've explained to your husband, that we're working with a number of interested parties in America who are looking for young, capable workers like your husband." The man smiled and took a sip from his mug. "If you're familiar with the redemptioner system, we're offering free passage to New York and places like Ohio and Indiana where you can start a new life, one of freedom and prosperity. The land is rich, the soil will bear good crops, you can move wherever you want, shoot your own game. It is a paradise, you'll see."

Roland patted Mina's hand. "We'll never have to starve again."

"How long would my husband have to work for this interested party?"

The man scratched his beard. "Four years, I assume, considering that you'll need to get to Bremerhaven, too."

"That seems like a long time." Mina eyed the man who seemed to her like a cheap peddler. Across the aisle, Augusta and her family rose. Mina immediately felt ashamed, not only had they left after being invited for dinner, Roland was utterly ignoring them.

Augusta threw her a curious glance. "We're turning in." There was no smile this time, rather something weary as if she wanted to warn Mina.

"I'm sorry," Mina hurried.

Augusta's hand landed on her forearm. "Watch yourself." Then she was gone.

"...you'll get a bonus payment at the end." The agent was just saying. "Then you can do whatever you want, go farther west where land is cheap, buy your own homestead."

"Only four years." Roland emptied his mug. "That'll pass in no time." He again patted Mina's hand and nodded enthusiastically. "Let's do this, I'm ready to sign."

"Can't we think about this first?" Mina said, "Decide tomorrow?"

The agent pulled out a pocket watch and frowned. "I'm afraid, I'm otherwise engaged tomorrow." He smiled and Mina recognized the lie in his eyes. "There are thousands interested in this once-in-a-lifetime opportunity."

"She doesn't know what she is talking about." Roland squeezed her hand so hard, the pain shot up to her elbow. "I'm ready."

Mina watched helplessly as Roland unfolded his passport and handed it to the man.

"What about the emigration permit?"

Roland looked at Mina who shook her head. "We don't have one...it was a quick decision."

Mina held her breath. This was her chance. They wouldn't be able to go without the proper document.

"I see," interrupted the bearded man her thoughts, smiled. "No problem, you wouldn't believe how many folks *forget*. He lowered his head and noted Roland's information on an official looking paper and in a little book.

The man stretched an arm across the table, opened his palm. "And yours, *Frau* Peters."

Mina looked at the agent, then Roland whose eyes shone from liquor and excitement. Both nodded at her. For a moment she considered getting up and leaving, or outright refusing. But she knew Roland wouldn't have it, would become violent and make a scene.

Ever so slowly she reached into the little pouch she carried on her chest beneath her dress. Her hands shook as she pulled out the paper and unfolded it. A coin, shiny and golden, rolled onto the table...her ducat, the nest egg, she'd kept since her wedding was lying in plain view.

Before she could pick it up, Roland snapped it away, bit on it and let out a sound, she didn't recognize.

"You bitch, you..." he started before catching himself. The eyes of the agent had grown large. Mina was sure it was greed, but then she was too busy to keep a straight face.

"It's mine." She held out a palm. "Please give it back."

A nasty grin appeared on Roland's face. "Right. I go to work every day while my wife is keeping gold coins."

"It was a gift from my father," Mina whispered. "For me, if I ever was in trouble."

"Why would you be in trouble, you're married to me."

Exactly. Helplessly, Mina watched how Roland put the coin into his jacket pocket. "I'll keep it for you. Wouldn't want some vagabond stealing it." Again, the grin. "Now let's finish this paperwork."

The agent wrote down Mina's information, then handed Roland the document. "This paper says that in exchange for your passage to America, you'll be working for the Iron Forge in Fort Wayne for four years. Sign here."

Roland labored through his signature. "I think that calls for another round, don't you think." He waved the bartender who appeared with two more mugs.

Mina felt lost. If she stayed up, she'd be able to watch over Roland, but she was so exhausted, she could hardly keep her eyes open. Besides, he'd do what he wanted, no matter what she said. "I'm turning in."

She slipped from the bench as the room began to whirl, her right hand just able to catch the table's edge. She blinked twice, waited for the room to steady. Roland hadn't even noticed. He was chatting with the agent as if they were the best of friends.

Despite her exhaustion, she couldn't sleep. Again, she was lying in a room with two dozen strangers, the blanket much too thin to keep out the cold. Worse was the uncertainty of what Roland would do when he returned. She must've fallen asleep, when a shout awoke her. Somewhere in the dark, a woman was screaming insults... "...drunkard...approaching an innocent woman...should be ashamed of yourself."

Mina recognized Roland's lulling voice. "Sorry, I made a mistake." A shadow appeared and Roland slumped next to her. "Could've given me a sign."

The next moment he rolled onto his back and began to snore while Mina listened to the whispers of her neighbors, cursing her husband.

Wherever he went, he made himself disliked and now he'd signed away their future.

CHAPTER TEN

Davin

Davin left the next morning after the old man cooked breakfast and handed him a few rolls of soda bread and a hunk of butter for the road. Davin realized how lucky he'd been because it had snowed all night. A fluffy white blanket lay across the path and covered the landscape with hardly a thing, his eyes could focus on. He could've frozen to death, idiot, he was. He'd better learn to plan or he'd never make it to Dublin, not to mention to the railroad in England.

The sky, pewter gray on the horizon, promised more snow. Along a field, he noticed the form of a human body covered under snow. Whoever it was had been caught in it and had been too weak or disoriented to find help. The old man had offered to shelter him for another night to wait out the weather, but Davin had declined. He was slow anyway, now that the snow reached above his ankles and every step required additional energy. Who in their right mind was traveling in this weather? But his parents were running out of time.

He passed an occasional farm, a few homes that were obviously deserted, no more than a gray lifeless cabin with a thatched roof and no smoke in the chimney, now surrounded by nothing but icy white. By midday it began to snow again. He knew there wouldn't be any larger town ahead, which meant there wouldn't be any soup kitchen. He'd have to rely on the kindness of strangers or trust in his luck to find a suitable barn, ideally with animals for heat. The pound note under his shirt rustled. So far so good. The way he looked nobody suspected him of having any money at all.

While he trudged along the path, his mind often returned to the pub, the scene with Finn and how stupid he'd been, waving his money around. He tried to recall the men and if any of them had acted suspicious, but his memory remained fuzzy.

In the early afternoon, he took a break, ate two apples and some bread with butter. He'd be all right for another day if he stretched his supplies, but he'd need shelter again, no matter what. He was coming around a bend in the road, when he noticed a dark speck on the horizon. Somebody was walking north like him.

Within the hour he caught up to the lone figure. It was snowing more heavily now, made worse by the wind, and the flakes crept under his collar and cooled him further.

"Hello sir," he called from behind. "I don't want to startle you."

The man turned and Davin did a double take. He recognized the checkered scarf, the ruddy face. It was the man who'd pulled him from the ground after the mugging. "Malcolm?"

The man looked at him, blinked. "The lad with the head wound. Where are you wandering on this fine day?"

"Dublin, then across to Liverpool."

"I suppose, we'll be traveling companions then, though I'm not as fast as you." As they resumed their walk, Davin noticed the bulky pack, Malcolm carried. "I'm a tinker, you see. It's been the worst year ever. People are out of money, they hardly have enough food or no food at all—why do they need pots for cooking? Every day I pass corpses, it's a crying shame."

Despite the freezing wind and snowflakes hitting them, Malcolm kept talking and Davin was glad for the distraction. "I'm afraid, we have to turn in," he said after a while, squinting at the darkening sky. "There's a vacant house up the road. Isn't much, but it'll keep out the wind."

They spent a miserable night, huddled together. There was no firewood, just a bit of dirty straw, while the wind howled around the little house. Davin imagined who'd lived here. Some family with children or an old couple, either way, they'd left nothing, not even a piece of wood. The space felt empty and yet, he sensed the presence of its former inhabitants. Likely, they'd moved or died recently, one more casualty of the famine. His toes were numb in the wet shoes, the skin of his entire body seemed to be covered in goosebumps. After a while, he got up and stamped his feet and waved his arms like the blades of a windmill. The one blanket he carried, was no match for these temperatures. Malcolm just sat huddled in his blanket—he seemed a lot tougher.

It soon turned out that he'd been lucky, because Malcolm knew every house, farm, barn, and store along the way. Sometimes, they'd stop while he'd offer to fix people's pots and pans, buckets and troughs. If Malcolm was successful, they'd stop while Malcolm prepared a fire and worked his magic with tin and copper. Davin hated to wait, but he was too afraid to continue on his own. The winter was just starting, but worse, he dreaded the loneliness and uncertainty.

Once, they were able to spend the night and receive a meal for payment, other times Malcolm collected a few farthings, a handful of onions or bread. These days, anything was better than nothing—everybody had to tighten their belts.

The main thing was that he stayed alive and safe through this weather. They passed by several quarries, men breaking stone to build or repair Ireland's roads. The men looked miserable and when Davin asked, they confirmed what he already suspected. Working paid just enough to fill a stomach, it certainly wasn't going to pay for his parents' lease.

In Mitchelstown, they stayed two days. Davin alerted the shop owners and inhabitants of Malcolm's presence, who in turn carried their vessels to him for repair. Davin even stopped at the castle, a huge structure occupied by one of the Earls of Kingston, but the butler immediately told him to get off the property.

Typical, Davin thought as he trudged back through the snow. Malcolm had set up shop in a horse barn and was using the black smith's fire to soften the metals. Davin helped by keeping track of the pots and pails, collecting payment and keeping a list. He even repaired a support beam that had caught fire a week ago and was threatening to crumble.

At night, after a hearty soup in the local pub, they remained there, warm for once.

"This is a good arrangement, lad," Malcolm said as they settled around the fire, wrapped in blankets. Davin had built a shallow platform of straw underneath and it felt almost as comfortable as his bed. "You let people know and offer some carpentry, I do my pots and pails."

"It's just taking so long," Davin said into the darkness.

"You're a third of the way there, lad. On the road, you've got to go with the flow."

But I need to earn money, Davin wanted to say, *for my parents*. Instead, he closed his eyes. He couldn't shake the feeling that destiny was taking him on a ride and that no matter what he planned, he had no control.

CHAPTER ELEVEN

Mina

Mina's father waved as he climbed on a horse and followed Mina's wagon, piled high with furniture and household goods. Next to her, a man she didn't recognize, swung a whip and called to the team of horses. He said something, his words drowned by the whistles and calls of the other wagons. In front and behind, the caravan of hundreds of travelers crept across the prairie, in the background rolling hills and farther still, snowcapped mountains. Mina pulled the shawl closer around her shoulders, the howling wind made her shiver. Hopefully, they'd stop soon for a fire, her toes were icy, too.

A snort awoke her. Next to her Roland lay on his back, his right arm twisted in her blanket, his own blanket beneath him. A cloud of alcohol vapors rose from his mouth with every breath. She blinked a couple of times, shaking off the dream, and sat up. The barn was already empty, travelers likely having breakfast or trying to snatch up one of the coveted spots on the ships.

She rose and rubbed her arms to shake off the cold. The memory of last night returned, Roland taking her gold coin, the strange combination of fury and giddy excitement in his expression. All this time, she'd told herself that it was a matter of a few weeks, before he'd come to his senses, and they'd return home. Whatever he'd done, surely it could be resolved. All she wanted was to see her father, make sure he was all right. Now Roland had not only made sure, they'd continue, he'd sold himself to the agent and some stranger in America. And she, by association, was trapped to join him. She'd never return home, never see her father again. The room blurred as she tried to get her bearings, push that sorrow away, forget it.

She had more important matters to attend.

She sank to her knees and watched her husband. Carefully, slowly, she pulled apart the blanket, her blanket, to search for his pockets, rather, what was inside them. Please don't wake. *Let me at least get some of that money, surely you haven't spent it all.*

Her fingers wandered across the folds of his jacket, into the right pocket. Nothing. Roland snorted again and mumbled something before resuming deep gurgling breaths. Watching him, Mina moved to the other pocket. Nothing. That left his pants.

Ever so slowly, she moved closer, until she thought she'd found his right pant pocket. Maybe that's why he always lost things. Other people carried secret pouches, hidden beneath their clothes or attached to their belts. Roland just stuffed things into his pockets and the wrong movement or a pocket thief could relieve him of his valuables. He'd lost money before, not just from drinking, but from being careless. He was like a five-year old, who had no sense.

A sharp pain made her cry out.

Roland was watching her, his hand squeezing hers like a vice. He bent back her fingers and her cry turned into a scream. He was breaking her bones. "What are you doing?", he seethed, still gripping her hand. Alcohol vapors mixed with bad breath hit her. "My own wife stealing from me."

"I'm looking for my coin." Mina pulled back and finally yanked free. "You took it. You had no right to."

In a swift movement, Roland sat up. "No right to? Who's keeping things from me? We're near starving and my wife carries ducats? Ha! Who knows what else you keep from me." His eyes carried that crazy shine again, she knew so well.

"It was all I'd left from my parents," Mina said. "It was for absolute emergencies."

"What do you call this?" Roland made a sweeping gesture with his arm. "We could've traveled well instead of exhausting ourselves."

"You would've wasted it on liquor months ago." It was out before Mina could stop herself. The fury about Roland's theft was making her forget caution.

"You little devil," he shouted, getting on his knees and then to his feet. He was towering over her now, ready to smash her to pieces.

"Mina?" Augusta's voice could be heard in the hallway. "Are you up? We're having breakfast."

Roland pulled Mina from her seat and shoved her forward. "Not a word, you hear me?"

Mina quickly rubbed her eyes dry, not that she was crying, but her right hand burned fiercely from the harsh bending. "I'm coming, just a minute." She folded her blanket and packed it into her bag, pulled her fingers through her curls to straighten them. She had the mahogany locks of her mother, even in the gloom of the barn it shone like fresh chestnuts. She pulled on her hat and coat and headed for the door.

Even without looking, she knew that Roland was right behind her.

Augusta hugged her with a smile and Mina almost lost her composure. She was used to Roland's abuses and had shuttered her heart, but the kindness of a near stranger was something that threatened to let in light. Right now, she couldn't have that, couldn't afford to. She pushed back a bit and nodded. "Did you sleep well?"

Augusta threw a curious glance at Roland, who was hovering behind Mina, before she took Mina's arm in hers. "Not well, I'm afraid. I'm just too excited and my thoughts galop like these wild prairie horses, they talk about." Augusta squeezed Mina's sore hand which made her groan. "What about you? What's wrong?"

Mina forced a smile. "Nothing. I'm just tired. It's hard to sleep with so many strangers." *Not nearly as hard as sleeping next to a drunk, thieving husband.*

The pub room bustled with guests, and they joined Augusta's family at a corner table.

Roland threw one glance at the bread and oatmeal and excused himself. They all knew the reason, but nobody commented.

Mina nodded at Stefan. "I wanted to thank you properly for inviting us to dinner last night. It was very kind of you."

"Not to worry." Stefan's smile turned into a frown. "Did I hear right that Roland got passage through the agent?"

"Why don't you let Mina order breakfast before you bother her with questions?" Augusta's mother nodded at the waiter who was picking up dishes at the next table.

Mina winced and ordered a bowl of cooked oats and herb tea, the cheapest items on the menu. Again, she was worried about paying. How could they afford to stay several more days if Roland spend everything on liquor? What would happen once they arrived in Bremerhaven?

She gave the ring on her finger a whirl, wishing not for the last time, she could take it off. Roland returned as the waiter brought Mina's food. Ignoring her, he slid next to Stefan, telling in an animated voice how he'd arranged travel. From his mouth, it sounded like he'd done the impossible, the agent being so impressed, he was anxious to get Roland because he was so valuable.

Next to Mina, Augusta whispered. "What happened to your hand?"

Mina had gripped the spoon with difficulty, but now in the light of the candle, she saw that her middle and ring fingers were swollen and turning purple. Self-conscious, Mina dropped the spoon and hid her hand under the table, only for Augusta to take it gently into hers.

"He did that, didn't he?" Augusta abruptly got up. "Excuse me, Mina and I are going to the ladies." She led Mina outside, gripped her shoulders, her face close. "He's no good, I knew it. What happened?"

At last, a sob escaped Mina, her throat tight now. She remembered the little white handkerchief and dapped her eyes. "I'd kept a ducat for emergencies, Roland didn't know about...he drinks...I was afraid." She met Augusta's eyes, which glittered with unshed tears. "Last night, the coin fell out when I showed my papers. Roland snapped it away." Mina took a deep breath to push away the lump in her throat. "This morning, I tried searching his pockets to see what he'd done, how much he'd spend...he caught me."

"And about broke your fingers?" Augusta's voice was full of venom. "He is crazy—"

"The drink makes him crazy."

"I'm speaking with *Vater*. He needs to know." Augusta took Mina's good hand in hers. "And we must figure out a way to retrieve your money or you'll not make it to Bremerhaven. It's a longer journey and we'll have to travel on foot again. The Rhine is only the beginning."

"I thought the agent would help—"

Mina shook her head. "The agent only does what's good for the rich man in America. He's not going to take care of your everyday needs."

When they returned to the pub room, Mina's oats and tea were cold, but her appetite was back. Finding a friend gave her hope, even if the looks, Roland threw her across the table were dark and lurking. He was sitting next to Stefan at the now empty table.

While Mina ate, Augusta moved to stand in front of the men. "*Vater*, I need to speak with you—in private."

Something in her voice made her father look up surprised. He excused himself and led his daughter away.

"You better keep your mouth shut," Roland said, scooching next to Mina.

Mina put down her spoon. "I just heard that it'll take a long time to get to Bremerhaven. After the Rhine River part, we walk again. It's at least another two weeks."

"The agent will—"

"The agent pays for our passage, not for everything." Mina forced herself to look at Roland. His eyes were red and he reeked of sweat. "How much money do you have left?"

Roland looked away as if he hadn't heard her. "Don't talk to me like that."

"Like what?"

"Like you're my mother. I'm in charge, don't forget that."

"Then act like a man." Stefan had silently come to the table, there was no sign of Augusta. He was a big man with massive shoulders and large, meaty hands. Mina had always seen him smiling, but right now, his expression was grave and his eyes hard. He sank across from Roland and studied him. "This trip is strenuous in the best of times. We've got months ahead of us. If you don't get your wits together, you won't make it, you hear. You'll get run down and die of fever or some other disease on the ships."

"How do you—"

Stefan smacked a fist on the table. "I wasn't done. It was your idea to leave, wasn't it?"

Roland nodded.

"Then listen to me. You take care of your woman, make sure she's got what she needs." He rose, "And quit drinking." With a kind nod at Mina, he left.

Mina trembled. What would he do to her now that it was obvious she'd shared their secret. To her surprise, Roland called the waiter and ordered oatmeal and tea...like her. Without looking at her, he ate silently, then dug into his left pant pocket and produced a Groschen.

"Let's take a walk."

They left the inn, neither of them speaking. It had stopped snowing, but the wind was fierce, and Mina soon shivered. Roland took her hand, came to a stop to face her.

It was hard to say what he thought, his eyes a mixture of regret, anger and uncertainty. "I'm sorry." Mina just stared at the man, she feared and didn't understand. It obviously took an outsider, a good, strong family man to put some sense into her husband. "I'm going to do better, the drink..." He spit into the snow, "It's the devil."

"Can we speak about the money?" Mina asked. "I'm worried, we'll run out long before—"

"It's mostly here." Roland pulled a hand from his pocket, an assembly of coins on his palm. "I only spent a little last night."

"I'd like half." Mina extended her hand, the ring and middle finger swollen like sausages now.

"I...I didn't mean to..." Roland stammered. He put three Taler into her hand. "I've got four Groschen left. We'll be frugal from now on. No more drink."

Mina didn't smile, couldn't. She'd seen and heard it all before and if things got tough and they inevitably did, he'd seek solace and oblivion. Not with her, but in the bottle. Together, they could've done a lot, but as it stood, she felt alone—a tiny rowboat on the vast ocean of life.

CHAPTER TWELVE

Davin

Two days before Christmas, Davin and Malcolm reached Rathcoole. It was after four and already getting dark, so they hurried along the single street, line with mud huts, their reed roofs gray and shaggy, and in need of repair. A couple of men were hobbling along, pulling a cart with peat.

"We're in need of a bed tonight," Malcolm called as soon as they reached them, displaying his professional grin, which Davin assumed was supposed to tell people that he was easy-going and non-threatening.

"Straw is fine," Davin added, regretting they hadn't hurried more to get to Dublin. From what he could tell it was only a few more hours walk to downtown. But Malcolm had trouble getting up in the morning, his knee joints stiff and his feet sore. Not only that, whenever they passed by a house that looked inhabited, he stopped to offer his services, even though it made no sense to stay for a single customer. Most of the time, he didn't get business anyway.

The two men, dressed in rags, eyed them suspiciously. "Much folk is coming through these days, all heading to Dublin. Why don't you try there?"

Malcolm shrugged, holding his smile. "Gents, we tried, you know we've been traveling our heels off. It's hard on a man day-after-day in this weather, surely you understand that."

"Not sure, we can help you," the villager said.

Davin bit his lower lip. It was easier to travel as a pair, but then Malcolm was so terribly slow. By coming along and helping out, he'd saved his pound note, even collected a few coins for his use, but time was the price he paid. Alone, he would've already been across to Liverpool, likely been working on the railroad, likely sending money to his parents.

"Just a barn, maybe?" Malcolm tried, but the two men mumbled and shuffled off.

"We better continue then." Davin glanced at the darkening sky, remembered the night he'd almost frozen to death, had it not been for the light, guiding him to the old man's house.

"You can stay with me," a voice said. The door of one of the mud houses gaped open, revealing a tiny woman of middle age. "It'd cost a farthing each."

Malcolm rushed over. "Dear woman, thank you for your hospitality. Would you have a soup, maybe, or some tea for us worn travelers?"

The woman shook her head. "No food, I can make bramble tea...from blackberry leaves."

Malcolm slapped Davin on the back. "Let's go."

The space was tiny, no more than a hundred square feet. Once they closed the door, it was near dark, the only light coming from the fire and a single tallow lamp on a shelf above. In the rafters hung bundles of dried plants and the woman now pulled leaves from one of them.

"I'm the midwife and doctor around here," she said, "but it's been a difficult year. Mothers are dying of hunger before their babes are born. Some days, I go to Dublin, just to get a warm meal."

Davin opened his pack and handed the woman a piece of bread and a sack, payment at one of the last successful stops. "Maybe you can cook the oats for us? We'll share."

The woman's eyes lit up as she got busy at the fire.

Davin looked around, it'd be a challenge to find space on the ground to lie down, nothing more than hardened dirt. The simple cot along one wall was covered with a couple of blankets. Never mind, tomorrow they'd reach the big city and he'd immediately look for a ship across to Liverpool. "What are you going to do once we get to Dublin?" he asked Malcolm.

"Rest for a day or two and head in a different direction." The older man gazed into the fire. "A tinker is never done traveling. It's part of life."

"Don't you get tired of it?"

Malcolm shrugged as their eyes met. "What choice do I have? It's the only craft I know."

"Couldn't you find a place in Dublin, open a shop? It'd be a lot easier."

"It's a thought." With a groan, he took off his shoes and inspected the bluish bruises on his heels and toes.

"I have something for that." The woman picked up a clay pot and opened it. "Calendula salve, heals the skin." She moved across from Malcolm and took a closer look. "No good, you need to wash them first."

It was true, the little room was filled with the foulest odor, not just from Malcolm. Davin felt self-conscious about taking off his boots. He hadn't washed properly since leaving home. They had no time to clean clothes and wait for them to dry.

The woman was up again, pouring water into a larger kettle. "We'll do it after dinner?"

She threw a glance at Davin. "What about you, young man? I suppose you've got a few things that ail you." She moved over to him and softly patted the back of his head. "You've got a bump."

Davin just nodded as the memory of that terrible afternoon returned. He'd been experiencing headaches, especially later in the day, when he was exhausted. Like now.

The woman's hands gently moved through his hair, around the crown and back down to his neck. "It was a mighty blow, I'd say." She pointed at the cot. "Lie down for me, will you?"

Davin lay down on his back while the woman began manipulating his shoulders, then upwards to the base of his skull all the way to his forehead. She mumbled while she worked and Malcolm later said, she'd closed her eyes. She pushed and pulled, pressed hard a few times, then held her hands a few inches above him. "Much better, energy is flowing. Your headache may get stronger tonight, but by tomorrow, it'll be gone."

They left in the morning, both giving the woman five farthings. Davin felt like a veil had lifted from his head, his vision was clear. He'd even slept well despite being cramped, the woman had crushed lavender flowers to help with the smell and apparently, to induce sleep.

"Stop by next time," she said to Malcolm who'd regained his biggest smile.

She patted Davin on the arm, "Farewell, may the winds be with you."

How did she know, Davin thought. They hadn't talked about his plans to sail to Liverpool. Whatever she was, she had a magic eye for the human condition. Malcolm even whistled as they headed out of the village. In his pack he carried a tiny pot of calendula salve.

Davin knew, Malcolm would return.

CHAPTER THIRTEEN

Mina

The line at the Rhine's quay seemed a mile long as they waited to board the Adeline. Bound for Rotterdam, Mina and Augusta's family would get off early to make the trek to Bremerhaven.

Mina nervously scanned the ship and its attached barge. It was one of the more modern steam ships and would make the journey in just a day. She was relieved that the agent had gotten them passage on the same ship as Augusta, but worried about the cramped conditions. Except for the back where wealthy travelers could take refuge under a roof and sit in comfort, the ship was tightly packed with passengers. Out in the open, they were exposed to the weather. Christmas was in two days, hard to believe, they'd already traveled for two weeks. As they finally reached the gangplank, the noise and bustle intensified. The smell of coal and the river mixed in the cold December air. When the line began to move toward the gangway, Mina shivered and had to hold on to Augusta, pulling her thin shawl tighter around her shoulders. She glanced up at the towering ship, its black smokestack already puffing out clouds of smoke.

Moving onto the boat irreversibly forced her onto a journey away from home and everything she knew. She did not share Augusta's excitement nor that of Roland. She'd left her father wondering about her whereabouts. What must he think of her? It was against anything, she'd ever done.

When they squeezed in-between a couple of families with small children and Roland followed Stefan to the bathroom, Mina asked Augusta for a piece of paper.

"I need to write to my father. He doesn't know we left." She tugged on her scarf as if it were choking her. "Roland mustn't know."

"He is running from something, isn't he?" Augusta's clear blue eyes lay on Mina's.

"He's not telling."

Augusta rummaged through her bag and produced a sheet of paper, ink and pen with a steel nib. "Hurry, before he sees you."

Mina gripped the pen tightly. In her mind, she'd written hundreds of letters explaining their hasty departure. Now she was at a loss for words.

After a few attempts, she wrote:

Dearest Father,

When you read this note, Roland and I are on our way to Bremerhaven. Roland wants to travel to America, though he did not ask my opinion. Words cannot describe how sorry I am to leave you behind. Take care of yourself, your daughter,

Wilhelmina

Her hands shook as she folded the paper and handed it to Augusta. "Here, hide it for me."

"I've got a better idea." Augusta stuffed the letter into her shawl and headed down the aisle, a difficult maneuver, since every inch of the boat's surface seemed to be covered with people. Mina thought she saw a glimpse of blond hair near the exit but wasn't sure. Across the way, she recognized the agent, they'd met a few days ago, take his seat under the roof. He was traveling with the rich. She wondered how many others had done, what Roland did: signed their lives away and venture into the unknown.

Swallowing the lump in her throat, she sat down and waited.

"Why aren't you excited?" Roland squeezed next to her on the ground. "Just think of the opportunities we'll have over there."

Mina nodded but couldn't make herself smile. If Roland were like other men, reliable and honest, she'd maybe feel better. But there was no telling what happened, once the next problem arose. If she were brave, she would excuse herself and jump off the ship, walk home to take care of her father. Let Roland go to some foreign land as a slave.

But she wasn't brave, she felt stuck.

The engine roared to life as Augusta fought her way back through hundreds of travelers, wrapped in an assortment of blankets and shawls. It was cold now, no telling what the wind and the approaching night would bring.

"Why don't you sit with Stefan?" she asked Roland. "We girls like to talk about female matters."

Roland made a face and half climbed, half crawled to the aisle where Stefan had wrapped an arm around Augusta's mom.

"It's gone," Augusta whispered. "I paid a man from the shipping company to mail your letter. At least, your father will know what happened and that you're safe."

I wouldn't call it safe. Aloud Mina said, "Thank you, I will pay you for the mailing."

Augusta threw her conspirative smile. "Later. Girls have to stick together."

The wind picked up as the ship steered toward middle of the river, the banks often more than fifty yards away. According to the news that traveled across deck, they would be making good time.

Mina spent nearly all night awake, not just because it the icy wind crept beneath her clothes and caused her to tremble, but the proximity of so many people made her uncomfortable. There wasn't even room to lie down or stretch out her legs. Every muscle ached as they rose in the morning and squeezed through the crowd to get off the ship. A third of the people left here to begin the journey to Bremerhaven.

Mina looked over the railing into the gray water of the river and suppressed a shudder. It'd be easy to jump in, it'd be quick, the watery grave would sweep her away. But she loathed the water, was afraid of it. Even if she hadn't chosen this path, she was going to deal with what destiny was handing her. Tomorrow was Christmas, a celebration she'd always enjoyed, especially when Mother was alive. They'd cut a tree in the forest and decorated it with straw stars and chestnut garlands. They'd gone to church and prepared a special meal. She pushed away the image of her father sitting alone in his messy kitchen.

Linking her arm with Augusta's, she lined up behind the others, following a trek of men, women and children north and east.

CHAPTER FOURTEEN

Davin

Dublin was bustling with people, every road and walkway was crowded so that Davin had to weave in and out, sometimes outright stop when the throng got too thick. People called out their wares, others begged, here too, the weak sat in a stupor, waiting to die.

He felt disoriented among the sea of houses and anxious to cross to Liverpool as soon as possible. Leaving Malcolm in town, he headed to the port where hundreds of boats of all sizes anchored.

"I'm looking for passage to Liverpool," he asked several times until he ended near the quays. Here the crowds were even thicker. The buildings carried names like the Dublin General Steam Shipping Company Ltd. or William J O'Toole Shipbrokers. Confused and tired, he entered one of the offices.

"I'm looking for passage to Liverpool," he said to the clerk.

The man, dressed in a black suit with long gray sideburns, studied him, the corners of his mouth turned down distastefully. "Steerage, I assume."

Davin patted his chest where the pound note still waited. "How much is it?"

"Not here, lad, ask at the B&I."

"B&I?"

"The British and Irish Steam Packet Company," the man said slowly as if Davin were a halfwit. He waved toward the door. "Take a right, can't miss it."

The B&I was located in a larger stone building, its doors as tall as Davin's entire home. A line of more than a hundred people snaked in front of it. Frustrated about the long wait ahead, Davin went to the back of the line. Along the quays, people mingled, many of them carrying boxes and suitcases. Some pulled carts with their belongings, all shared one thing: they looked anxious.

"Where are they all going?" Davin asked the man in front of him.

"Liverpool and then across the ocean to America."

"America?"

"Lad, half the country is moving out—at least those who still can. Where've you been?" The man eyed him curiously. Of course, Davin knew about people moving away and some had spoken about going to America or Australia. He'd seen his village dwindle, but he'd believed some went to Dublin or maybe across to work on the English railroad like himself.

"It seems pretty brave."

"Desperate, I'd say." The man shook his head. By the way he dressed, he was better off, while a lot of the mingling families looked poor and ragged.

When Davin arrived at the counter, it was after four o'clock. "I need passage to Liverpool."

The man nodded and studied a calendar. "January third, ten in the morning. One pound and ten shillings, I need your name and birthdate." His pen hovered on a book with a long list of names.

"Why so late? I thought I could go tomorrow," Davin stammered.

"Have you seen the crowds? Everybody wants to go to Liverpool."

Davin nodded. "Is there a cheaper fare?"

The man squinted and made a tsk sound. "You're welcome to row across. Do you want to travel or not?"

"Do I have to pay now?"

"If you want your ticket."

Behind Davin, a man called out, "Hurry up, man, you aren't the only one traveling."

Davin shook his head. "I'll need to come back tomorrow."

"Don't wait, lad, it'll be even a longer wait." He impatiently waved. "Next."

Head low, Davin made his way back to town. He'd so looked forward to getting on with his travels, but now he was stuck. The fare was much higher than he'd expected, whatever he'd expected. Worse, he'd soon use up the little he had, just by waiting. No, he had to do something, get money somehow, only he didn't know how.

Malcolm was nursing an ale in the pub adjacent to the workhouse. It was a dark, smelly place, not much better than the place they were staying.

"The way I see it," Malcolm said, "you've got to find a different boat. Surely, there're others that travel across."

"Surely, they're just as booked as B&I and just as expensive."

"Only one way to find out."

To save money, Davin didn't order anything and soon they stood in another line at the soup kitchen to save the few coins they had. The workhouse was so crowded that they slept fifteen to a room. Women, children, men, all mixed together, some were sneezing and coughing, some appearing lethargic and half dead. The air was stifling and reeked of everything, a human body could discharge.

"I'm not staying," Malcolm said after a near sleepless night. Davin rubbed his face to chase away the cobwebs of sleep. "I'll rather take my chances on the road. The resident tinkers surely leave little room for a man like me." He rose with effort and grabbed his pack. "Let's go before they steal it all." He threw a glance at some of the younger men lounging in the hall.

"I'll return to port," Davin said.

"At least let me buy you breakfast."

They ate boiled oats and bread with butter at a nearby joint that looked as rundown as the pub. "We could travel together, lad," Malcom said, cleaning the last of the oats with the remaining bread. "It's a good arrangement. You help with the organization, take a carpentry job here and there and it's a good life, a free life." He looked around, his usual smile absent. "This place is filthy, even filthier than I remember it."

Davin shook his head. "Sorry, man, I just can't. I've got to help my parents pay the lease. If I don't, they end up in the poorhouse like the place we stayed last night." Malcolm remained silent and studied the table. Davin knew he was disappointed. "You could come with me, get over there and earn a good living."

"Ah, lad, that work is for young people. Look at me." Malcolm's eyes glinted with tears. "I'm an old man, soon to settle somewhere because my legs and feet will give out."

"Maybe you should return to the herb witch. Her salve sure helped."

A sly grin came over Malcolm. "I may just do that."

Davin rose reluctantly. "That's it then." He hugged the older man and patted his back. "Farewell, my friend, take care of yourself."

Afraid, he'd grow even sadder, Davin hurried off to the port. He began asking around at the smaller ships and soon realized that it was impossible. Every vessel that looked half-way sound had other destinations or was booked for weeks.

Afternoon came and Davin had not made any progress. He was beginning to hate the crowded city, had somehow envisioned Dublin to be a beautiful place with big houses and great shops. It was all there, but the filth of the onslaught of desperate travelers turned it into a slum. Even the streets reeked because many relieved themselves in the open, refuse was left to rot, attracting rats as large as cats.

He had to get out of here, quickly, yet he saw no way forward. When he noticed a postal service, he stopped. He had to write to his parents, let them know that he was all right.

On a whim, he went inside, purchased paper and wrote:
Dear Mam and Da,
I'm in Dublin, waiting to travel to Liverpool. The journey here has taken longer than expected, but I'm in decent health and will soon be able to earn good money. Please send word to this post address. I'll be here for a few weeks.
Your loving son,
Davin

He paid for the letter with one of the coins he'd received from working with Malcolm. *You're going to be here forever and soon look like those wretches in the poorhouse, if you don't do something,* his mind commented. He'd always prided himself of his education, having learned a real trade. Already, his pants were filthy, and the cuffs frayed. His jacket had a hole in the elbow and his cap was grimy.

He meandered through the port again, but soon grew tired and worked his way back toward downtown. Some place he came upon another soup kitchen and waited his turn for a meal. He felt like a beggar, like he was losing himself in the shuffle. He also missed Malcolm. He hadn't realized how much confidence Malcolm had given him. Now he was truly alone. Worse was that he felt unsafe. Hordes of youths filled the streets, likely stealing anything in sight. What would keep them from mugging him, stealing his bag with the few carpentry tools, he'd carried and his money? He pulled up his collar and hurried back to the workhouse. It was horrible inside, but it was free.

Stuffing his bag under his head as a pillow, he wrapped himself in his blanket and in hopes of a good night's sleep. At least, when he slept, he didn't have to think about life.

But sleep wouldn't come. The room was noisy, the hallway never slowed down. It seemed like people stirred all night, some because they were ill, others because they were restless. He also noticed an itch under his armpits and in his crotch. Without question, he'd picked up lice from the filthy straw.

Bleary eyed and groggy, he got up in the early morning. It was Christmas, but the day he'd always celebrated had lost all meaning.

Unsure what to do, he wandered to the quays again. He was down to his last shilling and would soon have to break the pound note. He picked up bread and cheese from a street vendor and leaned against the wall of a two-story house.

Chewing slowly, he watched the hustle and bustle. Even this early in the day, the docks were crowded. Some families had obviously braved the cold and slept here, others wandered around in a stupor. Boats arrived to sell fish, others were leaving.

Right in front of Davin, a small fishing vessel moored, yet there was no activity on board except for a single bearded fellow with the same fiery red hair as Davin's. The man was sitting quietly, mending a net and smoking a pipe. Curious, why the man wasn't selling fish or preparing to leave for the day, he approached.

"Top of the morning, sir. Is it not a good day to fish?"

The man kept his eyes on the net, his fingers never slowing. "Not for me, it isn't."

Before, Davin would've left because the man's grumpy retort. But he'd learned a great deal from Malcolm and knew there were always reasons. "I'm sorry to hear it. Life is hard for the Irish, no matter where you look. I've been traveling a great deal, and it is a crying shame."

The man's hands slowed as he glanced at Davin. "Sure is." When Davin didn't move, he said, "What's a man to do when the only thing he is meant to do is impossible."

"You mean you can't fish?"

"Not anymore. Rudder is broke. I'm lucky I got back here in one piece."

"Why don't you fix it?"

The man scoffed and lifted his hands. "All these hands know is to catch fish and *drive* a boat, not fix it. At least not that."

"It's wood, isn't it?"

"Son, all you see here is made of wood."

Davin couldn't help but smile. "Then, sir, this is your lucky day. I'm a carpenter in need of work."

CHAPTER FIFTEEN

Mina

The trek to Bremerhaven crept along at a snail's pace. If it were up to Mina, she'd have walked faster, but Augusta's grandmother and many of the hundreds of people heading northeast were old or unfit and needed frequent rests.

Roland seemed subdued since that morning when he'd handed Mina the money. Not that they'd talked much before, but for the first time, he appeared to think about the severity of his decision. Their departure had been nothing but a panicked escape. He was also suffering, his forehead sweaty despite the icy temperatures, and his hands trembling. Mina suspected it was the missing liquor. To her surprise, a part of her felt sorry for him.

Mina watched her breath puff out in small clouds, her eyes occasionally darting to Roland, who walked with a noticeable effort, each step a battle against his own demons. She spent most of the time with Augusta, whose excitement had faded a bit. Maybe it was because of the seemingly endless hours on the road or the forbidding winter weather. Christmas had come and gone and the farther north they traveled, the worse the weather became.

The landscape consisted of unending fields, patches of woods and sprinkled throughout, red-bricked farmhouses. They crossed bogs and meadows, steps crunching on the frozen ground. Many nights they stayed in barns, the farmers rented out for a few *Pfennig*. If they were lucky, they received breakfast...oats with honey, fried potatoes, eggs and bread with butter and homemade preserves. Those were the lucky days. Many other nights, they spent huddled together, nibbling provisions they'd managed to save.

After ten days, Mina wished her way to the end. 1849 had started and she'd never in her life felt so miserably cold and lost.

Even Stefan seemed less certain these days. Mina heard him argue with his wife, discussing Augusta's grandmother who'd developed a nasty cough and seemed feverish. Mina helped Augusta, leading the old woman to a fallen log and wrap her in a blanket, then turned to check on Roland who was discussing what they'd find in Bremerhaven.

The wind picked up, biting at her exposed skin. Mina pulled her shawl tighter, wishing for the hundredth time, she'd have warmer clothes. Roland returned to sit next to her, his eyes a mixture of doubt and worry. Mina wished she could say something reassuring, but she had her own fears to contend with. The uncertainty of what awaited them in Bremerhaven weighed heavily on her mind.

"We should've left her," Stefan whispered to his wife, when he thought nobody was listening.

"How could we have left her, we were all she had?," Augusta's mom answered.

The next day, the old woman was worse. The cough deepened, resembling the bark of a dog, her eyes shone feverish. She'd trouble putting one foot in front of another and walking nearly ground to a halt. More and more travelers passed them, most passed silently, too exhausted to muster the energy for a greeting.

A couple of times, Stefan had managed to arrange passage on a wagon to the next town. Those days, they made better progress, but when they arrived, Augusta's grandmother was sitting lethargically in some corner.

"We'll have to take a break, I'm afraid," Stefan said one morning, after they'd hardly slept. The old woman was coughing and mumbling, keeping everybody up. Mina had offered what few herbs she'd saved, but nothing seemed to work.

Augusta was crying outright. "She's going to die," she told Mina on the way to the outhouse. They were staying at a large farm west of Cloppenburg.

Mina kept her thoughts to herself. She knew Augusta's grandmother would never arrive in Bremerhaven. She wasn't the only one. Already, they'd passed hastily dug graves along the path. At least, they'd died on German soil, not in some strange place on foreign soil. Aloud, she said, "The break will be good for her."

"How will we find you?" Augusta's question pulled Mina back to present. They'd agreed that Roland and Mina would go ahead to preserve precious resources.

"At the latest in Bremerhaven. I suspect we'll have to wait a few days until ..." *The ship sails.* Mina couldn't make herself say it out loud. A part of her still hoped that Roland would see reason and they'd turn back. She'd even considered asking her father to join them, but she knew better. He would soon look like Augusta's grandmother.

They parted with tears and promises to meet up soon. Roland began to whistle despite the blowing winds hitting them from the east. "Finally, we're making progress," he said, when they stopped for a break. Indeed, they'd passed numerous travelers, but Roland's new pace was too much for Mina.

"You'll need to slow down a bit. I'm quite tired," she said, inspecting the soles of her shoes. Never in her life, had she walked this much. She also felt lonely, missing Augusta's company.

"Didn't you see the sign, just forty miles and we'll be in Oldenburg. And then another forty and we'll arrive in Bremerhaven." Roland watched the passing travelers who walked, heads low against the biting wind. "Another six days, a week top."

"I feel bad for leaving them." It was true, Stefan had helped them and had kept Roland straight. Already, she was sensing a shift, his impatience was back, the searching look.

"Nonsense, you know we couldn't wait and waste the little money, we've left on some farm in the middle of nowhere. Who knows how long the old hag holds on, it could be weeks. Surely, she realizes what a burden she places on Stefan."

In that moment, Mina realized that Roland was incapable of empathy. She should've known by the way he treated her, but somehow it hadn't registered—or had she pushed away the thought? Hearing him speak about Augusta's dying grandmother made it clear. "She is not doing it on purpose, Roland, she is sick." *Likely, she misses her home.* The road blurred as Mina thought of Augusta's family who would bury a loved one on some unknown road, never to return.

"Ready?" Roland waved impatiently. "We've got at least three hours of daylight left."

When she rose, he charged ahead, leaving Mina no choice but to stumble after him. Luckily, the snow had been trampled flat by thousands of feet. But the relentless wind burned her eyes and made them teary, the skin on her cheeks grew numb, the insides of her nose hurt, and there was a burning sensation in her throat. Despite their brisk walk, she couldn't get warm, made worse by her damp feet.

At times, Roland was fifty or a hundred yards ahead. She called to him, causing other travelers to turn their heads. The wind carried away her words as easily as it dissipated smoke from a chimney. He finally stopped and waited for her, but not without throwing her an angry glance.

It was dusk when they reached another farm. Judging by the men and women in front of them, Mina and Roland weren't the only ones, seeking shelter. Mina had noticed how the roads were growing gradually busier.

"Come on," Roland cried, "Hurry up before they run out of room."

Heinzen Hof was written in large letters at the entrance. It smelled of cattle and pig dung, in an enclosure a dozen hens scratched in the icy dirt.

"Hey, wait your turn," a man in a black wool coat and matching hat called after Roland who'd charged toward the farmhouse door. "The line ends here."

"How much is it?" Mina asked anxiously, taking her place behind the man.

"No idea, all I care is that we get a spot in the barn," the man said.

"Damn crowds," Roland mumbled, appearing next to Mina. "I knew we were too slow, could've been here an hour ago."

Mina bit her lip, she was exhausted and hardly able to stand. "Maybe you should go ahead then, I cannot walk any faster."

Roland threw her a nasty look. "Maybe I should have—"

A noise by the door distracted him. A man in a felted wool jacket, bald and ruddy looking, waved his arms. "Sorry, folks, but we cannot take any more guests for the night. It's gotten so tight, people hardly have enough room to lie down."

Roland spit and charged forward. Mina heard him shout and argue with the farmer who soon grew tired and turned his back. Red in the face, Roland returned and roughly grabbed her elbow. "Come on then, hurry up." Around them people whined or complained loudly, others just turned to leave. "You'll have to walk faster," Roland said after a while. "It's getting dark, we have to be quicker than the others."

"I'm doing the best I can." Mina's breath came in spurts as she held her sides. Even her ribs ached now and all she wanted was to lie down. Except there was no place, just open country, relentless wind, and strangers stumbling into the approaching night.

"Your best isn't good enough. No moon, it's going to be pitch black soon," Roland barked over his shoulder. He was already thirty feet ahead as if he could somehow pull her forward.

"Maybe you could take my arm and help me?" Mina called after him. When he ignored her, she lowered her head and forced her aching body to move forward. For a minute or so, she was able to distract herself by thinking about her family, the way she'd lived protected behind the shield of her parents' care. But then a wind gust hit her, bringing her back to the icy cold night. The light was nearly gone now, and she could only guess at the road's outline. Only a shadow remained from Roland who had pulled away even farther.

Soon, she'd not see him at all. Panic gripped her, a tightening of her throat as if something was going to strangle her. He'd not even know if she fell or wandered off some place. By morning, she'd be frozen solid. Only when another farm came into view, did she discover Roland. "Where are you?" he yelled, waving at the looming buildings. "Let's try here."

But as soon as they drew closer, Mina saw the sign: "Fully booked—no vacancies." She was beyond exhausted now and could hardly stand. *What now*, she wanted to say, but no words left her mouth.

"Come on," Roland said after a tirade of curses. Mina looked at him, then the road, which lost itself in darkness. The wind was picking up further and the snow swirled into every crevice, cooling her to the bone.

That's when she saw it, a light somewhere off to the left. It was hard to say what it belonged to or how far away it was. "We should leave the main road, there must be places who can shelter us for the night." She pointed at the tiny twinkle. "Over there."

Roland squinted in the direction she'd pointed. "I don't see anything, besides, it's too far off the route and will throw us back."

"It'll do no good if we freeze to death."

"Shut your mouth, woman."

But Mina was done being nice. "We cannot continue like this. We'll lose our way and fall into some hole. You've seen the corpses along the way." She forced herself to touch Roland's sleeve. "Please, husband, let's try the light."

"And if it's nothing but a lantern or they refuse us?"

"It is a risk, but going on where hundreds are walking and searching for a bed may be worse."

Roland looked at the *no vacancy* sign, shook his head. "I never thought there'd be so many. To think how'd be in good weather." He extended a hand. "Let's go then."

At first, Mina was afraid she'd dreamed it, but then she discovered it again, growing larger as they approached. They walked cross-country, through what looked like fields or meadows, climbed over a fence, then another. The snow here was deeper and soon her shins throbbed with cold, her thighs felt as if they'd give any moment, and her breath came in spurts. Please don't turn off the light, Mina thought over and over.

The twinkle grew larger and brighter and after what seemed like an eternity, they entered another farm. She smelled it more than she saw it, but it didn't matter. A light shone behind a window and there were people inside.

Roland knocked on the door, "Hello?"

After a moment, a man in woolen underpants opened, a lantern in his hand. "Can I help you?"

"We're in desperate need for shelter," Roland said, for once sounding civil. Exhaustion had turned his voice low and gravelly. "The barn would be just fine."

Mina took a step forward, into the light. "Please, sir, we're afraid of freezing to death."

The man, who wore a thick beard but was bald on top, eyed her curiously, the squint disappeared, replaced by something like pity. "Ottilie, come quick," the man called over his shoulder, while stepping back and waving them inside.

A small woman with a gray bun and a shawl wrapped around her shoulders hurried to meet them. "Oh my goodness," she said, her hands aflutter like songbirds. "What are you doing out there at this hour? Take off your shoes and come in, please, to the fire."

Mina's hands were so cold, her fingers refused to untie the laces of her boots. In fact, once she bent low, she was afraid, she'd remain right here on the scrubbed wooden floor of the hallway. She sagged to the ground to keep herself from falling. The man and Roland had already left, but the old woman rushed up to her.

"Dear, dear, you're in quite a state. Let me help you." She quickly undid the knots, pulled off Mina's boots without commenting on the state of her socks and helped her straighten. "Nice and slow, dear, you rest by the fire."

It was a simple room with tall ceilings and straight heavy oak furniture, but to Mina, it was a palace. "Thank you," she whispered as Ottilie wrapped her in a blanket. While Roland told the man about their travels, Mina just sat and watched the dancing flames. She would've dozed off, had the woman not handed her a steaming mug of tea. Mina wrapped her hands around to thaw them and was soon distracted by the most delicious aromas. Two slices of fragrant rye bread and a piece of hard cheese lay on a board next to her.

"You must be starving," Ottilie said. She'd put on a woolen jacket and watched Mina curiously. "What in the world are you doing out there at this hour?" She squinted at Roland as if she wanted to scold him for his foolishness.

"We didn't know it'd be so crowded, all the farms along the road to Bremerhaven are filled with travelers. It grew late..."

Ottilie tsked a few times and shook her head. "It is a hard time for many." She patted Mina's hand. "How did you find us?"

"The light," Mina said. "It guided us. I thought we might perish out there." A shiver ran through her.

Ottilie threw another glance at Roland. "Your man, he should know better and take care of you."

Their eyes met. The old woman nodded slowly. "I thought so."

CHAPTER SIXTEEN

Davin

The fisherman, whose name was William, offered Davin a spot on his boat to sleep. It was cold and swayed beneath him all night, but it meant that Davin could hold on to his money, even earn a few extra shilling.

Over the next few days, he managed to lift the rudder into the boat, inspect and take it apart. He needed the right wood and some tools which he found, accompanying William to several fellow fisherman. It all took way longer than he'd anticipated, but after a week, the rudder was fixed. In his spare time, he built a new bunk for William, mended the broken fold-up table and various wooden crates, William used to keep his catch.

In exchange, the fisherman shared his boat, cooked and told stories. "Say, you still want to get to Liverpool?", he said one evening. They'd shared a bottle of poitín, and Davin felt light and woozy at the same time. "Why don't you stay and help me catch fish? We could share the work."

Davin put down his glass. "I've got to earn enough to send to my parents. As far as I know only the English railroad pays."

"You aren't afraid of the work?" William leaned back and rubbed his forehead. "It's back-breaking, I hear, lots of stonework." He pointed at Davin's chest. "You know your craft, but that body of yours will break along with the stone."

"I've got no choice."

"I could ask around, surely other men have repairs on their boats. You could stay in Ireland."

"I already asked some, they've got bits of jobs, but it's not enough.

Nobody has the means, not now that Ireland is in such bad shape."

"Thanks to the English." William emptied his glass. "Damn bloodsuckers."

"I'll help one of them tomorrow, then I'll have enough for the ferry across. All I ask is to stay until the ship leaves. I'll help you fish, if you like."

They shook hands. Davin felt relieved that his journey could finally continue. It was already January and soon the landlord would ask his parents to pay up. He always sent some agent to collect—with a pang he remembered the post office. Maybe, Ma had written. Tomorrow, he needed to find out.

But no letter had arrived, and Davin decided to write another. He'd have several more weeks to wait until he'd get a spot on the ferry, plenty of time to wait for the mail.

Dear Mam and Da,

I've managed to earn enough for the ferry across to Liverpool. Will soon start working on the railroad and sending you money. Just tell the landlord that I'll pay the interest and do not worry.

Your loving son,
Davin

After posting the letter, Davin headed to the docks to purchase his fare. Again, the line snaked around the building of B&I Steam Packet Company with hundreds of people waiting to book passage across to Liverpool. Never mind, that a freezing wind pushed across the sea, turning their faces red and their eyes teary.

The same man in black waited at the counter.

"One fare to Liverpool, as soon as possible," Davin said, keeping a tight fist around the pound note and coins in his pocket.

"Don't they all," the man said, "one pound, ten shillings." His forefinger, blackened with ink, ran along the lines of the book, listing each passenger by name. "January twenty, ten o'clock."

"But that's even longer."

"Yes, lad, there's too many people leaving. Look around."

Davin read the impatience in the man's eyes who peered over his spectacles. More than two weeks waiting, he'd have to find more jobs to cover expenses until departure. Hadn't he just written to his parents that he'd soon send money. Why hadn't he waited? It'd be at least another month before he'd have anything *to* send. He shoved the crumpled pound note and coins across the counter. "Here, one fare please."

"Name, final destination."

"Davin Callaghan, Liverpool."

The man dunked the nib into the ink and wrote in long skinny letters, then handed Davin a ticket. "Be there an hour early and bring your own food."

Head low, Davin hurried along the docks. Being able to continue his journey, he should've felt elated, yet, all he felt was dread. William's comment about the backbreaking work returned, paired with his own disdain for the English. He'd always wanted to work with wood and now he'd dig around in the earth to lay rail. Not what he'd wanted, not what he'd trained for.

He wiggled his hands inside his pockets, surely they were work hardened, but moving rock was an entirely different matter. How long would he last? At least long enough to pay the landlord and to outlast this insane famine. The main thing was not to get hurt.

For a moment he considered returning to the workhouse, but even William's wiggly boat was better than the foul-smelling, unsanitary conditions of the poorhouse. Truth was, he felt lonely among the thousands of people crowding the docks. They were strangers, and soon, he'd feel even more isolated. The English didn't care for Irish people, their feud hundreds of years old, their rule iron-clad and brutal.

A boy of no more than four scrambled across his way, chasing a crudely sewn lump of fabric, functioning as a ball. "Sorry, sir," his mother called. "Peter, come here this instant."

"No worries," Davin said, helping the boy retrieve his ball from beneath a stack of boxes. "Here you go."

The boy threw him a quick grin and scampered back to his mother. Safe in her arms, he watched Davin. "You going to Merica, too?"

"It's *A*-merica," his mother said.

"Just Liverpool." Something in the way the woman spoke made him hesitate. "You traveling alone?"

"My husband, Peter's father, died in the stone pit, you know, building roads. Blast went off wrong, he was hit in the head." The woman, sitting on a shipping box and cradling Peter in one hand and a ragged bag in the other, shook her head. "I'm not waiting to watch Peter starve to death."

"When are you going?"

"To Liverpool on the twentieth, and then I'll have to find a ship." She shrugged. "I'm worried about the fare. It's supposed to be several pounds."

"Me too, I mean, I'm going to Liverpool that day, maybe I'll see you on the ferry."

The woman smiled, a bright light in the dreary gray of the morning. "Peter would like it."

Indeed, the boy was beaming at Davin. "We can play ball."

"Sure thing," Davin heard himself say. "I look forward to it." He patted the boy's wool cap and asked, "Where're you staying until then, it's another two weeks."

The woman's smile disappeared. "The workhouse at night. A terrible place, but we can't afford an inn, besides, they're all booked for months." She gazed across the windswept bay. "Thing is, everybody steals. I lost my nightgown, just left it on the cot for a minute. That's why I take our things out every day. There's all sorts of vermin, too." She squeezed Peter tightly. "I don't want him to get lice."

Davin studied the older woman. She had to be in her late twenties, her nose too large to be pretty with an open honest expression. The best feature had to be her hair, she wore in a thick braid of copper red. She was clean, Peter, too, which had to be a herculean task in the dirty streets of Dublin. "Maybe there's another way."

Peter crawled out of his mother's arms and tucked at Davin's pant leg. "Do you want to play ball now?"

Davin got to his knees to be face-to-face with the boy. Somehow, Peter reminded him of himself. "I tell you what. Why don't we go and find you a bed first? Then, if there's time, we'll play."

Peter smiled and waved his little fist. "Deal."

"You're a savior." The woman extended a hand. "I'm Kate."

The closer they got to William's boat, the less confident Davin felt. What had he done? How could he promise a spot on a boat, he didn't own? He swallowed hard, readjusting the wooden trunk, he carried on his shoulder, wondering how Kate could manage such a load.

"I'm not sure, you see," he said as they walked along the quay.

"Sure about what?"

"I'm staying with a fisherman, William. He's allowed me to sleep on his boat."

Kate's steps slowed. "You don't know if he'll ..." Her gaze fell on Peter and the little pack he carried on his back.

Davin didn't answer and when they approached the spot, where William usually docked, was empty. "Let's wait, surely, he's out to fish." As soon as William returned, Davin would plead for them.

But the boat didn't show. The afternoon slipped away, dusk settled. Davin had left his pack and tools on the boat, figuring he'd return like he had for the last ten days. He'd been pacing for the last hour, going to the end of the dock, looking across the water, going the other way—searching.

Maybe William had tied his boat at another place. He hurried off to check each dock where hundreds of boats bobbed up and down. None looked familiar, the neighboring fishermen shook their heads.

"Maybe, he moved up the coast," one of them said.

"Most of us stayed here today," another said, squinting into the evening. "It's risky with the wind and high waves. He may have needed to wait it out some place."

Davin's imagined William's boat leaning and taking on water, slipping silently beneath the icy waves, taking his pack with him.

"We can't stay here," Kate said, when he returned. "Peter is half frozen."

"I know, I'm sorry." Davin felt embarrassed, worried he'd lost the few belongings he'd carried. Worse, he had just a few shilling left, figuring he'd sleep on the boat and share William's meals. "We better return to the workhouse."

"How long did you know this man...William?" Kate asked as they made their way back.

"Met him after I got here, helped him repair his boat. I figured..."

"You figured, he'd give us shelter, too?" Kate's voice was low and hard to read.

"I'm sorry, if I mislead you."

"You meant well, I know." Kate gazed ahead where the workhouse came into view. The crowds were thick here and Davin wished himself back on the boat. "You see, I'd be all right, but Peter needs care. He's only four."

Two men and a women clogged the entrance to the workhouse. "It's full," they said, looking dejected and panicky.

"Let me through," Kate demanded, the harshness of her voice cutting a path. The woman at the desk inside shook her head. "Sorry, there isn't room. Try tomorrow."

"Please," Kate said. "My little boy cannot sleep on the street. We have no place to go."

"Why did you come so late?"

Davin bit his lip. It was his fault, he'd convinced Kate that there'd be a spot for them and now—

"I must have a place, we'll sleep here in the front room, anywhere," Kate yelled, the red of her cheeks clashing with the copper hair.

The woman shook her head. "Not possible, we already have too many, the rooms are overfilled and—"

Kate gripped the woman's hand. "Please! For my boy's sake?"

Davin read the doubt in the woman's expression, but then she shook her head. "As I said, we're full. Come back tomorrow morning and we'll find a spot."

On the street, Kate faced Davin. "Give me by box."

"Let me carry it," he said quietly.

"You don't understand, give it to me and go." Kate's eyes flashed with anger. "We'd at least be safe inside, had we not listened to you."

"I'll help you."

"Ma, I'm cold," Peter said. His little face looked half frozen in the flickering shine of a street fire. Everywhere, people were gathering to spend the night, burning whatever they could find to keep warm.

"I never want to see you again." Kate turned her back to Davin and dragged the box with one hand, the other firmly tucked around Peter and the bag. He watched her disappear into the night, a lone mother out on the street because of him.

"You're so stupid," he shouted, a couple of people passing him jumped and threw him furious glances. The path blurred. Damn life, every time, he tried to do something good, he got kicked in the ass. Maybe it was better to just think about himself and forget about others. But how could he abandon his parents who'd taken care of him and made sacrifices their entire lives?

On a whim, he returned to the post office. Unlikely, something had arrived, but he craved to read a note from his mother, something to lift his spirits.

"Any mail for Davin Callaghan?"

The postal worker sorted through a stack of letters and handed Davin a gray note.

Fingers shaking, Davin hurried outside. He needed light, so he decided to enter a pub down the street. He didn't have much left after buying the ticket, but a bottle of ale had to be in the cards tonight.

After ordering, he tore open the seal, hesitated. The handwriting was short and stubby and uneven—this letter had been written by somebody else. His eyes began to search and race across the lines...

Dear Davin,

I'm writing to you on behalf of your parents. Just two weeks ago, after the new year began, they both fell sick with fever. One of your neighbors found them a couple of days later after they hadn't been seen. Both were delirious and didn't recognize any of us. We tried our best, several of the neighbors taking turns, caring for them. Not everybody helped, because they themselves were afraid of contracting the disease. We still don't know what happened, but first your mother passed and within a day, your father followed her. We're heartbroken as surely as you must be, reading these lines. Maybe it is time for you to return to help sort out their affairs. We buried your parents in the village graveyard, though I'm afraid it was a muted affair, having no money to go around.

I'm so sorry, your neighbor and friend, Steven McGregor

Davin's hand sank to the table, his bottle sat forgotten. His parents were dead, had been dead for weeks while he struggled to get to England to save the farm. Now it was all gone. His parents had no more use of their home, the English landlord would take what was left for himself.

Davin swallowed, but the lump in his throat grew larger by the second, choking him. He rose abruptly and pushed his way outside. He needed air, wanted to scream. His parents were gone, the only people, who'd cared for him, the two people who he'd loved the most in the world.

Again, the road blurred. Tears rolled down his cheeks and he felt too distraught to wipe them away. Nothing mattered, let them stare and comment. He wandered through the crowded streets, his feet taking him back to the docks. Maybe he should just continue walking...at some point, he'd drop into the water, the waves would close above his head, erase his existence. Who'd care? Not a soul, nobody would miss him or expect him back.

"Davin?" The voice sounded familiar, so he turned. Behind the haze of his tears, he recognized Kate. Peter had rolled up on a blanket on top of the travel box and was fast asleep. He just stood there staring at the young mother. "What happened?"

He cleared his throat, found that his mouth and tongue worked. "I...my parents are both gone."

Kate took another step, put a hand on his arm. "You mean...they're dead?"

Davin nodded. "Fever."

The grip on his arm tightened. "I'm sorry. Not just for your loss, but that I yelled at you. I know you meant well, tried to share your sleeping quarters." Her gaze traveled to the small figure on the box. "I'm just worried to lose him. He's all I've got."

"I don't blame you." Davin was surprised he could form normal words. "He's a good lad and deserves a decent bed." Becoming aware of the wetness of his cheeks, he pulled out the only handkerchief he possessed and wiped his face.

"What are you going to do now?" Kate's question hit him like a fist in the stomach.

What indeed? All this time, his purpose had been to travel to England and work the railroad, even if he hated everything the English stood for. Now he no longer needed to go. He was—in a sense—free. He looked at the small woman in front of him and shook his head.

"I don't have the faintest idea."

CHAPTER SEVENTEEN

Mina

Mina wondered if it showed—was her desperation, the dislike for her husband's plan written on her face? The old woman had helped her wash and change her clothes, taken care of her frostbitten feet while Roland kept talking to the old farmer. She'd slept well that night, buried under a feather bed, white and fluffy as a cloud, and reluctant to ever climb out again. But Roland had called to her at first light, and she detected the old impatience in his voice.

Now they were walking again. The wind and snow had stopped, it was a beautiful, clear day with a sky as blue as cornflowers. Only that it was far below freezing, each step crunched on the snow. The road was already busy again with travelers, many looked as bad or worse than Mina and Roland.

Mina's pace was even slower than yesterday, the scare of freezing to death still deeply in her bones. She understood Augusta's grandmother, how she'd stopped caring and just wanted to lie down and rest. Had she died by now? Were Augusta and her parents back on the road?

She caught herself, looking over her shoulder and scanning the crowds resting at the side of the road at all hours. None looked familiar. The feeling of loneliness returned—every step brought her farther from home, from her father and all she'd known.

Roland seemed to have no such feelings, he just charged ahead as if the police were chasing him. Maybe they were. He'd not talked about that night again, but Mina knew something had happened to make him run like that.

They reached Bremerhaven eight days later and Roland immediately headed toward the docks. They needed no directions because a steady stream of travelers marched the same way. Everybody carried suitcases and boxes, some rode on horses or steered wagons.

Roland had to find the office of the agent from Hapag Lloyd, the shipping company that had arranged their crossing. By the time, they found it, it was early afternoon. Two more hours passed until they reached the counter. Roland pulled out his papers which the man carefully studied and compared to an entry in a thick black book.

"Travel date is February 15, 1849. Two persons, steerage." He handed Roland two tickets. "Make sure you bring enough food for six weeks, just in case."

"But that's in a month," Roland cried. "What are we going to do all that time?"

The man shrugged and waved at the next person in line. "Rest up, I suppose. We're fully booked for months, good thing your agent registered you early."

Mina pushed her way next to Roland. "You know where we can stay?"

"We're a shipping company, miss," the man said. "Now make room, there're many more waiting."

Outside, Mina watched as Roland hid the tickets inside the leather pouch, he'd picked up on the road. At least he'd learned that much.

"We need to find a room," Mina cried. The damp and chilly air that smelled of salt and fish, and nothing like her home, was getting to her.

"Don't you think I know that?" Roland stomped off without looking at her. Mina followed as fast as she could.

Every inn and hostel was filled beyond capacity, most had signs out front—no vacancies.

"Head to the outskirts, they're building huge barns," a man in a ragged suit said when they were turned away for the seventeenth time.

All Mina wanted to do was to sit down in one of those pubs, eat a good meal and sleep for a week. But even the restaurants and taverns were crowded, so they stopped to buy bread and cabbage soup from a street vendor and ate leaning against the wall of a building. The wind tugged at Mina's hair, pulled it this way and that. She had to look like a wild woman by now, with holes in her shoes and soggy soles. The bottom rim of her dress was splattered with mud, her shawl stained, not to mention the state of her underthings. It was embarrassing. She'd always taken pride in her appearance, even when they'd had little thanks to Roland's meager and unreliable pay.

"Where are we getting that much durable food?," she asked as they walked along one of the canals, leading out of town. It was getting dark again and the old worry was back. The weather here seemed harsher because of the fierce wind that blew at them across the North Sea as if it wanted to send them back home.

Roland ignored her and charged ahead as usual. After asking several people and knocking on doors, they finally ended up on another farm five miles from town. A couple of barns looked brand-new and housed a hundred people each. There were two floors, each of them stuffed with straw. A sign proclaimed: *No fires permitted.*

Already the straw was soiled, the air thick with the odors of too many people, as Mina squeezed herself in-between a boy of maybe fourteen and Roland on the other side. She was so exhausted, she didn't even take off her shoes, which was a good thing because the air grew colder inside by the minute. Mina pulled her knees up to her belly and hugged herself to retain some of the warmth. She would've loved to cuddle up to somebody, but she had no desire to be near Roland. He may see it as an invitation. Every time, she awoke, people were snoring, coughing, and whispering, a constant rustling that kept her on edge.

How on earth was she going to survive here for weeks? It was cheap, yes, but she'd never get any rest. The farmer offered a simple breakfast of cooked oats and bread with jam, which Mina devoured in a matter of minutes, not looking up, only wondering how she could convince Roland to return home.

His mood grew worse over the day, and the next seemed worse than the day before. He'd wander off, mumbling something about "getting the lay of the land," while Mina sorted her pack and washed a couple of underthings in the water trough outside.

She listened to the excited voices of the women, standing together in groups, chatting about the new country, waiting for them on the other side of the ocean. Of course, not all of them seemed positive, some of the older men sat staring into the fire that roared outside and kept to themselves.

She grew bored that afternoon, surprised how she'd feel this way, when just the day before, she'd wished for quiet and rest. Now, she wandered among the hundreds of families, feeling displaced and weary. She'd been used to a busy schedule, keeping house and cooking, shopping and tending the garden, collecting herbs and flowers, she'd use for healing. Now she had nothing to tend, no house, not even a bed to make—nowhere to go. All she could do was to sit around and wait to be carried off into some unknown land.

According to the stories, she overheard, America was a land of opportunity, of unending forests filled with game, grasses twice as tall as a man, rich soil and friendly people. Some travelers clutched letters and pamphlets, reading them to their families over and over as if to assure themselves that it was all right to leave.

Mina couldn't imagine any of it, no matter the flowery descriptions. She followed a path, dotted with pine needles and cones to the beach. Above her the wind whispered in the trees, pine sap and sea salt mixed into an intoxicating aroma.

Beyond lay a beautiful patch of sand and colored stones, and under different circumstances, she'd enjoyed it. She breathed deeply, turning right, past boulders and driftwood.

Not a hundred yards away sat Roland on a log, staring into the distance.

"What are you doing out here?," she cried, drawing closer.

Roland turned to face her, his expression a mix of anger and sadness. "Nothing much."

"The crowds are getting on my nerves." Mina sank next to him. "Can we talk?"

"About what?"

"This...this journey. I'm not sure, it's the right thing. I never wanted—"

"Shush, woman. You're talking nonsense." Roland jumped up and turned to face her. "We've come all this way, there's opportunity in America, lots of fertile land."

But you never found any here, how will you find it there...in a different language. Aloud, Mina said, "I'm homesick. Why can't we talk more, see if there's another solution. I miss my father."

"I've signed a redemptioner contract, I'm going to America." Roland waved his arms toward the vastness of the sea. "We're going to start a new life over there, buy land and build a house."

Mina stared at the man, she was bound to, and realized, there was nothing she could say or do to change his mind.

CHAPTER EIGHTEEN

Davin
The days passed in a blur. Davin had trouble concentrating, was even numb to the cold and discomfort. In the mornings, he returned to the empty spot where William's boat had moored. To keep afloat, he did odd jobs for other boat owners, returning to the workhouse in midafternoon to make sure he'd have space to sleep.

Sometimes, Kate accompanied him on his jobs, watching from the dock while Peter played with his crooked ball. They'd eat cheap food from street vendors, cabbage and onion soup or soda bread with butter, cooked oats and on occasion, mutton stew. Food at the workhouse was worse and less filling, but it was free as long as they played along. Not that it mattered, Davin didn't really taste much, his mouth and tongue as numb as the rest of him.

The life he'd planned for the foreseeable future, saving the farm and eventually returning to take over for his parents had evaporated. While the famine continued, there was no point returning to Skibbereen. He had no place to live and there'd be even less work.

He often fell into a stupor, staring into the distance without seeing anything while memories of his past life ran through his mind. They'd never had much, but until the famine hit, he'd felt reasonably happy, had gone out on weekends, had danced and kissed a few girls, lost his virginity to a widow who'd hired him to fix her roof.

A small hand came into view. "Are you going to play now?" Peter held out his ball, his expression hopeful. They were sitting near one of the docks and the afternoon sun lit up the freckles on the boy's nose.

Fighting the darkness, Davin took the ball and led Peter to an open area next to a building. "All right, let's see what you can do."

Peter kicked the ball which flew every which way. Davin taught him how to use the side of his foot to direct the kicks, how to aim at a goal. It felt good to move and Peter had a way of distracting him from brooding.

He'd managed to trade a set of used clothes for fixing a leaky window, had fashioned a pack from scraps of fabric. What he needed was a decent project, something he'd get paid for enough to afford a room. But it was difficult to find such work when he didn't know anybody, and most companies employed local people. William had taken his tools when he'd left, so Davin had to work with what was available at each worksite. He needed to earn enough to buy another set, at a minimum a decent saw, chisels, level, planes, auger, and square. It'd taken him years to assemble a solid toolkit, without it, he'd never succeed.

He scoffed. Without tools, he couldn't work his magic and earn enough, but he needed money to buy tools in the first place. Something had to happen, except he didn't know what.

"Why don't you come with us?", Kate said, when they returned out of breath, but at least he felt warmer. Her cheeks had taken on the same red coloring as Peter's, her expression hard to read.

"To America?" Davin sank onto a mooring buoy, adjusting his hat. "What would I do there?"

Kate's cheeks grew darker. "Start over. They say it's a big country, much bigger than Ireland. You'd be away from English control, could start your own business, build houses for people." She took a deep breath. "I know you'd be good at it."

Davin gazed across the waves glistening in the sunshine. It was a pretty sight, seagulls flying above, the air fresh and salty. "Even if I wanted to, I've got no money to afford the passage." He shook his head. "I'd rather make a go of it here."

"But you said yourself, you need tools. And even if you had them, Ireland is dying." A shiver ran through Kate. "I feel it in my bones. First the English are sucking us dry, now the famine. I'm glad to leave."

Davin studied the little woman standing in front of him. He admired her strength, the way she took care of her son. It was hard enough to look after yourself, raising a small child seemed like an enormous task. "Maybe you're right," he heard himself say. "I'll think about it." He rose and offered Peter a hand. "We better get you some dinner and a bed before the workhouse fills up again."

That night, Davin couldn't sleep. It wasn't just the crowded, stinky room with the dozen or so people cramped on beds and the floor, the coughing, sighing, snoring, and whispering at all hours of the night. He was thinking about Kate's question. At least here he knew his way around, he was among fellow Irishmen. His parents were buried here. Buried. A tear squeezed through his closed eyelids. He'd failed them, had gotten drunk and been reckless. He'd not been there, when they took their last breaths, had not been able to give them comfort. Even his letter had arrived too late.

But he needed to think ahead, somehow get over his grief. Fact was, thousands of Irish were leaving, searching for a better life, not in England on the railroad, but across the seas, in some foreign land. For a moment he allowed himself to dream of running a business, employing a dozen men, building solid houses with porches and square windows.

The journey would be hard, no doubt, but hard had never scared him. What scared him was the unknown, the unfamiliar which even bothered him here in Dublin, not to mention the crowds of strangers, swarming every road, filling pubs, inns, and docks. But returning to Skibbereen was out of the question, so why not do something daring. He remembered William, how he'd openly approached any stranger and struck up a conversation, always jovial, always a smile on his lips and a compliment to bestow, no matter how dire his own situation had been and how urgently he'd needed to find the next pot to repair.

Why couldn't he be more like William, why did he have to weigh every decision and worry about its outcome? Planning obviously didn't work because fate threw him on a different path in an instant. He let out a sigh and turned to his side, his nose touching Kate's hair.

If fate wanted him to go to America, he'd go—provided he'd be able to afford it. A small smile crept onto his face. In the morning he'd tell Kate and Peter.

Over the next days, they discussed his options. Kate had enough traveling money from the company who had employed her husband, but Davin had no time to save.

"I heard some man talk about the redemptioner system," Kate said. They were having a watery soup in the workhouse, drinking it from dented tin cups, because it was so thin.

Davin had heard it, too. It was nothing but modern slavery, but it seemed the only way to afford the passage. As a carpenter, he'd be in high demand. He'd have to make a decision now, because the boat to

Liverpool was leaving the day after tomorrow. Who knew what he'd find over there.

"It's only for a few years, until you pay off the debt..." Kate was just saying, her eyes on Peter who sat between them. "In the meantime, you could plan your own business, line things up."

Davin shrugged. "Maybe. It reminds me of the English, though."

Kate's hand landed on his. "You'll never have to work for the English again."

A small consolation. He felt Kate's gaze on his temple but was unable to look at her. He knew she wanted a new husband. But he wasn't ready and while he felt he needed to help Kate and Peter, he couldn't quite imagine spending the rest of his life with them.

"I suppose it wouldn't hurt to find out," he heard himself say. There were signs all over the port, agencies looking for skilled men, willing to sign their lives away—at least for a few years. He thought of the news of more deaths, tens of thousands of Irish were starving until they were too weak to move. He wasn't going to be one of them.

When he boarded the ferry two days later, once again squeezed between hundreds of passengers, once again shivering and wishing for the trip to be over, it was all done.

Inside his pocket lay a contract, arranging his passage to America. In exchange he'd be working for some outfit in Indiana. What a strange name, was it full of wild Indians? He didn't even know where Indiana was. The agent had gotten excited, when Davin told him about being a carpenter and suggested Williams Construction. Apparently, they built houses and bridges all over the Midwest.

It was a longer trip than most, many Irish remaining in New York where a growing population, was settling, the man had said. But in exchange, he'd have provisions and travel to the final destination covered.

He no longer had to fret about what to do with himself, he even had a woman to keep him company. Why did he feel so lost then?

CHAPTER NINETEEN

Mina

Mina and Roland were scouring the area for the best deals on provisions. They needed to buy enough food to last six weeks, that's what the agent had said. But bread wouldn't last, fresh vegetables were unavailable. At the same time, they were paying for shelter and food while they waited for the ship to sail.

If they bought too early, they were liable to fall prey to some thief. Everything disappeared if they didn't carry it with them. If they waited, prices could rise. Every day, people left, more arrived, took the empty spots inside the barn, many more had to travel on. It was a constant coming and going.

"Why don't we settle with a farmer, buy enough grain to cook gruel? I heard there're stoves to share in steerage," Mina said one morning. They'd been there two weeks, and she was getting nervous about running out of money again.

Roland squinted at her, the idleness making him even grumpier. "I make the decisions around here."

"But if we wait—"

Roland's hand gripped her wrist. "Quit your whining, it's too early. Where would we store it safely?"

Mina opened her eyes wide, so he wouldn't see her tears. "You're hurting me. We could order and pick it up right before."

Without a word, he let go and walked off. Every day, he left her for hours at a time. Mina thought it was a good plan, but he was so weak, lacked all confidence that he couldn't allow her to have good ideas—a small man in a large body.

Mina rubbed her wrist and wandered toward the road where men, women and children passed in both directions, some still searching for shelter, others heading for the docks of Bremerhaven.

"Mina!"

Mina turned abruptly as Augusta ran toward her, arms waving and a broad smile on her face. It was as if sunshine were brightening the road.

They embraced, both of them teary-eyed. "You made it," Mina said breathlessly.

"We've been staying in town, but Papa says, it's getting too expensive. So, we're looking for a cheaper space."

Mina hugged Augusta to her. "You have lost weight."

"So have you. Where is Roland?"

Mina made a face and looked away. "Walking around. He's in a bad mood all the time."

Augusta was about to answer when Stefan drew near, Augusta's mother on his arm. "It's good to see you. You think they've got room for us?" He nodded toward the barns.

"People leave every day, it's utter luck these days."

While Stefan headed toward the farm, Mina shook hands with Augusta's mother. "I'm so sorry for your loss."

Augusta's mother swallowed, obviously trying to keep her composure. "It was quick. It's just...I wish I'd been able to bury her in her churchyard, next to her husband."

Mina patted her lower arm, realizing that at least her father would be laid to rest next to her mother and not on some strange road in the middle of nowhere. The thought comforted her a bit.

"How are you doing?" Augusta's mother was studying Mina. "The wait is rather difficult." She scoffed. "Everything is."

"I'm worried about getting supplies in time. We've got to have enough for weeks. How do we even know, how long the passage takes? Some people say four weeks, others say six or eight."

She felt Augusta's arm wrap around her shoulder. It was better than any shawl. "You should order now and pick up before you leave." She clapped her free hand on her mouth. "When are you leaving?"

"In two weeks, February 19."

"Our ship leaves on the 28th."

"Do you know where you'll head after arrival?"

Mina shrugged. "A place called Indiana. It is a state somewhere inland."

"Indiana." Augusta let the word roll of her tongue. "It sounds like a good name. Are there Indians there?"

Mina shrugged. "I don't know, only that Roland will work at an iron forge."

Stefan hurried toward them. "We can stay. Quick, let's get settled. We're in this first barn."

"I'll come with you," Mina said. "Then I'll know how to find you. This place must house many hundreds."

"Near seven hundred. I asked." Stefan grabbed the two suitcases and led the way while Mina helped Augusta with a pack.

They agreed to meet for dinner and Mina ran off to find Roland. He'd love to see Stefan, she was sure of it.

Every morning, Augusta would meet Mina for a walk. Together, they explored the coastline, investigated farms and paths. With Augusta by her side, Mina felt stronger and less afraid, though she could tell that Augusta was far less enthusiastic than when they'd met.

"Do you know where you'll settle?", Mina asked on one of their walks. It was an icy day with a bright sun and no warmth, their breaths steam clouds in the air.

"Papa talks about Ohio, apparently, we have family there, some distant cousin."

"I can't imagine any of it."

"Neither can I, but it has got to be better than Württemberg." Augusta's eyes clouded. "People are sick, starving, or dying of hunger. We met others from Westphalia and Bavaria. It's the same everywhere."

"How far is Ohio from Indiana?" Mina tried to imagine the landscape, visiting Augusta.

"I do not know. Papa says, America is much larger than anything we've seen. He says there are mountains as high as the Alps, wide open spaces, and lots of land to settle on."

"How does he know?"

"Before we made the decision to leave, he'd been writing letters with people from Ohio and other places. He's been planning this journey for two years."

Augusta tipped a gloved forefinger on her lower lip. "We should go in search of a map. At least we'll know where things are. I want to visit you."

Mina nodded though secretly she worried. Roland being a redemptioner meant, he'd not earn any money. They'd be dependent on what housing the employer provided. Surely, Augusta was used to a grand house. "You never told me what your father does," she said aloud.

A smile flitted across Augusta's face. "He is a master beer brewer, that's why he wants to go to Cincinnati. I guess lots of people are settling there to brew beer."

"Cincinnati." Mina tried out the strange word. "I've got to learn English."

Augusta clapped her hands. "Of course, we should practice together." She pulled a book from her pocket. *English without Teacher, help book for emigrants*, it said on the cover, above a sailing ship.

Mina realized quickly that she had a good memory for words though she wished somebody would tell her how to pronounce them. Soon, Augusta would point at something, and Mina would blurt out the English word. They switched back and forth and began forming simple sentences.

"What are you doing all day with Augusta?," Roland asked one evening, when Mina joined him in the barn. She had delayed entering until the last possible minute, because she loathed the thick, smelly air.

"Practicing."

Roland sank into the straw and adjusted his blanket. "Practicing what?"

"English, of course. We'll need to communicate with the American people."

Roland scoffed. "Nonsense. There'll be thousands of Germans, all speaking our language. I heard they're even naming streets and parks in German."

Mina squeezed next to her husband, hoping he'd leave her alone. It had been weeks since he touched her, one advantage of sleeping in such crowded conditions. She knew there were some who didn't care, listened to their moans and rustling. Roland was obviously too shy.

Just as well. She had not been able to bring the wild carrot seeds. The last thing she wanted was to get pregnant. She turned her back to him and closed her eyes. No need to answer, all she'd get was a nasty retort. She was glad to pass the time learning the language.

Tomorrow, they were going to order oats from the farm, Stefan had helped convince Roland that it was the right thing to do. Mina patted the pouch she wore on her chest where she kept the coins. Hopefully, the money would be enough.

CHAPTER TWENTY

Davin

If Dublin had been busy, Liverpool was worse. People were everywhere and though Davin recognized many fellow Irish men by their looks and accents, many more jabbered in all sorts of English and acted the part—arrogant.

The crossing had been bad enough, Kate became seasick and hung over the railing while Davin held on to Peter. Not that he could've gone anywhere, the deck was stuffed with passengers. Those unable to make it to the railing threw up on themselves, the ground, or their neighbors. Soon, everything reeked of vomit and Davin kept his nose in the wind as best he could.

He had to help Kate get off the boat because she was weak and unable to pull her trunk.

Now they were sitting on a side road near the port, devouring a loaf of bread, Davin had organized from a street vendor.

"I've got to find a room," he said. "And more importantly, a shipping company."

Kate nodded weakly, pressing Peter to her chest. "I'll wait here. Just hurry back. I don't like this neighborhood." Indeed, the docks were full of shady looking people, some lingering in front of pubs and inns, others just watching silently. It was well known that there were thieves and shysters preying on people, trying to lure a coin for some promised service that didn't exist.

Wilson & Sons was hard to miss, their offices large and roomy. As in Dublin, a line of people snaked out of its front door and along the path. Kate had given him her money to buy a ticket for the crossing.

According to the agent in Dublin, all Davin had to do was to show his redemptioner papers and he'd get a spot on the next available ship.

"You're in luck," the man behind the counter told him. "The New-Orleans keeps a few spots open for redemptioners. I'll reserve one."

"I need one for my friend and her son as well." Davin pushed Kate's passport across.

The man shook his head. "Sorry, your friend is going to have to wait a while longer. Ships are booked for months."

"But she can't, her boy is only four—"

The man vigorously shook his head. "Open your eyes, half of Ireland is leaving. She'll have to wait her turn. Unless..." The clerk's mouth twitched.

"Unless?"

"If you're married, you can take your family along."

"Married?"

The man's hand hovered above the book. "What will it be?"

Davin's thoughts raced. He'd have to marry Kate, a woman he hardly knew. He liked her well enough, but he'd seen what a loving relationship like that of his parents could do. He didn't feel love for this woman, only affection. Was that enough, would it grow? What did she want?

He knew what she wanted, had read the signs. She would *want* to get married and be taken care of. Again, life was throwing up a hurdle, another thing he'd have to overcome. He felt out of control once again.

Behind him, voices mumbled insults: "Hurry up, man...let's go...we're all waiting here."

"All right, I'll marry her." He swallowed away the worry. He'd explain it to Kate—to himself at the next opportunity.

The air felt different when he entered the street, the tickets subtly rustling against his chest. First, he'd signed away his life by accepting work as a redemptioner. Now he'd signed his private life away, too. He'd get married, already had a son in the bargain. Not that he didn't like Peter. But wasn't it different to father a child than to inherit one?

Get yourself back to Kate, his mind commented. *You'll have to sort it later.*

The roadside where he'd left her was empty. Davin asked a man lounging nearby, smoking a cigarette. "Have you seen a young woman and a little boy? They were sitting right here."

The man gave him a strange look and shook his head. "Saw none," he said. And when Davin turned to leave, "Better go back where you came from, *Paddy!*"

Was it that obvious? Of course, the way he looked and sounded had be strange to the snobby English. He caught sight of himself in the pub window and smirked. Not to mention that his hair and freckles gave it away. His wasn't copper like Kate's, much brighter like fresh rust, red enough to stick out anywhere he went.

He hurried off, relieved to reenter the busier quays where ships of all sizes, most of them sailboats, docked, the worry for Kate urging him to hurry. He turned left, weaved back and forth through the mingling and waiting crowds. The uneasiness grew, made him sweat despite the cold. What if some man had attacked her, dragged her inside a building, never to emerge gain? For all he knew, it could've been the grimy fellow he spoke to.

He turned abruptly and ran the other way. He'd have to go to the police, explain what had happened, when he realized that he didn't even know Kate's last name. Yes, officer, I met her in Dublin. No, I don't know her last name, but she has a son, Peter. He chewed his lower lip and hurried on, looking left and right. She wouldn't have gone far with the heavy wooden trunk. Not after the exhausting passage.

"Davin, over here!"

Through the line of people waiting to board a sailing ship named Esmeralda, he caught a peek of Kate sitting on her box. The next moment, Peter caught hold of his leg. "You're back," he cried. "We were scared." His blue eyes were filled with a mixture of anxiety and delight.

He took Peter's hand and guided him toward Kate. "I couldn't find you." To his surprise relief flooded him and he dropped on his knees in front of Kate. They were at eyelevel and for the first time, he imagined making love to her. Immediately, he felt his cheeks warm, so he straightened again and put down his pack. "I've got tickets." He fumbled through his pocket and handed Kate hers and the remainder of her money.

Kate warily sorted through the bills. "But that's six pounds less than they said." She looked up, suspicion in her eyes. "What happened?"

There it was, the moment he had to come clean.

"I...am sorry, it's complicated." He looked away, then back to Kate who squinted at him. "We've got to get married."

A mix of emotions showed on Kate's face: surprise, fear...and to his surprise, joy. When she remained silent, he continued, "I got a spot on an earlier ship because of the redemptioner contract. I suppose they want me as soon as possible. But you would have to wait another two months, unless..."

"Unless we married first."

"Right."

Kate's smile widened. "It's not the most romantic proposal, but I accept." She rose and took his hand. "I'd much rather travel with you than alone. Besides, what would I do here by myself?"

"Right," he said again, surprised how nice Kate's small hand felt in his.

"Then it's settled."

They married a week later in a small chapel on the outskirts of Liverpool, where they were staying in a boarding house. It was a small affair, Kate wearing a dress, he hadn't seen before and he his normal clothes. The priest had studied their papers and asked few questions. Apparently, it happened all the time, their kiss short and hurried. Already three other couples were waiting outside.

To celebrate they went to a pub and shared roast and potatoes, Peter sitting between them and smiling from ear to ear. "I'll call you 'Da now," he announced when the waiter brought them dessert, some kind of pudding with a red sauce.

Davin produced a smile though his mind was on the wedding night. He didn't feel particularly confident, his experience with the older woman, whose roof he'd repaired, a distant memory. He drank a second ale to chase away his nervousness.

They'd rented a private room just for one night, an hour's walk from the port. Nearer than that, rooms and barns were filled to overflowing. At least it was quieter here, a working neighborhood of thatched row houses.

The room was tiny, a bed with a flowery blanket, a tiny cot in the corner for Peter, a wash bowl and a wooden cabinet with a missing foot. They turned off the candle and undressed in the dark, Peter's voice drowsy from a long day. Kate tucked him in and slipped into bed while Davin hung his clothes over the only chair.

He was dead tired himself, but also strangely awake. Then Kate was there, in his arms, snuggling her body to his. She was wearing some kind of nightshirt that now scrunched against his skin. His hand wandered and soon remembered what needed to be done. Kate suppressed a moan, so he had to be on the right track. After a while she took off her shirt and pulled him toward her, and he soon forgot his apprehension.

Out of breath, he fit himself next to her and fell asleep. In the night, he awoke briefly and noticed that she'd redressed. Just as well. He put on his pants in case Peter would wake before him. He'd done it, gotten married and was going to America.

    He turned on his side and wrapped an arm around Kate...his wife. He was no longer alone, no longer without purpose—a new life was waiting for him.

CHAPTER TWENTY-ONE

Mina

The morning their ship departed, Mina and Roland left at dawn. Augusta, who'd waited for her at the road to say good-bye, pulled her close. "I'll miss you," she whispered. "Be safe." Mina's eyes spilled over, her throat too thick to utter a word. Augusta stuffed a piece of paper into her hand. "My dad's cousin in Cincinnati. Write to me."

"I will, I promise—"

"We've got to go." Roland's voice was gruff. "We'll be slow as it is." He squinted at Augusta, hoisted the sack of grain onto his shoulder, and turned to leave. Mina squeezed Augusta's hand, before she followed her husband into the morning.

The wind had died down for once, but Mina's steps crunched on the frozen ground, each breath burned in her lungs. Fog blanketed the fields as a feeble sun crept over the horizon behind them. Mina's arms ached from the unaccustomed weight of the grain sack, not as large as Roland's, but heavy enough to make her switch back and forth every few yards. They'd also purchased a bag of dried biscuit that was hard as rocks but supposed to withstand the damp conditions on the ship.

Every so often, they halted to rest, Roland cursing and massaging his shoulder. "Damn food, we should've gotten a cart."

Mina held her temper. They had no money for extras, certainly not a cart, they'd have to dispose of as soon as they stepped foot on board.

Roland stopped more and more often, and she realized how weak he'd gotten. Workdays at an iron forge in the new land would be hard and long and she already worried, how he'd cope. This time he couldn't quit, not when he'd signed a contract. Who knew what the employer would do to him...them?

By the time, they reached the docks of Bremerhaven, it was the middle of the morning. They were supposed to arrive by nine for the sailing and even without a watch, Mina knew they were late. Roland left to ask for the right ship and returned running toward her.

"They're almost ready to sail, let's go." He swung the sack back onto his shoulder and hurried off, Mina struggling to keep up like she had when they'd walked through the snow. Soon, he was fifty yards ahead, then a hundred, and she worried to lose sight of him.

But then he stopped abruptly near the water where several men were carrying packets, crates and elegant suitcases up a plank...to a ship.

Mina had expected to feel excited, but when she saw the boat, her heart sank. It was a sailing vessel, no more than forty yards long with the front deck so crowded, it seemed like a mass of bodies. Only the back space was shaded by a small, tarped roof, from which a handful of well-clothed men and a women with blond hair, laid in fashionable curls, looked down on them. For an instant, Mina thought it was Augusta. Such nonsense, Augusta was sitting in the barn, waiting for her ship to sail in two weeks. What space remained, was filled with kegs and wooden boxes, cords thick as her arm coiled every which way, all of it shadowed by a jumble of sails.

Roland was talking to a man guarding the plank walkway, waving his arms. "I know we're late, but I've got a contract," he yelled. "Surely, you don't want trouble. We've got tickets." He pulled the paper from his jacket and waved it in front of the man who was rubbing his beard.

Everything in Mina bristled against crossing the plank and squeezing onto this impossibly full ship that looked too small and too ramshackle to carry them across a vast ocean. She wanted to return home, move in with her father, if she had to. Anything was better than this. For a moment, she hesitated, saw herself turn away from the docks...hike the long way back...embrace her—

"Come here, hurry up." Roland's voice cut off her thoughts.

Mina picked up her sack and the small traveling bag, and joined Roland, hoping to hear that they'd be turned away.

"This is my wife, we're supposed to travel together, you surely wouldn't want her to return or wait any longer." He lowered his voice. "She's with child, you know. The sooner we get there, the better."

The bearded man's eyes traveled across Mina's body as if he were searching for signs of her pregnancy. Mina stared in shock at Roland's lying. Please let the man see through this ruse.

But to her dismay, he nodded. "All right, hurry up. Steerage, two levels down, you'll have to find room. Five to a section, no more, no less. You'll have to make it work."

Mina's knees nearly buckled as she crossed the swinging gangway above a dark, deep mass of water that cut her off from the land, then up a flight of stairs, onto the ship where people clogged every available space and stood before her like a wall. Without Roland, she would've simply gotten stuck, but he pushed his way through the crowd, yelling, "Coming through, step aside."

From deck, a set of stairs led into the belly of the ship. It was a temporary deck, installed only for the voyages to America, the ceiling no more than five feet eleven with no windows. Every compartment they entered was filled to capacity and soon, all they asked was, "Five?"

Near the end of the corridor, they found one spot each in separate sections. In front of each bunk, the space was packed with trunks and suitcases, kegs, storage boxes filled with food supplies, leaving no more than two feet to squeeze through. Since most people were on deck, Mina laid out her blanket and stored the sack of food at the foot of the bed. Other than a lantern, it was dark, the air stifling without the slightest breeze, she wanted to squeeze shut her nose and keep it from smelling the stench. No wonder, most people were outside.

At the end of the corridor, she discovered a couple of buckets used as a toilet. It wasn't even a private room, nor were there facilities to wash. A cast-iron stove with no utensils or pots stood in an alcove. It was tiny and she wondered, how they'd all prepare meals on such a small surface. She'd have to borrow a pot to cook the grain, goodness, they didn't even have spoons. How in the world was she going to survive four or even six weeks in here?

She decided to tell Roland and go upstairs. He was lying on the bunk and near filled out half the space, supposedly laid out for five passengers. "I'm going up," she said, relieved, he waved her away.

People stood on the top steps, trying to join the mass on deck, but Mina soon gave up. Instead, she climbed one level down. The sign on the door announced *no entry for steerage*. Frustrated she climbed back up and fought her way onto the deck. Next to the partitioned section where she'd seen the wealthier passengers earlier, a sign announced *no entry for steerage*. Never had she wished more to have enough money to travel with some comfort, some dignity, like a human being, not a rat subsisting on scraps. When she'd first met Roland at seventeen, she'd believed he'd move mountains. He'd been so enthusiastic and good looking, an easy smile on his face. It had taken her time to look through his stories, the great schemes he dreamed up and then dismissed just as fast.

She caught a glimpse of the dock, where two men were untying the arm-thick ropes, waving and yelling commands. On deck, a handful limber-looking crew were climbing around the masts, preparing ropes and sails.

Somewhere beneath her, she heard a grinding sound, a knocking like some machine. Augusta's father, Stefan, had explained to them that most sailing ships these days had small steam engines that helped maneuver them in and out of ports. He'd talked about big steam ships soon taking over and transporting passengers much faster.

Obviously, this vessel was older and would be dependent on the wind for most of its voyage. The dock began to move, rather it was the ship slid away from land. On the quay, men and women waved and called good-byes, above, passengers whistled and hollered, the woman next to Mina, wearing a severe black dress cried, silent tears rolling down her cheeks. She had to be in her late forties, the hair on her temples graying, the lines around her mouth deep as if she hadn't smiled in a long time. Despite the crowd, a shroud of loneliness surrounded her.

Mina swallowed repeatedly. She didn't want to cry, didn't want to give in to the feeling of helplessness. She was stuck now, dependent on the whims of the weather, the captain's abilities and her fellow passengers. Roland's abrupt escape had left them with nothing except a blanket and the clothes on their bodies. Head low, she abruptly turned and crept back to her quarters and pulled up her legs facing the wall. All she wanted was to sleep and escape this nightmare.

Mina awoke because somebody was kneeing her in the back of her legs. She half turned and grew aware of a man, lying next to her, his face inches from hers. Despite the gloom she knew that the compartment was filled with people, their odor sharp in her nose. She wanted to fall asleep again, but her stomach had other ideas.

She peeled out of her blanket and climbed off the platform in search of Roland. They'd have to prepare oats, but she had no idea how they'd cook. Roland was sitting in the aisle, his back against the outer wall, his eyelids puffy in the flickering light of an oil lamp.

"How are we going to eat the grain?", she asked, joining him. At least out here, the air was a bit better. Above, the floorboards creaked and the swooshing, whistling sounds of the wind hitting the sails could be heard. Worse was the constant shimmying of the ground as it cut through the waves, the shuddering of the wood. Up and down it went in an unending pattern.

"Not sure, we'll need to borrow a pot, I doubt, they'll allow us to make a fire while we've got such high waves."

"What do people eat then?"

He shrugged. "Half the people in my section are throwing up. It's impossible to stay in there without getting sick, too."

Indeed, the air was filled with the stench of vomit, moaning and crying voices. Mina had heard of seasickness, people throwing up for days on end because their bodies could not get used to the movement. She felt uneasy, but more hungry than nauseated.

"Why don't we go on deck?"

"Can't." He scoffed. "The opening is locked. Somebody said, the sea is too heavy, they're afraid, we'd get washed over bord or fall. I think they want us out of the way to work the sails."

Mina got up and wrapped her shawl across her nose and mouth. "But we've got to have air. It's already hard to breathe."

"I know." Roland rubbed his forehead and looked at her. "I'm sorry, I put you through this."

Mina swallowed. It was rather late for apologies, now that there was no turning back. Still, he was making an effort, so she nodded. "Can't we complain?"

"To whom? None of the crew are down here. They know why, it's unbearable."

Mina swallowed and realized that she was terribly thirsty. "What about water?"

Roland got up and held out a hand. "Come on, I'll show you."

By the staircase, two kegs had been fastened with belts. Above it, a sign read, *one ladle per person four times a day*. Roland filled the dipper and handed it to her. "Not too much. I wonder how clean the water is. Someone said, they'll give us watered-down ale or tea."

The fire in her throat extinguished, Mina followed Roland back down the aisle, holding on to the sides with every step. The ship swerved and bucked, trying to throw her off her feet. The semi-darkness made it worse, moans and retching came from various bunks. The rumbling in her belly continued, though she could not tell whether she was getting sick from the horrific stench or seasick. Her mind felt woozy, and it was hard to focus on more than keeping her balance.

A man in a long coat appeared in the aisle and stumbled past them toward the stairs. They heard banging and shouting, and shortly after, the man returned. "They've locked us in." He looked wild-eyed and fidgeted with his arms. "I can't stay in here, I'm going crazy."

"You're welcome to join us," Roland said. "The air is slightly better than in there." Retching and coughing sounds reverberated from the bunks. The man shook his head and stumbled off in the other direction.

"What are we going to do?" Mina whispered. "He's not the only one losing his mind."

CHAPTER TWENTY-TWO

Davin

The days passed in slow agony. Davin hadn't been able to find much work, the English suspicious of his accent and appearance, worse was the fact, he had no trade tools. They looked at him with that studying, half disgusted expression and then shook their heads. In a way, he didn't even blame them. He looked nothing like the man who'd worked in Skibbereen, dressed with care and always carrying his tool bag. Now, he appeared like a beggar—he was a beggar. No wonder, they didn't trust him.

Out of boredom, he accompanied Kate and Peter to the docks where they watched thousands of starved Irish depart on ships, he wouldn't have taken out to go fishing, let alone cross the Atlantic. The travelers crept up gangways, suitcases, sacks and boxes in one hand, small children and elderly men and women in the other. Most of them looked scared with wide open eyes like they'd seen a ghost or were going into purgatory.

That's what it had to feel like, a kind of hell. Or was it the fact that they left everything they'd ever known behind, the sense of belonging, the land they'd been born in? He'd asked around and knew that most people traveled in the middle deck, a narrow, temporary platform beneath the passenger deck, reserved for wealthier patrons, that maximized human loads. Typically, these were cargo ships, transporting goods to Ireland. To maximize profits for an otherwise empty ship on the return trip, the shipping companies had found a way to transport emigrants by stuffing them below deck like cattle. It was nothing different than slavery.

You're a slave, his mind commented. *You sold your life away, even got married. You've got control of absolutely nothing.*

Had it not been for Kate, he would've turned around. Even now he thought about joining the railroad, just disappearing into the English countryside. She'd never find him. But how could he do that to the young mother who was now his wife? It'd break her heart and Peter would never understand why the new man, he called Da', had vanished. As long as he remembered, he'd always taken care of the people around him. He'd have to do it a little longer.

How long? Would he ever get to do what he wanted? Which was what?

"Is everything all right?" Kate took his hand between hers, her gaze curious and worried. They were sitting in front of the hostel, catching a bit of frigid sun before turning in. Peter was building a corral from sticks for the wooden sheep, Davin had carved for him.

They hadn't lain together since that first night in the inn, there was no privacy in the hostel's room, they shared with a dozen others. Sometimes, at night, he listened to the moans around him. Obviously, others didn't feel as particular, but he couldn't muster the energy of fumbling around in the dark. Truth was, Kate was just as much a mystery to him as when they'd met.

She didn't seem to mind, content with an occasional hug or holding hands when nobody was looking.

He forced a smile. "Everything is fine," he lied. "I'm just tired of waiting. And we need to organize more food." He was proud to have organized a drum of sauerkraut as well as a bag of oats. With the help of Kate's pot and dishes, she kept in her traveling box, they'd be able to prepare warm meals.

Kate pressed his fingers and leaned in. "I'm so thankful, I met you. I can't imagine doing this on my own."

He squeezed her hand but kept staring straight ahead. It was getting too cold to sit still, yet, he didn't want to enter the overcrowded hostel.

In the morning, they set out to roam the stores in search of more supplies. Problem was that everything remotely suitable for travel was ten times the price, he remembered.

Smith's general store was no different. Already, the aisles swarmed with Irish travelers in search of bargains.

To Davin's surprise, the man behind the counter called out a hearty *Dia Duit*...the customary Irish greeting, meaning God be with you. But Davin would've recognized a fellow Irish man anywhere.

"Looking for something suitable to eat on the journey," he said, instantly feeling more confident.

"Going to America, I take it." The shopkeeper, wearing a long brown apron, slipped around the counter, signaling a young man to ring up another purchase. He had to be in his fifties, his head as bald as a baby's though the grayish beard made up for it.

"Indiana," Kate said, hanging on Davin's arm.

"A long journey, then." The man scratched his beard. "Salt pork, maybe, it's pricey though." He squinted at Davin, likely to size him up for what was in his coin purse. Davin knew how rough he looked, though still better than many of the families lingering along the streets, asking for handouts.

The shopkeeper led them around the side to an assembly of bins. "You could take onions, potatoes, maybe. They won't last the journey, though, spoil after a couple of weeks." He clucked more to himself. "It's the salt air."

He pointed at stacks of bags. "Flour or grain is best." He seemed to want to say more, but closed his mouth again. "You could make soup or bread."

"How much for the flour?"

"Ten shillings a bag, two for eighteen." He pointed at a shelf by the front door. "I'll throw in a glass of blackberry preserves."

"How much for the salt pork?", Kate asked.

"A pound, six shillings."

Davin shook his head, but Kate pulled out her purse and started counting the remaining bills. After the inn and hostel, the daily spent on food, they had little more than five pounds left.

"I'd like the pork." Kate eyed the stacked kegs with the shape of a pig burned into the wood.

"Maybe we should take more grain," Davin said. "It'll last longer."

"Oh, it'll last." The shopkeeper whistled and a boy of no more than twelve carried the pork to the counter.

"It'll be good for Peter," Kate said. "And more variety. We'll take two sacks of oatmeal, too."

Davin bit his tongue. It wasn't his money, he was the beggar, traveling on the apron strings of a woman. *You wouldn't be traveling in the first place*, the little voice in his head commented.

"This is your store?", Davin asked while Kate paid the young man.

"Married an English woman, this was her da's store. He's gone now...so is she." He crossed himself.

Davin nodded gravely, trying to imagine a younger version of the man, wooing an English dame. Why would anyone fall in love with a foreigner, let alone an English woman? Aloud, he said, "You've been here a while then."

"Twenty-five years." The shopkeeper lowered his voice. "It's more Irish now, with the famine, lots of people coming for a better life. But to tell you the truth, I've never gotten used to it, never will."

They parted with a friendly nod, Davin carrying the keg and one sack on his shoulders, Kate managing the other. In five days, the ship was supposed to leave. There was still time to take off.

In the early morning hours, when he lay awake, he made plans to slip out, get on a train or walk to the railroad…or take a ferry back to Dublin, search for William. By the time, breakfast came around, he was undecided. And so it went day after day. On the morning of the ship's departure, he was still there. They left early. With the last of Kate's money, Davin had hired a fellow Irish man to help carry their supplies to the ship.

Hundreds mingled on the docks when they arrived, most of them standing silently, their gaze on the three-mast sailing ship. The sound of hammering came from the inside, deep voices shouted commands, Davin didn't understand.

The ten o'clock departure time came and went. A light drizzle dampened the air and Kate wrapped a blanket around Peter's shoulders. Around them, people were whispering, their expressions as anxious as he felt.

"What's going on?" Davin addressed a man next to them. If they waited much longer, they'd be soaked through.

"I heard there's a delay because of repairs," the man said.

"What kind of repairs?"

"Didn't say."

Davin told Kate to stay put and squeezed his way to the front, collecting a series of choice words along the way. "What is going on?" he asked again when he reached the quay. "We were supposed to board hours ago."

The man, dressed in sailor's garb, guarded the plank way with his arms crossed. "Repairs."

"How much longer?"

"Don't know."

"I'm a carpenter, I could assist." The man eyed him suspiciously, the same expression Davin had seen on others when they sized him up. He didn't look anything like a man of knowledge, a representative of his profession. "Lost my tools on the journey."

"You'll have to wait," the sailor grumbled.

By the afternoon, the mumbles around them grew louder. "Let us board," some voices called. Whistles sounded, some women shouted that their children needed to lie down.

Kate was feeding Peter a piece from the bread they'd bought this morning. His little nose was red and he looked half frozen while he nibbled the food. The rain hadn't stopped and now the wind had joined, tugging on the ropes and sails above them.

Shouts rang out and then Davin saw it. Smoke billowed through an opening on deck, instantly torn apart by the wind and swept to sea.

"Fire," somebody shouted near the front. "The ship's burning, watch out."

The mumbles around them grew into screams. "Make room, move back." Men, women and children pushed against Davin, threatened to undo his carefully stacked boxes and supplies.

They were a reasonable distance from the ship, there was no need to move, but the people near the front seemed to be in a panic. "Hold your ground," he shouted to Kate. He grabbed Peter and placed him on top of their supplies. Like an island they stood in the middle of the shoving crowd.

He noticed how the rest of the crew had disappeared from deck, obviously helping to contain the fire. Something had gone terribly wrong. Which could mean only one thing. They wouldn't be traveling today. Not tomorrow either. Who knew how long they'd take to repair the ship. Their spots at the hostel were long filled with new travelers, intent to leave for America. Besides, they had no money left to afford more waiting.

On a whim, he told Kate to wait. He had to do something—and quick.

CHAPTER TWENTY-THREE

Mina

Mina awoke in the middle of the night, impossible to say what time it was. The air was so thick—a mix of body odor, throw-up and excrement, she had trouble breathing. She was facing the wall and though she squeezed herself so close, her forehead was only an inch from the rough wooden partition, she felt the body of the man behind her push against her backside.

She had to speak with Roland, ask him to have words with the man. She knew she should do it herself—Roland had a way to escalate conflicts, which was not a good idea when they were caught down here like rats.

She thought of Augusta and how she missed her, not just having a friend, but the lightness that seemed to surround her and make everything better. Mina vowed to write to her at the first opportunity.

The elderly woman at the opposite end of their compartment coughed incessantly—all day and through the night. Did she never sleep? She couldn't help it, of course. Already, she sounded weaker than yesterday.

Beneath her, the ship moved through the waves, up and down it went, not as extreme as earlier, but the waves crashed against the sides. Only a few inches separated her from the icy ocean. Any little thing could happen and take them all into an icy grave. In her mind, the ship had moved in total silence, in reality, the air was filled with the creaking of the wooden boat, the howling of the sails, the crashing of waves, not to mention the noise from the other travelers. Not in her worst imagination had she understood the misery of being stuck down here.

And with every minute, it was taking her farther from home...from her father and all she knew.

In the hall, voices mumbled and a light danced passed, waking Mina from her stupor. She climbed from the bunk and put on her shoes, threw a shawl around her shoulders and stepped into the aisle. The light had disappeared, a single lantern burned, hardly enough to show the way.

But wait, there were voices nearby. Mina turned right and followed, her ears on high alert. The voices grew louder. Three compartments down Mina stopped. Inside the room, people were arguing.

"You did this," a man said. "Something is wrong, I'm telling you."

"Calm down, sir," the other voice was much calmer yet authoritative. "When did the symptoms start?"

"As soon as she drank from the water, and it's not just my wife, my sister and mother are ill, too. For all I know, the entire ship is infected. You did this!"

"They may be seasick."

"They've been on the water before—"

"The conditions are rather extreme here."

"You don't say." The man's voice was sharp, angry. "I demand that you investigate. Quickly! And they need help. They've already grown weak."

In the momentary pause Mina heard groans and whimpers. Those had to be the sick women.

"I'm also sick," a man said from inside. "So is my wife."

Again, a pause, then the authoritative voice said, "All right, I'll look into it. Stay where you are and don't drink any of the water."

A man in sailor garb, the two black strings of his hat fluttering behind him, hurried from the room and rushed the other way, up the stairs and through the opening. A whiff of sea air traveled into steerage and Mina realized that the cover was unlocked. She followed quickly and climbed on deck. Above her, the sky sparkled with millions of stars and a quarter moon. She was immediately caught by the wind that cut through her with icy knives. But the air, oh glorious air, so fresh and good. She breathed deeply and carefully walked to the railing. The sails above her made a whooshing sound and for a brief moment, she felt like flying. In the semi-darkness she sensed movement behind her. Three men rushed across the deck and disappeared inside the door.

What was going on? She'd drank from the water earlier and felt fine. Well, not fine. The stench alone made her queasy, but it was not illness, that much she knew. She needed to speak to Roland and discuss what was happening. If there was some terrible disease going around, they'd all lie down soon, maybe die. Fear crept up in her, added itself to the unease of this impossible journey. At home, she would've studied her herbs, mixed potions and teas. Here, she had nothing.

Becoming aware of the cold once more, she slipped back into the hole. She'd expected it to be louder now with the additional men, but it was eerily quiet. Only when she closed in on the compartment, did she hear the whispering voice of another man, asking questions about what the passengers had eaten, what they'd done before they boarded.

She decided to wake Roland and tiptoed past, only to find the other two crew bent over the water barrel in the hall. It was a different barrel than the one Roland had taken her to—hers was in the very back, the other stood in front. Afraid to be yelled at she continued to Roland's bunk.

"What's going on?", he grumbled, when she patted his legs.

"Shhh. Come with me." Afraid to be overheard, Mina hurried back into the passageway.

"Something is wrong with the water," she whispered. "People are sick." She pointed down the aisle. "Or it is some disease, there're men from above looking around."

Roland rubbed the sleep from his eyes. "For that you woke me? You realize how hard it is to fall sleep in the first place?"

"What if we all get sick?"

"What if this...what if that?", he parroted. "They'll sort it, I'm sure."

How can you be sure, Mina wanted to say. *How can you trust these people who treat us like cattle and stuff us beneath deck for weeks?* Aloud, she said, "Can you at least ask them?"

"Ask them what? If they're searching, let them search. I'm going back to bed."

He turned on his heels and disappeared in his partition, leaving Mina standing alone. Unsure what to do, she hurried back to her bunk and climbed under the covers, pushing the arm of her bed neighbor aside to make room. Her toes were numb with cold, so were her hands and face. She furiously rubbed her skin and fell into a restless sleep.

She awoke to an almost empty room. Only the old woman at the opposite end was still there. At least she was quiet now. Curious, Mina moved closer. She knew nothing of the old woman, just that she was traveling with a couple from the next compartment. She seemed even older than Papa. In that moment, Mina was glad that she hadn't taken her father along. The elderly were not fit enough for the strains of this journey.

She peered at the woman and listened to her rattling breath that reminded her of a purring cat. Quietly, Mina put on her shawl and shoes, and went down the hallway. Only this time, the ship was moving more smoothly. But more so, there was nobody around and from the staircase, a cold draft caught her. The deck cover had to be open.

After taking a drink, she went back to her bunk and put on all the clothes, she owned, wrapped the shawl tightly around her head and went upstairs.

The light was so bright that she blinked, her eyes instantly teary. The deck was crowded with travelers, some standing and talking, others surrounding a couple of stoves, cooking, more of them clinging to the railing, eyes searching the horizon. Mina stepped to the railing and stared across the grayish waves. Somewhere out there was New York.

The woman next to her, dressed in an ankle-length black dress and matching hat, cried out. "Look, there are fish down there." Mina recognized her from the first day, the sad expression, the deep ridges around her mouth.

"Dolphins," a man on the other side said. "Look at the tales, they're horizontal."

For the first time, Mina smiled. The animals were jumping and sliding through the water so smoothly and easily, she wanted to join them. They were free, could move anywhere they wanted. Unlike her.

She lifted her gaze out to sea and closed her eyes, enjoying the brightness behind her closed lids and the fresh air in her lungs. She realized how hungry she was, starving was more like it.

"Where are you heading?", the woman in black asked her. She appeared even more severe than on the first day, her eyes almost a match to the clear blue above, except they were hooded and exuded sadness.

"Indiana," Mina said, trying out the strange word once more. "You?"

"To join a second cousin in Illinois."

"You're traveling alone."

The woman nodded. "My husband was supposed to be with me. He died two months ago." Her upper lip trembled, but she caught herself. "We'd already sold everything, so I decided to go anyway."

Mina patted the woman's forearm. "I'm so sorry, what a terrible time to travel alone."

The woman smiled weakly. "I'm Regine Graf, glad to meet you."

Mina introduced herself. "I'm afraid I've got to leave you. I haven't eaten a thing since yesterday noon and have got to find somebody with a cooking pot."

"You traveled without cooking utensils?" Regine eyed her curiously. But when Mina didn't answer, she continued, "You can borrow mine. Or we can cook together."

An hour later, Mina had managed to boil oats in Regine's pot, she and Roland squatted on a stack of ropes, taking turns eating gruel and gnawing the biscuit. A glorious warmth filled Mina's belly as they scraped out the bowl, she'd also borrowed while Regine prepared herself a soup. Unlike Mina and Roland, the widow seemed as prepared as Augusta's family.

Sleepy now, her eyes half closed, Mina grew aware of movement near the staircase leading to steerage.

Two sailors appeared, carrying a human form, wrapped in cloth. Sleepiness forgotten, Mina jumped to her feet. The two men were carrying a dead body. She wasn't the only one alerted, mumbles traveled across the deck, every person watching the two sailors carrying the corpse to the railing in back. They hesitated a moment, spoke a few words, and then hoisted it overboard.

Mina swallowed, the comforting taste of the oats replaced by bitterness. They hadn't been on board for two days and already a person was dead.

"I wonder what happened," Regine said.

Mina remained silent, her thoughts on the argument, she'd overheard in the night. Within minutes, the sailors reappeared with another body between them. Then another. Were those the people, she'd listened to in the night? What had they died of?

Something cold rose inside her, a shivering fear that settled in her belly, threatening to kick out the food she'd just eaten.

"I heard them talk about the water last night," Mina said, focusing her gaze on the horizon. "Several people said they'd gotten sick from it."

Around them the mumbling grew louder. Three people had died in the night and were tossed over overboard like pieces of garbage.

"What is going on?" A burly man in a better cut suit shouted when the two crew members passed him.

"You'll have to ask the captain," one of the sailors said.

"Then get him, we demand answers."

"We'll ask." The seamen disappeared with a nod, while the burly man led a group of men toward a second door, off-limits to steerage passengers.

"Coffin ship," somebody said next to Mina. "We'll all die long before we reach America."

"Coffin ship," the whispers traveled across the deck in waves until the last of the travelers had heard the terrible words.

We are doomed, Mina thought. Hardly two days on the water and already we fear to die. Not from the sea's power, but from some unknown enemy that made them sick.

Roland materialized next to her. "Did you hear? I'm going to see what the captain has to say."

He didn't even bother to ask how I'm feeling. Mina swallowed her comment and turned to Regine. "I want to hear it, too. Will you join me?"

After what seemed like an hour of waiting—the noise on deck was growing, a mixture of loud discussions and angry shouts—the captain appeared and immediately lifted his arms.

"Folks, calm yourselves."

The mumbles and shouts reluctantly died down though Mina felt the anger like a thick cloud engulfing her, feeding her own fears. Roland stood near the front, and she worried about his tendency to stir the anxiety further or take a swing at the captain.

"What is the meaning of this?", thundered the burly man.

"We're as concerned as you are," the captain said. "At this time, it is unclear what happened, likely, the three deceased were already sick when they boarded. We can't be sure—"

"Nonsense," Roland cried. "Your water is bad! We know all about it."

"The water?", whispered Regine and gripped Mina's hand. "I knew it."

"The water is poisoned...we're doomed...we will all die," people cried while the captain upfront again raised his arms again.

"Please, folks, we don't know that. Right now, it is but one theory."

"What are you going to do about it?" Roland's tone was aggressive. "We paid good money and have given up a lot to start new lives."

"Exactly...he's right," came the echoes from the crowd.

"We're prepared to make a stop. It'll be a delay, but your safety is most important to us." Mina could no longer see the captain but detected a note of uncertainty in his voice. "We will stop in Liverpool to replace the water. Just in case. From now on we will provide tea to drink and water only for cooking."

"How long will it take?" The burly man asked. "We have limited food."

"An extra week, maybe less. You can leave the ship and buy more food."

Hollers and shouts rang out. "We're broke as it is...are you kidding—"

"That is your responsibility," Roland shouted. "Your bad water is the cause, now you take care of our extra food needs."

Again, the crowd cried, "Exactly right...it's your job."

The captain shook his head. "That is all, folks." He rushed off, followed by a couple of seamen, who'd undoubtedly been there to protect the captain.

"Another week." Regine shook her head. "As if it isn't hell already."

Mina felt the same, yet the alternative of drinking bad water and getting sick or not drinking at all was worse. "We will help each other." She extended a hand and led her new friend to the railing.

CHAPTER TWENTY-FOUR

Davin

By the time Davin returned to the docks, it was early evening. He'd raced to the shipping office, standing in line for hours, thinking what he should say.

In the end, he said little except ask what they intended to do about the burned ship.

The man behind the counter shook his head. "You'll have to be patient. From what I hear, the repairs will be extensive. It may take a few weeks until—"

"A few weeks? We're out of food, we have no place to sleep," Davin shouted. "Everything is rationed exactly and I'm sure, we're not the only ones."

The clerk's expression hardened. "I have no answer, check back with us every few days."

Seeing that this way was not going to work, Davin tried again. "I've got a young wife and a little boy. They can't be on the street. What are we going to eat?"

The man eyed him across the counter as if his marriage were written on Davin's forehead. "You're young, see if you can work."

"I'm a carpenter. Nobody will hire me, not when there're all these established companies in Liverpool, not without my tools."

The clerk's eyes widened in surprise. "Wait here. I'll be right back." He slipped to the back and disappeared in an office, only to emerge minutes later. Meanwhile, the crowd behind Davin was getting impatient. Obviously, other passengers from the burned ship were waiting.

To his surprise, another man in a suit and top hat waved him to a separate counter. "You are a carpenter?"

"I am."

"You can help repair the ship. Half of steerage burned to a crisp." He wrote down Davin's name and gave him a piece of paper. "Hand that to the captain. You'll be paid and receive three meals."

"What about beds? I've got a wife and son."

"We'll have to see. Go now." He waved Davin away like an unruly child.

Half relieved, half worried, Davin returned to port. He'd wanted to search for another inn or hostel, but now he'd have to work instead. Kate would have to do it on her own.

The damage to the ship was extensive. The fire had started in steerage, but moved upward and spread to the mess hall, private cabins, and crew quarters above. These had windows and open spaces to walk around. The stench of charcoaled wood took his breath as soon as he climbed beneath and by evening he was covered in black oily residue.

The team of woodworkers assembled on deck where the ship's cook had set out soup, bread and ale. Davin stuffed several pieces of bread into his pocket and slurped down his soup, his mind on Kate and Peter. They were out there on the dock, exposed to the cold, waiting for him while he sat here, stuffing himself. He abruptly rose and approached the boss, a man, the shipping company had sent to oversee the repairs.

"Sir, I've got a wife and child waiting out there. We were supposed to travel with the ship, and we have no place to sleep. You know how it is."

The man eyed him curiously. "Going to America, eh?"

Davin nodded. "I want to build something, make a good life."

"You do good work. I didn't think it, but..." he nodded, more to himself. "How old is the child?"

"Peter is four."

"Small lad, then. I've got a handful me self." He scratched his head. "I tell you what. Bring 'em up, they can sleep in the back end of steerage. It's dark and smelly, but it's better than the streets."

"Thank you, sir. I'll not forget it." Davin turned to leave.

"Just for the night. Tomorrow, you better find someplace else. Make sure, they stay out of the way. Don't want any accidents."

In the early morning, before anybody was up, Davin left the docks to search for another space. He'd get paid tonight, but as he had learned, it was not only an issue of money, but one of luck and timing.

By the time he returned to work, it was after nine, but he'd secured a space in a hostel half an hour's walk from the port. Kate and Peter were waiting in front of the ship, wrapped in a blanket, Peter's nose red and his eyes droopy.

"I've found a place," he called from afar.

Kate pressed her son to her chest. "He's sick, I need to get him out of the cold."

Now that he drew close, he recognized the signs of fever. Peter's eyes appeared glassy, his cheeks were flushed. Worse, he remained still in his mother's arms when he'd usually jump up to greet him.

"Let me get you some of the breakfast, then you go ahead to the inn." He explained the address and rushed up the plank. "I'll bring our luggage tonight."

"You're late," the supervisor grumbled when he hurried into the mess where the remnants of bread, cheese, and oatmeal lay scattered among dirty bowls and cups.

Davin straightened his shoulders and faced the older man. "Had to find a place for my family. Peter is sick. Please let me give them some food, so they can leave?"

"Hurry then."

Stuffing bread into his mouth, Davin rushed back to the dock, handed Kate two fists full of bread and sent them on their way.

"I'll work late tonight to make up," he called after them. "We'll get paid, I'll bring food."

Kate appeared to hardly listen and carried Peter on her shoulders. Remembering his work, Davin hurried back. He couldn't afford to lose his job, or they'd be on the street once more.

Working in those tight quarters, removing the oily stinky remnants of the fire felt like he'd entered hell himself. The air seemed stuck down here, the only opening at the far end of the deck. He'd covered nose and mouth with a rag to avoid the stench, but it was no good. Every breath was a chore and he soon wished himself far away.

By lunchtime, he and the others emerged, covered in soot. Glad to escape the stench, Davin washed in a bucket, just to avoid getting the bread and soup blackened as well. When he searched the dock, he did not see Kate. By evening, they'd removed the burned remnants of steerage and the flooring above.

After a hurried dinner and pocketing his pay for two days, he rushed off to find Kate. Somehow, he'd expected her to wait for him outside, but there was no sign which could only mean one thing: Peter was too sick.

He stopped to purchase three meat pies, cheese, an apple pastry for Peter and enough bread to last through tomorrow. With the remaining money, he bought a shirt, pants and a jacket. He'd discard his work clothes—already beyond repair—as soon as he'd finish the job.

"Kate?", he called, entering the hostel's second floor family sleeping quarters. Every square inch of the room was filled with sleeping, sitting and lounging people. He pushed his way through and discovered Kate in the back corner, her back to the room, cradling Peter in her arms.

"Kate," Davin said again, kneeling next to her. Even in the gloom, he noticed Peter's burning face. He seemed to have lost weight in a day, his nose pointy in his thin face, and all of a sudden, Davin was afraid. It was bad enough to get sick at home, but this place could kill. The air was filthy, the straw no better. People coughed and sniffed everywhere he looked. What they needed was a doctor or at least somebody with herbs to help Peter.

Kate had hardly acknowledged him and continued to hold her son. He knew he reeked of soot and worse, not that it mattered in a place like this.

"How is he doing?"

A small sob rose from Kate. "He's so hot, I don't know what to do."

"I'll go and look for a doctor," he said, bone tired and well aware that he had no more money to pay for one. But he couldn't sit here and watch, he'd never forgive himself, if something happened to Peter.

He moved through the crowd, asking if any of them knew a doctor. Of course, none did, each of them appearing as retched, as he had to look. The proprietor sent him down the street, but the doctor's office was locked. He knocked and called a couple of times to no avail.

Dejected, he continued down the street, passed pubs, inns and hotels. Surely, some of the travelers were doctors and they likely could afford to stay in places like these. Swallowing his pride, he entered an inn and was immediately stopped by the proprietor.

"What do you want?"

"I'm looking for a doctor, my little boy is sick."

"Does this place look like a hospital?," the man said, his gaze stuck on Davin's blackened pantlegs. "Please leave, you can't bother my guests."

Davin turned and tried the next place, and again, didn't get past the entry hall. As he stumbled back onto the street, a woman took him by the arm. "Lad, try the Old Liverpool Hospital on College Street. It's a walk from here, but they have doctors." She pointed down the road. "Ask around, everybody knows it."

Davin thanked the woman and took off. He was so tired after working all day, his feet refused to walk in a straight line. The panic inside him grew, squeezing his heart and taking the last of his energy. He looked like a mess, but what choice did he have? Head low, he asked until the long four-story brick building of Old Liverpool Hospital came into view.

"Waiting room is straight ahead," the man at the door told him.

He obviously looked sick himself, Davin mused. He followed the signs and soon realized; he'd be here all night. The waiting area was cramped full of coughing, sneezing and lethargic men, women, and children. Just being here was a risk to contract a new disease.

He hurried back into the hall, climbed up the stairs and found the same overcrowded conditions. Beds lined the hallways filled with mostly very still patients. The smells of urine and excrement made him sick, but worse was the cloak of sickness that lay like a suffocating blanket above everything. Frustrated, he stumbled back down and stopped at a desk where a nurse was sorting through charts.

"I need a doctor for my son. He's got a fever. We don't know—"

"Bring him here," the woman said, "I'll see that he's helped."

"I was hoping, we need a doctor to come..."

The nurse studied him. "No doctors are free to make house calls, we are overwhelmed as it is. You should find a doctor's office near your place or bring him."

Davin mumbled "thanks" and hurried back outside. Cold rain greeted him as he turned back toward the docks. All this running around had been useless. He'd exhausted himself and soon would lie down himself. But how could he return to Kate without help, some kind of cure. The next moment, he was convinced that Peter had already died.

Scenes of the boy playing soccer with his crooked ball returned and Davin blinked to chase away the tears. He slowed down, weaving around a group of men exiting a pub.

At some point, he stopped, his legs plain refused to take another step. All evening, he'd been running across this godforsaken city and what had it gotten him?

He spit and sank to the curb. Damn life, what had he gotten

himself into? Regret spread like poison through his veins, choked him. He'd made nothing but bad decisions, had wasted his time, gone this way and that to do what exactly—land in the gutter in front of some pub. He felt the urge to go inside and get as drunk as the men crowding the street. At least he'd forget for a while.

A bitter smile crossed his face. With what? He was broke once again. Like Ireland.

A few feet from him two men pissed into the gutter, so he jumped to his feet, turned and smacked into somebody.

"Don't you have eyes?" a sharp voice yelled as a leather bag clattered to the ground and landed on in front of his feet.

Davin shook off his frustration and focused on the person in front of him, a woman who reminded him of the poor lady, making tea and offering Malcolm and him a space in her cabin. Except this woman wasn't as old, just tiny with a stubborn chin and large green eyes like the Irish hills he so loved. He pulled off his hat and said, "Excuse me, miss, I did not see you."

"That much is clear." She gave him a look of disdain mixed with curiosity. She was Irish, that much was clear, and Davin felt himself smile.

"You are far from home, I take it."

The small woman shrugged as she bent low to pick up her bag. "Wee place in County Cork, if you must know." She carefully dusted off the bag and gave it a little pat.

"I'm from County Cork, Skibbereen."

She squinted at him, again the flash of curiosity. "I know it, I'm from Ballylinch." She studied him. "What's a lad doing here in the gutter in the middle of the night?" She sniffed. "You aren't drinking."

"I've got a sick boy, have been searching everywhere for a doctor, somebody who can help him."

"What's wrong with him?"

"He's got a fever, is hardly awake. Is small as it is. I even asked at the hospital, but they can't send a doctor."

A "tsk" escaped the woman's lips. "Hospital is a morgue. People go in for help and end up dead in a few days."

Davin rubbed his face to chase away the exhaustion. "It did smell something awful."

"Where is your son?"

"We're staying at a hostel, waiting to travel to America."

She seemed to wrangle with herself, gripped the bag's handle tighter. In the flickering light, he noticed the tired lines around her eyes.

She wasn't as young as she seemed or maybe just weary. He tipped his hat and turned to leave. "I better go, it's late—"

"I can take a look."

He did a double take, felt a spark of energy. "You're a doctor?"

"Midwife. Just delivered a babe." She studied him. "At home, I worked as a healer mostly except people just moved or died of hunger. I couldn't take it any longer."

Davin looked down at the small woman who likely wanted to crawl into bed instead of spending more hours helping strangers. "I'd be forever grateful. Let me carry your bag."

CHAPTER TWENTY-FIVE

Mina

The port of Liverpool was a mess of ships, barges, and boats of all sizes. Thick fog lay across the bay this morning and Mina and her fellow passengers were asked to leave the ship while the crew smoked out the quarters and organized new supplies, especially fresh water. Six more people had died and been buried at sea, among them the old woman in Mina's compartment.

Mina already loathed returning to steerage, the idea of spending weeks beneath deck made her queasy. The passengers had insisted that the water was bad, but Mina wasn't so sure. These days, people died of all sorts of diseases, consumption, typhus, dysentery, diseases of the lungs and who knew what else. They'd barely been on board for a week and she felt weak herself.

Roland was restless and charged ahead again. She knew he missed drinking, a welcome escape from the world and whatever demons possessed him. Every time, they passed a pub, she noticed his searching look, the way he licked his lips like a starving animal.

They stopped at a street vendor for cabbage soup and bread and continued toward the bustling shops. The air was thick with cookfires, various foods from street vendors, garbage and worse in the gutters. They passed shop windows, offering fine woolen clothing, a sign promising suits and dresses tailored to the highest requirement, shoes and boots made of leather, handmade paper and fine ink pens, delicacies from around the world. The shops went on, a dizzying display of things, she would never be able to afford. That she didn't fit was made clear by the arrogant looks of the men and women gallivanting past, exiting elegant carriages while burying their dainty noses in lacy handkerchiefs.

"Let's go back to the docks." Mina wrapped her shawl tighter around her shoulders and head. The damp air was getting to her. "I want to keep the ship in my sights." They'd been told to leave their belongings and that they'd be able to reboard in the evening. How could she trust it? But Regine and most of the other passengers had done what they were told. As much as she loathed returning on board, a part of her couldn't wait to get this entire journey behind her.

Liverpool seemed as crowded and even dirtier than Bremerhaven. People were everywhere and the closer they got to the water, the shadier the people seemed. They'd been warned about vendors taking advantage of travelers, promising to show them warm rooms and hot soups for a penny, only to disappear a moment after they'd pocketed the money. Thieves and bandits also preyed on the unsuspecting, though Mina felt she had nothing to give.

"Come on, hurry up," Roland called as he once again charged ahead. He'd hardly spoken a word.

Mina followed, searching for Regine, who'd planned to purchase a pocket watch to help her keep track of time. She would've loved to accompany her new friend, but Roland didn't allow it. "You're staying with me," he'd said. "Gallivanting all over town by yourself, what are you thinking, woman?"

What did he even see in her other than *owning* a wife? He didn't love her, likely never had. What were his dreams? They never talked about anything other than Roland's lofty idea of buying a homestead. How and where he never discussed. If she were honest with herself, she was ready to leave him.

You're crazy, her mind commented. *What is a single woman in a foreign land to do? You have no money.*

Head low, she scrambled after her husband, glad when the docks came into sight. The ship appeared as empty as when they'd left it, and the guard sent them off as soon as they approached. "Try in a couple of hours. Water hasn't arrived yet."

Roland cursed and wandered off along the quay, not even turning to see if she followed. Mina sank onto a wooden box and mumbled more to herself, "I'll wait here." Her ankles throbbed and she felt exhausted.

Around her, other passengers waited, one of them a woman not much older with a little boy. She held him like a baby though he had to be at least four or five.

"You're sitting on our luggage," a voice behind her said.

Even though Mina hadn't understood the man, she jumped to her feet and turned, facing a man with fiery hair, his nose freckled as if God had tossed a few golden dots over his face. He studied her carefully, his eyes most striking, reminding her of a stroll in the dense evergreen forests of her home village. He had to be Irish, not just because of the eyes, but because of the hair, not copper like the boy's and his mother's, but like the rich warm red of a hot fire.

"I didn't mean anything," she said in German. She scrambled for something she could say in English, some of the words and sentences, she'd practiced with Augusta, but all she remembered was, "Sorry."

He nodded and turned back to the woman with the little boy, before hurrying off. Looking after him, she noticed Roland standing with a group of men. Some of them gesticulated, others talked or laughed. They were playing some kind of game with dice and to her horror, Roland joined them. Not that it mattered, he couldn't bet anything because they had nothing of value. At least he'd pass the time without being short-tempered with her.

"... to America?" The boy, the woman had cradled earlier, studied her. He was very thin, his skin almost translucent.

"Sorry," Mina said, then added, "Yes, America."

The boy said something else, she didn't understand. That's how it had to feel, living in a foreign country. The people spoke gibberish. Of course, it was the same to them. German wasn't exactly an easy language. She pulled out her English book, searching for a fitting phrase.

"I am going to America," she said slowly.

The boy's face brightened. "Me too. I'm Peter."

Mina waved. "Mina." She searched for a fitting answer. "Nice to meet you."

Peter pointed at his mom. "This is my mother, Kate. Da' has gone to work."

Mina formed the word in her mouth. "Work—what is that?" She searched again until she found the translation, vowing to spend every available minute, studying English.

A horse cart stopped in front of the ship, accompanied by the captain. He was talking to a couple of seamen who immediately began carrying kegs up the plank. He was about to follow them, when the man with the forest eyes reappeared and began speaking to him.

Peter had obviously discovered his father and ran to him with waving arms. The man stopped talking and wrapped an arm around the child. A sharp twinge ran through Mina as if something had nipped her heart. That was what love looked like. A simple wrapping of arms, a bit of attention. The next moment, the man pulled out a paper and handed it to the captain who nodded.

Mina's gaze wandered to Roland who was throwing up his arms, apparently winning a round. She was about to wander over, when the Irish man hurried near, shouting excitedly. Mina only understood "ship" and "room," but it wasn't difficult to discern that Peter's family would join them.

After some excited chatter, the man passed Mina and tipped his hat. This time he smiled which changed his entire being into something bright and cheerful. Without intending to, Mina smiled back.

She watched him run off past Roland's game and disappear in the crowd. Strangely, her spirits felt lighter than they had in days.

"You're looking almost jolly. What happened?" Regine stood before her, carrying a couple of boxes, tied with string.

Mina shook her head. "Nonsense, I'm just glad when we can continue on our journey. What did you find?"

"A wool shawl and socks. You won't believe the wool garments, these English make. It is a shame that I have no more money."

Mina knew that it wasn't true. Regine's husband had been wealthy, but she likely didn't want to exchange more money. It was rumored that the banks took advantage of all the travelers by overpricing the English currency.

"I did get a pocket watch." Regine lowered her voice. "I'll show you later, it was made in London."

"I better check on Roland." Mina led Regine to the Irish woman with her son. "Will you wait here? I'll be back soon."

But it wasn't necessary because Roland was walking toward them, his expression as ill-tempered as the first days on the journey. *What happened*, Mina wanted to ask. But she bit her lip, guessing that he'd lost and afraid to find out what he'd promised.

"Look," Regine said, taking Mina's arm in hers. "The captain is waving. We can reboard—finally."

CHAPTER TWENTY-SIX

Davin

Davin held Peter in his arms. The boy slept while he was wide awake—impossible to know what time it was, the gloom in steerage always the same no matter the time of day. He felt trapped like a caged animal. When he'd worked on the other ship, the deck's door had been open, and he'd moved around freely. A bit of air had passed through.

This place was filled to capacity with men, women and children, judging by the way they looked, most of them as poor or poorer than he was. At least, he and Kate had plenty of provisions, but the air down here was so foul, it was like dipping his nose into an overflowing outhouse. While he'd gotten used to the burn smell on the English ship, this vessel of mostly German passengers stunk to high heaven. And there was the noise, a constant cacophony of wheezes, coughs, whispers, and snores.

This was only the third day and he already felt like losing his mind. On top of that they'd reached open water, and the mighty Atlantic Ocean was tossing them about like some toy boat in a hurricane. And that despite Davin having overheard one of the seamen remarking how calm the waves were for late February.

How would it be in bad weather? The walls and bunks creaked with every wave, and he felt the urge to inspect the woodwork. He'd already noticed the sloppy workmanship of the steerage deck, but knew they only installed it temporarily for the voyage to America.

He'd forsaken half a day's pay because of the hasty departure from Liverpool, but they'd save at least four days, maybe a week by not waiting. The captain of the German ship had seemed glad to take them on, though Davin wondered why there'd been room when every ship was filled to capacity.

He'd hardly talked to anyone besides Kate and Peter because every person other than some of the crew were Germans. Only that strange woman, who'd nearly mowed him down on the docks, had spoken to Kate and Peter.

Earlier today, he'd noticed her studying a book, then speaking to herself, her words torn away by the wind. He suspected she was learning English, a smart move. She wasn't as small as Kate, but pretty in her own way with a perky nose and nicely shaped lips. What confused him was her appearance, her dress torn and mended in several places and though surprisingly clean despite the rigors of travel, she looked poor—a stark contrast to her intelligent eyes and the fact she was reading and studying. Truth was, he couldn't figure her out.

Why should you? You've got a wife and son.

Davin let out a sigh. Thankfully, Peter had somewhat recovered after the healer visited. In wonder he'd watched her open her bag and sort through vials and cloth sacks until she found the right one, sniffed and demanded hot water.

She'd prepared yarrow tea and instructed Kate to cool Peter's calves with cold rags. By the following evening, as Davin hurried back from work, worried what he'd find, Peter was sitting in bed, playing with wooden marbles, one of the other mothers had gifted him.

The healer had visited a second time and though she'd declined, Davin paid her well.

Maybe he should trust in the divine. Ever since completing the roof in Skibbereen a hundred years ago, he'd been thrown from one challenge to the next.

Was he really his own man? Hardly.

It felt more like he was showing up to a theatre act, somebody else was directing. His entire life he'd envisioned himself living and growing old in County Cork, building a nice home, raising a family. Look at him now.

A scoff rose into the air as Davin turned on his back, immediately hitting Kate's shoulder. The space was so tight, they all had to sleep on their sides. He assumed his earlier position, even though his right shoulder ached from the hard surface.

Something crawled across his wrist, likely the place was infested with lice and bedbugs. The urge to run returned and his lungs felt like someone was sitting on them. *Think of something else*, his mind commented.

The strange German woman with the mahogany braid was the last thing he remembered before he dozed off.

The following morning, they were allowed on deck. Davin hurried past the foremast, as far to the bow as he could get and peeked across the heads of his fellow passengers. Luckily, he was taller than most, the damp wind hitting his face. Air had never felt so good. He closed his eyes and breathed deeply...slowly, expelling the foul air, he'd carried all night, from his lungs.

He knew he should return to Kate, who was waiting to cook their breakfast at one of the stoves, but his legs refused to move. Despite the chill creeping across his skin, he kept standing there, staring at the horizon, urging fate to tell him what it had in store for him next.

Somewhere ahead lay America, a vast country, populated with Europeans, English and Natives. He'd overheard people speak of New York, a large city where many Irish were settling. Whenever he'd mentioned Indiana, the faces of the people had grown blank. It lay somewhere to the west, another journey on land, they'd have to master.

"One thing at a time," he mumbled to himself. Hadn't he learned by now that it made little sense to plan or anticipate?

"Hallo." He turned and was face to face with a man, he'd seen accompanying the German woman. The man said something like "help" and waved his arms.

Davin nodded and shoved his way back to the two stoves where he'd left Kate earlier, but none of the people nearby looked familiar.

"Kate?"

"Over here."

He found her leaning against a pile of rope, holding her right hand while Peter clung to her leg.

Next to her kneeled the German woman, dunking Kate's hand into a bucket of water.

"I burned myself," Kate cried. "There was a shove from behind, I lost my balance and touched the stove top. Mina helped me. It's much better already." She pulled out her hand and extended it toward Davin. The skin on her right palm was beet red and shiny.

"She need...fat...," Mina said. Obviously, she was searching for the right word. "Sheep fat or honey." She gently took Kate's hand and returned it to the water, looking up at Davin. Gray eyes, calm and reassuring, met his. They weren't just one color, but several shades, some so light, they seemed to sparkle.

He thought of the gray shades of the Blarney Stone, he'd once visited with a couple of friends, at Blarney Castle. It was said that kissing the rock upside down provided the person with eloquence and wit. He'd never thought that it worked, but when he'd returned home, he'd told his parents that he wanted to become a carpenter.

He felt her eyes on him still, realizing he hadn't answered. "Fat...maybe. I will ask."

"Wait," Mina called after him. She rose and faced, signaling Kate to leave her hand in the bucket. "I ask."

Not waiting for his answer, she began speaking German to her fellow travelers, returning within minutes, a clay jar in her hand. While Davin helped Peter eat the gruel, Kate had cooked earlier, Mina gently dried Kate's hand and administered the fat that smelled strongly of sheep.

"Thank you," Davin said, when the woman closed the jar. "I really appreciate your help." Mina smiled though he had no idea what she understood. He pointed at himself and spoke slowly. "I help with English?" The little voice in his head chuckled. *Since when are you a teacher?* Ignoring it, he extended a hand. "I—am—Davin."

The woman firmly gripped his. "I—am—Mina."

She gave him a small smile and was about to turn, when her husband called to her. The smile vanished as she faced him, their conversation quick and unfriendly. Something was going on, something Davin didn't understand. The woman followed her husband and disappeared in the crowd.

"She was nice," Kate said, inspecting the reddened skin on her palm. "The pain is much better."

Davin nodded, helped his wife eat, then scraped out the burned remains while keeping an eye on Peter, while his thoughts were on the woman with the gray-speckled eyes.

CHAPTER TWENTY-SEVEN

Mina

The days crept along in painful slowness and after a while, day and night merged, especially when Mina was forced to remain below deck. In the near darkness, the foul air grew thicker by the minute, it seemed to Mina as if ghostly hands choked her, her stomach often vacillating between hunger and nausea.

To distract herself, she chewed on a biscuit, first removing the weevils that had inhabited each one of them, and crept to one of the oil lamps in the corridor to study her book. Her eyes would soon ache from the strain, so she'd close it and mumble the words...house, ship, person, food. She recounted vegetables, animals, the days of the week, months, and numbers. Then she moved on to simple sentences. "My name is Mina...how are you?...I eat bread...I like birds..."

Augusta had gifted her the English book when they parted. Augusta. How she missed her friend, her optimism and love for life. Down here, in this dungeon, it was easy to lose your way and succumb to hopelessness, the ship creaking and aching in the strong winds, trying to buck them from its innards.

Regine often joined Mina, but was always severe or downright depressed, and now, in this terrible space, and they often remained silent, neither of them mustering the energy to keep a conversation going. Roland hardly looked at her and often didn't show for hours, only when she fixed food, did he appear, staring into space while he gulped down the tasteless gruel.

"*Haus*—house," Mina said out loud, "*Tisch*—table...*Bier*—beer."

"That's an important one." The Irish man, Davin, whose wife had burned her hand, stood before her, a half-smile on his lips. To her surprise, she returned it.

"Im—port—tant."

"Right." He pointed at himself, then at her. "We study?"

She nodded. "How is...Kate?"

He pointed at his palm. "Better."

Mina began repeating the words, the Irish man said, trying them with her tongue, sometimes shaking her head. He'd get up and point at things like his shoes or his nose and say the English words, she then repeated over and over. They worked on body parts and clothing, on simple verbs.

Whistles and calls came from down the corridor. Even without checking, Mina knew that Roland was gambling again. Every available minute he hung out with the same group of men who played dice and *Bavarian Schafkopf*, a card game, he'd told her, he was learning and enjoying.

Mina had bit her lip, suppressing a comment though she worried what the constant idleness and playing was doing to him. The only good thing was that there was just about no alcohol. Most travelers were poor, the few wealthy passengers stayed among themselves in a separate cabin.

Communication with Davin was halting, yet Mina enjoyed challenging her mind, searching for words and forming the unaccustomed sounds. Especially, the words with *t h* gave her trouble and she often kept her tongue between her teeth to practice.

At the end of the lesson, the Irish man got up, his forest eyes nearly black in the gloom. "Tomorrow?"

She nodded, finding herself smile once more. "Yes, thank...you."

"You're spending a lot of time with the Irish," Regine said when they met at the stove to cook afterwards. "Isn't he married?"

Mina ignored the accusatory tone of the widow. "He is teaching me English. I think he is glad, I helped with his wife's injury."

"Hmm."

Mina poured two helpings of grain into the pot, added water and asked, "Don't you think it is important to know the new language?"

"Of course, but shouldn't you study with your husband?"

"Roland isn't interested." Mina sighed, pushing away her worries how he'd fare once they entered the new country and he went to work. Supposedly, Fort Wayne in Indiana was home to a number of German families already. Maybe, he'd get by.

Silence descended between them as Mina finished cooking and

handed the pot to Regine. "Thank you," she said in English.

Regine's eyes widened in surprise. "No need to show off."

"I can teach you...or you can study with us." Mina watched Regine prepare her pot and return it to the stove. Next to them several women were stirring their vessels, others waiting their turns. It was a constant shuffling for position and took hours to get everyone's meals prepared.

"I cannot concentrate." Regine looked thoughtful. "Not here. I'm surprised how well you are doing."

Mina nodded. She was pleased that she could remember the words, even speak them well enough for the Irish man to understand. If she were honest, she'd admit that studying was enjoyable because of him.

Shaking her head, she made her way down the aisle in search of Roland, trying not to spill the bowl of gruel. Usually, he'd find her about now because he surely had to be starving.

She found him still sitting where he'd gambled earlier. He was alone, staring into space.

"Did you have fun?", she asked, settling next to him on the ground. They'd take turns eating, since Regine had only loaned them one spoon and the bowl. Still, Mina was grateful for the widow's help.

Roland seemed to wake from his stupor. "With what?"

"Playing your games."

"It's not fun." He jumped up, his expression wild, before he seemed to realize that Mina had brought food. With a sigh, he sank down next to her and began to eat.

"I am learning English," Mina said after a while.

"Good for you."

"I can help you, we can study together."

He licked the spoon and handed it to her. "No, thanks."

As so often, Mina kept her thoughts to herself, afraid she'd ignite the tinder box, smoldering inside him. He jumped up again and began to pace, a task by itself because the aisle was full of travelers, tired of sitting in their bunks.

Roland tucked at his shirt. "I need air. Damn ship, damn ocean. I cannot stand it."

This once, he was right. Mina tried to remember how many days they'd been down here. Three at least. "Maybe you should knock on the door, remind them that we're still down here." Without a word, Roland took off, and Mina returned the bowl and spoon to her corner.

The large man who'd slept next to her, had moved to the other end, where the old woman had died. Roland had moved into his spot which also worried Mina. Already, he'd pushed himself onto her twice, always in the night, when most people slept. Of course, they weren't the only ones, even in this hellhole, people still found ways to lie together.

It wasn't so much the rough treatment, he used, never asking before, never touching her in a loving way, not even kissing her first. No, it was her fear of getting pregnant. She could only hope that the conditions down here were keeping her body from accepting his seed.

She didn't want to be tied to him, didn't want to live in constant fear what he'd do and how to take care of her child without money. It was hard enough to survive as a couple.

Shouting and pounding erupted outside. Roland's voice and that of several others boomed. "We need air, let us out. Toilet buckets are overflowing."

It was true, the toilets were so bad now that Mina put off going as long as possible. After leaving Liverpool, the water was also rationed and she had little need, albeit the soiled air left a constant thirst and wish to flush away the awful taste.

Mina followed the men and women into the hallway, but got stuck in the crowd, filling every available space.

Voices could be heard from deck, but they were too low to understand. Instead, the crowd whispered and carried the conversation from person to person. "Soon," they said.

What did it mean? Mina returned to her bunk and laid down. Face to the wall, her thoughts returned to the English lesson, then to the Irish man who so patiently taught her. She couldn't imagine him being rough with the little woman. Mina had watched him care for the boy, Peter, his movements gentle and loving. Something inside her ached then, a kind of pain or yearning for something, she couldn't define.

When she awoke, the bunks were empty, and she immediately noticed a breeze and lightening of the air. The deck had to be open. She crawled from her bunk and hurried up the ladder. The entire surface was stuffed with people, everybody sticking their nose into the wind.

Mina worked her way to the railing where she found Regine.

"I can't decide what is worse," Regine said, "freezing to death up here or suffocating below deck."

Mina chuckled grimly. Already, the wind and damp air were cutting through her, her cheeks and nose growing numb. It had to be near freezing though the prospect of going below seemed worse. "Let's move a bit," she said, holding out a forearm. "It'll warm us up."

They shuffled, weaved and pushed through the crowd, went to the bow, then back to stern. It was slow going, but at least Mina felt her muscles wake and her spirits lift.

Even Regine found her voice. "Hard to imagine that we'll be out here another three or four weeks." They were standing at the bow again, looking at the horizon where the sky met the ocean with nothing but water between them.

Beneath, the ship cut through the waves. Up and down it went, though Mina hardly noticed the movement now. She was thankful for having been spared the seasickness so many of them suffered from. Even now, she caught a whiff of vomit once in a while.

"Where is your husband," Regine asked after a while. "I never see him with you."

"Only when there's food."

Mina felt Regine's gaze on her temple. "He succumbs to gambling, doesn't he?"

"And drink, if he finds any."

A "tsk" rose from Regine's lips as she crossed herself. They hadn't talked about it, but Mina knew that the widow was devout. "Shame on him. He entered into a marriage vow."

"What about your husband?"

Regine sighed as her gaze returned to the sea. "He was a virtuous man, a bit boring, maybe, but a good soul. If anything, he worked too much, just loved numbers, and kept the books for people." Her eyes sparkled with tears. "We had a respectable home until two years ago, when things grew tough. People couldn't afford to hire him any longer. They lost their own businesses, couldn't afford to buy bread. That's when he came up with the idea to move to America."

Mina squeezed Regine's hand. "You had it all planned." *Unlike you,* the voice in her head commented. *You planned nothing, you followed your husband as blindly as if you'd run into a mine.*

CHAPTER TWENTY-EIGHT

Davin

Every day, when they were stuck below deck, Davin met the German woman to study English. Sometimes, Kate would accompany him, not participating, just joining to listen with Peter playing nearby.

Kate's hand was heeling well, the skin still sensitive, but otherwise intact. Davin knew that without Mina's help, it may have been quite different. He wondered how she knew such things, where she'd lived and what she'd done. He was also curious about her husband, who was never around. But it wasn't proper to ask such things and besides, her English wasn't yet good enough.

He realized, he was teaching her English with an Irish dialect, but it couldn't be helped. At least, she'd be able to communicate, once they arrived. They were plenty Irish already there and as far as he knew, many Germans.

Mina seemed subdued this morning, somehow sad or maybe upset. He asked her simply, "Are you sad?"

"Sad?"

He made a face, pulled down the corners of his mouth which elicited a chuckle from her. He smiled back, then grew serious again. "Not happy, sad."

The woman didn't answer, just shook her head, and avoided his gaze. "I want to learn English."

"Good."

She opened her book, and they were soon engaged in speaking and repeating words, some simple sentences.

When he finished and guided Kate back to their compartment, she eyed him curiously. "You like the German."

"She's a good woman, trying to learn the language," hurried Davin.

"You're still helping because she took care of my hand?" Kate's voice had a slight edge. "It's been eight or nine days, that should've paid for it."

"Who does it hurt?", he said, lifting Peter onto their bunk. "It's easier to pass the time this way."

"You can pass the time with me."

We're spending every breathing minute together as it is. Aloud, he said, "Why not help somebody who needs it? You didn't mind me helping you."

Kate's mouth opened, but then she nodded, so he covered her with the blanket and returned to the hallway...down the aisle to what served as the outhouse.

A line had formed, the stench growing stronger with every step. He was also itching from head to toe, especially at night, when he tried to sleep and had no way to distract himself. Water was rationed and barely enough to drink and cook with. Not a drop could be wasted on washing or cleaning clothes.

Davin noticed multiple welts on the neck of the man in front of him, the way his own skin had to look.

He'd never known such filth, such conditions, not fit for a rat, let alone families with children. They deserved better. All of them. Was that why he still helped the German woman? Kate was right, the debt was surely paid, yet, every day, something drew him into the corridor or in good weather on deck to spend time with Mina.

He hardly knew her, their conversation as limited as speaking to a three-year old. But...

But what? He couldn't explain it other than that he felt in her a kindred spirit.

Don't be daft, the voice in his head commented. *She's from a different country, you have nothing in common*. Maybe he felt sorry for her...for the way, her husband treated her. It was in plain sight, how he preferred to gamble and boast. Even if Davin didn't understand the words, he knew when a man was pretending.

How had Mina met this man, bound herself to him?

Somebody patted his shoulder. It was his turn to use the buckets. Every night, they were overflowing and sloshed their contents across the floor, being emptied first thing in the morning. He hurried to do his business and returned to Kate, only took off his shoes before joining her in bed. To his surprise, she felt her hand on his, guiding him to her breast. Peter was asleep against the wall, so he followed her lead.

He shielded his eyes against the low sun as he heard a laugh. He knew it was her even without turning, but then she stood in front of him, breathless, her lips turned into a smirk, a dimple on her right cheek. She took his right hand in hers, placed the other against his chest, and looked up at him, her face so close...he was kissing her, a long kiss, after which he pressed her close and buried his nose into her chestnut curls. Everywhere they touched, he felt hot and alive, an urge to explore more and more of her...

Davin awoke, his heart pounded. He remembered where he was, felt Kate's back against his belly, his excitement hard between them. Hadn't they just lain together? And here he was like some dog in heat. He moved backwards the slightest bit, well knowing there was no room to his neighbor, some bearded man in his fifties, who traveled with his wife and adult son.

What was the matter with him? He still heard the German woman's laugh in his mind, light and happy like church bells on a spring day. Two bunks down, a woman coughed incessantly, her breathing raspy in-between. He'd seen her off and on, coming and going and didn't know her name, hadn't bothered, but he knew that she was quite sick. Already three passengers had died, a young girl of twelve and two older men. Undoubtedly, there'd be more.

The worry returned, worry for Peter who seemed more fragile since the fever. He had to protect him, make sure, he got enough to eat and play with him. Worry for Kate, the woman, he'd vowed to take care of. He felt helpless, trapped in the belly of this ship, sitting in the dark, not knowing where he was going, when he was arriving or what would happen once he did—if he did. And then he dreamed such nonsense about a woman he hardly knew. The ship was twisting his mind, making him crazy.

He was still awake when the people in his compartment began to stir. The woman continued coughing, but now there were whispers and rustles, someone got up, then another. On a whim, he slipped from his bunk and headed for the deck opening. The movement of the ship was calm this morning and sure enough, a grayish light wafted toward him and when he climbed to the top, he was engulfed in fog.

Even the sails above were losing themselves in a whitish cloud, the sails fully extended, yet hanging limp, sometimes slapping a bit like a feeble attempt at catching the air. The splashing of the waves was muted as if a blanket had been thrown over the ship to shut out all sounds. He hurried to the railing, for once able to move freely. Below him lay the waters of the Atlantic Ocean, not churning waves with white caps, being pushed into a frenzy by the harsh wind, but a flat board of grayness that lost itself within a few yards.

Davin trembled, his face and hair covered in a fine, cold mist, yet he cherished the peacefulness. When a seaman passed him, he asked, "How long will it last...the lull?"

The man gazed at the slack sails that hung weakly above them. "Who knows, maybe a day, maybe three." He tipped his cap and hurried off.

Davin wandered to the bow. He may as well have been blind, the fog impenetrable. It seemed he could grip the whiteness with his fingers. From here, he couldn't even see the other side of the deck, let alone the stern of the ship. It was like floating in nothing.

He wandered on and almost smashed into a man who crossed his way without looking.

"Excuse me," he addressed the man he recognized as Mina's husband.

Roland stopped and flashed him an angry look, said something in German that was no doubt an insult.

Davin tried a smile, but the man just squinted before disappearing in the fog. Mina was right, her husband wasn't even learning the simplest words like *sorry*. Davin's gut told him to stay away, that this man was carrying trouble wherever he went. Mina seemed so sweet and eager to learn and help. How had she ended up with such a man? He longed to learn more about her life, what she'd done before ending up on this rat trap of a ship.

"You're up early." Kate materialized in front of him, Peter in tow.

Shaking off his thoughts, Davin wrapped an arm around her. "Couldn't sleep. Let's take advantage of the quiet and cook before everybody wakes."

In the afternoon, a feeble sun tried to dissolve the fog, but the wind did not return. Everybody who could manage, was on deck, walking, sitting, talking or just enjoying air on their faces.

Davin had been dozing, his back leaning against the captain's cabin, when he grew aware of raised voices. He chased away the cobwebs of sleep and, leaving Kate and Peter behind, wandered to see what was going on. His mind was so starved for entertainment that he'd welcome even a fight.

Near the entrance to steerage, Mina's husband was shouting, the three men, he was with, eyeing him with care. Neither seemed to want to engage.

Roland yelled something, theatrically threw down the cards, he'd been kneading, and jumped up.

Davin suspected he'd lost and now owed money. Davin turned to search for Mina who could hopefully calm down her husband because he looked ready to strangle somebody. Somebody else had already found her because she rushed to her husband's side. The arguing didn't stop though, just the opposite. The men were speaking, Roland was shouting, and Mina seemed to have trouble making herself heard.

Without thought, Davin moved to her side. "What happened?" he asked.

Mina, two flames reddening her cheeks, threw him a helpless glance. "The men say...Roland," she seemed to search for the right words, "lied with cards, that he owes them three...Thaler."

"Thaler?"

"German coin."

Meanwhile all men were standing, the three of them glaring at Roland who seemed to have second thoughts.

Mina's hand wandered to her mouth. "They want to tell the Captain, have him arrested."

At that moment, Roland grabbed Mina's hand, but so roughly that she cried out. He pulled at her finger, obviously keen on the gold ring she wore.

Again, Mina screeched. Davin jumped forward and removed Roland's hand. "Stop!"

Roland looked like he'd take a swing at Davin, but then his arm sank because Davin's work-hardened fingers, clamped down more firmly. Though Roland was three inches taller, Davin had no doubt, he'd win any fight.

Mina was rubbing her fingers, her gaze going back and forth between Roland and Davin.

One of the three players held out a palm.

"What do they want?" Davin asked.

Mina stuck her hands behind her back. "My ring?"

Roland turned back to Mina but didn't touch her. "Give it to him."

Mina set her jaw, the expression of defiance surprised Davin. "It's mine."

Keeping an eye on Roland, Davin turned to the three men. "That's not yours to take."

One of them, a man with the bushy eyebrows of a woodcutter,

seemed to understand and answered in rough English. "They are married, they share."

Mina shook her head. "My father gave it to me."

Davin didn't understand much more than father, but he placed a calming hand on Mina's forearm. "Your bet is with her husband, not with a helpless woman."

The thick browed man said something to his friends, then pointed a forefinger at Roland's chest, said something menacing and walked off with his friends in tow.

Roland, eyes flashing murderously, turned back on Mina. But Davin was prepared and though not a single word was said, Mina's husband wandered away as well.

Mina was still massaging her fingers, and instead of looking relieved, she appeared fearful. "He is very...angry, dangerous."

Davin nodded. He'd met men like Mina's husband before. He wasn't afraid. Holding out a hand, he said, "Come and sit with us."

CHAPTER TWENTY-NINE

Mina

What had just happened? In Mina's mind the scene on deck repeated: Roland being accused of cheating, his anger turning towards her, his demand to hand over the ring, Davin, the Irish man, coming to her rescue, protecting the only valuable thing, she'd kept from her family.

Her heart lifted and fell at the same time. A virtual stranger had helped her, but she knew that Roland's wrath would be unpredictable. He'd fight for the perceived wrong, he'd experienced. She had no doubt, he'd cheated, likely had done it for days. Now they'd caught him and to protect himself, he'd tried to steal her father's ring.

Coldness spread through her chest, and it wasn't from the damp air this afternoon, she was deathly afraid, Roland would attack her in the night, steal the ring from her finger while she slept...and for the Irish man. There was no telling what Roland would do to get even. If she knew one thing, it was that Roland never forgot. He carried a grudge for years, even it had been a minor thing. This wasn't minor. Roland was embarrassed, had been called out in front of the entire ship.

She already worried returning to her bunk.

Now she sat next to Kate, the woman she'd helped earlier. The Irish man had left, apparently to cook for them. "Can I see your hand?", she asked to distract herself.

Kate nodded and extended her palm. "Your English is getting better."

Mina nodded. "I try." She inspected the skin that was darker and shinier than the rest. "Does it still hurt?"

"Not much. Though I'm afraid of fire now."

"It will pass," Mina said. She looked up and discovered Regine, the widow, waving at her. When Mina motioned her to approach, Regine shook her head. With a sigh, Mina rose. "I come back." Her smile froze as she approached the widow, because Regine looked as severe as attending a funeral.

"They're talking, the entire ship is talking," she exclaimed, keeping three feet distance.

"He is a difficult man."

"I'm not talking about your husband, I'm talking about *you*!" Mina opened her mouth, yet no words came out. "How could you do that?"

"What did I do? He about ripped off my finger to steal my ring."

Regine's voice rose, something Mina had not seen before. "He's your husband, you *share* your life...everything."

"He wasn't sharing, he was taking." Mina's throat grew tight from anger. "He is violent and moody."

"You are his wife and rather spend time with that Irish goon? People say you're a strumpet." Her gaze wandered toward Kate and her boy. "Isn't he married too?"

Mina stared at the widow who appeared so righteous, as if she herself were administering God's will. "Davin merely helped protect me from my husband's wrath. What is wrong about that?"

To her surprise, Regine leaned closer. "I suggest that you return to your husband at once. Support him, take care of him. That is your purpose." She gave Mina a little shove. "Go on, cook his dinner or you can get your pot someplace else."

With a last look at Kate who'd watched but likely not understood, she stumbled off. To her horror, many of the women she passed stared at her, some whispered to their neighbors. "Witch...tart," some called after her. Mina kept her head high, even if she felt sick to her stomach. Was it because Davin was Irish? Was it because she was spending time with another man to study English? Nothing had happened except that a man had taken her side and helped her. She'd been grateful...was grateful for keeping her ring, for this support, fending off a violent man. What was wrong about it?

She almost fell, climbing down to steerage, the stench welcoming her and making her even sicker. Waiting for her eyes to adjust to the gloom, she hurried to fetch Regine's cookware. When she entered her own compartment and began measuring out the grain, Roland gripped her shoulder. "Damn woman. In front of everybody," he seethed.

Mina, having fought tears over the hurtful treatment of the women on deck, straightened to face her husband. "It appears everyone is on *your* side. No matter that you beat and mistreat me, no matter that you were going to take the one thing I've got left from my father." The words just bubbled to the surface, words she'd thought a thousand times and never had the courage to speak out loud. It no longer mattered. Let him beat her. All she wanted was to lie down and disappear. Roland's eyes had narrowed though he'd let go of her shoulder. "No matter, you forced me to go on this impossible journey with nothing but the clothes on our bodies."

The air had left her lungs and she prepared for a blow. But it didn't come. Roland just stood there, towering over her, staring at her face, his expression hard to read. There was contempt there, but also self-loathing and fury.

Mina swallowed once more. "If you don't mind, I'll cook our meal now." She straightened and turning her back, marched off. In the corridor, she wiped her eyes, then climbed to the top to find a free stove.

Ignoring the stares and whispers, she busied herself with the pot. It felt good to face Roland and tell him off. He hadn't said anything, hadn't touched her. She had no idea what would happen now. Only one thing was clear: she couldn't speak with Davin anymore, certainly not study. All of a sudden, she felt sad...disappointed. Spending time with the Irish man had felt special, they'd laughed, but more importantly, he'd made her feel special, like she was worth teaching the new language.

"You about done here?" An elderly woman in a cinnamon brown dress and ruffled hat squinted at her.

"She'll be done when her food is cooked." A gloved hand appeared on Mina's forearm. "You take your time like everyone else."

Mina looked up in surprise. A woman of maybe thirty with blond curls that she'd seen the first day looking down at her from the deck of the privileged travelers and who reminded her of Augusta smiled at her. "Thank you." And in a low voice. "Are you sure you want to talk to me. I'm apparently a loose woman." For whatever reason, she felt herself smile. It sure didn't take much to rile up the entire ship.

"All you did is speak up for yourself," the other woman said and extended a hand so remarkably clean, Mina just stared at the white skin and perfect shiny nails. "Margarete Weber, glad to meet you." Louder she said, "It'd be helpful for us females if we spoke our mind more often."

Mina shook. "Wilhelmina...Mina—"

"Already know all about you." Margarete grinned. "Well, what those wagging tongues think they know about you." She leaned in as the aroma of roses reached Mina's nose. It was so surprising, she inhaled deeply, instantly taken back to her parents' cottage where her mother had tended a half dozen rose bushes. "Don't let them bother you."

Mina felt instantly better while she gave the oats another whirl, then pulled away the pot with a rag. "I know you as well. The first time, when we boarded, I saw you on deck. And later...your blonde hair reminds me of a friend." Mina's thoughts traveled to Augusta who was surely crossing the ocean by now. She pushed away the twinge of sadness. "I'm surprised you'd set foot here. We have no access to water, sleeping below is a horror."

Mina felt the eyes of the other women, but all remained silent, maybe because this woman looked so unusually proper among the filth of steerage. Indeed, she had nothing in common with the families who barely survived below deck, her dress was clean and elegant with lace around the neck and front, her hair swept up in neat curls below a tiny hat.

Margarete lifted a gloved hand to point at the back of the ship. "We remain among ourselves...mostly in the sitting room. But I'm dying of boredom and the tight space is unbearable."

"You have a sitting room?"

Margarete chuckled. "And a nice dining hall. It's small, but then, there are only a few of us."

"Everybody here stinks, there isn't even water to wash. I'm ashamed of the state I'm in."

"It'll pass. The main thing is to get through the passage, everything else washes off." She scoffed. "Just like those ugly comments."

"Where are you going?"

"Chicago." The smirk was back. "I'm traveling alone, quite scandalous, don't you think?"

Again, Mina was reminded of Augusta. "Why did you leave?"

"Father meant to marry me to some ancient earl, and when I refused, he suggested, I take a long trip not to embarrass him further. Especially, because I'm long past marrying age." Margarete smiled. "He thinks I'm hopeless...which I am. I don't want to have children, I don't want a husband."

"Me neither." It slipped out so fast, Mina clapped a hand on her mouth. But Margarete just laughed.

"At least the one you currently have."

Their eyes met, an understanding between them. It didn't need words, yet it was as strong as if they'd spoken. Mina was in awe how open the elegant woman expressed her disdain for societal expectations. She didn't even want a family, wanted to remain independent. Not something women did.

"Here you are." Roland towered over them. "I'm starving and you dawdle like a market wench."

Mina wordlessly held out the now cooled pot, she'd placed on the ground. "I haven't eaten either."

"It is time to return to my cabin anyway," Margarete said. "I will look for you again." She lightly patted Mina on the arm and said in a low voice. "Chin up, you are strong."

Mina swallowed, suddenly, she had a lump in her throat. "You are very kind."

But the elegant woman just waved and disappeared in a door, Mina had never set foot in. She only knew that the captain and crew stayed down there, one level above steerage, and apparently wealthy passengers stayed in private cabins.

By the time, she focused on Roland, he'd more than half emptied the food. Wordlessly, she held out a hand and he turned over the spoon they shared. Mina expected that the widow would soon demand back her pot, but maybe Margarete could help. Not that she looked like she'd ever cooked a meal herself, though the world operated differently when you had money. Mina had seen rich men visiting the mayor, had once by chance come upon a wedding party passing to the nearby castle. She still remembered the black wagons and perfectly cared for horses, their woven manes and shiny leather tack. The liveried staff had kept watch to make sure no commoner would get in the way of the carriages.

She'd never experience something like this, you had to be born into it. Still, Margarete had been nice, something Mina had not expected. In her mind, all rich people were arrogant and condescending, treating people like her badly or ignoring them altogether.

"What are you doing with that fancy dunce?", Roland said. Mina had forgotten he was still standing next to her, just as she'd not realized she'd finished the oats.

"She is nice," Mina said simply. *Unlike everybody else.*

Roland eyed the empty pot. "You could've left me some."

"You ate more than your share already," Mina shot back, surprised at herself for telling it like it was. Immediately, she braced herself for some insult or a blow, but Roland just squinted angrily before he left her standing alone. Remembering the empty pot, she had to return to Regine, she headed downstairs.

Margarete had said she was strong. She didn't feel strong, just tired of the ordeal of living this impossible life.

CHAPTER THIRTY

Davin

"People are talking," Kate cried when Davin returned with their meal. He'd prepared an extra portion, expecting to share with Mina.

"About what?" Davin sat down, momentarily distracted, and wondering where the German woman had gone.

Kate took two bowls and handed one to Peter. "You and that German. She's preying on you, playing the helpless girl. And now you fix her food?"

Davin bit his lip. Not so long ago, he'd jumped to Kate's help. *You chose that,* his mind commented. *You chose to marry her.* "You believe I should've let that husband of hers rip the ring from her finger, so he could pay his gambling debt?"

Kate shrugged. "She's none of your concern. I don't understand why you meddle."

"She helped you with your injury."

"It was a kindness and I'm grateful." She waved the spoon in his face. "But you've done enough. I overheard one of the Germans speak English...that she's a loose woman, spending time with you when she should take care of her husband."

Davin wanted to shout back, the anger surprising him. Stupid people. It was none of their business, but this ship was like a miniature world swimming on a vast ocean in the middle of nowhere. They could make any rules they wanted. He'd check on Mina later, secretly hoping she'd do more studying with him.

Above him, a sail puffed out, then snapped loudly. The seamen began shouting, hurrying around the crowds, working to adjust the tension. The planks creaked as the ship bucked and pushed forward. Several things happened at once: the ship listed sideways, Kate cried out, Peter slid away and Davin jumped after him, barely grabbing his jacket...people screamed, sliding, stumbling and falling toward the left railing.

As Davin held on to Kate and Peter, shoving the bowls into the bag between them, he thought about the German woman, envisioned her falling overboard. Nobody would save *her*.

More people screamed and then the captain shouted for them to immediately return to their bunks. The wind was back, so was their imprisonment in steerage.

All evening, Davin stayed with Kate and Peter who'd scraped his hands but was fine otherwise. The ship's wooden structure creaked with every up and down movement as the waves pounded and the wind howled above. Between the icy sea and certain death lay no more than a thin wooden wall, at some point having been crafted by carpenters like himself. Out of practice, he'd inspected the walls and seams of the vessel, most of them in decent shape. Steerage was another matter. It had been erected in a hurry, the bunks crooked and built with rough wood, the floors uneven. As soon as they'd arrive, the captain would have everything ripped out to fill the ship's belly with valuable cargo.

Down here misery had returned. People were seasick, returning their precious meals to the buckets and more often to the floor. The air turned into a foul stench, the floor slippery with vomit. To distract himself, Davin climbed from his bunk and picked his way into the corridor.

Maybe Mina would show herself and he could speak with her for a moment, make sure, she was all right. He had to hold on to the ceiling that was barely higher than the top of his head and walls to stay upright, the waves so strong, he heard them slosh on the other side of the wall. It wouldn't take much to sink this ship. He looked upward, sent a prayer, something he hadn't done in a while. The corridor was deserted, the captain had urged them to remain in their bunks because it was too dangerous to move about, running the risk of falling and breaking a bone.

The ship bucked, pulling the legs from under him and throwing him on his side. He crashed painfully on his shoulder and slid to the floor, fumbled for a post or beam to catch himself. Finally, he managed to crawl to the entrance of another compartment and, still sitting, held on to the sidewall to clear his head.

Nothing was broken, but his shoulder burned and throbbed. He'd turned his thumb somehow which now felt painful to move or even touch. Damn ship. He swallowed a curse and tried to decide what to do next. It was obvious that nobody in their right mind was leaving their bunk and his plan to casually run into the German woman wasn't going to work. But returning to Kate and the stench of the bunks was out of the question. At least out here, the air was a bit better. If he had to, he'd just sit here until the weather changed.

The groaning beneath and above him continued, sometimes he heard voices or was it the wind screaming in the sails. He smiled grimly. At least they'd make excellent time in this storm.

What good did it do them, if they became sick? Some would not see the new world, instead find an early grave in the ocean. Was it worth all that? Was it worth risking your life in hopes for a better one? He didn't know anymore. Maybe it was too hard to imagine America, the vast land and fertile ground, people had talked and written about, not to mention Indiana, some place seven hundred miles west of New York, where he'd work one day, paying off a voyage that caused nothing but suffering. Again, he questioned his sanity, binding himself to a woman, binding himself to an unknown employer. The choices he'd made didn't feel good or right. If he were honest, he felt trapped, as trapped as sitting in the belly of this ship.

"Davin?" Mina, holding onto the wall with both hands, stood above him. "What are you doing here? You break your head."

"Your neck."

"What?"

Davin grinned and pointed to the base of his skull. "It's called neck."

Mina returned his smile. "I miss our lessons."

Davin patted the ground. "How about now?"

Mina hastily scanned the corridor which appeared empty. "No. People are saying things...about me."

"I heard. Let them talk."

Mina shook her head as a new wave made the ship shudder. She nearly lost her balance, caught herself and hugged the wall. "I can't."

"Your husband?" Their eyes met in the gloom. They'd looked at each other a thousand times by now, but something had changed. It was just as gloomy, just as stinky, but he no longer cared to be someplace else. Heat curled in the pit of his stomach, and he wanted to jump up and embrace her. He breathed through his nose to calm the turmoil inside him, looked away.

Mina hadn't noticed his confusion. "He is...fine. I mean, he leaves me alone."

Again, he pointed at the ground next to him. "Better sit or you'll hurt yourself."

"I cannot, I meant to use the bathroom. But it is too dangerous. I return to my bunk."

No, Davin wanted to cry, but all he did was nod. "Be careful."

He remained in his spot, anticipating the waves and the movements of the ship. He grew tired from the stale air and yet, he remained. Somehow, he could not return to Kate and lie down next to her. It felt like a betrayal.

To whom, his mind mocked. *You are married and bound to Kate.* At the same time, he yearned to be near the German woman. The ship was playing tricks on him, the unending slapping of the waves, the gloominess was making him crazy. All he needed was some fresh air and a full day's work and he'd come to his senses.

CHAPTER THIRTY-ONE

Mina

Mina lay awake in her bunk. The encounter with Davin sitting out there by himself had disturbed her. She would've loved nothing more than to sit down and practice English, not only to prepare for the new land, but to distract herself and pass the time.

The ugly tongues would wag though, and she did not feel up to it. It was one thing to be on deck and be able to walk away, maybe have the support of the elegant woman, Margarete. But down here was a different matter. They were stuck together so tight, she felt like suffocating as it was. The terrible air and the small rations were making her feel weak and tired. But they couldn't afford to eat more, there was no telling how much longer they'd travel.

Regine had asked the captain and he'd refused to give an answer. She had told Mina, angry, that he would refuse to give an estimate. Mina knew that others had tried. Most everything down here was overheard, and word traveled from front to back in a matter of minutes. Roland hadn't spoken to her since the last meal, but at least he was leaving her alone. The waiting and idleness were poison for a man like him, especially now that he no longer could distract himself with gambling. Unlike some of the passengers who played fiddle or harmonica or sang, Roland did not care for music.

Mina worried the other men would do something drastic to collect the debt, either punish him or try to take her ring by force. She considered taking it off and hiding it. Already it was so loose, it nearly slipped off when she wiped her hands. She decided to ask Margarete for a length of string or wool to weave together and secure the ring around her neck.

If she'd ever get out on deck again. A child wailed not two yards from her. It was small, no more than three or four and seemed as sickly as its mother. They'd been throwing up every time, the ship hit heavy seas and barely moved anymore. At home, Mina could've administered to them with her herbs. Chamomile to soothe the stomach, the purple cone flower for strength, peppermint to freshen and lift the mood. But she had nothing to work with and the ship didn't even have a doctor, just some medical kit that she'd seen once, a few instruments and brown bottles, nobody knew how to use.

The feeling of helplessness returned. At home, they'd been poor, but she'd been free to move about, work the cabin and garden, stroll in the forest or visit the market. Here she was stuck, lying between Roland and some stranger, stuck in the belly of the ship. She turned her face into the pillow to muffle the stench of vomit and fell asleep.

In her dream she walked through a vast garden of medicinal herbs. She knew she'd planted them, the air filled with the scent of lavender and lemon balm. The sun shone hotly, yet she felt herself smile. In the distance, a man plowed a field with a couple of oxen. She waved to him, shouted, but he never looked at her. When she left the flower garden, the man and his oxen grew hazy as if a wall of fog had moved between them. She called out again, but her voice didn't carry and when she ran toward him, she found herself at the edge of a canyon, the precipice in front of her filled with clouds, hiding the bottom. When she turned, she realized she was standing on an island, surrounded by a giant gorge. In an instant, the flowers died and withered, turned to dust...

She awoke with a start. The skin on her chest and back itched, the bed bugs doing their work. Every day she collected all she could find. But they simply moved over from the neighboring straw to find her. She scratched and turned to her back, staring into the darkness. The dream had left her feeling desolate and alone once more.

The wind subsided enough for them to emerge two days later. Mina just stood, facing the ocean, urging her eyes to see past the horizon. They'd been traveling for more than four weeks now which meant they'd crossed at least two thirds of the way. The air was mild this morning and Mina removed her wrap to allow the sun to touch her neck and face.

She forced herself to be in the moment, just enjoy breathing fresh air, feeling the wind. This morning, the crew had carried out the young mother and her child who'd died in the night, two more casualties. Mina felt her throat tighten with anger and sadness. Such a waste!

Because the ships wanted to maximize profits, they offered near impossible traveling conditions.

She felt a movement behind her as Regine joined her at the railing. Her face appeared gray this morning, her eyes sunken. A strong, unpleasant smell emanated from her, the fabric of her dress stained.

"What happened?" Mina asked, supporting the widow's elbow.

"I cannot keep anything down," she panted, "I am weak, but lying in that bunk makes me lose my mind." The widow tried to smile, but failed, the skin around her mouth a weave of wrinkles, Mina had never noticed before.

"Let me get you some water."

Regine shook her head. "No use. My stomach turns even at a drop."

Mina swallowed her comment. Not taking in any liquid was life-threatening, but she didn't want to add to the widow's distress. Regine had been nice enough to share her cooking utensils, even if her strict morals were hard to take. Of course, what she needed was a decent tea, maybe chamomile or peppermint, something to soothe her innards. Again, Mina felt at a loss. She remembered the elegant woman, Margarete, and decided to search for her.

"Can you hold on for a while? I will try to find you some tea."

Regine nodded though Mina worried, the widow could teeter at any moment. That's when she noticed Davin leading his wife and son to a spot beneath the main mast. She hurried to him, and a bit out of breath, explained that the woman in the black dress was too weak to stand on her own.

"Could you please, I mean..."

"I'll help her," Davin said simply.

Mina threw him a quick smile before she pushed her way into the crowd. It was unlikely that Margarete was mingling with the likes of steerage. It had been pure coincidence that they'd met at all. Mina suspected that Margarete stayed in the small section, cordoned off on the side. Unfortunately, she wasn't allowed there.

"I need to speak to the lady, Frau Weber, traveling in first class," she addressed the first seaman, crossing her path.

"Sorry, I've got to work," the boy said. He was no more than sixteen, his chin still smooth as a child's.

"Who can help me then?" she called after him, but the boy ignored her and quick as a monkey climbed up one of the masts.

Frustrated she knocked on the door of the main cabin. When nobody answered, she opened the door, well aware that she'd be in deep trouble the moment somebody discovered her. She smelled herself, her dress and skin covered in a layer of grime, she'd never thought possible on a human being, let alone herself.

Swallowing her anxiety, she took a step to the deck below, then another, trying to guess where Margarete was staying. The air was filled with the appetizing aroma of frying meat, reminding her that she hadn't eaten breakfast. Somewhere down the hall, dishes clanged.

Disheartened, she stopped. To the people up here, a sick passenger meant nothing, just somebody from steerage, no more important than a rat.

"Mina?" Mina swiveled on her heels and stood face-to-face with Margarete, dressed in a cream-white gown and a matching hat. "I was about to go to breakfast."

"I was looking for you, hoping you could help."

Margarete threw a glance down the hall, then pulled Mina into her chamber, a smallish room with a narrow cot, a tiny window sending a stream of light onto the table and chair. A desk on the opposite wall was covered in paper, books and an assortments of quills. To Mina, it looked like heaven on earth.

"Quickly, what is it? I don't want you to get in trouble."

Mina, well aware of her dirtiness, kept her distance. "I'm sorry, the widow, Regine, is very ill. I'm wondering if you have access to chamomile or peppermint tea to soothe her stomach. I'm afraid, she'll die if she doesn't drink something soon."

Margarete gripped Mina's filthy hand with her clean one. "I will ask at once. How should I find you?"

"I will wait outside the cabin upstairs."

"Give me a few minutes." Margarete quietly opened the door and scanned the hall, then waved Mina through.

Mina hurried back on deck, relieved, she'd remained undiscovered. She hurried to steerage to fetch the widow's pot, just in case, Margarete would be successful. If not, she'd at least cook breakfast.

The ovens were surrounded by a dozen women, trying to fix whatever food they'd brought onboard as Mina moved toward the cabin door. The young seaman, she'd asked earlier was standing next to it, watching the crowd. She had no doubt, he'd stop her from entering.

A moment later, Margarete slipped onto the deck, a teapot made of porcelain in her hand. "Here," she said as soon as Mina approached. "It is some kind of herb." She poured the content with some kind of seed swimming in it into Mina's pot.

"I better return this." Margarete glanced at the young seaman standing watch. "You won't give me away, will you?"

The boy's cheeks grew pink as she slipped back inside. Mina detected a soft anis smell and immediately knew that this was fennel tea, perfect for upset stomachs. Careful, not to spill a drop, she weaved through the mingling horde, searching for Regine.

The widow sat with eyes closed, her back to the railing.

"She was too weak to remain standing," Davin said as soon as Mina drew close. "She is only half conscious."

"She must drink this," Mina said, falling to her knees. Davin moved to Regine's other side and gently lifted Regine's head.

"Let me sleep," she mumbled as their eyes met. "It is all right."

Mina moved the pot to Regine's closed lips. "Please open your mouth, just a little." From somewhere, a spoon appeared. A crowd was building around them, most of the people just staring, others whispering. A man prayed.

Mina used the spoon, tipped it lightly on Regine's mouth. "It is fennel tea. You will like it."

The lips didn't open. Only when Mina dropped the spoon back into the pot, Regine spoke. "I'm ready to join my husband." She took Mina's hand, held it to her chest. "Do not fret. It is fine. Tell them, I want *you* to have my things. I wrote it down. Say a prayer...for..." Regine's eyes stared straight ahead, the last word evaporated, her expression almost cheerful and free of the sadness, she'd carried in life.

Davin placed two fingers on Regine's neck, then shook his head. "She is gone."

Mina's eyes blurred as she closed Regine's lids. Roland, who'd appeared out of nowhere, announced he'd fetch the captain.

Davin held out a hand, but Mina remained on the ground and crossed Regine's hands on her belly. Pushing away the lump in her throat, she addressed the crowd. "Will you say a prayer, I know Regine would've wanted it."

"*Vater unser im Himmel...*," they began the Lord's prayer, more and more voices falling in until everybody on deck was shouting the words except for Mina and Davin, who just watched over the dead woman.

They'd silently watched as the captain and four crew lowered Regine's body into the sea, they had even lowered a couple of sails to slow down the ship. Mina, who'd shared the tea with Roland, at some point remembered that she hadn't eaten yet and went in search of their grain bag.

"Miss?" The captain stopped her at the entry to steerage. "The people tell me that Frau Graf bequeathed her belongings to you. We also found a note. Your name?"

Mina cleared her throat. "I...yes. I'm Wilhelmina Peters."

"How well did you know Frau Graf?"

"We met on the ship."

The captain watched her carefully, his bushy white brows in stark contrast to his leathery face. "It is only...your husband has been accused of cheating at cards. I'm concerned—"

"My husband has nothing to do with this," Mina cried. "He didn't even know Regine."

The captain coughed. "Right. Be that as it may, I'm required to keep order and make sure that your dealings are above board."

"Dealings?", Mina cried, new heat rising from her belly. "I tried to be there for a woman who'd lost her husband. I had no idea she would leave me her things until moments before she passed."

"Calm down, Frau Peters, we'll go downstairs now."

Regine's bunk space was a mess, but her travel bag and a box with household goods and food were in perfect order.

"There's also a trunk in the storage compartment, you can pick up when we arrive." The captain instructed one of the seaman to transport the travel bag and household items to Mina's bunk. "Before I forget," the captain said, pulling a linen sack from an inside pocket. "These items were on Frau Graf when we prepared her for burial. I didn't think it prudent to waste such fineries." He hesitated. "And this." He handed her a belt made of cloth which jingled softly. "Make sure you inform your husband. It is highly unusual to see him absent in such matters."

Mina remembered Margarete's words and said, "I'm perfectly capable...my husband has nothing to do with this..."

The captain nodded wordlessly.

Did he understand, Mina wondered. *Surely, he met thousands of people on these ships and learned to read them.* Numb from the back and forth, she stuffed bag and belt into her shawl and returned to her bunk.

Thankfully, Roland was absent, likely upstairs, searching for a way to pass the time. She sank onto her bed and poured the contents of the bag onto her lap. A brooch with a ruby, two wedding rings, one small, one larger, a gold necklace with a diamond pendant, its stone sparkling golden in the lantern's light, and a matching diamond ring. Mina stared at the jewels in disbelief. The widow had been wealthy, despite her plain dress. She could've traveled much more comfortably like Margarete but had preferred to remain unobserved. Mina only remembered seeing the golden wedding band. Everything else had been hidden, likely beneath her severe dark dress. She remembered the cloth belt and when she opened it, something sparkled yellow: dozens of gold ducats nestled inside. She let out a sigh. Regine had mentioned that her husband had done well until two years ago. Mina had assumed that he'd lost his income...

Hearing movement, Mina scrambled to stuff everything back and into her bodice. Such wealth would give the desperate reason to steal or worse. If Roland got wind of Regine's gift, he'd gamble it all away before they reached land.

Mina quickly rose from the bunk and pretended to tie her shoe as a man with his young son entered. Now she was really curious what the large trunk contained. Had the widow hidden other treasures?

Acutely aware of the heavy packages touching her skin, she made her way back on deck.

CHAPTER THIRTY-TWO

Davin

In the evening Davin remained on deck. Kate had taken Peter below after dinner, most other passengers had also returned to their bunks. The wind carried a light rain that seemed to mist and swirl around him, not enough to soak, but to cool and creep into his skin.

Still, he remained, his back against the base of the foremast, staring straight ahead. There was nothing to see, of course, just the darkening sky above an even darker ocean. But the regular up and down of the ship, the creaking mast and wind pushing the sails, soothed him somehow.

He wondered if they'd forget him up here and if he'd be forced to spend the night outside. Spring had arrived, the temperatures no longer forbidding, yet an entire night would be hard to take. He thought about the German woman saying farewell to her friend, the way she'd tried to get help, even breaking a few rules to do the right thing. Kate would never do that, she always waited for him to take the initiative, expected him to take care of everything.

He sighed loudly, the wind seemed to pull the sound from his lips and carry it off into the approaching night. He needed to stop thinking about women and concentrate on what lay ahead. Another week or so and they'd arrive in New York, all of them going their own ways. He'd never see the German woman again. The heaviness in his chest returned, the conviction that he'd made a mistake...many mistakes.

Somewhere a bell clanged and brought him back. He rose slowly then, his legs stiff with cold, the fabric of his jacket and pants damp. A few straggling passengers were heading toward the door to steerage where a seaman was waiting to lock them in.

It felt like going to his grave, descending into the darkness. The door smacked shut behind him, the filthy air swallowed him and took his breath. At the bottom, he sank onto the stairs, when he noticed Mina coming his way. She hadn't seen him yet, seemed deep in thought, keeping one hand on the wall of the ship for balance.

"Mina?" In his ears, his voice sounded weak and desperate.

She looked up then, their eyes meeting, crossing the distance easily. "You are wet," she said when she reached him. They were at eyelevel, him still sitting on a lower step, she standing in front of him. She wore a different dress, sleeves covering half her hands, dark and too loose, which made her skin appear much paler, likely bequeathed by the dead woman.

He wiped his face with a sleeve and said, "And you must be sad."

"I am. Regine should not have died. Not here...like this." She half-heartedly waved at the dark space behind her, when the ship bucked and send her flying forward.

Davin's reflexes, quick from years of working in dangerous environments, automatically opened his arms to catch her. She was close now, pressed against his chest, her face mere inches from his. Neither of them spoke, but the response of his body was immediate, a wave of heat like lava flowed through him, his breath caught. He half shook his head, confused about what to do, fighting the urge to pull her closer yet, wrap his arms around her...kiss her.

The moment passed as she pushed off his chest. "Sorry." Her cheeks were flushed as she took hold of the wall once more. With a "you should dry yourself" she turned abruptly and made her way down the corridor.

Davin remained, frozen in place, the scene repeating in his head, Mina flying towards him, the feel of her touching him. Just thinking about her, made him breathless all over again. "Get a grip," he mumbled.

"Who are you talking to?" Kate stood before him, holding Peter with one hand, the other on the wall. When Davin shook his head, she continued, "Where were you? I've been looking all over for you." Her brown eyes flashed. "Peter is bored. I thought you should play with him a while."

Davin swallowed a nasty remark and turned his attention to the boy. It wasn't his fault they were stuck down here. But playing ball while the ship was constantly shifting was too dangerous. "What do you have in mind?", he asked.

"Don't know."

Davin offered him a hand. "All right, come here." He patted his knee. Peter climbed on, looking immediately excited again. "Let's ride." Davin wiggled his knees up and down like a bucking horse. Peter screamed with delight as Davin pretend through him off, caught him again. At some point, he stopped, throwing a glance at Kate who still watched them. "You can go, I'll take care of him."

Kate looked surprised, seemed to want to say something, closed her mouth and wordlessly wandered away.

Davin watched her go while he kept Peter entertained.

"You think I'll get a horse?", Peter asked after a particularly wild ride.

Davin smiled. "We'll see if there's room. A horse needs lots of space, it needs grass and somebody to clean and feed it."

"I can feed it."

"Of course, you can. But we want it to be happy and it's too early to make plans." He paused, looking earnestly at the small boy. "I promise we'll discuss it once we're settled." Peter took Davin's outstretched hand and shook it.

Eventually, Peter grew cranky, and Davin carried him to their bunk where Kate was already sleeping. He was glad to slip next to them silently. His clothes were still damp but the heat in here, albeit thick with stench, warmed him eventually.

Sleep was another matter. He was tired, his bones felt old as time, and yet, his mind refused to shut down. Was Mina awake? He imagined her lying in her bunk, pressed against her husband who...

He sucked air. They were married just like he and Kate. Why had Mina left so abruptly? Did she feel something for him as well?

He longed to be alone with her and just talk, learn more about her, make her smile. Impossible, especially now that people watched them.

It was early morning before he fell asleep.

CHAPTER THIRTY-THREE

Mina

As exciting as Regine's gift had been, now it presented Mina with another reason to worry. If Roland touched her somehow in the wrong spot, he'd find out and take the jewels and gold from her. She'd placed the belt with the gold around her waist beneath her dress, invisible to the eyes of others. But nights were a different matter, when Roland slept so close and his arm sometimes landed on her. Not to mention, if he wanted to lie with her. If anyone else found out, they'd steal or maybe attack her. People had been killed for less. At the same time, she felt guilty for carrying such wealth when Roland owed money to people on the ship.

In the morning, she made a decision. When Roland got up, she quickly sorted through the bag and picked out one of the wedding rings and switched it with the one on her finger. Luckily it wasn't much wider. Now she needed an opportunity to speak with the gambling men who still played cards, now with another fourth man.

Midmorning, she discovered them in the corridor. Luckily, Roland kept his distance these days and spent time talking to other passengers. After scanning the area, Mina quickly approached.

"I'm going to give you my ring," she said quietly to the man with the thick brows, "provided you keep it a secret from my husband. I don't want him to know that I paid his debt."

The man eyed her curiously, then placed his cards face down and got up. "You're afraid, he'll continue gambling."

"He has a problem. I never knew you were playing for money and that he owed…"

The man grinned and revealed crooked teeth in bad need of cleaning. "That's mighty nice of you."

Mina pulled the ring from her finger and handed it over. "Not a word."

Again, the man grinned, pocketed the ring and sat back down. "Glad to know you're doing the right thing."

Mina hurried away, sweating. If they only knew, if any of them knew that she was rich underneath those clothes. Already, Roland had urged her to search through the widow's luggage, but she had refused, saying it was unsafe when everybody could watch. She shuddered. Finding her knowingly carrying such riches would make him angrier than anything she'd ever seen.

Why hadn't she just left things alone? Surely, those men wouldn't have hurt Roland, not here where everybody was watching. But then, some men carried grudges forever. Maybe they'd wait for him to leave the ship and punish him. She couldn't live with herself if anything happened to him. Even if she despised him most of the time.

Down the corridor, she recognized Davin walking alongside his wife and boy. Could she trust him? What about Margarete upstairs? She was wealthy, but did that mean, she could be trusted with gold and jewels?

Listen to your gut, her mind commented. *Who do you know?*

But did one ever know somebody? They all carried armor and hid their thoughts and feelings. Adding greed to the equation was a recipe for disaster. Men murdered others to gain what they coveted. Should she have left Regine's treasure with the captain?

The heavy belt pressed her middle. She needed to do something quickly—before Roland found out.

In the afternoon she ran into Davin fetching water. They were on strict rations now, a seaman distributing even amounts to each passenger.

"I need a talk," she said when he passed her.

"I'll meet you upstairs later." The sea had calmed enough that they were promised an evening on deck.

Mina downed her ration, well knowing that she'd be thirsty before long. In fact, she was thirsty all the time these days. She suspected that the water kegs were almost used up and they'd soon receive even less. In the beginning they'd enjoyed a bit of tea or watery beer, but that had stopped after a few weeks. Mina suspected that the cabin passengers above had no shortage of beverages.

Clutching her shawl tighter around her chest, she climbed upstairs.

Already, the deck was getting crowded. If every passenger was up here, there was barely enough standing room. She decided to move to the forward mast, step behind it and wait.

The air was mild tonight, the wind almost calm. All sails were up to catch the last bit of breeze. Less wind meant more days on the ship. Mina briefly closed her eyes. *Please let it be over soon.* She wanted a bath, soap, and clean underthings.

"How are you?" Davin's voice was soft, yet clear and very close to her right ear.

She opened her eyes, surprised at the flutter in her middle. "Well enough." She looked around but nobody seemed to pay attention and Roland was likely still talking to the men, he'd been spending time with.

Fighting the urge to lean in closer, she whispered, "I need advice. Can I trust you?"

Davin nodded. "Of course."

"I received..." What was the word for valuables in English. She pointed at her empty ring finger.

"Ring...jewels?"

"Yes, jewels. I don't know how to protect." Their eyes met. In Davin's lay surprise and a bit of curiosity, but she found no greed. Encouraged, she continued, "I cannot trust Roland. He likes to play..."

"Gamble?"

"Yes, gamble." She looked at him once more. "If he finds out, I'm worried... He waste it all instead of helping us get a good start in America."

"You want me to protect your valuables."

"I can trust you, right?"

"Yes."

It was one small word, but she knew in that moment that he'd never betray her. "Will you take things and hide them well?"

He stared at her. Above them the sail billowed, shreds of conversation drifted across. "I don't know if I can...people are everywhere."

Mina kept her eyes on him. How good he looked...earnest, too. "Please?" She gripped his hand. "If he finds it, I will be in trouble. At the very least, he may play...gamble."

He nodded slowly then. "Not now. I'll go and find you again here at dusk."

After Mina watched him leave, she turned her attention toward the horizon. There was still no sign of land, but it wouldn't be long now. The gold belt weight heavily on her, the jewelry bag pressed against her chest. How had the widow endured such burdens?

Because she'd appeared modest in her dark clothes, had kept a low profile. *The way you look these days, nobody expects you of any riches*, her mind commented. Why had she endured such hardship when she could've traveled in a cabin upstairs? One never knew about people, maybe she was afraid to be robbed. Or she wanted to have the best possible start into her new life.

The itch from the unwashed skin was a constant now, a different dress was not going to fix that.

After preparing dinner, Roland appeared by her side and wordlessly slung down his porridge that Mina had enhanced with a bit of sugar from Regine's stores.

"Aren't you the least bit curious, what she left you?", Roland said, putting down the empty bowl.

"I am, of course, but I don't want the others watching. It's none of their business, what's inside and they'll say, I'm greedy."

"They say that anyway. First you get involved with that Mick and now you inherit the dead woman's things. Certainly convenient, don't you think? For all I know, you mixed something in her food?"

Mina nearly dropped the bowl. "Is that what people say?"

"No, but they say you're a witch, always looking for herbs and concoctions." He paused. "We'll put an end to that when we settle in Indiana."

Mina looked at the man, she'd married. How ugly he was. Not on the outside, but his being, his thoughts were as rotten as apples in spring. "I'm not involved with anyone, merely try to learn English, so we can find things, better connect to the locals."

Roland spit. "Hah, I saw him ogling you."

Deciding to ignore his comment, Mina bent forward to collect the cook ware. "I'm going to clean up now."

His fingers bit painfully into her arm. "That's all you're going to say?" Roland's voice was low and full of menace.

Mina straightened once more and faced him. "You're hurting me." She abruptly pulled her arm back and to her surprise, he let go. "What do you want me to say? I know you're unhappy...bored. None of us have anything to do, so you're not alone." She looked up at him, proud of her strong voice. "Soon, we'll arrive and another journey awaits, more than a thousand kilometers. Maybe you should find out about the way we'll travel. Speak to some of the men."

Roland's expression was hard to read. "Don't tell me what to do."

Despite his words, he sounded uncertain. Mina picked up pot and bowls. This time, he let her be.

Without another look, she hurried toward the stairs. He must not see the turmoil on her face. People were talking...the Irish man, Davin, was attentive, but was there more? She thought back at the moment, when he'd caught her in his arms during the rough seas. She'd felt him soften against her, sensed a reluctance to let her go.

She had felt it, too, her own body betraying her, responding to the touch of this man in a way, that made her blush. She was not going to give in, couldn't. He was married, so was she.

She shoved the cookware back into the case and took a deep breath. *Calm yourself. He is not ogling.*

Too nervous to remain and worried, they'd close the door, she hurried on deck once more. It was quieter now, the dinner hour behind them, some already settling in for the night. In a way, she understood why. It was easier to pass time sleeping, an escape from the reality of unmentionable filth and crowdedness. Not even the poorest of them had lived like that in Germany.

Ever so slowly, she made her way to the foremast, sometimes stopping to gaze at the waves, searching for dolphins that accompanied them for miles, sometimes watching the wind stretching the sails above. The entire time, she kept watch on the people around her, hoping that none would remain up front, where the wind was strongest.

The sun was low but still quite visible, the days getting longer. At home it would've been spring now, the trees and bushes flowering and she...likely searching the forest and meadows for edibles and her beloved herbs.

Roland's hurtful words returned, calling her a witch. Maybe he hadn't called her that, had pretended other passengers spoke of her in those terms, but she knew better, knew he was envious of anything she did...or did better or different. He was smallminded, and the longer they traveled together, the surer she was that she'd search for a different life, once they arrived.

She leaned against the base of the foresail to steady herself. The sun was gliding beneath the waves now, turning the edge of the horizon into a glorious orange and golden spectacle.

She shrieked when a shadow moved toward her, then recognized Davin.

"I'm sorry," he hurried. "Didn't mean to scare you." He pulled the hood from his head and smiled at her.

"I am distracted," she offered, unsure if the word was even the right one.

"We better hurry, they're closing the deck soon."

"Promise not to tell any person."

He gripped her fingers then, held them firmly between his. The touch calmed her, his face close now, indecently close. She heaved a breath. *Focus*, her mind commented. She pulled away her hand and removed the linen sack from beneath her shawl, handed it to him.

"Here, the jewels." He was about to tuck the bag into his jacket, when she stopped him, her hand landing on his forearm. "Wait. I want to keep my ring." She'd put her father's ring with the other pieces, when she'd handed one of the widow's wedding bands to the gambling men. Eventually, Roland would notice her ring missing and get suspicious. She rummaged through the bag and stuck her father's ring back on her finger. "Here. And this." She'd already removed the belt with the gold coins from beneath her dress and now handed it to him.

If he was surprised, he didn't show it. Like the bag, he stuck the belt inside his jacket. "I've got an idea. Once I hide everything, I'll let you know." Again, his hand found hers. "Please do not worry. I will return everything to you as soon as we arrive."

Their fingers intertwined as if they had a mind of their own. Mina's palm grew instantly warm, her breath sped up. All she wanted was to stand here with this man, lean against him, feel the goodness of his heart.

Somewhere behind them a seaman shouted that it was time to return below deck. A bell rang.

Davin peeked around the side, bent toward her and whispered, "You better go." He was so close now, she felt his breath touch her cheek. It was the most exciting thing, she'd ever experienced.

With a last squeeze, she let go and hurried across the deck, not looking left or right. Behind her, the door banged shut. The Irish man had chosen to remain outside. Surely, he'd get somebody to open for him later.

CHAPTER THIRTY-FOUR

Davin

Davin felt Mina's sack and belt push against his chest. They were of considerable weight. The widow had been wealthy, at least compared to the likes of him. He felt happy for the German woman, her life would become considerably easier. If only her husband weren't a gambler. Davin understood why Mina didn't want the valuables on her person. Most people down there had little to nothing, but if any of them found out, there would be theft.

He returned his thoughts to the plan, shaping in his mind, ever since Mina had mentioned the jewels. All he needed was a decent tool and he'd take care of things. At least until they arrived.

Darkness was settling on deck, and he carefully peered around the mast. Nothing was moving, the crew likely having a meal during these somewhat calm seas. Someplace near the stern, was the wheel that was always manned. He'd watched the crew and inspected the deck, knew there were hidden compartments with tools and tackle. All he needed was a chisel or screwdriver, ideally also a hammer. He tiptoed to a wooden box near the stairs and opened it carefully. Unable to see what was inside, he picked the oil lamp from the hook by the door and peeked inside.

Beneath coils of rope in various thicknesses, he saw something glint, some kind of metal hook. Better than nothing. He stuck it inside his coat and returned everything to its place, then began to whistle loudly.

"You...what are you still doing out here?", came the prompt shout from the back. In the shine of another oil lamp, the helmsman tied up the ship's wheel and hurried to meet him. "Steerage, I presume?"

"Sorry, sir, I fell asleep up front. The air was good and—"

"Yeah, yeah." The helmsman unlocked the door and let Davin pass. "Don't let it happen again."

Davin tipped his hat and climbed into steerage, the air growing thicker and nastier by the second. In back, in the corridor across from the last compartment, he'd noticed a door that except for a padlock was almost indistinguishable from the wall around it. He'd once seen it open when crew members had carried boxes and cases to stash there, so he knew it was an additional storage space. He walked casually to the end of the hall, quickly set the iron tool against the edge and applied pressure. Held by a nail, the metal loop, holding the lock, broke from the wood. He quickly opened the door and closed it behind him, stopped and retraced his steps. He had forgotten a light.

He plucked one of the two oil lamps that did little to brighten the corridor from the wall and returned, hoping nobody had seen him. It was a risk, but he could not leave such valuables in his bed or case, he had to find a spot few people would ever see.

The room was stuffed to the ceiling with wooden boxes, leather cases, trunks of all sizes. He crawled toward the outer wall and knocked on the paneling, which sounded hollow. He applied pressure behind each nail along the seam, and carefully pulled them out until the wooden board came loose. Behind it was a space of a foot-and-a half, strengthened by cross boards. He pushed against them...solid. Quickly, he placed Mina's treasure inside and replaced the board, used the tool to replace the nails. One bent, so he straightened it, glad for the knowledge he had, working with wood and building things.

Straightening, he pulled several boxes in front of the wall. On the last day, he'd return to retrieve the gold. Until then, it would be safe.

He stuck his head through the door. Good, the corridor was still almost empty, most people in a stupor at this hour. He quickly hammered the nail, he'd pulled from the lock, back into place with two hard swings. Done. Sometimes, darkness was a good thing.

He fought the urge to find Mina and tell her that he'd hidden her treasure, but knew it was unwise. He'd have to wait until tomorrow.

CHAPTER THIRTY-FIVE

Mina

Mina awoke, relieved Roland had already gotten up. What time was it? Down here, it was perpetually gloomy, but judging by the many empty beds, it had to be late morning. She realized she'd slept well for the first time in days, knowing that she didn't have to protect Regine's inheritance.

She wiped her hands on a rag and decided to cook breakfast. Roland would find her as soon as there was food to be had.

Luckily, the good weather was holding, so she took her spot in the line to cook, glad for the fresh air and wind on her skin. Some passengers had barely anything left, looking haggard and sickly. Still, there was no sign of land. In her mind, Mina counted backwards. They'd been on the ship for nearly six weeks now. If all went perfectly, the voyage took six weeks. But they'd had two days of no wind.

Behind the barrier, she noticed Margarete walking with a man in an elegant suit. They were involved in a conversation, and she didn't look up. Mina wanted to call to her and stopped herself. A rich woman like Margarete wouldn't want to be interrupted by some mongrel from steerage, no matter her kind words earlier. *But you are no longer poor*, her mind commented. *At least not destitute like most of the other passengers.* It didn't matter. She saw herself as poor and that's how she acted.

She'd just finished cooking and was looking for Roland, when he appeared out of nowhere, his eyes burning with anger.

"How did you do it?", he shouted, oblivious to the staring eyes of the other travelers. He gripped her hand like the other time, when he'd tried to remove her ring. Only this time, he tapped on it.

"What do you mean—"

"Your wedding band, how come you wear it, when you gave it to the men?"

Mina's mouth opened and closed. She'd asked the heavy-browed man to keep her secret, obviously he'd told Roland anyway.

Roland still hovered above her, his voice low. "Where did you get it? It's from the widow, isn't it?"

"What?"

"The ring you paid my debt with. What else are you hiding? She had more jewelry, didn't she? Except you wanted to keep it all to yourself." The menace in his voice cut through Mina. She wouldn't have been surprised, if he'd thrown her overboard. Instead, he began wrenching on the wrap, she wore to protect her shoulders and chest. Just a day ago, he would've found her hiding place. Now, his hands came away empty. Mina wanted to smile then, but she looked down instead. He could not learn about Regine's gift. Not ever. At least not here when she felt so alone despite all the people.

A crowd had assembled around them, welcome distraction from the boredom of the passage.

"It was Regine's ring," Mina said finally. "I wanted to pay your debt, so the men would leave you alone."

"I don't believe you," Roland said, his voice calmer now, his eyes still as seething. "You hid the gold coin from me on our trip. Now you sneak around, making deals with other men."

"I don't make deals, I paid off what you owed." Mina had spoken quietly, but other than the wind in the sails, nobody made a sound to catch every last word. Her thoughts wandered to Davin who stood nearby watching. In his expression she read his wish to interfere, to come to her side, even if he didn't understand the argument. Doing so, would make everything worse.

She nodded in his direction, then turned back to Roland. "I did not want you to come to harm." It was almost a lie. No, she didn't want him to get hurt, but at the same time, she wished for her freedom from him. Right now, trapped on the ship, it was a moot point.

Wordlessly, Roland gripped the bowl of food, she had cooked, and pushed through the crowd, undoubtedly licking his wounds.

Conversations began anew, a man started up his fiddle, another sang. The entertainment of the warring couple was over.

Mina readjusted her scarf and found a place to eat beneath the foremast. It seemed no more than fitting to sit where she'd met Davin.

She had just taken a bite, when Davin, Kate and Peter in tow, approached. "What happened?", he asked, helping his wife sit down next to her.

"Roland was angry," Mina said, well aware that she'd have to choose her words carefully. Not that she spoke that well yet anyway. But she didn't want Davin's wife to know anything, casually scanned Davin's body for signs of bulging pockets. What if he still carried her jewels? "I paid for the gambling. He thinks, I'm hiding something."

As if he'd heard her, he said, "So sorry, all is *well* with us." Their eyes met and he winked. "Maybe we can enjoy the nice weather."

"I can't wait for this darned ship to arrive," Kate said, her attention on Peter who was investigating a rope thick as his arm.

Mina mouthed a silent "thank you," and leaned back to finish her meal, her thoughts on the Irish man in front of her. He'd turned sideways, so she could see his profile, the fiery hair, much redder than her own, the straight nose and strong chin. He would do well, wherever he went.

In an instant, her inside ached, the envy for the woman next to her like a fist to her sternum. But her gaze continued traveling...down his neck, the strong shoulders and broad chest, lower still... Her cheeks grew hot. *What is wrong with you*, the voice in her head remarked.

In that moment, Davin turned to face her. No words were spoken, Kate still watching Peter, the air between them filled with tension, an invisible line connecting them like an intimate touch. In the sunlight, his eyes were a lighter shade of forest green, a spring day when the leaves are fresh and juicy.

Mina's cheeks grew even hotter, and she turned her attention to the bowl and pot. "I better clean up," she said, scrambling to her feet and hurrying away. She could've sworn, she felt Davin's eyes burning a hole into her back.

Near the entrance to steerage, she grew aware of Roland sitting with the men, playing cards as if nothing had happened. How was it that they accepted him back, after he'd owed them, only to be rescued by his own wife? The old anger about his impulsiveness and disrespect, her inability to rely on him, returned. She hesitated, the rawness of her emotions for the Irish man still fresh. She needed time and space to collect herself, not get into another fight.

Ignoring her husband, she hurried below deck, stuffed the cookware into the box and slumped down on her bunk. The compartment was completely empty for once, so she lay back and stared at the ceiling.

What had Davin meant to communicate when he looked at her

that way? Making her sweat and uncomfortable, her stomach a whirlwind which made it near impossible to finish breakfast. She recalled the night before, when he'd touched her hands, the electricity she'd felt between them. She was going mad. And for the first time, she acknowledged that the man from Ireland was capturing her heart. It hadn't needed long discussions, walks in the park or doing social visits. A spark had ignited and created a blaze of emotions, she had never before experienced.

How could she pretend that nothing was going on? But she had to...play Roland's wife, the unhappy woman who stuck with her husband through thick and thin, even paid his debts. A life with a virtual stranger, a man from a different country, who was married on top and had a son was as impossible as swimming to America. If she understood him correctly, Peter was not his natural son, but nonetheless, the boy loved his father. How could she come in-between them?

A sigh rose and she realized, it was her own. What craziness? She had to distract herself, avoid seeing Davin, avoid talking to him. He'd saved her from Roland's wrath, protected her newly found wealth. But this, whatever this was, had to be stopped. Now!

She rolled on her side and tried to sleep. No such luck. Instead, Davin's face swam in her vision, sometimes so close, she saw his reddish beard glowing in the sun, then farther through a fog, unreal and floating.

Her skin was awake, tingled and buzzed as if a swarm of bees had descended. Next to her the compartment was filling with passengers. It had to be evening, yet she felt no hunger. Roland would be expecting her to cook or would he forget for the gambling he so loved. She remembered a time when he'd stayed out all night drinking and playing.

She decided to investigate and found him and the men in the corridor, the bushy eyed man dealing while Roland watched intently. Was he losing again? It was possible, likely. He didn't notice her passing and when she turned on the stairs, he was picking up his cards.

With another sigh, she climbed on deck. The sun stood low on the horizon, so it had to be after seven o'clock. She wandered along the railing, one hand outstretched to catch herself, should the ship buck too wildly. The wind had increased once more and she already dreaded, being sent below, maybe for days. *Please let it be over*, she mumbled. Almost automatically, she walked past the foremast, but the spot was empty. Maybe Davin was lying down next to Kate right now, his body pressed against hers, his—

"Mina?"

She turned as Davin rushed up to her. "I didn't see you all afternoon. Is something wrong. Are you well?"

"Just fine." She tugged at her wrap, hardly able to look at him after her lewd thoughts.

He took her hand, squeezed her fingers gently. "I hid your things in the storage room in back...behind a wall. It should be safe until we arrive." He was speaking hurriedly as if he were out of breath. She tried to focus on his words, but his hand on hers was distracting. He was still holding on, the skin of his fingers work toughened. "Mina? Are you listening?"

She returned her attention to his voice, the deep strong tone, she'd come to crave. "Yes, sorry. It is...I am very thankful." Did he notice the quiver in her voice? His face was so close, she longed to touch the red beard, stroke the line of his jaw. Embarrassed once more, she forced her gaze past his shoulder. "We better go inside."

He was still holding on to her hand, nodded and in an instant, bent closer, touched her mouth with his lips. Just lightly, no more than a flutter. A storm unleashed then as Mina reached for his neck and pulled him toward her. This time their lips met fully, the kiss deepened until she felt nothing but his chest touching hers, his warmth enveloping her like her best winter comforter.

Somebody called, the bell rang. Mina drew back, their eyes on each other. She felt hungry now, not for food, but for this man...to learn all she could about him, to spend time with him, lie with him...

"We must go," he whispered, his voice hoarse. His cheeks glowed and his eyes sparkled with life. "I want to see you. Alone." He sighed, then looked at her again. "It is difficult, I don't know what is going on, all I know is that there is something unique here...you—"

Mina heard a movement and then a crew member appeared behind Davin. She quickly turned toward the railing, wondering what the man had witnessed.

"Sir...time to go. You, too, ma'am."

Mina hurried off without another look. She had to get to her bunk without being seen and found out. Surely, what had happened was written plainly on her face.

CHAPTER THIRTY-SIX

Davin
Davin awoke, feeling Kate's hand on his belly. It had to be the middle of the night, for once all bunks were silent except for the occasional snoring.

He lay still, waiting, hoping she'd leave him be. Two days had passed since he'd kissed the German woman, had felt her body press against his, listened to her quickened breath. In her eyes, he'd read what he himself was feeling. However wrong, however ill-placed, they wanted each other. Was this love? Was that constant yearning, the feeling of wanting to take flight and be in each other's company, what songs and stories talked about?

The hand wandered toward his chest, then back down. He was instantly hard, his need for relief so strong, he wanted to cry out. At the same time, he felt guilty. Hadn't he just shown Mina how he felt? Now he was lying with his wife.

Kate's hand felt hot and something inside of him gave.

Minutes later he lay back, gasping for breath. He'd hardly known what to do with the intensity of his feelings and he knew, their source wasn't Kate. She'd been the outlet, a way to make it through the day without losing his mind.

After kissing Mina he'd tried in vain to see her again, had waited for her at the foremast both evenings, had passed her in the corridor, hoping to speak to her. She'd barely looked at him and worked on a sewing project instead, sat with a few other women or cooked for her husband.

From the looks of it, Roland was gambling once more and soon there'd be another blow-up. He'd considered stopping her, but he didn't want to appear desperate. Especially, since he was sure that anybody would read the emotions on his face. He felt that Kate was watching him carefully these days, her lingering gaze thoughtful and somewhat suspicious. He distracted himself by playing with Peter, teaching him the alphabet and doing word games.

On the third evening, he wandered back on deck after dinner while Kate was putting Peter to bed. In the distance, another sailboat was visible, hardly more than a speck, but a sign that they were not alone on the vast ocean.

Already, his heart ached, thinking that he'd not see her again once they arrived in New York. All that yearning would just fizzle, and he'd forever wonder what would become of her. Part of him wished to stay out here so he could hold on to the hope of seeing her, even in passing. He'd turned into a fool.

He continued down the railing when he noticed her standing near the foremast, hair wrapped in the shawl, her back to him. But he would've recognized her anywhere, the straight shoulders and narrow waistline, partially hidden in the too large dress of the widow.

He hurried over, making sure that nobody was near. "I missed you," he whispered.

Her eyes met his, immediately setting his insides on fire. "I miss you, too."

He touched her hand, then her cheek. "What will we do?"

She shook her head. "Nothing, we are stuck, both of us." She turned to look over her shoulder, faced him again. "Maybe we can write."

"Neither of us has an address."

"But we settle in Fort Wayne. We may meet in the street."

Davin scoffed. "That is not what I envisioned."

Again, she looked away, this time toward the ocean. "It's of no use."

"What if we tell them?"

"You mean, tell Roland and Kate?" Mina sighed. "He kill me before he lets me be with another man."

"Will you meet me?", he asked. "Tonight?"

"People are everywhere—"

"In the luggage room in back. I can show you where your valuables are hidden." The thought had come to him earlier today.

Mina seemed to hesitate, her eyes large with worry. "I do not know."

"Please?"
She nodded then. "After dark...the end of the hall."

Davin tiptoed noiselessly into the corridor, down the hall, the iron tool, he'd kept hidden in his bunk, stuffed inside his shirt. Except for the shine of a single oil lap, it was dark. He lit a second lamp from the wall and carried it to the locked door, removed the nails a second time and slipped inside, pushing the door closed behind him.

Except for a narrow space at the entry, the room was nearly filled to the ceiling with luggage. His heart hammered fiercely in his neck, his breath sounded loud in the stillness. The air in here smelled faintly of damp leather. *Get a grip.* He returned to the door and peeked through. What if she had changed her mind, what if she fell asleep or Roland was awake?

He closed the door again and took one of the boxes from a pile to sit down. They hadn't said a particular time, neither of them had a watch, so he'd wait a while, all night, if he had to.

Despite his nervousness, he must have dozed off, because a noise at the door startled him. He jumped up when a shadow slipped inside and then Mina stood in front of him.

"I'm late," she said, her voice shaky.

Davin checked that the door was closed and embraced her. "You are here." For the first time, he could solely concentrate on the woman in front of him, didn't have to be afraid to be overheard or watched. "Let me show you where your jewels—"

Mina's hand cradled his cheek and smiled at him. It was the first full smile he'd seen. "Later."

The next moment, their embrace tightened, and their lips met, warm and soft. Davin's body began to tingle and buzz, as he explored her mouth. Her breath quickened, her hand moved down his neck to his shoulder, lower.

He responded, his fingers having a mind of their own, began to wander, then stopped as he whispered, "I am in love with you, Mina Peters. I can show you the hiding place and then you should return. It was wrong of me—"

"We may never see each other again. This tonight," Mina placed a palm on his chest, "is all we shall ever have. Something to remember when times are difficult." Without waiting for his answer, she began untying his pants.

Davin pretended to be asleep when Kate and Peter got up. His body was so sensitive, he hardly knew what to do with himself. What had happened in that luggage room was beyond anything, he'd ever felt. It overwhelmed him to think that he'd been so ignorant. With Kate, he'd been performing his duty, but he'd never connected with her on an emotional level. With Mina, the world had stopped, their bodies had danced together, skin on skin, each inch of him alive and glowing.

This was what songs and stories were all about. Now he knew...and was equally elated and devastated. Already, he yearned for her again, wanted to see and speak with her, touch her to elicit those delicious sounds, he'd heard her utter. And knew that he'd never get to do it again, even if they traveled in the same direction to Indiana. From what he'd learned speaking to several of the men, most people traveled by ship on the Erie Canal. But the distance was mind-boggling and there were thousands of travelers. Who knew what plans Roland had made?

He'd found love and lost it already. She belonged to somebody else, so did he. Not that he felt guilty toward Kate, well, maybe a little, but he felt that she'd manipulated him somehow.

Nonsense, you had a choice. You could've gone back to Ireland or gone to work for the English railroad, nobody forced you to marry her. No, this was entirely his own doing and if he hadn't joined Kate, he wouldn't have met Mina. It was obviously fate for him to find and lose love at the same time.

Outside, a bell began to ring, followed by shouts. He slowly rose from the bunk, put on his shoes and climbed on deck where every single passenger was pointing, waving, and talking at once.

In the distance rose the skyline of New York.

CHAPTER THIRTY-SEVEN

Mina
Mina hadn't slept much that night after sneaking back to her bunk. She was reasonably sure, Roland hadn't noticed, he slept like the dead most of the time, especially after having gambled all day, but her mind and body were in such turmoil, she couldn't calm herself. What had she done? Aside from finding out that *this* was what love felt like, a monumental shift of what she'd known—until now. She'd considered herself fairly smart, at least in comparison to many in her village. But this new knowledge of bodily pleasures was overwhelming. How had she missed this, how could it be that with one man it was a chore, and with another it was heaven?

And the other thing...she'd committed adultery, had been with another man, breaking her marriage vows. It was a sin. Then why did it feel so good, so right? Why did *this* man feel so right? Would God see that she'd made a mistake and married the wrong person?

She'd hardly dozed off, when shouts and clanging woke her. She quickly followed the other passengers on deck where everybody was looking in one direction.

"New York...we've arrived...finally...", they shouted. Some had tears in their eyes, others hugged. The man with the fiddle played *Das Wandern ist des Müllers Lust* about a miller delighting in hiking the country. Some people sang along, others just hummed or stood silently as the ship crept closer to the shoreline.

She remembered Roland and discovered him up front, his eyes peeled on the new world. He gave her a rare smile when she joined him, her heart heavy and confused, not only about what she'd done, but the sadness she felt. She quickly wiped her eyes and forced herself to smile back.

Roland mistook her tears for joy. "Isn't it grand?", he cried, wrapping an arm around her shoulder, something he hadn't done in months. "Finally, we can leave this godforsaken ship."

Mina didn't answer, couldn't. Another voyage lay before them, one that would take many more weeks. Deep down, she hoped that Davin, who was also heading for Indiana, would be on the same journey—somehow.

She did not dare look around for fear that they'd make eye contact and she'd give herself away. Her heart pounded, just knowing he was up here, within fifty feet, breathing the same air. She pushed away the thoughts of last night, their skin touching in the most intimate way, his kisses caressing her, his fingers knowing.

At least now she knew what she'd been missing, she could dream about it, cradle the memory of him like a precious stone.

Her insides cramped. The gold...Regine's jewelry. She'd have to retrieve it before leaving the ship...before leaving Davin behind forever.

The captain appeared on deck and shouted instructions... "It'd take a few more hours...they'd dock at South Street Seaport in Lower Manhattan...everybody had to wait their turn. They'd collect the remainder of their luggage, form a line and exit the ship, papers in hand..."

"Where are we going next?", she asked, remembering Roland by her side.

"I believe an agent from Hapag-Lloyd will be waiting at port...with instructions on how to continue to Indiana."

But Mina was only half listening, because of the spectacle in front of her, the line of tall houses stretched for miles, ships of all sizes, vessels like theirs, fishing boats and steamers were coming and going. She'd never seen so many houses, such busyness. The air was a mix of smoke and fish and salt. This was New York...America, a foreign world she'd somehow have to get used to.

"We better sort and collect our bags," Roland said, meaning Regine's things. When they arrived below deck, she noticed that the door to the luggage room, the very spot, she'd been at with Davin a few hours ago, stood wide open and people were emerging with a variety of boxes and cases.

She indicated for Roland to follow her to retrieve Regine's trunk, the captain had mentioned. The wall was now exposed and there was no sign that something was amiss. Davin would need to sneak inside when everybody was done, which in the mayhem of things wouldn't be hard. But how was he going to hand her Regine's gifts? How could she return the belt with the gold coins to her waist in broad daylight?

They'd soon go their different ways, Roland would make sure of that. Or was Davin planning to keep everything anyway? The little voice in her head nagged as she followed Roland along the corridor, back to their compartment where people chattered animatedly while packing up and moving out.

"Maybe you should go back on deck," Mina said, "I'll watch over things."

"Sure." Roland flashed another smile, obviously glad to be able to watch the ship's arrival in port. "I'll get you when we're close."

Mina remained, hoping that the others, most had few belongings, would leave, hoping that Davin would come and search for her. She sat back down on the bunk to darn a hole in her wrap. Thanks to the widow, she now owned a complete sewing kit and was able to make repairs. The light was bad, which made her squint.

"I've been looking for you." Davin seemed out of breath but remained a few feet away. In the last bunk, a man was sorting through his bag. Nodding at him, Davin continued, "I still need to get my things from the luggage room."

Just the word luggage room sent heat to Mina's cheeks. "We are to move on deck," she said, watching as the other passenger hoisted his bag and nodded good-bye to them.

Davin immediately slipped inside and hurried to Mina. "Finally. I'm sorry." He took her hands, the warmth immediate on her skin. "It's been mayhem inside that storage room. I've got to wait until they're all gone. Where will I find you?"

"I wait here as long as possible."

"I mean when we leave the ship."

"Roland plans to find an agent, so we can arrange for the remaining passage."

"Me too. It's quite a ways, I understand."

She felt his eyes on her, his face so close, she wanted to lean into him, feel his strength. "We need to get the jewels now...before Roland sees—"

"Before Roland sees what?" Roland stood behind them, his eyes menacing.

Mina flinched as Davin let go of her hands and turned to face her husband. "Nothing. I'm just saying farewell, is all."

Of course, Roland didn't understand a word, so Mina stepped in. "He's saying good-bye."

"Is that it?" Roland's voice dripped with sarcasm. "I always knew something was going on with you two. Obviously, you've been messing around behind my back." He stepped forward and took a swing at Davin who easily swerved and light as a boxer slipped around him.

"I thanked him for teaching me English," Mina cried.

Roland scoffed, his expression a mixture of aggression and disgust.

"Everything is fine, I'm leaving." Davin meant to walk around him, when Roland took a swing that landed, thanks to Davin's quick reflexes, harmlessly on his shoulder. In an instant, Davin gripped Roland's wrist and bent it down and behind his back, obviously painfully because Roland's furious expression turned into a pained one.

"I am leaving," Davin said again, quietly and yet full of energy, leaving no doubt what would happen if Roland tried attacking again. He nodded at Mina and vanished down the hallway.

Mina remained, trying to get her composure, not letting Roland see, how upset she was. "We better pick up Regine's trunk from storage and get these things on deck."

Roland squinted, then took hold of the kitchen box. "I'll deal with you later."

Mina followed slowly with the remaining bags. The corridor was empty, the door to the luggage compartment wide open. Regine's trunk with her name and now Mina's added beneath in black letters stood in the middle of the nearly empty room. She hoped that Davin would retrieve her things. Should she find an excuse and return here? Roland took hold and dragged the heavy piece into the corridor, then asked one of the card players to help him lift it on deck.

Mina followed. Already a line had formed to exit the ship and the first cabin passengers were heading down a gangway. The air smelled of salt, garbage and fish, yet compared to steerage, it was heavenly. She took deep breaths, trying to take it all in. To the left and right, ships were docked between various buildings. Horse carriages, wagons, and people were everywhere. This was the new world, America, a vast land, she'd soon call home.

Home, what nonsense. She'd left it the moment she followed Roland into the night.

The twenty some crew were folding up sails and scrubbing the deck. The captain stood silently watching. Down below on the dock, Margarete was walking toward a building. Of course, the wealthy were allowed to leave first.

Mina sighed. What did it matter? They'd survived this impossible journey across the ocean, a few boards of wood separating them from a liquid grave.

Roland stood next to her, watching everything, but she did not see Davin or Kate and Peter. Had they already gone down the plank? How could he hand over Regine's gold without being seen. Aside from Roland, it wasn't safe to show such valuables in broad daylight. They'd been warned over and over to watch out for thieves and opportunists, fast-talking salesmen who had only one goal: to extract the last coins from weary travelers.

Her doubt from earlier returned. Maybe Davin had meant to keep it for himself all along, had pretended his affection.

Mina closed her eyes, realizing how starved she'd been for a shred of love, a bit of kindness. Her heart hammered as the line slowly moved ahead. She'd opened herself fully, maybe she'd fallen prey to a con man. Her chest ached as she remembered his eyes, the way he looked at her. Had he just played her, and she'd been too green to notice?

The line snaked closer to the exit. Not much longer. The captain had instructed them to enter the flat long building to their right to show their papers and register. Afterwards they'd report to the agent at Hapag Lloyd to get instructions on how to continue to Indiana, so Roland could fulfill the redemptioner contract.

Again, she scanned the docks, looked over her shoulder, but did not see Davin. With every minute they crept closer to the exit, her heart sank a little more. She'd been taken for a fool, her mind foggy with confusion as her body yearned for the Irish man. She was in love with him. And now he'd gone off with her inheritance. Not that she'd deserved special treatment from the widow, she hadn't earned it, she'd been lucky.

The gangway shook beneath her feet as they descended toward the quay. And then she stood on firm ground, both feet planted without the least bit of movement. Except her mind was playing tricks and it felt as if the earth they stood on were trembling. Tears shot into her eyes. The country she'd loved was gone. Here she stood in America, her new home except it felt so strange, so alien, voices shouting in English, speaking way too fast for her to understand. Several of the couples around them were hugging and crying with delight. They'd wanted to come here, wanted to start a new life—together.

She blinked a couple of times to chase away the tears and hurried to catch up with Roland, who'd taken down the trunk and pushed it a few feet every time, the line advanced.

Port authority it said above the door. Mina formed the words in her mouth, said them out loud. It sounded strange, not like her at all.

The man behind the desk wore a black cap and a bushy moustache that covered half his cheeks. He pointed a forefinger in front of him. "Papers please."

Roland didn't understand, so Mina told him to hand over their passports and the redemptioner document.

"Going to Indiana, right?"

"Indiana," Roland said, nodding at the man.

"You need to see your agent for your travel instructions."

Roland stared at the man, so Mina stepped in again. "Yes, sir, we see the agent. Thank you."

The man stamped their papers and handed them back. "Next."

They stumbled through the door and found themselves on the street. "Why don't you find the agent, so we know where to go next?" Mina said, looking for a spot where she wasn't in the way. People hurried this way and that, horses and carriages passed them.

"Don't you think I know that?" Roland had the usual squint on his face, the one he got when he was nervous and didn't want to admit it. He placed trunk and box next to her and rubbed his back. "Damn heavy. Don't think I can carry that for long."

Mina didn't listen. She was flagging a man in a suit, well aware that she had to look horrendous. "Excuse me, sir, we are looking for Hapag-Lloyd."

The man made a face like biting on a lemon and pointed down the street toward a brick building. "Over there..."

"How about a bathhouse?"

But the man hurried off as fast as he could, waving his arm as if to dismiss her.

"What did he say?"

"I asked him where we can bathe."

"We can't afford a bathhouse," Roland said. "Nor anything else...let me find that agent."

Mina remained silent. They had just a few German coins left which were useless here anyway. They needed to find an exchange, some place where they could get a dollar or two. She had no idea how much a dollar was worth, but she'd not eat if it meant clean skin. She wouldn't wait another day to bathe.

The thought of Davin returned, the man who'd run off with her money. With it, they could've lived well and traveled in style. Now they were destitute again, like in Germany. Roland didn't notice and squinted down the street again. "Where is the damn office?"

"The man said it's in the brick building."

Roland scanned the street and shook his head, mumbled something, Mina didn't understand. She searched his face, a terrible suspicion rising inside of her.

"Do you not see the brick building? The sign above says Hapag Lloyd."

"Of course, I see it," Roland scoffed. "I'm going then."

Mina looked after him. It wasn't the first time she'd thought that something was wrong with his eyes. She watched him meander through the crowd, stop a couple of times, and finally cross the street, stop again in front of the building, and finally disappear inside.

"Ma'am, looking to exchange dollars?" In front of Mina stood a man in a dusty suit and a full gray beard. "I'll make you a deal." When Mina didn't answer, he continued. "You want dollar?"

Mina shook her head. The captain had warned them about crooks, preying on newly arrived immigrants. "Sorry, no."

With a shrug, the man walked off, addressing another group who'd been on the ship with Mina. They began haggling, but Mina didn't pay attention. She felt bone-tired again, her stomach an empty pouch, her skin so itchy, she wanted to tear the dress from her body. The sun felt hot on her face, and she longed for a hat and a glass of cool water. All winter they'd been freezing, constantly searching for shelter or a hot meal. The boat trip had been cold due to the wind and damp, salty air. Now it was April and New York felt like summer at home.

She looked longingly at a building down the street. Vandyke and Brinley Dining Saloon it said above the glass doors. For a moment, she imagined herself walking inside, a waiter showing her to a table with porcelain dishes and real glasses.

"Looking for accommodations?" The man, stopping in front of Mina, looked like the coin trader—sleezy. "Cheap rooms, comfortable beds," he continued, ignoring her disgusted look. "From Europe?" he said knowingly. "This good country...the best."

"I don't have money," Mina said slowly. That obviously did it, because the man hurried off to find his next victim. Mina smiled grimly. Whatever the man offered had to be better than steerage. Where was Roland, what took him so long? She scanned the street for the hundredth time. Likely, he had trouble communicating, never expressing any interest in learning the language.

"Mina?" Hearing Davin's voice, she almost fell off the trunk. There he stood, his wife and son next to him. She looked up at his face, struggling to control her emotions. She wanted to scream, tell him what a scoundrel he was, at the same time, she longed for his embrace. "I'm sorry, I looked for you and then, the men in the immigration office wouldn't allow us to stay. So, we went out and I took care of a few things, got Peter some food." He was speaking so fast, she hardly could keep up, her eyes locked with his, refusing to move.

"I thought you left," she said simply. Again, she fought the urge to pound his chest and then throw herself into his arms.

He threw her a half-smile. "I would never betray you."

"What are you talking about?" Kate looked back and forth between them. "Davin, what is going on?"

"Nothing, I kept something safe and am now returning it." He bent low and quickly handed Mina the bag with the jewels and the gold-filled belt. "I meant to wait, but it was difficult with the crowd and everybody watching." Mina stuffed the items into her wrap, she now held on her lap. "Thank you."

Davin rose quickly. "We better go, have to catch a carriage to Albany."

Mina wanted to ask him other things, make him stand here with her, forget about Kate and Roland, just the two of them, holding hands...finding a room. *Get a grip.* Her cheeks blazed as she nodded. "Farewell then."

"Farewell." He straightened, his voice heavy, his eyes dark as an evergreen forest in the rain and full of secrets.

Secrets they'd keep between them forever.

"Wait!" She rose and pulled three gold coins from the belt. "For your travels."

He shook his head. "Keep it."

"I want you to have it."

Davin hesitated, then extended his hand. Skin touching hot against hers. "Thank you." There was a lot more written in his face...worry for her, longing. He gave a final nod, abruptly turned, and lifted Peter on his shoulders.

Helplessly, Mina watched Davin and his family walk off, down the street, around a corner. They were gone. From sight...and her life.

A sob rose from her then, harsh and loud, and full of sorrow. She knew with certainty that he'd been the one for her, even if he belonged to somebody else—

"What happened?" Roland's hand landed on her shoulder. "Are you sick?"

She looked up at him, wiped her face. "Everything is fine. I'm just homesick."

He shook his head and gruffly said, "Straighten up. We don't have time for that now. Need to find the stagecoach," he eyed the paper in his hand, "to Albany." He waved another paper. "Have a voucher for a meal at the depot. Let's go."

Mina remained seated, Regine's inheritance heavy on her lap. "Take a break. I've got to tell you something."

CHAPTER THIRTY-EIGHT

Davin

Walk, the voice inside Davin ordered. *Forget her, there's no future here, you must continue and get to your new home...Indiana.*

"Whatever did you do with that woman's things?" Kate asked as they marched up the street. The agent had explained where they'd catch the Albany post carriage that would bring them to the Erie Canal. "Please slow down."

Davin, Peter on his shoulders, dragging Kate's box with the other, looked at his wife who was out of breath and red in the face. "Sorry, it's complicated."

"You acted very strange with her." The irritated tone was back. "She looked at you like she was in love."

"Nonsense," Davin barked, and quieter, "I'm just tired and so is she."

"Then why were you handing her all those valuables?"

"I helped her hide them from her husband. He has a gambling problem."

"That's why she gave you the gold coins...for payment?"

"Yes." Davin didn't feel like talking and sped up again. "We may still catch the evening post."

But that was wishful thinking because when they arrived, a line of people snaked around the depot's office. Leaving Kate and Peter on a bench, Davin joined the line, only to be told an hour later that there would be no room for the next two days.

"Sorry, sir, I can book you the day after tomorrow, nine o'clock. Provisions will be covered during the trip."

"How long is the journey?"

"Figure a day and a half, give or take, with breaks, change of horses."

Davin suppressed a shudder. Sitting squeezed inside a carriage wasn't his idea of travel. "I've got a young son, we need a place to stay then."

The man who reminded Davin of his own father nodded. "Try Mabel's boarding house. They get most of our passengers."

"One more thing. I need a reputable place to exchange money."

The man tapped a forefinger on his lips. "Hmmm, I'd try the Bank of New York, oldest bank in the country."

Davin deposited the tickets inside his jacket and led Kate and Peter to the boarding house.

A woman in a charcoal-colored dress hurried to meet them. "Top of the morning, a young family, how darling, I'm Mabel."

"We need a room, two nights," Davin said, feeling self-conscious in the squeaky-clean reception room. His hands were gray with filth, so was the rest of him. Why hadn't he at least cleaned his fingers and face?

The woman didn't seem to notice his distress. "We've got a vacancy. Bath is extra." She slipped behind a desk. "I need you to fill this out, two nights, that's a dollar twenty cents including food." She smiled at Peter. "Don't suppose the little fellow eats much." She opened a glass bowl and placed a piece of what looked like a huge crystal on a piece of paper. "Here you go, little man, rock candy. Try it. Just watch your teeth, suck on it."

While Kate handed Peter the candy, Davin addressed the woman. "Excuse me, I've got a German gold coin, but need to exchange it first." He handed it to the woman who inspected it and gave it back.

"How 'bout I get you settled and while your wife takes a nice bath, you get dollars." She swept around the desk and placed an arm around Kate who looked surprised and thankful."

In the evening, they gathered at one of the tables while Mabel and two young girls dished up potato soup, meatloaf, roast chicken, lamb and rice, followed by custard and apple pie. Davin would've wished for a whiskey or strong Irish ale, something to remind him of home, but Mabel's establishment did not serve alcohol.

Other than that, he felt almost happy. He'd taken a bath, changed clothes, had his hair and beard attended to at the barber shop next door, his skin smelled of nothing but soap and the permanent itch was gone. But on the way to the bank, while he sat in the tub and scrubbed months-old filth from his skin, had his beard shaved off, and now, sat in the merry round of travelers, his thoughts went to the German woman.

He'd left her there on the street, dumped the gold into her lap and run off when all he'd wanted was to remain by her side, keep an eye on her, hold her hand...

She likely took the same route as him to Indiana and from what he gathered, they'd live in the general vicinity of Fort Wayne. How far apart, he had no idea. But there was a chance they'd meet again one day and that, right now, had to be enough to sustain him.

Most of the other travelers were heading west, some to Indiana, others farther to Illinois and beyond. Some of them spoke no English, the conversation between them reduced to an occasional word or greeting, hand signals and smiles.

As before he had little to say to Kate, nor she to him. When Peter fell asleep at the table, Davin carried him upstairs. Their room was small, but as clean as his mother's home. His stomach pressed painfully against his ribs, he'd eaten way more than was good for him.

When they laid down, Kate's hand landed on his chest which meant an invitation. Davin ignored it, but the hand began to wander up to his neck and then down...below. He finally gave in and crawled onto Kate. But something was off, his body uninterested.

"Something wrong?", Kate asked, her breath quicker than usual.

"Nothing is wrong." Davin moved back to the side of his bed and stared at the ceiling. "I'm tired, is all."

But the next morning, while Peter was still asleep, Kate's attempt fell flat a second time. It was as if there were some barrier between them, he could not break through. His body didn't feel like his own, his mind distracted.

If Kate was angry, she didn't say, except her expression seemed more aloof than usual. They didn't speak during breakfast and only what was needed to keep Peter entertained. They went out to purchase a set of clothes and shoes for each of them, including hats to keep away the sun, a few necessities like a comb, soap and skin cream, a new ball for Peter and a traveling bag. Everywhere they went, Davin searched the streets and shops for signs of Mina or Roland, but there were none, just hundreds of strangers, many of them immigrants, their eyes full of wonder, pointing this way and that.

By the time, they climbed into the carriage, Davin was glad to leave the busy town. He wasn't used to such crowds, the narrow, bustling streets made him nervous and uneasy. He couldn't imagine living here, even if thousands of Irish had already settled. No, he needed space to breathe, fresh air and a home with a garden.

They stopped every few hours and while the drivers switched horses, Davin took Kate and Peter into the depots to freshen up or get a bite to eat. Their money was dwindling fast again, but he'd soon earn something, maybe work on the side. His backside felt sore from the bumpy road that shook the carriage mercilessly and he felt grimy all over again from the dust and heat inside the carriage.

They were squeezed on a bench next to a single man and another couple with a little girl, not much older than Peter. Off and on, he dozed off or escaped into a daydream where he was walking hand-in-hand with Mina, only to realize that that could never happen.

They arrived in New Albany the following evening, spent another night in a boarding house, and embarked on the packet boat in the morning. It was a strange looking ship, long and skinny and low on the water with a single room, they'd live in together for several days. Supposedly, traveling the canal was the fastest way to get to the Midwest. Hard to believe they'd make progress at all, Davin thought, after seeing the mules strung to the boat. Apparently, they'd pull the vessel all the way to Lake Erie, more than three hundred miles. And the canal was so narrow and low, the boat barely fit, an utterly different experience than crossing the mighty Atlantic.

At least he felt safe. They may be slow, but there was no rough sea, no threat of drowning or seasickness. Kate seemed in better spirits too, talking to the family with the girl who also boarded the boat.

For mealtime, the fifty or so travelers set up a long table that ran almost the length of the room. The ship's cook provided all the food, another luxury, Davin appreciated after eating cooked grain for weeks. At night, Kate and Peter slept in the forward part behind a curtain with the other female travelers, a fact he liked. Since their failed attempts in bed, he had even less interest in trying again.

Maybe something is wrong with me. He was lying on a narrow cot that was hanging from the wall of the boat, one of dozens, folded out at night and tucked away during the day. Now that they were approaching the final destination, he was growing more and more nervous, wondering where they'd live—he'd forgotten to ask the agent for details—and what sort of work he'd perform.

CHAPTER THIRTY-NINE

Mina

Mina had told Roland about Regine's inheritance with reservation, knowing full well that he may go crazy gambling. But to her surprise, the most extravagant thing he did, was to order red wine with dinner.

After Mina had spent the afternoon in a bathhouse and shopping for a new wardrobe, they were staying at a small hotel. Roland had exchanged some of the gold ducats for American coins, a few gold and mostly silver, keeping some of it for himself. How much exactly, he hadn't told her, but she didn't want to argue again.

"Imagine what we can do with the money," Roland said, emptying the bottle into his glass. "No more scraping." He smacked a hand on the table. "Maybe I'll get a horse. Shouldn't be that expensive. I'll learn to ride, maybe raise horses."

Mina sipped thoughtfully from her wine. "You'll have to work, too. That agent said it is an iron forge and you won't get paid the entire time."

Roland's expression darkened for a moment. "Not sure what I'll do there." He took another sip and waved the waiter to bring a whiskey. "I can't believe that old hag carried all that cash with her."

"She was no hag, her husband did well before he died suddenly."

"And to think she left it to you, just like that," Roland continued as if he hadn't heard her.

"It was coincidence. I was there, trying to help her, when she fell ill. It all happened so fast."

"You and your witchcraft."

Mina felt the old anger rise. "It isn't witchcraft to know about the healing powers of herbs."

Roland downed the whiskey in one swig. "Why don't you leave it to the doctors?"

"I enjoy it. Not everyone can afford a doctor and we've had to supplement our meals often enough." Roland's eyes searched the room and Mina asked herself, if he was going to order more alcohol. "I'd like to pay and go to bed."

"Just one more," Roland said, half rising from his seat, calling loudly. "Where can a man get a decent drink around here?"

Mina noticed the couple from the neighboring table watch them. "Why don't you sit? I'm sure the waiter will return any moment."

"Don't tell me what to do," Roland said. The demons were back, and Mina knew she'd made a mistake. It would've been better to hide the money indefinitely, at least until they arrived in Fort Wayne. "Over here," he yelled when the waiter entered the dining room. "Whiskey, please...or better yet, I'll find a real pub where the service is better."

"We'd like to pay," Mina said quietly, her cheeks aflame with embarrassment and fury.

Roland threw down a few of the unfamiliar coins, hardly bothering to count them out. It was way more than they owed, and Mina was tempted to count them. At this rate, they'd go through the money in a matter of months or even weeks, if Roland decided to gamble again.

She had to do something to stop him.

"You go to bed, don't wait for me," he said as they walked out. Already his gait was wobbly from the unfamiliar liquor.

"How about I'll accompany you," Mina said. All she wanted was to go and rest, but the thought of Roland getting himself into trouble wouldn't let her sleep anyway.

"Suit yourself."

It was pure revulsion to watch her husband ordering one drink after another, his words slurred, his eyes glassy. He slammed the fistful of gold and silver coins on the table, everything he had kept for himself. "That should last a while," he mumbled.

Of course, the bartender didn't hesitate to supply him with liquor. Soon, half a dozen leeches joined him, each of them accepting free drinks from Roland.

"Let's go home," she said several times, but he'd just wave at her as if she were some bothersome mosquito. "Quit your nagging, I'm having fun," he cried, eliciting loud laughs from his new friends.

Mina watched and wondered why he wouldn't pass out, why he would continue drinking, no matter how intoxicated he was. The only saving grace was that nobody here knew them and tomorrow, they'd travel far away.

While Roland staggered to the outhouse, she slipped the remaining coins still lying on the table into her pocket, walked to the bartender, paid the bill and said, "If you serve my husband one more drink, I'll call the police. Tell them, that I received lewd advances and that you are preying on unsuspecting immigrants."

The man behind the counter eyed her curiously, then smiled and nodded. "No worries, missy, I'll help you carry him out myself."

When Roland staggered back to the table and blared at the top of his lungs that he was thirsty, the barkeep, a colleague in tow, asked him to leave. "Go home and take care of your wife."

"She can go home by herself," Roland slurred, eyeing the man.

"In that case, we'll help you outside." Without another word, they took Roland by the arms and escorted him to the door, Mina rushing after them, while Roland's newfound friends slinked back to their tables.

"You did that, didn't you," Roland said, walking off.

Mina kept her distance, trying to remember which way they'd come. It was late, the street empty except for a couple of cats chasing each other and a man snoring on a bench. This big unruly city gave her the creeps and she wanted nothing more than to be in her bed.

"This way," she repeated several times as he stumbled along. The alcohol was finally slowing him down and she worried, he'd lie down someplace. "Come on, not much farther."

She breathed a sigh of relief, when the hotel came into sight. Roland passed out immediately, so all she did was take off his shoes. Then she fell into a chair and inventoried their money. He'd spent at least four dollars on liquor, a fortune, where they'd come from.

New worry crept up inside her. She needed to find a safe place for the money, one he couldn't get to. But until they arrived, there was no option but to carry and hide everything. Under no circumstances could Roland repeat what he did today.

Roland refused breakfast, his face puffy and white, his forehead pearling with sweat. Serves you right, Mina thought, stuffing herself before the long ride on the stagecoach.

Not long after they took off, Roland got sick, hanging his head out the window. The other passengers looked at him and Mina with disgust, the small sticky hot space reeked with vomit. Mina wanted to disappear into the ground and hoped, none of those four passengers would take the boat, especially, the pointy-nosed woman with the black lace hat and bulging blue eyes, who kept watching her. Mina could just about read her face that spoke of her snoopiness.

But no such luck, when they arrived in Albany and lined up for the packet boat, the nosy woman was waiting in front of them.

At least Roland was doing better by now, though he said little and the glances, he threw her, made her shiver all over again. He'd undoubtedly found his pockets empty and now wondered, what had happened. Given their previous fights about money and Mina's tendency to hide what he thought was his, he'd just wait for an opportunity to steal it back. If nothing else, he'd threaten or hurt her.

Already, Mina studied the faces of the other men to guess if they were interested in gambling or carried strong liquor with them. She realized that Roland would never rid himself of his demons, he wasn't strong enough and lacked the discipline. If she wanted to succeed in this new country of America, she'd have to do it on her own, preferably without him.

CHAPTER FORTY

Davin

Davin was equally bored and anxious as days turned to nights, turned to days, as the boat crept through the lands, stopping every few hours to change mules, stopping at the more than a dozen locks. While a part of him couldn't wait for the journey to end and to finally arrive, the other part of him dreaded what was next. For months, he'd been running and searching, now he was almost at this destination where he'd have to create a life for Kate and Peter, for himself.

He'd live and work among strangers, Americans and other immigrants, likely Germans. What if he hated it? Kate with her passive ways had nothing to add to their relationship. Only with Peter did she come to life, cared for him like only a mother could. He was relieved, he was sleeping with the men in the back of the boat, a safe distance from her perusing hands.

Even if he craved privacy, he was not looking forward to being alone again with her. He couldn't even exactly say why. Surely, the German woman hadn't bewitched him, only that for the first time in his life, he'd understood what bodily *love* actually meant when it was in unison with mutual feelings of respect, love, and care. Heat rose inside him if he only thought about the way her kisses felt on his lips...his skin. Not to mention the other things they had done. Things that had carried him away like the wings of an eagle.

It seemed not worth it to go through the motions with somebody else, not even if that somebody was his wife. Or would he somehow develop feelings for her after a time out of convenience, maybe friendship and was that enough?

He'd simply concentrate on the important issues, learning to fit in at his job, whatever that was, joining the community, building relationships...taking care of his family by providing them with a roof and food.

They arrived in Buffalo five days later, more rested than he'd thought possible, and continued on with another ship, a steamboat across Lake Erie to Toledo. Thankfully, the agent had provided them with the necessary paperwork and traveling plan, of course, they wanted to take advantage of his skills.

And then, after another day and night, on the morning of May 12, 1849, Davin, Kate and Peter set foot on the docks of the Wabash and Erie Canal in Fort Wayne. Somehow, Davin had expected a quiet place, a port of sorts sure, but not this...mess of warehouses, hotels, pubs, depots, and assorted businesses, offering everything from a ten-minute hair cut to a dress-made-to-order in a day.

This was their new home and it reminded him of Dublin and New York with its busy, noisy streets.

He asked Kate and Peter to wait for him in a small eatery and headed down Water Street. The offices of Williams Construction were supposed to be located on Pearl Street. After asking for directions, he finally entered a two-story brick building.

He knew he didn't look particularly trustworthy or skilled, his suit once again covered in dust, his hair shaggy and his shoes scuffed.

"Sir, I'm here to report for employment," he addressed a narrow-chested man behind a desk who was entering numbers into a book.

The man gave him a once over but didn't move. "You have an appointment?"

"I just arrived on a packet boat from Ireland."

"Wait here." The man carefully put down his ink pen and walked in measured steps to an adjacent office.

Words drifted through the open door..."...another immigrant, Irish, I think...yes...who knows."

Tired and out of patience, Davin marched past a handful of employees and entered the office where a man with gray sideburns, nearly as bushy as his beard, occupied a massive desk. A sign said P.F. Williams—the boss, "Sir, my name is Davin Callaghan, I've traveled six months and thousands of miles and I'm ready to settle." He pushed his redemptioner contract across the desk. "If you don't mind, I'd like to get started as soon as I'm moved in." According to the agent, the contract provided room and board, but no other income. In exchange Davin would work for the company for three years to pay off the passage.

The man with the sideburns adjusted his golden spectacles and studied the paper. "Carpenter, eh? What did you do there...in Ireland?"

"Built houses, roofs, windows, furniture. It's made with wood, I can do it."

"That we shall see." The man mumbled something to his underling who waved at Davin to follow him.

"I'm sending somebody to show you to your place, wait here." He disappeared and shortly returned with a rough looking character in ragged pants and a sweat-stained shirt. "Billy here will take you. Report to work tomorrow morning, seven o'clock sharp. We'll discuss everything then."

He waved Davin's contract. "I'll keep it...for review."

Davin, exhausted and confused, followed Billy outside and down the street. They kept walking at a fast clip, the streets growing narrow and jagged, the homes alongside small and in ill repair.

"Where are we going?"

"Camp," Billy said, hurling a wad of tobacco spit at Davin's feet. "You fellows live together."

Davin ignored it. "Which fellows?"

"Redemptioners, you immigrants, German and Irish folk."

"I thought we get a house."

Billy grinned, revealing an assortment of brownish stumps. "House, haha. You get a villa and I'll shit on a golden throne." Davin was so perplexed that he almost didn't notice when Billy stopped and pointed at five cabins, a couple of rickety tables between them, the ground covered in high grass and refuse. "I thinks there's a free bunk in the one on the right."

Without another word he turned to leave, but Davin was faster. "Wait a minute! I've got a wife and son, we can't live here. We need a separate house, some place safe." He imagined Kate and Peter waiting for him at the river, impossible to bring them to this dump.

Billy shrugged. "You take it up with the boss tomorrow. I've got to report to work, or I'll be in trouble. Is late as it is."

Davin shook his head, then followed Billy. "I'm taking it up with the boss now." Billy abruptly stopped, spit again, this time right on the top of Davin's shoe, a brown glob that gradually slid off and disappeared in the dust. Davin took a deep breath. "Give me one good reason, why I shouldn't smack you in the nose right now." He glared at Billy, who was six inches shorter, but stout as a tree trunk. "It better not happen again, I haven't come here to be insulted by the likes of you."

Billy grin froze, then disappeared. "You looking for trouble, you found it. Boss won't put up with your insub...nation."

"Insubordination. None of your business, you go back to your job, I'll take care of mine." With that, Davin marched off, leaving Billy standing there open-mouthed.

"I need to speak with Mr. Williams," he said upon entering the company once more. The little man behind the desk looked up surprised. This time, he hurried off.

"Mr. Williams will see you now," he said moments later. "He has another appointment in five minutes, so be quick about it."

"I haven't come all this way to be treated like a slave," Davin said as soon as he entered, the room filled with smoke from Williams' cigar. "I've got a wife and child, and my contract says that we will be provided with adequate housing."

"Wife and child, I see," Williams said, sucking on his cigar. He leaned back and squinted at Davin. "A little hot-headed, aren't you, Mr. Callaghan. Heard that about you Irish." He flicked a piece of ash from his too tight suit that stretched over an ample belly. Abruptly, he leaned forward. "I tell you one thing, Mr. Callaghan. I haven't made it to the largest construction firm in the area by listening to the likes of you. You signed a contract to work for me. Need I remind you, I paid for your passage. You came from nothing, otherwise you wouldn't be here. That country of yours is going down the drain. Crops dead for years, folk dying by the millions." He puffed a cloud of smoke in Davin's direction. "You will fulfill your contract or I'm calling the police to arrest you. Is that understood?"

Davin was tempted to ring the man's neck and tell him how the English had exploited Ireland, caused his fellow countrymen to die because they took every kernel of grain for themselves, but it would be a mistake and he was here to start a new life...a better life. "I'm prepared to fulfill my contract, sir," he said calmly. "I simply need a place for my family. They can't bunk with a bunch of men."

Williams eyed him from across the desk, puffed more smoke...the moment extending. Davin remained...waiting. *Come on you fat blob.*

"I've got no place right now, the men will clear one of the cabins."

"Right now, what does that mean?"

"I'll think of something." He waved a dismissive arm. "Now scoot." Davin swallowed an insult and turned on his heels. He needed to get Kate and Peter off the street, out of the heat. "And Callaghan, don't ever walk into my office again uninvited."

Ignoring his boss, Davin marched past the desks, outside where he let out a shout. His new life was already a disaster.

CHAPTER FORTY-ONE

Mina

"You hid it, didn't you?" Roland was sitting next to her on the deck of the packet boat, where the travelers were watching the landscape pass by in excruciating slowness. The sun shone high in the sky, but the cabin felt like an oven right now and Mina was glad for the slightest breeze, her dress way too warm for the unaccustomed heat. Worse was the humidity that seemed to permeate her skin and made her woozy. Once in a while, they were ordered to lie flat, when the boat passed beneath one of the low bridges. Somebody had told a gruesome story, where a young woman had died, her head being squashed after ignoring the captain's orders.

Mina opened her eyes, her mind foggy. "What?"

Roland looked at her, that look he had, when he was spoiling for a fight. Once again, he was forced to be idle, a state he could not tolerate. To Mina's relief, nobody had offered to play cards or dice, the men on the boat an older crowd. "The money, you took it from me."

Mina thought of the belt, she wore beneath her dress that contained most of the remaining ducats, Regine's jewelry and the American money. "You spent it on liquor, remember." She knew full well that Roland remembered very little from that night. "You ordered many rounds for the men, people you didn't even know." She paused, contemplating whether she should continue. She hated making a scene up here where everybody could listen in. The nosy woman was watching them enough as it was. "Anyway, I hope you'll like your new job."

"Answer me."

"I'm keeping things safe...until we get there." Against her better judgment, she leaned closer. "We don't want somebody to steal from us."

"Give the money to me," Roland said. "I'll keep it safe, I'm the man."

What a man you are. "Please keep your voice low," she whispered. "Nobody needs to know." Why did he always make a scene in the middle of a crowd?

His hand closed around her wrist. "Don't think I don't know what you're doing. It won't work. As soon as we arrive, I'm taking over. Understood?"

Mina forced herself to nod, then looked pointedly to the front while she shook off his hand. Tears pressed, not only from the pain in her arm, but the fight she had to continue constantly, Roland's abuse and unpredictability. All she could hope for now was that very soon he'd be tired after working all day, too tired to gamble or drink. Why had she told him about the money? It was like a slow poison, dripping into his brain, making him lose his mind.

The sun beat down on them when the boat dropped them off in Fort Wayne. It was early afternoon, Mina's forehead pounded under a hammer, an unusual phenomena, because she did not tend to get headaches. All she wanted, was to lie down in a cool place. Of course, there was none, the river front bustled with people, each one of them knowing where to go. Except the two of them. Roland was supposed to report to the iron forge where he'd work for the next four years. Supposedly, they'd also provide housing.

What kind, she'd wanted to ask, had planned to accompany her husband, but she felt weak and tired. After a refreshment in one of the eateries on Water Street, she remained behind while Roland took off.

Mina closed her eyes and dozed. It wasn't proper, but she couldn't help herself today. The proprietress, a woman in her forties with blond hair swept into a loose bun, had been watching her, she'd likely be kicked out. How she missed Augusta. She'd have taken care of the situation and done something to help. She was about to order another lemonade, when the owner waved away the waitress and stopped by her table.

"You're feeling ill, aren't you?"

Mina opened her eyes wider, all of a sudden feeling weepy. What was the matter with her? "It is the heat, I am new to the area."

The woman chuckled. "You don't say. Of course, you are new."

She stepped closer. "I've got a parlor in back, why don't come and lie down for a bit, while your husband gets his employment sorted out." Mina was about to say something, but the woman continued. "People arrive every day and from the looks of you, you've come a long way." She extended a hand. "I'm Paula Arends, call me Polly." She lowered her voice. "Once upon a time from Mannheim."

"You are German," Mina said, surprised she'd not picked up on Polly's accent.

"I try hard to fit in," Polly said. "It's better for business."

Mina introduced herself and followed Polly to the back. It was dark here and a breeze came through the open windows. She immediately felt better and accepted the chaise, Polly offered her. "I'll get you a pitcher, just to yourself." She patted Mina on the shoulder. "Don't you worry, it will all right itself.

How long will it take to lose the homesickness, to feel like you belong, Mina wanted to ask. But as soon as she leaned back, her eyes closed and she dozed off.

In her dream she was walking across a meadow, a basket of wildflowers in her hand. Bees swarmed, butterflies danced, she hummed a tune, something about birds in the spring. She felt light, almost weightless, as she hiked to the crest of a hill. Beyond lay a cabin, surrounded by a garden with corn and beans. Bed sheets billowed in the breeze and beneath them sat a little girl of no more than three with long curly red hair. Mina called out to draw the girl's attention, but it remained sitting there, playing with some imaginary toy. Mina began to run then, down the hill, but the faster she ran, the farther the cabin moved away. By the time she stopped, she was out of breath, her legs weak and achy—the cabin no more than a dot on the horizon.

She awoke, her mind reeling from the dream. Somehow, she knew that what she'd seen was the life, she should've let, had she lived with Davin—a happy fulfilled life in the country, raising a daughter.

"Better get up." Roland towered above her, his forehead and cheeks glowing with sunburn and heat.

Mina pushed away the sadness and rose slowly. The pitcher was still sitting there, so she filled her glass and drank, filled it a second time and handed it to Roland.

"Ready?" he asked, not once inquiring how she felt. She nodded and reattached her hat.

"I need to find the owner, I want to thank her."

"Can't it wait? I want to get to our place."

Mina sighed. "It can't wait." Leaving Roland standing in the entry hall, she found Polly behind a desk in the office. "I really appreciate your kindness."

She opened her purse, but Polly waved at her. "No worries, you come and see me any time, you hear?"

Mina nodded, again she felt weepy. "Did you learn something?", she asked Roland, trying to distract herself.

"I start tomorrow." He pulled out a piece of paper. "Here's the address of our place. Better help me find it." He lifted the trunk to his shoulder while Mina carried their bags.

Several times, she asked passers-by, again and again, they had to rest because they grew too tired to carry their things. At some point, they arrived on Reed Street. Narrow cabins squatted on either side, each of the identical except for the occasional flower in the front. Dust from the dirt road covered everything and Mina had the strong urge to turn back.

Their place was number fifteen and when Mina climbed the rickety steps to the front door, she discovered that several of the boards on the tiny porch were missing. Somebody had obviously needed to make repairs and helped themselves to more firewood.

Roland unlocked the door and stepped inside where he let go of Regine's trunk. The room was as small as their cabin in the homeland but in much worse shape. One of the two panes in the window was missing and had been patched with tarpaper.

The cupboards were as empty and filthy as the floor. A layer of dust had also wandered inside, Mina felt like she had grit between her teeth. A bird's nest lay in the fireplace, long cold since somebody had lived here. The bed in the corner had seen better days, too, the only good thing was the headboard, carved from a single piece of oak. There were neither sheets nor pillows, just an old straw-filled mattress, where, she suspected, mice had been taken up house.

This was supposed to be home...for the next four years? Right. She shook her head to chase away the image of her working and living here.

Roland opened the back door that led into a ten-by-twelve-foot backyard, filled with rubbish, weeds and an outhouse. "It isn't that bad," he said, when he returned. "You'll make it cozy, I know it." He patted her on the shoulder like one pats a dirty dog.

Mina's throat was dry with thirst again and afraid, what she'd say to him, searched for a bucket. She found a dented one made of tin and returned to the street. Three houses down, she discovered a woman sweeping the front step. She looked thin as a rail, but the broom seemed to dance as if possessed.

Mina shielded her eyes against the afternoon sun. "Excuse me, I'm looking for a well."

"Let me show you," the woman said in German, apparently glad to take a break. "You are new, from Germany, I take it?"

"Löwenstein in Württemberg, you won't know it."

The woman giggled and extended a hand. "We lived in Heilbronn, almost down the street, I'm Annie."

Mina introduced herself, explained that Roland would work for the forge.

"They all do, dear, we arrived last fall. It's a drag, living here, but Willibald signed a contract, so we're stuck until he's paid up." She pointed at the pump. "I remember arriving and wishing to return on the spot." She giggled again. "You'll get used to it."

Annie operated the pump. "Water is good, laundry a drag. But we help each other, best we can." She eyed the bucket, Mina was lifting. A thin stream ran out of the bottom. "Oh my, you'll need a new one. That is only good for storing something dry." She waved. "Quick, quick, wash your hands and face, take a drink. I'll loan you mine until tomorrow." She tipped a forefinger on her lip. "Better yet, I'll take you to the general store. You'll need a few things."

By evening Mina and Roland sat in the middle of a mess of boxes and household goods, sheets and blankets for the bed, a set of dishes, cutlery, glasses, linen and cotton towels, rags, a cast iron pot and pan, shovel and rake for the garden, broom, and a tin tub and new bucket. A lot of it had come from Regine's trunk and Mina had also bought cans of meat, lard, bags of flour, oats, potatoes, rice, salt and sugar and assorted spices, thanking Regine more than once for saving her.

Roland hadn't said a thing as she went around the store, picking this and that from the shelf, asking the storekeeper, Mr Philipps, for advice. As a thank you for her large purchase, he added a jar of molasses and delivered everything with his horse-drawn wagon.

Still, the gold she carried was substantial and she was anxious to hide it—before Roland would drink and gamble it away.

CHAPTER FORTY-TWO

Davin

Three days after their arrival, Davin, Kate, and Peter were still stuck at camp. Supposedly, there was no housing available because of the influx of immigrants and the rapid growth of Fort Wayne. Kate looked murderous and hardly spoke when Davin returned home after work and he knew, she blamed him for their situation. The cabin was rudimentary at best, a set of cots along the wall, a table and four chairs across from a sooty fireplace, a hodge-podge of dishes on a rickety shelf. Everything was filthy, the two pots covered in ash and burned in grease, the pottery crusted, not to mention the cabin itself that hadn't seen a good cleaning in months if not years.

The only thing they'd gotten new was bedding—Kate had insisted—and a set of towels. The grocer had delivered various cans and jars, sacks of dry goods and cleaning supplies. Most of what was left of the two gold coins was now gone as well.

Billy had told Davin that breakfasts and dinners were served as a group meal at camp, during the day, his work crew joined together to eat lunch. He'd been detailed to support the building of a warehouse near the river, nothing sophisticated. His work was even less glamorous, mostly cutting timber and joining boards together to frame simple walls. The crew boss Joe Dickins was local, a burly fellow with a pockmarked face and a thick nose, and naturally suspicious of newcomers, especially immigrants. At least Davin was able to communicate well while most of the German laborers struggled.

In the late afternoon, Joe called Davin to him. "Micky, what'd you learn in Ireland?" He nodded at the saw in Davin's hand.

"Carpentry," Davin said. "I've always enjoyed working with wood."

Joe eyed him curiously. "Then you didn't suffer from the potato famine. What's a fellow like you doing over here?"

"Indirectly, yes. People had no money to build homes anymore, not even for a simple bench."

"I hear you're staying in camp with your wife and son. That's no place for a young family."

"I've been trying to find a different place, but Mr. Williams isn't helping. He knew all along that we'd come together."

Joe spit. "He's got nothing but dollar signs in his eyes. Too bad you don't have money. I've got my eye on some land west of here. Perfect for a small farm."

"I'd love that."

Joe slapped him on the shoulder. "Say, I've got a little side job, if you're interested. Nothing fancy but pays a bit extra." He blinked. "Boss doesn't need to know."

"Sure, what is it?"

An hour later, Davin had decided to follow Joe to another worksite at the edge of town. He quickly understood that Joe was running a side business, building cabins for anybody able to afford them.

Tonight, a young couple from Indianapolis was meeting with Joe to discuss the building of a home, a twelve-by-sixteen-foot cabin with a small bedroom and an adjacent stall for life stock.

"When would it be ready?" The woman was patting her swollen belly.

"A month, two at the most," Joe said. "If I can get the wood in quickly and provided, you'll pay an advance...for supplies."

The young couple looked at each other.

"I've got a lot of demand for places like these?" Joe pointed at Davin. "He'd be able to hurry it along—especially for you."

Davin opened his mouth. He knew nothing about Joe's pay or the extra hours, the work would demand. He was also fairly sure that Williams would be livid if he found out. In effect, Joe was competing, even if his projects were tiny in comparison.

"Sure...I think, yes," the young man said. "We want our child to grow up in a home." He hesitated. "How much are you thinking?"

Joe blinked with his right eye again, then smiled. "Let's sit down and crunch some numbers, shall we?"

Davin was excused and began walking around the site. Two cabins were in various stages of building, both had no roofs yet. He walked inside and inspected the walls, door and window frames. None were up to his standards, even a blind man could see that the angles weren't plumb, the floor uneven around the fireplace.

Whoever was buying these would soon struggle opening the door or experience serious drafts in the winter. He wandered down the lane, where five more lots had been marked.

"And?" Joe said, when Davin returned. The young couple had left, likely having paid Joe handsomely. "You ready to join? I could use a good carpenter."

Their eyes met. "You've got a good scheme going, Joe. I might join you—"

"Let me tell you about the pay," Joe said, patting the table. "Have a seat."

Davin shook his head and sat to face his boss. "I've got a better idea." He paused. "I don't want money, I want to buy one of the lots, build our own place in my spare time."

Joe cackled. "Spare time. You might as well sleep here."

"I don't care." Davin straightened. "Take it or leave it. I need to get out of that camp and the sooner I start, the better."

"Which one?"

"What?"

"Which lot do you want?" Joe had risen too.

Davin smiled. "Can you show them to me?"

"You're late," Kate cried when Davin returned. "Peter and I ate hours ago." He was beat, the unfamiliar heat and humidity were getting to him. Already, the backs of his hands and his nose were sunburned. He didn't dare take off his shirt during the day like some of the men, afraid, he'd turn into a lobster. And it was only May, the summer lay in front of them.

"I've got a surprise."

Kate put a plate of overcooked rice with sweet potatoes and ham in front of him. "I can't get used to the rice, it's either hard or too soft."

"Come and sit with me." Davin took a bite of the mush and chewed mechanically. The camp's cook was terrible, but the food was included since redemptioners didn't get paid. He told her about his deal with Joe, working extra hours and in return acquiring one of Joe's properties. They'd agreed on a price and the number of hours it'd take to pay it off, an ungodly number, he'd have to chisel away at over time. Joe would give him the deed and a private contract and every week, he'd deduct the hours, Davin had worked.

"But that will take forever," Kate said, her gaze on Peter sleeping peacefully on his cot. "I'd rather you'd take the money, so we can buy things." Her eyes narrowed. "Look at me, we have nothing, this place is terrible. I can't buy a dress or shoes. Peter is growing, too."

"Just for a while." Davin took another bite, swallowed. "It'll be our own place."

Kate made a face. "How long am I supposed to deal with this...the men and their comments, the whistles?"

"I'm sure they don't mean anything, you'll get used to it. I'll ask Williams again to give us a different place. But first he has to understand that I'm good and needs me...like Joe."

"And if Williams finds out? Surely, this side business of yours isn't allowed."

Davin shrugged, not wanting Kate to see his worry. He'd thought about it on the way home. Williams would fire Joe if he knew, his little enterprise in direct competition with Williams' construction firm. And Davin's redemptioner contract was clear, he was bound to exclusively work for Williams—for three years...an eternity.

"...will you come to bed?" Kate's question brought him back.

"In a minute, I'm going to wash." On his way to the pump, Davin nodded a greeting to the men, some had worked on the Erie and Wabash canal and now worked in Williams' company as laborers, some he didn't know, redemptioners like him. All were single Irish men.

"Come and join us," they called, waving bottles of beer at him. When he shook his head, they cackled and whistled. "Has to take care of his wifey...keep her in line..."

Davin ignored them. All he needed was sleep. If he was lucky, he'd dream of the German woman.

CHAPTER FORTY-THREE

Mina

Mina worked all morning, cleaning and scrubbing every inch of the cabin. She washed the curtains, organized fresh straw for the mattress from a neighbor, cleaned out the fireplace until her fingers ached. It was still a shack, but now the place smelled a lot better. She kept the only window open to let in the fresh air.

When she was satisfied, she changed into her best outfit, a brown taffeta dress with ruffles from Regine and headed to town. She was glad for the breeze, making the walk just about tolerable. She needed a light summer dress or at least some fabric, she could sew one with. But first, she needed to take care of business.

Before she reached downtown, she was drenched, the taffeta stuck to her skin like peel to a sausage. She silently cursed the fashion, women had to endure in public. At least at home she could take off socks and shoes, open the top of her dress.

"I'm looking for the bank," she said, passing an old man, resting in the shade of a house.

He nodded thoughtfully, chewing on a pipe. "Main and Clinton Streets, that way." He pointed down the path.

Mina wished she'd taken something to fan herself, her legs already felt wobbly, and she had trouble focusing. She asked twice more until she reached Main Street, which bustled with horse carriages, men dragging loads on carts, and a handful of women hurrying along. She stopped to study a poster, attached to the side of a building.

Attention
Citizens of Fort Wayne

THE LIFE WE REMEMBER: BETWEEN WORLDS

The scourge is nearly upon us, the council instructs all men and women to be on the lookout for the sickness that is ravaging our lands. Take care of your home and family and use lime liberally whenever possible to prevent the spread of cholera.
Fort Wayne, City Council

Mina's thoughts raced. She'd heard of cholera, a sickness that could kill in a day. Wouldn't it be a cruel joke, if she'd come all this way, only to fall prey to some epidemic? She vowed to explore the area to search for herbs and roots to refill her stores. Most of all she needed to look for wild carrot and begin her regiment again. It was only a matter of time before Roland would demand attention and she did not want to get pregnant. Not while they were settling, not for a while.

Across from her the sign read *State Bank of Indiana*.

"What can I do for you?" a man in a formal suit addressed her as soon as she stepped inside.

Mina had prepared her words carefully. "Sir, I would like to deposit an inheritance for safekeeping. I believe I need an account."

The banker nodded eagerly. "Of course, ma'am." He gaze fell on her hand. "Your husband will join you, I suppose?"

"The account is just for me alone." Mina opened her mouth, closed it. How could she explain to the man that it'd be foolish to involve Roland, that she might as well toss the gold into the river?

"I see. In that case I ask you to wait a moment." He tipped his hat and hurried to speak to a a man in a top hat, obviously the director. Moments later, they returned together.

"Ma'am," the other man said. "I'm sorry to inform you, it is against Indiana state law to open an account for a married woman. You are married, are you not?"

Mina nodded.

"Now if you were in New York...the law there has changed recently, women are permitted to open their own accounts." He chuckled. "I'm afraid, we aren't there yet. Perhaps, if you'd bring your husband...we'd be happy to be of service."

Not a chance. "Thank you," she said aloud and hurried outside. The afternoon sun hit her and for a moment, she felt feint. What was the matter with her? All this work after months of idleness, the unfamiliar climate were wearing her out. And now the men of Fort Wayne, of Indiana, forbid her to have an account. She scoffed. The next moment the edges of her vision grew fuzzy, her legs so weak, she had the urge to sit down. *Pull yourself together.*

She remembered the friendly proprietress on Water Street, Polly, from Mannheim. She'd ask her for advice, have a cool lemonade and a rest.

It only took a few minutes to reach Polly's diner, but to Mina it felt like hours. Every step was like balancing on a tightrope, her vision foggy and her body so hot, she wanted to rip off her dress. Something was wrong with her, maybe she had that cholera, the poster spoke of.

"I'm looking for..." was the last thing she said before her legs gave.

A couple of men inside the diner hurried to help her up and that's when Polly rushed toward her. "Mina." Her hand felt cool on Mina's burning one as she directed the men to help Mina to the backroom.

Once on the chaise, the room stopped spinning and Mina leaned back.

"Drink that." Polly held a glass of lemonade to Mina's lips. "Nice and slow."

Mina did as she was told. "I meant to..." she said after a moment.

"Hush." Polly sat down the glass. "Close your eyes and take deep breaths. I'll be right back."

The dizziness subsided as Mina rested. A breeze was moving the curtains like last time, cooling her forehead.

Polly returned with a bowl of water and a cloth. "Let me put that on your neck. It will help you cool down."

"I'm making a fool of myself," Mina whispered.

"Nonsense." Polly sat down across from her. "A woman in your condition...you should take it slow, the summer will be even hotter."

Mina's thoughts reeled. "My condition...I don't understand."

Polly smiled knowingly. "You are with child...I am never wrong about those things." Her gaze wandered to the windows and for a moment she was far away. "I used to be a midwife...at home," she said, her focus returning to Mina.

"But..." Mina shook her head. Scenes of the ship returned, Roland pushing himself onto her...the luggage room. Davin. A sigh escaped from her chest, loud and rattled. It hadn't been that long, surely Polly was wrong. But then she'd never felt this weak, her breasts sensitive.

The room blurred as she realized she had no idea who the father was, had pushed the memory of the Irish man far away. Now he was back. If the baby looked like Davin, Roland would kill her. She tried to smile, but the tears kept coming.

Polly moved to her side and took her hand. "Nah, nah, it'll all work out, you'll see."

It was late afternoon when Mina returned home. She had to hurry with dinner before Roland arrived, but first she needed to change out of the darn dress. She pulled off the garment and placed the money belt, she'd been carrying since Regine's death, on the bed. She'd stuck the jewelry inside the mattress when she'd exchanged the straw, but if Roland had a chance, he'd find it.

No, she needed to find a place good enough, he'd never suspect. And she needed time to think about Polly's words which she knew were true. Now that she thought about it, she realized her body had been telling her things except she'd been too busy and distracted to listen.

Instead of lighting the logs in the fireplace and add more heat to the place, she'd cook outside tonight. She started a fire and while rummaging for a triangle holder for the pot, noticed the shovel. She could bury everything, but there was always a risk of losing the spot or worse, somebody watching her. It was an obvious choice, too obvious.

She fastened a pot with water and added onions, leek, and potatoes over the fire and returned inside. There was no time to prepare something elaborate, but Roland couldn't know where she'd been and why. Most of all, he couldn't know about the child.

You must be daft, her mind commented. *He'll find out soon enough.* But right now, she needed time to think.

She sank on the bed, her body heavy and her mind overwhelmed. The last thing, she thought of was that she would've loved to tell Davin the news—immediately.

"Mina? Wake up!" Roland's face swam above as she awoke from a heavy sleep. "What is wrong with you? Where is my dinner?"

Mina fought her way back through the fog, "backyard," was all she uttered. Roland disappeared while Mina realized that the money belt was still lying next to her. Feeling panicky, she stuck it beneath her pillow. She knew without a doubt that Roland would never give it back, once he had Regine's gold in his grasp.

Roland reappeared, hands on his hips. "It's cooked to mush and burned on the bottom, whatever it was. You dawdle all day and can't even cook a single meal while I break my back in the forge?" Indeed, he looked terrible, his eyes red and watery, the skin of his face puffy and damp with sweat. "It must've been two-hundred degrees in there."

Mina rose slowly. She wanted to tell him to leave her alone. He'd been responsible for them being here in the first place. "I wasn't feeling well this afternoon. I'll fix something else while you wash."

Roland's mood didn't improve after dinner. He'd eaten silently, shoveled the food down in a matter of minutes while Mina watched.

"You're not eating?" he said, throwing down his spoon.

"Not hungry. The heat is getting to me."

Roland scoffed. "I heard it's going to get much worse...hundred degrees and higher in July and August. "What are you going to do then?"

"I have to get used to it." Her thoughts were on the pregnancy and that the baby would arrive in the middle of winter, a time that would be equally horrid.

Roland jumped up. "They don't pay us a dime. I talked to some of the other redemptioners, all we get is some food allowance and shared meals. Everything else is extra. His gaze was on her. "Maybe you could do some work, earn money." He paused. "Or part with some of that gold."

"To do what?"

"Why do you ask, woman?" Roland started pacing back and forth. They were in the backyard and Mina immediately worried about the neighbors. "A man can't even have a beer. I'm a slave to the forge. For four years." He stopped in front of her, looked down. "Either you start working or you share, is that clear?"

As Mina looked up, their eyes met. "I will think it over."

"Do that." Roland climbed the stairs. "I'm going to bed. Got to be back at six o'clock."

"Will you ever tell me what happened in that pub at home?" She noticed the hesitation his his step, the tightening of his fingers on the railing.

To her surprise, he turned to face her. "It's history, so leave it be."

"Something else happened, didn't it? You stole the money, killed Harald intentionally." The words flowed from Mina's mouth. "That's why you had to leave."

In a flash Roland jumped down the stairs and leaned over her. "I said, leave it be."

But Mina was done cowering. She stood straight-backed, met his gaze. "Or what? You'll hit me again?" For an instant, she expected to feel his fist in her belly.

Instead, he silently looked down on her, then spit. "Goodness woman, how ugly you've become. Look at yourself, the hair all stringy, your face puffy. You should take better care of yourself." With that he turned and disappeared in the house, the door banging shut behind him.

Mina took a deep breath and sagged onto the bottom step of the stairs. Why couldn't she control herself? She could lose the baby...like last time...

It had been a year ago, early, almost too early to know for sure. But she'd known, had felt her breasts tighten and become sensitive. Despite their situation, she'd been happy...excited. And then Roland had had a fit over not finding his hat, had accused her of hiding it. The fist had come out of nowhere, hit her in the lower belly, the pain sharp and dull at the same time. She crumpled to the floor while he'd clattered out of the cabin. Later that night, she'd begun to bleed. She'd stuffed the memory deep into her heart.

A gold finch settled on the little fence across from her, his eyes on her. He remained quite still as if to tell her that things would work out in the end. What glorious colors he had, like a ray of sunshine just for her. A smile crept onto her face then.

With a pang she remembered the gold belt under her pillow and hurried after Roland. One little shove would reveal it.

In a way it had been easier being poor.

CHAPTER FORTY-FOUR

Davin

June arrived with more hot weather and Davin quickly learned that the additional work at Joe's development was bringing him to his limits. He'd hoped that he could do planning and measuring jobs for Williams, maybe even oversee some of the unskilled crew, but most everything he did was labor, lugging wood, cutting and fitting doors and windows.

He never made a mistake, his measurements precise, frames straight and level. But neither Joe nor anybody else seemed to take notice. All they cared about, was to work fast and to an unrealistic schedule. And as the weeks went by, Davin grew more and more exhausted, his legs shaky at times, his arms weak after a day's work. The food they received during the day was subpar, not helping him keep strong. It was hard enough to get through the long days, but then Joe expected him to show up at the other site.

The three men who helped were unskilled and unless Davin stepped in, nothing was done to his liking. Sunday, the only day, he could rest was reserved for the property, he was buying. But he was too tired to even dig a foundation and he hadn't thought about the fact that he needed money to buy lumber and tools. Kate would have to endure the camp for a lot longer and he didn't have the heart to tell her.

Williams showed up every so often like an evil ghost, a cigar stuck between his lips, waving around a cane. "What are you working on?," he'd ask Davin. They were placing walls on the second floor of a new building, and Davin was in charge of framing the windows.

"Office rooms, sir," Davin said, keeping his eyes on the ruler he was using to mark a board.

A puff of smoke stung Davin's nose like an answer. "I hear you do good work. Not the fastest, but good."

Davin paused to look at his boss. "Sir, I appreciate it. I'm wondering if I can get one of those circular saws, it'd make cutting straight, accurate lines much easier."

Williams' small eyes narrowed further. "What for? We're managing just fine."

"Sir, if I may, it's a great way to cut long pieces of lumber, even slim strips for baseboards or window trim."

"How does it work?"

"Let me show you." Davin turned to a worktable and began drawing the outline of the machine. He explained the wheel, the paddle mechanism, some woman had invented by using a sewing machine.

"How do you know these things?"

Davin grinned. "Saw one on a job in Ireland."

"Not such a dumb Irish after all," Williams said, sucking on his cigar. "I'll see what I can do."

Davin swallowed a nasty comment and returned to his work. First, the Americans wanted help and obviously benefited greatly from the labor they imported. Besides, Williams wasn't a native either, according to Joe, he'd come from England as a young boy. What gave him the right to be so arrogant?

Davin had planned to ask Williams about another house again, but the way the boss treated him, he didn't think he'd succeed. He'd spoken with other men, mostly Irish, and learned that a lot of employers were taking advantage, forcing immigrants to live in horrid conditions. Some of the contracts ran six and seven years and men and women were even sold like slaves between companies.

The saw arrived by the end of June, and Joe instructed Davin to train everybody on it. The blade stuck out of the table and when operated with a paddle, turned rather fast. A wrong move could take a hand or at least cause serious injuries.

For several days, Davin instructed the men every morning. Each of them had to cut lumber, each of them was amazed, how straight the cuts were and how narrow the wood strips. By the end of the week, everybody knew what to do and Davin should've been pleased.

But he was feeling strange, kind of light-headed and hot. The summer had arrived with even hotter temperatures and the air carried such high humidity, it felt like breathing steamy hot water. By ten o'clock, Davin's shirt was drenched and all he wanted was to sit somewhere in the shade and drink water. But the construction downtown went on unabated. Already exhausted, Davin continued late into the night at Joe's development until he was hardly able to lift his arms.

Kate was already in bed when he arrived home, so he washed and ate, hung his work clothes out to dry and collapsed on the mattress. They never saw each other and spoke less. Even on Sunday, on his day off. He'd asked her several times to accompany him to the property, he was buying through his labors, but she refused. Didn't she understand that he was doing this for them?

At the same time, he knew he wouldn't be able to continue at this pace. His body was breaking down, he'd lost weight. The food was not enough to keep him strong, the heat and workload did the rest. He just didn't know what he could change. Williams had him over a barrel, expected him to perform, even if many of the men at the construction site weren't half as capable. And Joe had made promises to his customers that were impossible to keep. Davin had tried to explain that good construction took time and attention, but Joe only cared about the bottom line. Like Williams.

And now he'd maneuvered himself in the middle. *Because you're too ambitious*, the voice in his head commented. *You could've taken a few small side jobs and earned money for Kate. Instead, you wanted the land. Why are you blaming her then?*

He had to make changes and fast, before he broke down or had an accident.

CHAPTER FORTY-FIVE

Mina

Her neighbor, Annie, had been by several times, providing Mina with tomato plants and corn, cucumber and carrot seeds.

Now her garden, however tiny, was taking shape. Annie had already tried crops and collected seeds for the past two years. Now she sat watching Mina water the fragile seedlings. In exchange, Mina had taken Annie into the nearby woods to search for herbs and medicinal plants.

They'd harvested chamomile, yarrow, sage and mint, Mina sharing their uses with Annie and instructing her how to prepare them for storage. She also collected wild carrot seed though didn't want to brace the subject of prevention with her new friend.

Except for Polly, nobody knew she was pregnant, and she wasn't ready to talk about it, even if she'd detected a gentle bump on her lower belly. At night, when Roland slept, she massaged it, imagining the baby inside—surely it was a girl—to feel her hand. In her head, she spoke to her about Germany and her grandfather who she'd abandoned without a word. Now that she was settled somewhat, she wanted to write to him, explain what had happened and assure him of her well-being. Roland wouldn't like it, but the farther her pregnancy progressed, the less she cared. Especially now that she'd found the perfect hiding place for the gold.

After the near-miss earlier, she'd decided against burying and instead, loosened a floorboard. She'd studied the shack and decided to use one beneath the oak headboard. It had taken her all day to move the bed and pry out the wood. The space beneath was hollow, so she attached a nail underneath and hung the belt from it. For daily use, she kept an assortment of coins in two kitchen jars, hoping that Roland wouldn't find them.

Most nights, he was too tired to do more than eat and go to bed, but on Sundays, he grew nervous and antsy. She'd suggested taking excursions to explore the city and its surroundings, but soon found that the heat was wearing her out. Worse, she did not enjoy spending time with Roland. He hardly spoke and when he did, complained about the forge, his coworkers, the house, and the weather. Nothing was ever good. After a few Sundays, they'd stopped going out together. By late morning, he disappeared, and she did not know where he went.

"Just as well," she said to herself, testing the soil's moisture with a forefinger.

"Don't water the tomatoes from above, they don't like water on their leaves." Annie sat in the shade of the house, fanning herself. It wasn't even ten o'clock and the sun was beating down. "You should plant a tree for shade," she said.

Mina smiled. "It'll be years before it's tall enough."

"A willow grows quickly."

"Don't they need lots of water?"

Annie kept fanning herself. "True. Maybe a maple. I've seen them sprout up all over."

"Shall we look for one?"

Instead of an answer, Annie abruptly jumped from the bench and rushed into the outhouse.

Mina moved into the shade herself and waited and when Annie returned, her eyes appeared glassy. "Sorry, I think I ate something wrong. My belly is twisting in a knot." She'd hardly spoken the words when she jumped up a second time, only this time she made it halfway to the outhouse before she vomited.

Alarm bells went on in Mina's head. Something was seriously wrong with Annie. The poster, she'd seen in town, had spoken of cholera. What if Annie had contracted it?

"Sor...sorry," Annie moaned. "I'll clean it up as soon as I feel better."

"Let me get you some water." By the time, Mina returned, Annie was in the outhouse again. Nobody in their right mind spent much time in there in summer, the stench was too great, and the flies kept bothering.

"I think I need to lie down," Annie said, when she reappeared. She took a couple of sips which reappeared in a matter of minutes.

Mina had seen enough. "Listen, I think you may have cholera. At the very least, you should get checked out. I will take you to the new hospital farm, all right?"

Annie weakly shook her head. "I just want to go home and rest."

Mina placed a hand on Annie's forearm. "I'm afraid this is dangerous. I'd rather you get help right away." *Before it is too late.* Aloud, she said, "You think you can walk?"

"If we go slowly." Annie rose, holding her belly. "Isn't there one in town at Berry and Calhoun? It's closer."

"All right."

By the time they approached the newly erected log house, it was midday and unbearably hot. Annie had stopped several times to vomit and twice, she'd leaned against a wall or a fence because her bowels gave.

Mina kept breathing through her mouth to avoid the stench. Her stomach was sensitive anyway and the farther they walked, the smellier Annie grew. She was red in the face and breathing quickly, her steps wobbly and her gaze unfocused.

"Just a little farther," Mina said, leading Annie to the entrance. "We need help," she cried as soon as the door opened. The smell of vomit and diarrhea intensified, a fact, the older woman dressed in black with a white apron, did not seem to notice.

Without much ado, she led Annie to a partition, helped her undress and wash, before she guided her to a bed on the opposite wall.

Unsure of what to do, Mina remained standing near the door. Her throat was burning up with thirst and she wondered, if she herself would fall ill. The symptoms of cholera let the body dry up in a matter of hours, all liquids were expelled violently. A body without fluids would not work. Her mind galloped through the remedies and herbs, she knew, and settled on chamomile. It calmed the innards and was good for any intestinal issues. Why not for cholera?

When the lady in black and white returned to fetch water, Mina stopped her. "I'm wondering if I may return with chamomile, we could prepare tea to soothe the stomach, hopefully stop the nausea."

The woman who had to be in her sixties threw her a knowing glance and nodded. "Sure, dear, anything that helps those wretches. You are trained in such matters?"

"I use herbs for healing," Mina said. "If I could get some wat—" Her gaze stopped at a figure on the other side of the room. The man lying on his back had a reddish beard and matching hair, cut short for the summer. She blinked and shook her head.

"You need water? Are you unwell, please sit, it's dreadfully hot." The woman pointed at a chair by the little desk in front, but Mina just shook her head. She had to be mistaken, her mind was playing tricks, no wonder. People spoke of heatstroke.

"May I look around?", she asked, glad to find her voice. "Make sure that my friend is all right? Her name is Annie."

"Of course, take your time, but be aware that you don't want the sickness, not in your condition." The woman smiled, her eyes for a tiny moment straying to Mina's belly. There was nothing to see and yet, some people just knew. Like Polly.

"I'll be careful and not touch anything." Mina left the woman preparing a document about Annie and wandered past the beds. She looked this way and that, but her eyes were inevitably drawn back to the bed across the room. She stopped briefly at Annie's cot. Her neighbor had her eyes closed and seemed to be asleep, but Mina didn't like the pale skin which seemed almost translucent.

"I'll be back," she whispered. The bed in back called to her, she had to know. And then she stood at the man's feet, expecting to see some stranger with a certain likeness. But it wasn't a stranger, it was Davin, the man she had fallen in love with on the ship to America. The man who'd taught her English and what love felt like.

She tiptoed to his side, hardly able to breathe. "Davin?" Her voice sounded shaky and desperate. He looked so thin and pale as if he'd lost twenty pounds in the last two months. His eyes were closed and when she bent low, all she heard, was a raspy breath. "Can you hear me?" she tried again. "It's Mina...from the ship."

His eyes fluttered a bit, but he did not wake.

Mina swallowed as a thousand thoughts rushed through her mind. He was very sick. She needed to help him, had to, he couldn't die. Not now that she'd found him again.

She gently touched his cheek and forced herself to withdraw. She had work to do, no matter the heat, no matter the tiredness. She hurried to the woman, afraid to ask the question. No, she was terrified. Gripping her own hands to keep them from fluttering, she said, "Ma'am, the man back there, how long has he been here?"

"You know him?"

"Yes, he was on the ship from Liverpool. He is Irish, his name is Davin—"

"Davin Callaghan, yes, he came yesterday, had collapsed at work. Mr. Williams had him brought here and wants to be informed."

"What about his wife?"

"He is married?" The woman seemed surprised. "I have not seen anybody. Surely, they have informed her of his whereabouts."

Mina nodded. "I could tell her, if you like, or send my husband. To make sure, I mean..."

The woman rifled through her papers and wrote down the address. "Poor gent, he's in a bad way for someone so young."

Mina hurried to the door. She didn't want to hear anymore, needed to get home, and find something to soothe his suffering.

"Where have you been?" Roland was pacing back and forth in the cabin, sweat pearled off his forehead and his shirt was drenched.

"Annie fell ill, she has cholera. I took her to the sick house in town."

"What about my dinner? I'm starving."

"It's early," Mina said. "Can you fix something yourself for once, I've got to return with—"

"Why on earth would you go back there? All you do is get yourself sick—and me."

As usual it's all about you. Mina turned toward her jars to hide her disgust. "I'm going back, Annie and the other patients need help. And I can give it." She sat the bag of oats and a pint of wild blackberries, she'd picked this morning, in front of him. "Here. I've got work to do."

She rushed to make a fire and heat water, she needed to make tea, lots of tea. Luckily, she'd picked loads of chamomile last week. She loved the herb for its many healing properties, particularly useful against diseases of the intestines, diarrhea, and nausea. It calmed the system and with its sweet and pleasant taste and gentle virtue would not upset the body further.

But she needed bottles or other containers to carry the tea in. Why hadn't she asked the woman, if she could heat water there? She'd not be able to carry a heavy load and if the container wasn't closed well, she'd slosh half of it onto the street.

Davin's pale face returned to her. He could not die.

She decided to make a smaller amount and carry an earthen jar in her basket, along with a liberal helping of dried chamomile, a spoon, mug and cloth.

By the time, she returned to the ward, she was drenched anew. The air had cooled some, but the stickiness remained. She'd ignored Roland's angry face and just left. Let him be upset, she didn't care, not now.

The older woman was still there, administering to another arrival, a young girl of maybe twelve. Annie was sleeping and Mina rushed to Davin's bed. She was afraid what she'd find, afraid to lose the one person, she cared about in this new world.

As before he laid on his back, his eyes closed, breathing with a slight rasp. She gently took his hand and squeezed it. "I'm here now, my love," she whispered. "I'll take care of you."

CHAPTER FORTY-SIX

Davin

A voice spoke in Davin's dreams, soft and gentle, and yet urgent. He wanted to ignore it, tell it, to leave him alone and let him drift away. But the voice kept saying things, he didn't understand. At some point, it sang. He didn't understand the meaning, its words foreign and strange and yet, beautiful.

He felt his hand move, his fingers being massaged. Kate must've come to see him and was taking care of him. He wanted to turn to his side then, tell her to leave him alone. But his body didn't respond, didn't obey.

"Davin," the voice said again, "wake up. You need to drink."

He swallowed and realized that his throat was so parched, his mouth burned. He smacked his lips, and something landed there, cool and smooth and then his mouth grew wet. He wanted to open his eyes then, see what was happening, but oh, he was so tired.

"Good, one more, come on. It's chamomile," the voice said. "It'll help your belly." The cool metal returned, the wet repeated, he swallowed a few drops. After a bit, the spoon stopped. "Now we'll wait a bit, make sure, it stays down." The voice was soft and so calm, he felt instantly drawn to it. There was a familiar tone to it, he couldn't place.

He dozed.

The voice returned, then the spoon and the liquid. "Let's try again. You are doing great."

He smacked his lips, swallowed, moved his tongue which had felt like a giant slug in his mouth.

"Maybe you can sit up a bit?" the voice asked. "I'll help you."

Davin struggled to open his eyes, it was like they were filled with sand, all scrapy and painful. The room came into focus, the wooden ceiling made of logs. He blinked, the light ached him, but he needed to see who the voice belonged to.

"Hey, I'm here. I found you."

A face appeared in his vision, gray eyes like a walk under rain clouds. He knew these eyes, had fallen in love with them months ago...

His mouth formed the word then, his tongue unwieldy. "Mina," he mumbled. Maybe he'd gone to heaven, and this was an angel, pretending to be her. Why was his body so heavy, every muscle hurt?

The gray eyes sparkled with tears. "Hi."

He focused on her, wanted to touch her cheeks, the lips he'd kissed, but his arm barely rose from the blanket. "I'm a mess," he managed.

A smile joined the tears. "You *are* a mess. But now I'm here and will take care of you."

She helped him prop up his head on the pillow and like a baby, fed him tea. He felt strange, childlike, and sore and comforted. Mina had come to save him. He believed that.

He dozed off and when he awoke and the log ceiling came into focus, she was gone. He'd had a dream, a wonderful dream about the German girl. Her ghost had been here to talk to him, encourage him. He smiled, his throat a bit less sore, his tongue almost normal. He was unbearable thirsty and raised his head.

He counted twelve beds, most of them occupied. A woman was sitting next to one, another moved about the room. The light of a glorious sunset bathed the room orange. He raised his hand, cleared his throat. "Water, please." His voice sounded strange, deep and gravelly.

The woman who'd been sitting nearby hurried to his side. Her hair was auburn and shiny like the chestnuts he'd collected as a boy, her eyes gray. He had not dreamed it. She was here.

"Davin," she cried. "You are better."

He managed a grin. "Thirsty." The spoon felt cool against his lips, his mouth welcomed the tea. "Let me have a cup." He drank it down in tiny sips and leaned back, his gaze on the woman he'd thought lost. She looked different somehow, her face softer, the skin glowing. "How are you?"

Mina bent lower and touched his cheek, fingertips light as feathers. "I am all right. It is a struggle at home."

"You live nearby?"

"In a tiny cabin next to other immigrants."

"Roland?"

"Is his usual self." Her smile faded. "He struggles with work...with himself."

Davin nodded and for a while they didn't speak. Her hand found his and their fingers intertwined, a simple touch and yet, his heart filled with joy and made him smile. "I cannot believe, you are here."

"I about fainted when I saw you."

"How long have you been here?"

"Since yesterday. I went back to fetch herbs. I think they're helping. You have not vomited."

He touched his throat, felt his belly—the pain was gone, the need to purge himself. "You saved me."

"I am working on it." Mina poured another cup of tea. "Here, drink this. If it stays down, we'll try cooked oats."

As she rose, he caught her hand. "I missed you terribly."

She smiled at him, her eyes wet again. "I'll be back, I have to check on Annie."

He followed her around the room with his eyes, it grew dark, and an oil lamp was lit. He fell asleep, a feeling of peacefulness the last thing he noticed.

Mina sat by his bed when he awoke. It was morning, the windows stood open and outside, a blackbird sang. He breathed deeply as he watched her sleep, head bent forward, her lips slightly open, hands in her lap. She'd gained a bit of weight, her cheeks less gaunt and softer.

At some point, she opened her eyes, found him, her expression moving from anxiety to gladness. "You are awake."

"I'm hungry."

Mina raised her arms and stretched. "In that case, I better fix your oats." She looked around the room and pecked a quick kiss on his cheek.

They ate together, him propped against the pillow, her sitting next to him. They didn't need to speak, her presence fulfilling him in a way, Kate never could. Kate! Where was she? He couldn't remember what had happened, only that he'd been at work and blacked out. "Where is Kate?"

"I assume she is at home. I haven't had time to visit and tell her anything."

He handed her his bowl. "Nor should you."

"She is probably afraid to catch the sickness...or infect your little boy. Cholera can be deadly."

Davin shook his head. "She never even checked on me?"

Mina took his hand. "Let's not assume. I will speak to her, if you wish."

"Not sure that's a good idea. I think she was jealous on the ship. If she knows you've been here with me..."

Mina smiled. "You are hardly in shape..." Her cheeks reddened as she looked at him. "But I don't care what shape you are in as long as I can be near you."

"You were not afraid to enter this ward and help the people here—me." He squeezed her fingers, suppressed the sudden wish to pull her onto the bed. "I felt I'd arrived in paradise, thought you weren't real, an angel of my imagination." He returned her smile and lowered his voice. "I cannot think of a better place than here with you."

Davin was out of danger, he was holding down fluids, mostly drinking tea, and solids. Mildred had told Mina that he'd have to leave in the evening to make room for new arrivals. Annie was also doing better, in fact more than half the patients, seemed to respond to Mina's slow feeding of tea, followed by plain cooked oats. The young girl had died within hours, so had an older man and his wife.

"I better walk you home?", Mina said as Davin was putting on his clothes which had been washed by volunteers. "I don't think you should be alone."

"But you're tired, you need rest." He slowly straightened his back, let out a groan.

I've got good reason, she wanted to say. But this was not the place to tell him about the baby. Besides, she didn't even know if it was his.

"I feel like an old man." He took her hand. "Maybe Mildred can find somebody to accompany me."

"I'd like to see where you live."

He scoffed. "It's a work camp for redemptioners, mostly single Irish men. Believe me, you don't want to see that."

"I'm more worried about running into your wife."

"Kate?" He let out another groan, putting on his shoes. "She has no right. Where was she when I was lying here?" He looked up.

"True, but remember, she does have a young son. Roland didn't want to risk it either and he has no good reason."

Davin stepped in front of her, his face close. She had forgotten that he was half a foot taller. All she wanted was to lean against his chest, kiss him... "You are so kind," he whispered, then stepped back to put distance between them.

Anybody with eyes could see that there was more between them than friendship. But to her credit Mildred had kept her mouth shut. Even Annie, who'd been awake most of the day, had not commented on Mina spending so much time near the Irish man.

Davin ambled to the desk and nodded at Mildred. "I thank you kindly for taking care of me when I was on death's door."

Mildred produced a rare smile. "You are most welcome, it is a joy to see you walk out of here." She looked at Mina. "I think your true savior stands next to you."

"Would you have somebody to walk me home?," Davin asked. "I don't trust myself."

"I'm afraid not, looks like Mina may do you the honor. She should get rest anyway." Once again Mildred's eyes swept past Mina's belly, then came to rest on her face. "I think your friend Annie can return tomorrow. Will you be back for her?"

"Of course." Mina waved Annie good-bye and followed Davin out the door. Finally, they'd be alone. She wouldn't mind walking no matter how long it took. There'd be time for a kiss. She craved his touch like she wanted fresh air.

"Davin?" Kate materialized next to them just as Davin was grasping Mina's hand. He let go and swung around. "You are well. They told me—"

"Who told you what?" Davin's voice was soft yet angry.

Kate seemed confused, looked at Mina. "What are *you* doing here?" Her gaze snapped back to Davin. "Is that what this is...you two continuing your love affair behind my back?" She rounded back on Mina. "Leave him alone, you hear. I've got—"

"Stop it!" Davin stepped in front of Kate. "I almost died...you couldn't be bothered to visit. Mina here helped me...many of the patients. She saved my life." He gave Kate a little shove. "Why don't you take a look inside and see for yourself?"

"No, thank you." Kate squinted at him, then Mina. "I want her to go."

"Why?" Davin asked, his tone just as demanding as hers. "She has every right to be here, actually, more so. How come you show up now?"

"Billy, the man who works for Mr. Williams, told me that you were coming home. I thought I'd surprise you."

"Why didn't you surprise me when I was lying in there?"

"I wasn't going to risk Peter's life with this pestilence."

"It's cholera." Davin hesitated, obviously searching for the right words. "I would've at least expected you to send a note, ask about me. Apparently, you did neither."

"I thought they'd take care of you here." Kate seemed less sure now, her eyes large and begging. "Please come home. Peter misses you."

Mina knew what Kate was doing, Davin likely did as well, but he was a man who took responsibility and right now, however conflicted he had to feel, he was married and had a son. *What about my baby?* Mina wanted to ask. *You don't even know if it's his, you have no right.* Fighting for composure, she turned to Davin, proud, her eyes remained dry. "I think you better go, I've got to get home myself. Roland will be worried and I need rest."

Davin knew as well as she did that Roland didn't much care if Mina came to harm, but to his credit he played along. Extending a hand, he said, "Thank you again for your help, I owe you my life."

Mina shook, thinking that she had to pay attention to the way, his fingers felt on hers, the warmth of his skin touching. She wanted to always remember this moment, not let it slip away into distant memory. But time was cruel that way, it just went along without feeling, without a sense of which moments mattered and carried weight for eternity.

She quickly nodded at Kate and turned away, her legs urging her forward. Away from the couple, she could never be with him, would never enjoy his love and respect. Again, she told herself that this had to be enough, to know that he'd survived and lived near her. To know that there could be chance to run into him. And maybe one day show him her baby.

To her surprise, the cabin seemed deserted. "Roland," she called, "I'm home. Annie is doing better and will come home tomorrow."

That's when she noticed the mess in the kitchen. Plates and bowls lay helter-skelter on the floor, the flour pot had broken and dusted everything white. She recognized the earthen ware pot, she'd kept their spending money in, broken in two...empty, the vase with the remaining coins also broken. Roland had raided the cabin and gone out, either to drink or to gamble—or both.

Panic gripped her as she ran to their bed, but it stood in place as usual. Gold and jewelry were safe. For now.

She sank on the bed then, tired to the bone, welcoming the exhaustion that hurled her away from this impossible life into deep, all-forgetting sleep.

CHAPTER FORTY-SEVEN

Davin

Davin lay next to Kate, his legs achy from the exhaustion of hiking home. He hadn't wanted her touch, but at some point, he leaned on her to give his body a sense of balance. He'd been on death's door and there was no easy or fast way back. He wouldn't be fit enough to work for a week or longer, would have to tell Williams and Joe that he needed time.

He also needed to think about his work situation. The reason why he had likely gotten so sick was his own stupidity, ignoring his body, demanding too much of it. He had an idea how to reduce his workload, if Williams would go for it.

He turned on his side, away from Kate, his eyes wide open. Part of him was rejoicing. He'd found Mina again, or rather, she'd found him and nursed him back from the dead. Their connection was as strong if not stronger than on the ship, just touching her fingers or being near her felt like coming home. Kate had arrived at the worst possible moment. He'd hoped for some privacy, to be able to talk to her while they walked, maybe find some way, however unlikely to meet again.

You are married and so is she, his mind commented. True. Was he just self-indulgent? Was he supposed to ignore the one thing that made life worth living: to share it with the woman he loved? What were her thoughts? They'd not been able to speak about important matters. Why not at least find out her wishes? He needed to have clarity. If she sent him packing, he'd deal with it, but let her at least tell him in person.

Suddenly, he knew what he needed to do.

It was before eight in the morning, when he left. He'd told Kate that he needed fresh air and to strengthen his body with a walk. He knew it was too early after a hundred yards when his legs grew tired and wobbly. *Turn around, you can go tomorrow or next week. You know where she lives.* But he couldn't...could not wait another hour, let alone another day.

So, he walked like old men did, slowly, with an uncertain gait, sweat on his forehead. Please let me get there. He perused the scrap of paper with her address, Mina had given him.

It was in the south of town, a row of modest cabins, all the same narrow front porch, no more than a rocking chair could fit, shingled roofs and mismatched windows and doors. He imagined making improvements, enlarging the porch, straightening the walls and windows, repairing the stairs.

He'd do no such thing. Not ever. He paused before climbing the two stairs. He was parched, the sun already hot. What time was it? Never mind, she'd hopefully be home, otherwise he'd wait up here on the porch.

But he hadn't even knocked, when the door flew open. Mina stood there in her nightshirt, her hair aglow and wild, reflecting the morning sun.

"You came," she cried and threw herself at his chest. He nearly fell backwards, caught himself, while she drew back and laughed nervously. "Sorry," she cried.

"I'm a mess," he said at the same time. She pulled him inside, threw closed the front door, and drew him to her again. No more words were spoken as they found each other. His mouth met hers, their lips danced, searched...their bodies recognizing each other.

Abruptly, Mina's palm landed on his chest as she pulled back. "Wait, I can't."

Davin just looked at her, the straight nose and those luminous eyes that now showed a mixture of pain and regret. "What's wrong?"

She heaved a sigh and took a step back, forcing him to drop his arms. The emptiness was immediate, a hollow feeling that threatened to swallow him. He lifted his arms, dropped them again. Helpless, frustrated. His body wanted her, no matter that his legs hardly supported him.

"This...this is wrong. We're both married, I can't...your wife."

"Who is afraid of being close to me." He couldn't keep the bitterness from his voice.

"Still, we have to wait, find a different way, an honorable way."

Her gaze met his. "Please understand."

How, he wanted to cry. But all he did was look at her. She was right, of course. Even if her words hurt and drove him crazy. It wasn't proper, not by a long shot. "I love you," he whispered. "Is Roland...does he come home for lunch?"

She hesitated, then shook her head. "He didn't come home last night, left me this."

That's when he noticed the broken shards in front of the cupboard. "He took our food money. You know he doesn't get paid. We're supposed to eat what they give us, which isn't enough."

"Me neither. But my goodness, did he have to destroy your kitchen?"

"He's angry. Remember the gold?"

"He didn't find it."

"Not yet." Mina stepped in front of the tiny looking glass to straighten her hair, pull it into a knot. "I tried depositing at the bank, but they require the husband to open the account." She scoffed. "I might as well throw it in the river."

Davin remembered his plan from last night. "We should talk about what you would like to do, how we should proceed. This...place," he threw up his arms, "is beneath you. We need to find a solution—"

"I need to tell you something as well—"

The door flew open and banged against the opposite wall. "Tell you what?" Roland lulled in terrible English, coming to a stop in front of Mina. His reddened eyes squinted at her, then at Davin. "My home is a love nest now. How quaint." He wobbled and caught himself. "While I bust my bones, you are whoring?" He spit on the floor and smacked Mina in the face, knuckles hitting cheekbone. The sound was dull, a thud of sort, but it had come so fast and surprising that Mina had not reacted at all.

In horror Davin watched her stumble backwards and smack on the floor, her head barely missing the table's edge. Flour rose like fog between the shards. Her eyes were closed now, and she did not move. "Mina!" he cried, being torn between checking on her and wanting to kill her husband. His vision grew narrow...into a tunnel and all he saw was Roland, who swayed back and forth, a nasty grin on his face. "You swine." He jumped forward, wrapped an arm around Roland's neck, intend to pull him to the floor, but he wasn't the man he'd been on the ship. His muscles had shrunken, he'd lost weight and was weak.

Roland slapped Davin across the cheek, his second swing missed altogether. Davin landed a fist on Roland's chin, finally sending him to the ground. He lay there for a moment, looking dazed and Davin jumped on top, intent on taking another swing. But Roland, being taller and heavier, found Davin's neck and squeezed, his strong sinewy fingers like iron ropes. Davin's vision blurred and it took both his hands to pry the fingers away. Roland twisted beneath him, and Davin lost his balance, a knee hit his stomach and he groaned. Then Roland was on top, the fingers back. Again, Davin's vision grew fuzzy. As crazy drunk as Roland was, he'd kill Davin without even remembering it.

"Fucking my wife," Roland wheezed. "I show you..."

Davin had no air left, white stars burst behind his eye lids. His hand was no match for Roland, whose full weight leaned on him. Davin's arm swung backwards, intent on hitting Roland in the face, but there was something on the ground, a jar from the kitchen mess. He picked it up and smashed it against Roland's temple.

Roland made a choking sound, eyes wide, he let go of Davin's neck before he collapsed and buried Davin beneath him. A cloud of alcohol engulfed Davin, the weight took his breath. Something warm trickled onto his cheek...blood.

He struggled sideways, crept away, and still on his knees, he leaned over Mina to listen for her breath. A faint rattle rose from her throat, her lids fluttered a bit.

"Can you hear me?" he whispered, his voice raspy. He gripped his neck, massaged the skin while he touched Mina's cheek with the other. He threw a quick glance at Roland who lay still as a puddle of red collected beneath his head.

Panic set in. He'd hurt Mina's husband.

"Davin?" Mina's eyes were open, studying him.

"Are you all right?"

She moved her limbs and nodded. Relief beyond anything he'd ever known flooded him and he fell forward, into her arms. They lay in the middle of the rubble, his head on her chest, her arm wrapped around him.

Until Mina asked, "Where is Roland?"

Davin abruptly sat up. "I...we had a fight." His gaze returned to Roland, his still figure like a dark ghost taking over the room.

Mina sat up. "What happened?"

Davin said nothing. "I was angry, I'm sorry," he cried. He scrambled to his feet, then helped Mina. Together, they approached Roland. Mina kneeled back down, placed a hand on his neck and listened.

"He's alive, just has a nasty cut on his temple," she said. "Help me place him on the bed."

Davin nodded and together they dragged him to the bed. All the happiness he'd felt earlier had evaporated. He'd messed up big time. Roland would go after him, accuse him of adultery and attempted murder.

"...do?"

"What?" He hadn't heard a word.

"I asked what we should do." Mina took his hand. "I'll say, he attacked me and fell from drunkenness. I'll ask one of the neighbors to come over, as a witness. Maybe I'll get a doctor." She felt the back of her head. "Good thing, I've got a thick head."

Despite the situation, Davin smiled. "You mean a thick skull."

Mina threw herself at his chest. He wrapped her into his arms like he'd always dreamed, except it couldn't last. "I better go, we'll find a way," he whispered into her hair. It was a lie. There was no solution to their predicament. They couldn't meet anymore.

She leaned back and nodded. Ever so slowly, every muscle in his body in pain, his heart pounding and aching, he let go, slunk to the door, opened it and scanned the quiet street.

Don't look back.

But he could not. He had to see her one last time, make sure that she was all right.

Their eyes met, hers filled with tears and longing. Sadness lay there too, in the way her shoulders slumped, her lips trembled. All he wanted was to run back to her, embrace her, tell her that everything would be all right. But he couldn't, he had to leave. Now, before Roland awoke and accused him of attempted murder!

Struggling to keep himself from crying out, he nodded a greeting—and ran into the street.

EPILOGUE

October 1849

Every time Mina visited town, or there was a knock on the door, or she saw somebody moving in the distance while she collected herbs and roots, she imagined it to be Davin. But it never was. She visited Polly every Saturday, went on excursions with healthy-again Annie, the thought of Davin never far from her mind. Despite her friendship with both women, she never mentioned him. He was like some encapsulated treasure deeply buried in her heart.

Roland had recovered quickly and other than a minor scar on his temple, nothing reminded of that afternoon. He'd not mentioned their fight nor the altercation with Davin. Mina wasn't even sure he remembered anything. She'd cleaned up the cabin and taken care of Roland's head. He'd gone back to work, and though the weather was growing cooler, she sensed there was trouble brewing. Surely, his employer demanded better attendance, but he never spoke about work either. They both existed next to each other, lives lived in a vacuum, nearby, but separate.

Over and over, she saw herself visit Davin's home, tell him that all was well, and that Roland had fully recovered. But she never went. He was married and had to take care of his wife and son, so was she. Their future together was nothing but a silly dream without merit.

Had it not been for Annie who'd been telling everybody about Mina's healing powers, sending scores of women and children to her door for treatment, she'd have despaired. But every day, somebody was needing her help with cuts and sprains, burns, ingrown nails, bites from various insects, snakes and an occasional dog, boils, women's issues, intestinal upset, and headaches, she was even asked to counsel on infestations of lice and bed bugs.

So, she transformed her kitchen area into a sitting area, added shelves with potions and dried herbs, tinctures, teas, and salves. With Annie by her side, they welcomed the wounded and desperate. Payment often consisted of some form of food: a few onions, carrots or a cabbage, potatoes, flour, grain, sometimes of assorted household articles like a piece of fabric, some yarn or a set of knitting needles, and rarely of a few pennies. Nobody had much, but they were all thankful to receive her treatment. And helping the unfortunate saved her.

And there was that other thing—her pregnancy, a life she had to prepare for. About a month after the incident, she's told Roland. She could've kept it a secret much longer, Roland was neither observant, nor did they ever see each other much without clothes. But she was tired of pretending, even excited to pass the three-months mark without having lost her baby. More importantly, she wanted him to leave her alone and stop his visits in the night.

"Why now?" Roland had asked with a frown. "It's hard enough to get by without another mouth to feed."

"It happened," Mina said, hoping that the doubts she carried about who the father was, didn't show on her face. "I thought you'd be happy. Besides, I'm receiving payment from the people I help."

"Some payment. Why don't they pay with money?"

"Because they're struggling like we are, and we can use the food to supplement."

Doubt and suspicion were written on Roland's face, she knew he wanted to ask her about the gold. But for once he kept quiet. "I suppose I'll build a crib. Let's hope it's a boy."

Mina nodded though she was hoping for a girl. "We'll know soon enough."

The news of becoming a father seemed to calm Roland. Or maybe it was the lack of coin to get drunk or gamble. Either way, Mina was thankful that he returned home after work to sort out the garden space, repair the steps to the porch, or collect firewood. Even spoke civilly to the neighbors and Annie's husband.

On mild evenings, as they sat on the porch, as Mina knitted or sewed garments for the baby, and Roland whittled on a set of wooden animals, it felt almost like they were a couple.

She'd convinced herself that she had to focus on her growing family, on building a life in this new world—that this was enough.

To expect more was foolish.

AUTHOR NOTE

Famine and Impoverishment in 19th Century Europe
The Irish famine (1845-1851), which was caused by years of poor potato harvests and cost more than a million people their lives, causing a further two million Irish to emigrate, is world-famous. Especially since the effects of this catastrophic period, which was not only exploited by the English in a shameful manner, but could have been largely avoided, continue to this day.

Potatoes, blighted by the fungus *Phytophthora infestans*, and the main food source for the Irish, perished before the eyes of the tenant farmers. Grains and animal products continued to be exported to England, and aid for the starving Irish population was withdrawn under the Tories – they wanted to prevent dependence on England and higher expenses to support Ireland. The prison-like poorhouses *(workhouses)* set up by the English had to finance themselves and had weekly death rates of over four percent; work programs were cruel and often so strenuous that the weakened Irish could no longer participate.

But a growing impoverishment, called *pauperism*, also occurred in Germany in the first half of the 19th century. Reasons included:
- the rapid growth of the population, which was able to feed its families cheaply thanks to the cheap potato
- industrialization, which sent many people to the cities but then led to rising unemployment rates

- the land inheritance system, in which the eldest son inherited everything, was abolished—instead, all sons received equal shares, enabling them all to make a living, albeit a meager one.

Between 1820 and 1928, more than sixty million people emigrated from Europe, including almost six million Germans, mainly to North America, but also to South America, Australia and New Zealand.

Fort Wayne, Indiana, USA

"I wish you by all means if you possibly can to send me Germans. I prefer the Wurtembergers as they are the most industrious and temperate."
—Henry Rudisill to John Barr, 1830

During the fourteen years (2003-2017) that I lived in Indiana, nothing drew me to Fort Wayne, which is located in the northeast of the state. But when I ended up there during a visit in the fall of 2023, my interest was immediately piqued. At the *History Center*, I discovered a collection of artifacts and descriptions that deal with the history of the city's creation. German immigrants were mentioned there in particular, who brought brewing, labor at the iron forges for the railway lines, and various trained craftsmen here. There were so many German immigrants back then, many streets and even parks had German names. That only changed during the World War I, when "being German" became unpopular. Much of what I saw and learned contributed to this book.

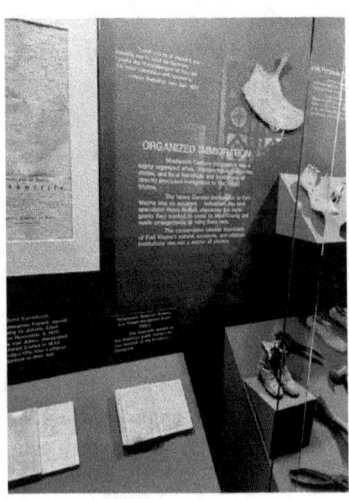

Redemptioner System

Redemptioners are people who, in the 18th and 19th centuries, hired themselves out as debtors by signing a contract to finance their passage to the new country. The employer, for example in North America, paid for the rather expensive passage from Germany, and in return the redemptioner worked for several years, usually three or four, without pay. He received room and board, but no salary. Sometimes he received a piece of land at the end of his contract. This worked because the American companies were looking for trained craftsmen who could not be found in the new and growing America. Suitable redemptioners were recruited through a system of agents who operated in Germany and promised the moon to the often desperate people. Once in the new country, they were often exposed to the worst working and living conditions.

Women's Rights
Women were subject to strict rules and had few rights well into the 20th century. This was the situation in 1848:

- Married women were legally nonexistent in the eyes of the law
- Women were not allowed to vote (women did not receive the right to vote in Germany until 1918 and in the USA in 1920)
- Women had to submit to laws in whose drafting they had not participated
- Married women had no property rights
- Husbands had legal authority and responsibility over their wives, so they could imprison or beat them with impunity
- Women were not allowed to pursue professions such as medicine or law
- Women had no opportunity to pursue an education because no college or university admitted female students
- Women were robbed of their self-confidence and self-esteem and brought into complete dependence on men.

Today, there are movements, even in the industrialized societies of the United States and parts of Europe, and even worse in countries such as Afghanistan, Iran, Pakistan, Somalia, Sudan and Syria, to restrict women's rights or suppress their human rights.

Girls and women deserve equality!

ABOUT THE AUTHOR

Perhaps Annette Oppenlander became a writer of historical novels because she likes to dig in the past. It all started when she asked her parents about their experiences as war children. Over many years, these emotional memories developed into the biographical novel "Surviving the Fatherland." Not only did this story win many awards, it also served as the springboard to a successful writing career.

Ms. Oppenlander likes to shed light on difficult subjects such as World War II from the perspective of civilian Germany, walks alongside ordinary people in the American Civil War or the Middle Ages. To create an authentic historical world, she often uses biographical information, interviews contemporary witnesses and unearths little known facts in the archives.

After studying business administration at the University of Cologne, Germany, Ms. Oppenlander spent 30 years in various parts of the United States. She writes her novels in German and English, and also shares her knowledge – writing workshops, entertaining presentations and author visits to universities and schools, libraries, retirement homes and organizations dedicated to literature – in German and English. She now lives with her American husband and dog Zelda in the beautiful Münsterland in Germany.

"Nearly every place holds some kind of secret, something that makes history come alive. When we scrutinize people and places closely, history is no longer a date or number, it turns into a story."

From the Author
Thank you for reading The Life We Remember: Between Worlds. My sincere hope is that you derived as much entertainment from reading this story as I enjoyed in researching and creating it. If you have a few moments, please feel free to add your review of the book at your favorite online site for feedback (Amazon, Apple iTunes Store, Goodreads, etc.). Also, if you would like to connect with previous or upcoming

books, please visit my website for information and to sign up for e-news:
http://www.annetteoppenlander.com.
   Sincerely, Annette

Contact Me
Website: annetteoppenlander.com
Facebook: www.facebook.com/annetteoppenlanderauthor
Email: hello@annetteoppenlander.com
Instagram: @annette.oppenlander
Twitter: @aoppenlander
Pinterest: @annoppenlander

READING SAMPLE

24 HOURS

THE TRADE

hun·ger /ˈhəNGgər/ *a feeling of discomfort or weakness caused by lack of food, coupled with the desire to eat, a weakened condition brought about by prolonged lack of food.*

TUESDAY, DECEMBER 19, 1944

EIGHT O'CLOCK

I awoke from Mother's knocking. Why couldn't she let me sleep? At least when I slept, I forgot about life for a bit. My gaze wandered to the empty bed across from me. My brother, Hans, had been gone for nearly three months. Just yesterday, we'd received a postcard with a scribbled note that he was stationed across the Rhine, less than forty miles from here. None of his cards said much, as if he were in too much of a hurry. The truth was that he wasn't allowed to write things. Like Father, who'd been gone for four and a half years, the field post of soldiers was censured. Not just to hide any news of the war, but because the government intended to hide the real state of the country.

As if that was necessary, as if we didn't realize how bad things were. Everything was rationed... Food, clothes, shoes, coal, and every month those rations grew smaller. You couldn't buy sewing needles, paper, pens or light bulbs. They just didn't exist anymore. Of course, since the city had been bombed six weeks ago, we had no electricity anyway. Nor running water. Life was a disaster from start to finish.

I sighed, the noise strange in the stillness, along with my steaming breath. Our apartment was freezing cold and gloomy, thanks to the boarded-up window, a patchwork of linoleum, tarpaper and wood scraps—my handiwork. The bombing had also destroyed every piece of glass or mirror and for a week afterwards, I'd hammered together whatever I could find to keep the icy winter air at bay.

"Are you up?" Mother's voice crept through the closed door. "I could use some help."

"Coming." Reluctantly, I crept out of bed, pulling on the one outfit that still fit somewhat. My big toe stuck through the tip of the sock Mother had already darned three times. Already, I dreaded the walk to the public water hole where we fetched drinking water. It was a ten-minute walk, fifteen with full buckets. But it was one thing to carry water to drink or cook with, another entirely to fill a tub for a bath.

Not only did I have to go three times, but a good portion of that water also had to be heated. And firewood was another issue. Usually, Helmut, my best friend, and I went into the woods to cut trees down—which was forbidden, or we searched bombsites, which was also forbidden. Beneath the rubble was plenty of torn-apart wood... Floorboards, pieces of furniture, roof trusses. But each piece had to be cut and carried home. My little brother, Siegfried, was only eight and no help. And Mother?

Another sigh rose into the air. Mother had enough on her plate to keep us going. First, she'd seen Father being drafted into this endless war, then Hans. I knew she worried about me going as well. When she felt unobserved, she paced around the room or patted the stack of field post, tied with a blue ribbon. It was the only piece of color that remained in the house, a fragile piece of fabric that could fall apart at any moment.

Pulling on my sweater, I entered the kitchen, where Mother was washing dishes in a zinc bowl and Siegfried was awkwardly drying them.

My gaze immediately wandered to the table where 'breakfast' was waiting for me. What a joke. I sat down, eyeing the piece of cornbread, thinly scraped with something red, passing itself off as strawberry jam. As a reminder, my stomach rumbled.

"I wanted to make tea," Mother said, drying her hands. "But firewood is low, and I was going to save it for dinner."

"I'll grab some this morning," I said, taking a careful bite of the bread. It tasted bland, because we had no salt, and the red goo scraped on top had no flavor at all.

Mother slumped on the chair across from me. "You also need to pick up rations." She pushed several coupon cards across the table. Bread, it said on one, meat and eggs on others. "Supposedly, we're getting sugar this week."

I stuffed the cards into my pant pocket, keeping my thoughts to myself. Every week they told us what food we were going to receive and how much. Most of the time, the store shelves were long empty when I got there and the allotments, we did receive were much smaller than announced.

The last bite of bread disappeared. To chase away the rumbles, I downed a cup of water, then another.

Mother's small hand landed on mine. "I'm sorry, Günter. I wish you'd not have to work all the time. I wish we had more to eat." She fidgeted and tugged at her hair she wore in a loose knot. Women no longer visited the hairdresser because a while back, it had been forbidden—most hairdressers had long been drafted anyway.

When had those creases appeared on her forehead? When had she stopped smiling? I couldn't remember, couldn't remember the last time we'd all sat at a dinner table together as a family, or the last time I'd eaten a full meal.

I pushed away the anger that accompanied me through most days. It wasn't Mother's fault that we starved. Or that Father and Hans fought some place for a man who was insane. Nobody said it aloud, but we all knew that the war was lost and that it was just a matter of time before…

Before what? Would we starve to death, or would I be called to serve, too? Maybe the bombs would do their job next time and finish us all. And to think that tomorrow was my sixteenth birthday. What a joke. Not that I cared for any gifts, but how I longed for a little celebration... A candle, a piece of apple pie.

Rising abruptly, I said, "I'll get firewood first."

Mother followed me to the door and touched my cheek. "Be careful."

NINE O'CLOCK—MORNING

I was already tired before I began. And cold. Being hungry did something to the body, something that surprised me every time. It robbed my breath, took my energy to the point that I was shivering. A general feeling of weakness crept into my legs, and starting at the ankles it crawled higher, to my knees and into my thighs until I moved like that war vet living next door, the one with the crutches and the grayish skin.

Father's voice resounded in my head. *Work yourself warm*, he'd said, trying for a smile.

He'd returned for a visit five weeks ago. They called it *Bombenurlaub*—'bomb vacation.' When a soldier's family at home had suffered bomb attacks, soldiers were allowed to leave their troops to visit and inspect what was left.

Laughable, right? Father had received Category B, which meant that living quarters needed substantial work, but family members were healthy. For fourteen days, he'd helped us repair the apartment house, had climbed onto the roof with me, because the other neighbors were too old or feeble to collect and reinstall what was left of the clay shingles and patch up holes with tarpaper. We'd picked up firewood and sorted through broken china, swept up the remains of flour and sugar. There was only one thing Father had been unable to do: fill our cupboards and our stomachs. He'd been appalled at our rations, and ultimately helpless.

Yet, for those fourteen days I'd allowed myself to dream of him being home... Staying home. Like a family. Like we used to be.

Inevitably, the day had come when he'd left once more.

Somewhere to the Balkans, he'd said when we hugged. Mother had cried, Siegfried too. Only I had kept it together, swallowing and breathing through my nose. The tears came later when I was lying alone in my bed.

In a way, I resented his visit. For a while, I'd gone through the motions without him, kind of gotten used to things. But now, with the memory of him here with us fresh in my mind, the difference had become clear. Missing him hurt like a fresh wound. The scab had been removed; new blood was flowing.

I trudged to Brühler Straße, where several houses had been reduced to rubble. To my left towered the four-story bunker, completed two years ago, where Mother and Siegfried hid whenever the air raid sirens warned of approaching enemy planes. I never went with them, not since that one day when I'd come along and found out that I couldn't stand being locked in.

Invisible hands had choked me to the point I thought I'd pass out. Now, I just glared at the monstrous building with the narrow slots for windows. The walls had to be six feet thick and reminded me of a giant stone grave. To bring in enough oxygen, the people inside had to turn the crank of a fan. It still wasn't enough, the air thick as soup. After a few minutes it became difficult to form a thought, and all I wanted to do was lie down and never get up again.

To my right, the remnants of several former houses rose to a mountain of rubble. A couple of women, hair wrapped in scarves, hands wrapped with strips of fabric, were picking up bricks in search of treasure, maybe a pot or some silverware, something that could be used or traded.

I crept to the edges in the back, where a former garden shed had been crushed and buried. Glass splinters sparkled in the sunlight, strangely beautiful among the wreckage. I pulled out a piece of framing, a precarious task because at any second the ground could shift, making me lose my balance, slide into a hole or get stuck. Already the skin on my palms ached from the rough edges. I needed Helmut to help. He lived up the street, not more than a five-minute walk from here, yet I couldn't make myself go up there. It took energy to stop and climb down, energy I didn't have.

My stomach rumbled once more, reminding me that the slice of bread this morning had long since been digested. I took a deep breath and sat down, letting the wave of dizziness pass that often accompanied the hunger pangs. I inspected my hands, the skin on my fingers dusty and chafed. To chase away the stiffness from the cold, I blew into them.

Nothing got accomplished sitting here, so I rose once more to continue. The pile of wood grew, though some pieces were too large to carry. I had brought Father's saw and began to cut a beam into two three-foot pieces. I'd have to cut them again in order to fit them into the oven, but for now that could wait.

At last, I wrapped them with a piece of cord I always carried for such tasks. The pack was heavy, almost too heavy to manage, especially across the rubble. I bent forward, set my feet carefully to keep my balance.

After a hundred yards, I rested again. The ache in my back had joined the ache in my belly. How much longer could I work like this on almost nothing to eat? My body was protesting, telling me to either feed it or quit moving so much. I could do neither. I had to endure. Somehow.

End Sample

Novella
ISBN: 978-3-948100-49-0
Paperback, eBook and audiobook

www.ingramcontent.com/pod-product-compliance
Lightning Source LLC
LaVergne TN
LVHW011931070526
838202LV00054B/4586